THE END OF SORROW

A Novel of the Siege of Leningrad in WWII

JV Love

THE END OF SORROW

The poem "Prayer" in Chapter Eight is from *The Complete Poems of Anna Akhmatova* by Anna Akhmatova, Zephyr Press (from the Russian by Judith Hemschemeyer; edited and introduced by Roberta Reeder).

Information contact: www.Facebook.com/ThereArisethLight

Originally published in 2007 by WingSpan Press

Second Edition: May 2019

10 9 8 7 6 5 4 3 2 1

And to all those involved in that fateful 900-day siege: the citizens of Leningrad, the Soviet soldiers who fought to defend it, and to the German soldiers who fought to take it. Good or bad, right or wrong, they were all in it together. It has always been this way, and always will be. This shared existence is the ground we stand on, and the actions we take today create the world we'll live in tomorrow. May we have the courage to understand those that would harm us, and the honesty to admit our fears.

Note on the Second Edition

The first edition of this book was—truth be told—little more than an unedited, second draft hastily released by a young, naive writer. An older, marginally wiser writer seeks to correct those shortcomings with this second edition. It includes a new cover, a cast of characters, an enhanced layout, substantial editing, and 40,000 fewer words.

Contents

Author's Note

This historical fiction novel attempts in every way to remain true to the events and circumstances history has recorded for the siege of Leningrad. Some real-life characters may be obvious. Others not so. For the real-life characters, the novel stays as close as possible to the historic events they were involved in, whether it be, for example, deserting to the enemy lines, or buying tickets to a soccer game before the war started.

Acknowledgments

I am deeply grateful to Harrison Salisbury and his book "The 900 Days," to Kyra Petrovskaya Wayne for her novel "Shurik," and to Elena Skrjabina for her diary entries from the war ("Siege and Survival: The Odyssey of a Leningrader"). Without their superb details and stories from the siege, this novel would not have been possible.

A special thanks goes to Felix Chevtchinskii for sharing his vast knowledge of all things, and also to Lydia Chevtchinskaia. I am grateful to Kermit Moyer, Michael Neff, Charles Salzberg, Lihong Ma, Jack Mangold, Elisabeth Dearborn and Jeanine Cogan. And a special thanks to Susan Hadler for her unwavering encouragement and support.

Cast of Primary Characters

ALFRED LISKOF — (German) Axis soldier stationed on the Polish border.

FELIX VARILENSKY — (Soviet Jew) Leningrader originally from Ukraine

DIMA — (Russian) Felix's best friend.

MISHA BORISOV — (Russian) Soviet soldier stationed on western border.

KATYA SELENAYA — (Russian) Felix's girlfriend.

IGOR — (Russian) Katya's cousin.

PETYA SOYONOVICH — (Russian) Katya's neighbor.

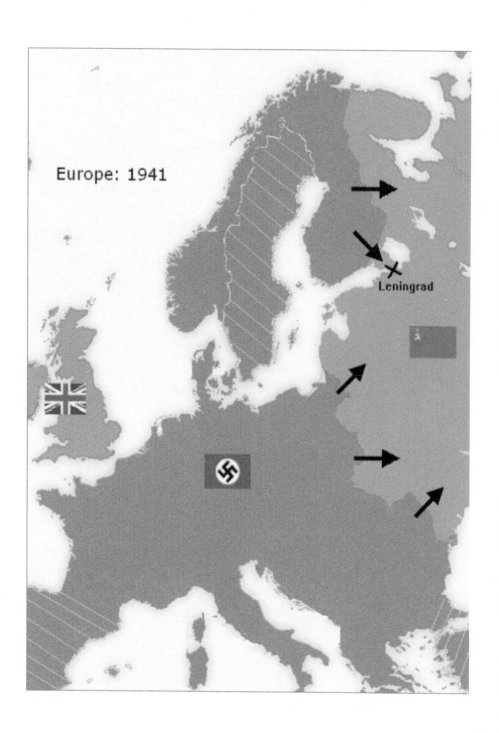

Europe: 1941

Leningrad

PROLOGUE

The two German soldiers huddled together and tried to deny their shivering by discussing the bitter cold and the strange blue tint of the moon. They spoke in soft, sad voices that the stillness of the night carried far and wide over the freshly fallen snow. They wondered how much longer it would be before the sun once again emerged from the horizon. Of all the unusual things in this country, they agreed, that was the one that took the most getting used to—the shortest days and longest nights they'd ever known.

The moon was suddenly gone again, swallowed whole by another of the enormous dark clouds floating through the black, winter sky. One of the soldiers took out a flask, cursed the city of Leningrad, and then took a long swig. A small hole in the cloud allowed the moon to shine through, and for a few seconds, the entire area glowed pale blue. Tall, somber evergreens cast eerie shadows a hundred feet long, and a solitary tree stump in the middle of a white field stood out like a tiger on an iceberg.

When the stump appeared to move, the strangeness of the night threatened to become surreal.

"Dietrich, did you see that?"

"See what?"

"That dark spot out there," he said, motioning toward the open field in front of them. "I think it moved."

No sooner had they begun to examine the spot when the light was again lost, and everything settled uncomfortably back into the dark.

"There's nothing there. I knew you couldn't handle your liquor."

"To hell with you! I'm telling you I saw something move."

"All right, let's go to the nest. The moon should be back out in a minute. You'd better be right this time. I'm getting tired of your false alarms."

What had been vague, borderless figures only an hour before could now be seen clearly by the Soviet soldier. Felix Varilensky had excellent nighttime vision, and even without the help of the moon, he could make out the two Germans as they trudged through the snow over to the machine-gun nest and disappeared inside. Under his breath, he cussed at whoever it was that had been spotted. For most of the men, there had been no training in how to crawl in thick snow across an open field in the middle of the night. For most of the men, there had been no training at all.

Felix studied the night sky and calculated how much time he had in between the clouds—in between the dark and the light. In the dark, he was invisible, immeasurable. In the light, he was just another man.

It wasn't long before the moon began showing its ashen face again. It crept along the edge of the monstrous black cloud, its frail light spilling over the rim and down to the frozen ground below. The light moved faintly from the top of the field where the Germans were, toward the middle of the field where he was. He dug a few more inches into the snow and stopped all movement as the light treaded up to, then around, and finally over him.

The machine-gun nest was off to his right on a slight hill, no more than ninety feet away. As he lay motionless in the moonlight, he tried to wiggle his toes, but they were too numb from the cold for him to tell if he'd moved them or not. He needed the dark to return. That was where he lived now.

And when it did, he slowly aimed his rifle at the machine-gun nest. The ghostly light returned a few seconds later, just as he calculated it would, and he found his target—a dim figure with binoculars looking out from behind the sandbags. Felix gripped his rifle tighter and slowly clenched his jaw until the gums around his loose upper tooth once again flooded his mouth with that thick, salty sensation he craved. He closed his eyes for a short second to concentrate on the sourness of his own blood. Then he opened his eyes and pulled the trigger. The bullet went straight through the German's hand to his cheek, and one after the other, the binoculars, and then the man, fell from sight.

The other German soldier quickly engaged the machine gun and bullets flew frantically in every direction. They struck all around Felix, but he remained still. Even when one of the bullets burned a hole straight through his left arm, he did not move.

After several minutes, the tat-tat-tat of the machine gun ceased and additional German soldiers could be heard arriving—barking out orders and demanding answers.

The snow underneath him turning red and the frigid air so intense it was difficult to breathe, Felix waited. In his mind, he was in that warm, familiar place where the sun refused to set, where the lazy afternoons went on forever, and where the shade of a tree was proof of God's unconditional love. In that peaceful place, he lay on the soft grass, Katya beside him—her seductive hips next to his, her outstretched forearm resting lightly on his bare chest. When he kissed the small of her wrist, the tender scent of lilacs stayed on his lips. He listened as she recited a poem she'd written for him, the final words of it repeating themselves unremittingly in his mind: *Love is the beginning, and Love is the end, and here in the middle is where we must mend.*

It was all so real: that bright yellow sun, that clear blue sky, that cool green grass. But that warm day was long past. That warm day was before it all began....

ОДИН — Part I

A man's character is his destiny. — **Heraclitus**

Глава Первая — Chapter One

TWO DAYS IN JUNE

Eyes that pierce,
    Beauty so rare.
Thoughts that intrigue me,
    love to share.
I with my body, a mind, and a soul,
    I am but parts, you make me whole.
Will so strong,
    with good intention.
The road is long,
    our journey in question.

Day 1: June 21, 1941

Sunlight soaked every inch of Felix Varilensky's muscular back. His fair skin glistened with tiny beads of sweat as his shoulder blades tucked in and out of his torso in a mechanical rhythm. He was deep within himself, shutting out all sounds, all feelings, all thought. This focus—this inordinate ability to concentrate solely on what he wanted to—was his gift. In addition to helping him survive life as a Jew in the Soviet Union, it also made him a fearsome competitor.

He counted to himself as he lowered his body to the ground and pushed it back up again. Fifty-six, fifty-seven, fifty-eight. Even when his muscles were tired and wanted to quit, there was still nothing but the count. Sixty-one, sixty-two, sixty-three.

"You've got him, Felix! He's slowing down!" one of his friends yelled.

"Let's go, Dima! Don't let Felix win again!" called another.

But it was too late. Dima collapsed midway through a push-up, and the cheers exploded.

"I knew I shouldn't have bet on you, Dima!" someone jested.

"How about pull-ups?" Dima said, very much out of breath. "I know I can beat him at that."

"No. It's hopeless. You'd think we'd know by now not to bet against a Jew. Felix always wins."

But even after the applause faded away, Felix continued his silent counting. Sixty-nine, seventy, seventy-one. He hadn't heard the shouting or the clapping, nor the quiet that announced the end of the bet. There was only the one voice he heard, and it was that voice he remained true to. He had no idea whose voice it was, nor did he care much. It was simply there, in his head, and it never left him. It reassured him when things weren't going well, complimented him when no one else would, and pushed him when he could push no further himself.

The group—four young men and four young women—gathered around and hollered for Felix's attention.

"You can stop now, you show-off!"

"Hey, Felix! It's over. Let's eat now."

Even Dima, his conquered foe, joined in. "Felix, I'm done. You beat me."

But Felix, eyes tightly shut, arms bulging, a silent voice counting, kept doing push-up after push-up in a perfect, unbroken cadence.

A young woman made her way through the group, and when she got to the front, she paused to watch the scene of Felix doing his seemingly effortless push-ups and his friends trying in vain to get his attention. She smiled for a brief second, and the inherent sorrow of her chestnut-brown eyes nearly disappeared.

"Katya, tell him to stop," a girl pleaded to her.

"No," injected a young man. "Let's see how many he can do!"

Everyone was laughing. Half the group was yelling for Felix to stop, and half was yelling for him to keep going. Gracefully bending her knees until she was atop her ankles and her head next to his, she called softly to him, "Felix, you've won. It's over."

He opened his eyes immediately and stopped at the top of a push-up. And as his eyes met hers, he held the entire world inside his heart. In Katya's eyes—in those beautiful brown eyes that looked sad even when she was happy—he saw himself, and knew he could do anything with her by his side.

He wanted nothing more than to remain in that moment, but the pandemonium around him wouldn't allow it. Noticing for the first time his boisterous friends gathered near, he also realized how vigorously his heart was pounding and how tired he was.

"Let's see how many more you can do!" Dima shouted as he sat on Felix's back.

"Yeah!" the others joined in. They all piled on top of him, and his arms finally gave way, sending the whole group tumbling to the ground amid a chorus of laughter.

Overhead, the late afternoon sun sailed through a bright aqua-blue sky, and in front of them, tiny waves from the Neva River lapped at the shore. Summer had finally arrived, and it brought Felix more joy than he'd ever known in his life. And when the thought occurred to him that it might be more than he ever would know, he quickly banished that thought from his mind.

A soft breeze picked up the scent of freshly cut hay and blew it across the Neva River, past the towering oak tree where the picnickers sat, and on to the forest of birch trees that lay beyond. In the other direction, they could still see their home—the stalwart, yet elegant Leningrad.

Katya sat with her back against the tree and watched a column of ants above her march into a black hole underneath one of the branches. It was a hot day, though comfortable in the shade, and after the spring that had been more like winter, no one was complaining.

"I'm hungry. Let's eat."

"No. We have to toast first."

"Who brought the champagne?"

"Dima did. Dima, open the champagne!"

After popping the cork out, Dima began filling glasses as they interrogated him about where he got it.

"My father gave it to me," he explained. "But only after he found out it was for Felix's birthday. He loves him like he was his own son."

After he'd poured a glass for everyone, Dima led them in a toast. "Felix, may your next eighteen years be as happy as your first eighteen years."

Felix grinned as he indulged in a glance at the vast, wide-open space ahead of him where he could see for miles on end. *Only in Russia*, he thought. Only in Russia could there be so much beauty crammed into one glimpse: the long, narrow fields of wheat with their scattered blue flowers, the peacefulness of the birch trees swaying in the wind, the calm authority of the Neva River. And what better time to be in Leningrad than during the White Nights, when the sun graced the sky both day and night. It was all his to savor.

"Thank you," he said. "It's a good time to be alive. Now, let's eat!"

Spread out before them was a delicious medley of foods. All nine of them had brought something, and with very little planning, a festive meal had been fashioned. A large smoked fish provided the centerpiece. It was surrounded by hard-boiled eggs, pickles, dark Russian bread, boiled potatoes with salt, thick eggplant spread, and a cucumber and tomato salad. For dessert, a large Napoleon cake awaited the picnickers.

"Felix, I see Katya brought some real Ukrainian salo for you. I thought Jews weren't supposed to eat pork."

Felix shrugged. He didn't know much about his Jewish roots.

"She must really love you to let you eat that."

"What do you mean?" Felix laughed. "Salo is very good for you. You should try some."

"Salted pork fat is good for you? You Ukrainians are crazy."

"You saw how I won the push-up contest, didn't you? It's because I eat salo."

"Either that or all that vodka you drink!" someone quipped, and everyone laughed.

A large black fly landed briefly on the cake before Dima swatted it away. It then buzzed in front of Felix's face for a few seconds until he snatched it from the air.

"Did you catch it?" Katya asked incredulously.

He nodded yes and began to squeeze his hand tighter, but Katya stopped him. "Let it go," she urged.

Knowing he could do no harm under that gaze, Felix opened his hand and the fly buzzed away.

As Katya gently stroked her fingers through his dark, curly hair, he thought back to that day thirteen months ago when they'd first met. She'd been carrying a sunflower-sized portrait of Lenin, and he'd had a big sign that read: "Glory to the Workers of the World." It was the first May Day parade where he hadn't been overcome with feelings of patriotism. His love for his country had been trounced by a different sensation altogether—nausea. And it only worsened the more he watched the beautiful woman at the end of his row with her shoulder-length brown hair and her fluid, effortless way of moving through time and space. Three times along the parade route, he'd run into the plump peasant girl in front of him, because he couldn't keep from staring over his left shoulder.

All during the parade, he'd memorized the words and gestures to approach her with. But when the time came, he walked up to her and promptly forgot everything. "Hi," she'd said apprehensively before turning to rejoin her friends. Grabbing her by the arm, he'd forced himself to say something—anything—so as not to lose the moment.

"You were great in the parade," he'd said, and immediately felt embarrassed by such a dim-witted statement.

"Um, thanks," she said, then added quite seriously, "You've got a nice sign."

It took him a second to realize she was gently poking fun at him, and when he laughed, she laughed too. She had a secretive, restrained laugh, and much like her delicate smile, it conveyed a sense of vulnerability. Even now, Felix wondered how anyone could say a harsh word to her with those doe-like, rueful eyes looking back at them.

Katya brought him out of his reverie by tickling his cheek with the sprig of lilacs she'd picked on their hike earlier that day.

"Look, here's one with five petals," Felix said, pulling the tiny branch from her hand. "That means you have to make a wish."

Katya closed her eyes, but only for a second. "All right. I did."

"You have to eat the flower now," said Felix.

"What? No, you don't."

"Of course you do. If you don't eat the flower, your wish won't come true."

"I think you're making it up," she said, but then plucked the tiny purple flower and put it in her mouth anyway.

"What did you wish for?"

"I'm not telling. If you say what your wish was, it won't come true."

He chuckled and kissed the underside of her wrist.

Their friends were busy doing what most everyone did these days—chattering about the possibilities of war with Germany.

"... but my brother is in the army, and he's on that border. He's on one side, and the Germans are on the other. He tells me he sees more German troops arriving every day. And he says he hears tanks and trucks moving at all hours of the night, up and down the riverbank."

"Pipe down, you provocateur!" someone jested, and everyone snickered nervously. They all knew someone who had been arrested for "panic-mongering." The position of the government of the Soviet Union was unmistakable. Only eight days ago, the official news agency, Tass, printed a statement in the newspapers denying rumors of impending war.

"There's no way the Germans will attack. They learned their lesson fifteen years ago. They can't fight and win a war on two fronts. They'll finish off Britain before they look our way."

"I heard that Britain warned Stalin the Germans would attack tomorrow."

"You can't trust the British," Dima chimed in. "They want to drag us into the war because they're finished unless they get help. They want the Germans to attack us to relieve the pressure on them. But it's ridiculous for us to speculate on whether or not the Germans will attack. The Party has said there won't be a war. Stalin made the pact with Hitler to guarantee peace."

"So how do you explain all the German troops massed on the border?"

"I don't have to explain," Dima replied defiantly. "The Party knows more than we do. That's why they make the decisions. I just have to have faith in the Party, and I do. I'm beginning to wonder how much faith the rest of you have in the Party." The challenge was implicit in his voice.

"Dima, calm down," Felix intervened. "We all have faith in the Party. Most of us are in the Komsomol. But there's no reason why we can't talk about things, that's what students do. That's what they *teach* us to do. Besides, we're all friends here."

"Yes, friends who don't trust in the wisdom of the Party and who gossip like peasants in a village!" Dima said as he stormed away to smoke a cigarette.

"Don't worry," Felix reassured everyone. "You know how he is. He'll calm down in a few minutes."

"Felix," one of his friends called, "what will you do if the Germans attack?"

"He'll run to the front and fight them off with his grandfather's sword!" someone joked.

"No," a young woman contended. "Katya wouldn't let him. She'd make him be a chauffeur for General Zhukov." Everyone laughed. "Hitler himself couldn't keep those two apart," she added.

Felix agreed with her. Nothing in the world could separate him from Katya. Their unbounded love could surely overcome anything the world had to throw at them.

Alfred Liskof wrapped his calloused, sweaty index finger around the trigger and began to squeeze. Perspiration gathered around the barrel of the gun where it met the soft, white skin of his temple. But something wasn't right, and he could neither squeeze nor release.

"Why do you keep doing that?" Franz yelled from behind in an exasperated tone. He was catching up quickly now that Alfred had stopped. "I hate it when you put that pistol to your head. What kind of a sick game is that?"

Alfred lowered the handgun from the side of his head and noticed a small deer and her fawn grazing at the bottom of the wooded hill. It was 7:30 p.m. and soft beams of sunlight squeezed through the young leaves of the trees, splashing the ground around them. Alfred's left eye began to irritate him. This strange sensation focused his attention, and then he felt it—something gathering and racing down the side of his cheek.

"Are you crying?" Franz asked incredulously as he approached.

Alfred scoffed at the ludicrous accusation. He never cried.

But then he felt it again—a warm drop of water rolling down his right cheek— and there could be no doubt. In bewilderment, he watched the teardrop plummet to the forest floor.

"What's the matter?" asked Franz.

"Nothing," Alfred replied, putting his Luger pistol back in its holster.

"Don't give me that. What the hell is your problem? Why are you always putting that damn gun to your head? It's the third time today. And now you're crying too."

"I'm not crying. Something got in my eye, that's all."

"In *both* of them?"

Alfred, at thirty-two, was over a decade older than Franz, a foot taller, and at least fifty pounds heavier. He glared at Franz with his practiced stare, both eyebrows furrowed tightly toward the bridge of his nose and low over his eyes. "Yes," he said coolly, "in *both* of them."

"Why do you even have a pistol?" asked Franz. "I thought only officers got them."

Alfred ignored the question and watched the two deer lazily rip grass from the ground while a squirrel chattered from somewhere in the treetops. The Polish forest they stood in was similar to the ones Alfred knew and loved in the Fatherland. Grabbing his rifle, he began marching again. Franz hesitated, but then followed.

Alfred had so many unanswered questions today. They surrounded him, swirled about, taunted and mocked him.

"Is it about tomorrow?" Franz asked.

"Is what about tomorrow?"

"Whatever's bothering you."

"Yeah," Alfred answered, "and about the day after that, and the day after that, and the day after that."

He regretted answering already. He never should have told Franz his opinions or what he'd overheard that morning—that they'd be attacking the Soviet Union tomorrow at sunup. He should have learned by now that his fellow Germans, soldiers or not, weren't interested in hearing any contrary viewpoints.

Franz, with his short legs, struggled to keep up. "What's there to fear? You see how poorly defended their borders are. The Poles put up a harder fight than the Russians will. We'll be in Moscow before the leaves turn color."

Alfred recalled when he was Franz's age and how he'd been just as arrogant.

"We were outnumbered in the last war," continued Franz, "and we still annihilated them. I don't understand you. We have all of Europe now. Who wants that miserable little island? The Brits can keep it as far as I'm concerned."

Alfred knew history well, and he understood perfectly what had happened to the last army to conquer the whole of Europe and then forge on to Moscow. That army had been led by one of the greatest military leaders of all time, and yet Napoleon and his army had been devastated by their attempted conquest. They had been destroyed slowly and methodically, day in and out, by the cold, the hunger, and the shrapnel ripping through their backs as they desperately retreated.

"Besides," Franz said, "we need living space and natural resources. That means going east."

Alfred remembered reading how in 1814, only two years after Napoleon had retreated, victorious Russian armies and their allies celebrated the fall of France by marching down the Champs-Elysées and through the Arc de Triomphe in the center of Paris.

"And we'll be doing the world a favor," added Franz, "by taking Russia and slaughtering all the communists. They're not human."

"I suppose they think the same about us," Alfred said as he stopped to look around.

"Well, they're wrong. And we'll prove it to them real soon." Franz glanced at his watch. "In eight and a half hours to be exact."

Alfred studied his compass for several seconds while Franz took a drink of water from his canteen.

"Are you sure we're not lost?" Franz asked. "Shouldn't we be close by now?"

"I know exactly where we are. We're right on schedule," replied Alfred.

The border to the Soviet Union was three miles ahead; Leningrad, more than seven hundred miles to the north; their native Germany so very far behind them. When Alfred thought of Dresden and his beautiful brick home with its little garden out back, the despair and helplessness threatened to overwhelm him once again.

"It's not like Russia is going to cease to be anytime soon," commented Franz. "We'll never be safe with these monsters on our borders."

"You're right," Alfred said sarcastically. "The killing isn't going to cease anytime soon."

Franz studied Alfred's face for a moment before answering. "That's not what I said."

"We were promised *peace*," countered Alfred. But of course he knew better now. The wars would continue, and the Third Reich wouldn't stop until it brought about the destruction of everything Alfred held dear.

"We don't need peace. We need oil."

"That argument is entirely illogical. First of all, there's—" Alfred stopped in mid-sentence, deciding he'd had enough of arguing. There was no point to it. He wasn't going to convince Franz, or anyone else for that matter, of the error of their views. After wiping his bald head with the green rag he kept in his pocket, he placed his right hand firmly around the handle of his pistol. He thought how nice it would be to cry some more, if only his tears hadn't dried up already.

It was time for him to make a decision: to continue living in a world of destruction, hatred, and fear, where death was waiting impatiently around every corner; or to put the gun to his head and end his suffering.

"What's today?" he asked.

Franz eyed him nervously. "It's the twenty-first."

"Hmm, so it is. Have you ever seen the incredible palaces in Leningrad?"

"No. Never," replied Franz and stepped closer to the wide trunk of a nearby tree.

"What a pity," said Alfred, pulling his handgun from its holster. "They're works of art. Very majestic."

It was a few minutes past 8:00 p.m., but the northern sun was still shining brightly. Misha Borisov focused his binoculars on the lone German plane gliding lazily through the blue sky. The plane veered wide left for half a minute, then wide right, and then climbed up toward the sun before diving back to its former altitude.

Misha set the binoculars down and lit one of his precious few cigarettes. His duty had only started five minutes ago, and he knew that having a cigarette so early meant he'd have to be extremely conservative to make the remaining three last until the end of his shift. He wondered if it was the same plane as two days ago. It probably was. That plane had done the same maneuvers—most likely out of boredom, Misha guessed. There wasn't anything new in this area the Germans hadn't already seen.

The German planes performed the same routine every time. They would cross the border into the Soviet Union, fly over military installations, cities, rivers, lakes, roads, railroads, and whatever else they wanted to, then return to their base on the other side of the border. Misha leaned back in his chair and concentrated on his cigarette. It was one of the few pleasures he had at his disposal while on duty. From 8:00 p.m. to 2:00 a.m., his job was to guard the ninety-three planes lining the sides of the runway and be on the lookout for enemy planes. It was a boring job and one entirely unsuitable to a nineteen-year-old who knew exactly how things should and should not be in the world. The planes were chained to the ground to prevent anyone from stealing them, and Misha hadn't seen so much as a stray dog near them.

Grinding out his cigarette, he caught out of the corner of his eye his commanding officer and another soldier coming his way. His commanding officer, a captain, was a tall, slender man who was inordinately quiet. His dark skin suggested he was from either the far North or the far South, but he spoke perfect Russian, with no trace of an accent. Misha didn't recognize the man walking next to the captain. He was wearing the same uniform Misha was, so he definitely wasn't an officer. He walked with an air of indifference that only came with connections or stupidity.

Misha rose to his feet, chastising himself for not reporting the plane sighting yet. It was not only within eyesight now, but also earshot. As he cleared his throat in preparation to make the announcement, the captain spotted it.

"Comrade Private, why haven't you reported that plane?"

"I was just about to, Comrade Captain. It's another German reconnaissance plane."

After an abrupt descent, the plane was less than seventy-five feet off the ground. The three men stood together and watched it approach. The captain took out his pistol, but did not aim it. And just before the plane roared over their heads, it tilted to the right and the pilot waved at them. Misha waved back.

"What the hell was that? Do you want to get twenty-five years?" the captain chastised Misha.

"But, Comrade Captain," protested Misha, "surely waving cannot be considered a provocation? We see German planes deep in our territory every day. We're not allowed to shoot them. What else is there to do?"

"You're a lunatic. You're going to get yourself killed or sent to Siberia one day."

"Siberia? But Stalin loves me. He only sends provocateurs, kulaks, and Trotskyites to Siberia. Not workers like me." The soldier next to the captain arched his eyebrows at this, though in amusement or consternation, Misha couldn't tell.

"Shut up, Borisov!" the captain yelled.

Misha was perplexed by the captain's demeanor as he wasn't usually so quick to anger. He studied the captain's nose yet again. It was the flat, crooked nose of a brawler, and it didn't fit the captain's personality at all.

"I've been patient with you because you're new," the captain explained. "Consider yourself warned. Your insolent remarks will no longer be tolerated." He glared at Misha for several seconds, as if to emphasize the point.

Finally, he turned to the soldier who accompanied him and introduced him as Comrade Stepanovich. "I want you to show him the ropes," the captain explained. "You two will be working together from now on."

The captain left without another word. Stepanovich watched him walk away and then turned his head slowly from the far right to the far left, seemingly looking for something that wasn't supposed to be there. Misha could smell garlic on his breath, and perhaps alcohol, though he wasn't sure about that.

Stepanovich looked intently at the rows of planes ahead of them. He poked his pinkie in his ear and twisted his wrist slowly one way and then the other. Misha couldn't help but notice what disproportionately wide and flat fingernails he had. They were grotesque.

"So, where you from?" asked Misha.

Stepanovich turned toward him with a look of surprise on his face. "What?"

"Where are you from?"

"Moscow."

"Ah, I thought so!" Misha said with a smile. "A fellow Muscovite! You've definitely got that Moscow look about you. It'll be nice to have someone with half a brain to talk to—not like these simpletons from the villages. The guy before you was a complete idiot. He was so gullible that one time I told him the moon was actually the old sun that had burned out five hundred years ago, and he believed me!"

Stepanovich scratched his nose and looked grimly in Misha's direction, but said nothing in response.

Misha had to force himself not to stare at those inhuman fingernails. "Don't you just hate people like that? They're not like you and me. We're from the city. We know Jupiter from Saturn, and geometry from geography. But these people from the villages, you have to tell them what's what."

To escape the sweltering heat of the late-day sun, the two of them stepped off to the right and into the long shadow of one of the hangars. Stepanovich pulled a rag from his pocket and wiped the sweat off his forehead.

"You know the kind, right?" asked Misha, casting a hopeful glance. "The ones who can't think for themselves, who buy everything the Party sells them."

A short silence made Misha uneasy, and he recalled the warnings his mother had given him about his "dangerous habit" of always saying what was on his mind.

"I hate those fuckers from the villages," Stepanovich finally answered.

Misha snickered nervously in response, but Stepanovich neither laughed nor smiled.

"You know today—June twenty-first—is my three-month anniversary of being stationed here," announced Misha.

"So?"

"So, I just thought I'd tell you. It's nice being able to talk to someone without having to worry about every word you say." Misha cracked his knuckles as he stretched his arms. "Have you heard anything about the war? They tell us that Hitler's going to invade England, but I'm not so sure. If they're going to do that, then why are they flying all these reconnaissance flights over us?"

"I guess Hitler doesn't trust us," replied Stepanovich.

"Maybe," Misha said as he swatted a fly away from his ear. "Back in March, a German reconnaissance plane made a forced landing here. I figured we'd arrest him, but instead we received orders to tow his plane in, give him dinner, refuel his plane, and then send him on his way. Makes no sense to me."

Stepanovich grunted and gaped skeptically at Misha.

"It's true!" exclaimed Misha. "Ask anybody."

Gnats began flying around Stepanovich's head, but he made no effort to swat them away.

"You want me to show you what we have to do for the next five-and-a-half hours?" Misha asked.

Though there was no response, Misha continued anyway. "Every seventeen minutes, we have to do rounds and check the hangars and planes, and—"

"Why?" interrupted Stepanovich.

"Why? Because that's what we have to do, that's why. Sure it's stupid, but you and I both know that that doesn't matter. If you ask me, it's because there's only one damn viewpoint allowed. Don't get me wrong, I was in the Komsomol in school, I just think this top-down order is bad for us. I mean, you can't even take a piss around here without permission."

"Is that so?" Stepanovich said. Then he smiled for the first time, looking satisfied, as though he'd just finished an exam and done well.

Misha hung his head, deciding he wouldn't talk anymore. He'd said too much already. His mother had taught him that honesty was a virtue, but in this day and age, it was sometimes a crime.

Alfred's hand trembled ever so slightly as he pointed the pistol at Franz's chest. "Put your gun on the ground," he repeated slowly and in no uncertain terms.

Franz did as he was told. "What are you going to do?"

"Keep your mouth shut," Alfred said as he removed a rope from his backpack. "Put your hands on your head and get on your knees." He forced Franz to sit against a tree, then tied his wrists together behind it.

"What have I done to you to deserve this?"

"You didn't do anything."

"Then you're simply insane? Is that it? Do you know that you've gone crazy?"

"I'm through arguing with you."

"So you agree with me then? You actually know that you're crazy?"

"Enough with the questions!" screamed Alfred.

"Or else what? You'll tie me up and leave me to die?"

"You'll be all right," Alfred said. "We're close enough to the road that someone will find you."

"Nobody travels down that road, and you know it," Franz shot back.

"Not true. There's at least two or three vehicles a day. Besides, it'll be overflowing with tanks and jeeps soon enough." He picked up his backpack and put it on.

"Where are you going?"

"To stop this stupid war before it starts," replied Alfred.

"What? What are you talking about? You can't do anything to stop it. It's the will of the German people—their God-given right to defend themselves."

"You don't defend yourself by invading another country," Alfred said as he walked away.

"We're not *starting* anything. We're protecting the Fatherland."

Alfred continued on his way, stepping over a large fallen tree and ducking underneath the low-hanging branch of a giant evergreen.

"You're no German!" he heard Franz yell after him. "You're a coward! A traitor!"

Alfred paid him no attention. He was reflecting on his irrevocable decision. It meant being ostracized, or maybe even death, but he had to take a stand. He was sure it would bring solace and comfort, rather than regret, on his deathbed.

He'd never again see his home in Dresden. Never again enjoy his aunt's homemade spaetzel. Never again taste the splendidly bitter lager beer brewed by the old farmer up the road. This was the price he'd have to pay. And maybe, just maybe, he could prevent Germany, the country of his birth—the country he loved with all his soul—from making what he was sure was a tragic mistake.

The Soviet guardpost at the foot of the bridge was nothing more than a rickety, wooden shack. Alfred spied one soldier sitting inside—his head down, weapon leaning against the wall. Another soldier sulked outside, shifting his weight from one foot to the other at ten-second intervals.

After trekking through the Polish woods in the heat and humidity of late June, Alfred's army fatigues were drenched. He tried to wipe down his hairless head, but the rag was already too saturated with sweat to do much good. The back of his neck and his muscular forearms were dotted with red mosquito bites that he scratched absent-mindedly from time to time.

While the Soviet soldiers smoldered in their boredom, Alfred gently set his gun on the ground and took his army-issue knife from its sheath. Clenching it in his left hand, he squatted behind large bushes, breathing deeply.

Familiar images came to him of that day eleven years ago when he'd finally gathered the courage to confront his father about the miserable childhood he'd had. The conversation hadn't gone the way Alfred had rehearsed it in his mind. Instead of sympathy and regret from his father, he'd received recriminations and denial. He could still see his father standing next to the fireplace with his arms folded, fists clenched, face red. "You ungrateful bastard!" he'd yelled. "I fed you, and clothed you, and put a roof over your head, and all you can do is complain." Alfred had wanted to tell his father how extremely critical he'd always been, how he never spent any time with him, how *he never seemed to give a damn* about him. But he didn't say any of that. Instead, he'd stood there facing his father—arms folded, fists clenched, face red—and said nothing. After his father's tirade, Alfred went home, broke three of his knuckles punching the wall, and vowed to never speak to his father again.

The sun was coming in at such a low angle in front of Alfred now that he had to look straight into it if he wanted to see the guardpost. It was almost 9:00 p.m., and the sunset would be complete in a few more minutes.

The Soviet soldier standing outside the guardpost stepped inside and kicked the other one to wake him up. Alfred—who understood Russian fairly well—heard the man explain that he was going to take a piss.

As the soldier approached, Alfred hid further behind the bushes. The man had his rifle slung haphazardly over his shoulder, and with one quick move,

Alfred knew he could jump him and slit his throat. But Alfred hadn't come to kill, he'd come to surrender.

When the man finished urinating, Alfred stood up with his arms over his head. The startled Soviet soldier stepped backward and tripped over a stone. When he got back to his feet, he pointed his gun at Alfred and motioned him toward the guardpost.

Alfred marched the forty yards in pride, in determination, and in fear of whether he'd made the right decision.

Lying on his stomach with a guard's foot pressing hard between his shoulder blades, Alfred did his best to understand what the Soviet soldier was saying into the phone. "That's correct. I said that I have a German soldier here who has surrendered."

After a short pause and an exasperated sigh, he heard, "Yes, comrade, you are correct that he could not have surrendered when we are not at war. That was my mistake. We have a German soldier here who has *deserted*. He says that the German army will commence an assault tomorrow at 4:00 a.m. What shall I do with him?"

Alfred again heard muted mumbling from the other end of the line, then another sigh from the guard and a response. "Yes, Comrade Captain, I understand that any provocations against Germans will be dealt with severely, but he approached us with his arms in the air and said he had important information. He says he's a member of the 222nd Infantry Regiment of the 74th Infantry Division. And he says he heard his commander, a Lieutenant Schultz, state the date and time of the attack. He has also observed troops being deployed."

All was quiet for several seconds, then Alfred heard the guard explain, "No. He doesn't speak Russian. He speaks German, and no, I don't think it's a trick."

It wasn't true that Alfred didn't speak Russian, although he mangled it so badly that it might as well be.

The longer the phone conversation went on, the more distinctly Alfred could hear the irritation in the guard's voice. "I learned how to speak German at the university, sir. It's in my records if you care to check."

When the guard finally disconnected, he whispered into the other soldier's ear, "Ohn durak."

Alfred understood that he was the one being referred to, and understood all too well what the guard had said, *"He's a fool."*

In the center of Leningrad, the Cathedral of Our Lady of Kazan sits quietly on the main thoroughfare of the city. The proud Romanesque structure, more commonly called the Kazansky Cathedral, has held a quiet authority over the city ever since the first stone of its foundation was set by Tsar Alexander I on August 27, 1801. Stretching its massive wings out to the east and west, it always seems to be ready to fly away to the more perfect place it surely must have come from. But it never leaves, and perhaps that's why it holds such a special place in the heart of so many Leningraders. It's always there, in repose, patiently watching the cars, buses, and pedestrians as they move in steady streams up and down the stately Nevsky Prospekt.

In 1931, the cathedral was shut down and transformed into the "Museum of the History of Religion and Atheism." But for Felix, it would always be known as Kazansky Cathedral. He'd fallen in love with it the first time he laid eyes on it, promptly learning every detail of its storied history.

The setting sun colored the sky beyond the cathedral with soft pastel hues of violet, gold, and crimson. It was after 11:00 p.m., and Felix and Katya walked slowly by the rose bushes lining the front of the cathedral. It had been a long, but fun day, and Felix hated to see it come to an end. He was escorting Katya to her apartment building, trying to squeeze a few more moments from the summer day. Reaching his arm out, he pulled her close and ran his hand up and down her side, feeling how her waist seductively curved into her hips. Leaning over to give her a quick kiss on the cheek, he abruptly changed his mind, dropping the picnic basket and taking her in his arms. He kissed her on the lips and pulled her body tight to his—delighting in the firmness of her breasts as they pressed against him. She wrapped her arms around his neck and kissed him back.

After a few seconds, Felix heard a mother with small children approaching and reluctantly ended their embrace. As he and Katya prepared to cross the street, he glanced over his shoulder at the cathedral and the dozens of giant Podoust stone columns that marked the front facade. Members of the Romanov royal family had been married within Kazansky's majestic confines, and Felix wished he could have witnessed that.

Holding Katya's hand as they crossed the street, he asked her, "Did you talk to your father?"

"About what?"

"You know perfectly well what," he said, annoyed that the pleasure of a minute ago was gone so quickly. "Don't make this into an argument again."

"Don't talk to me like that," she said crossly.

"Like what?"

"In that tone. You talk to me sometimes as if I'm a child and you're the parent, and I hate it."

Felix reflected for a second. "You're right," he concluded. "I'm sorry. It's just that I get tense even thinking about this. Have you talked to him yet?"

"What's there to talk about? I know what his answer will be—the same as last time."

"So you're not even going to try anymore?" Felix stopped and turned to face her.

She shrugged her shoulders.

"But Katya, why do you need his approval? We're both eighteen now."

"Why do you ask questions like that? It's annoying."

"Come on, so what if he sits on the City Soviet. He's only one man."

"Felix," she said, the volume of her voice climbing a notch. "He's friends with Party Secretaries. He doesn't just know powerful people. He plays chess with Kuznetsov; he has tea with Zhukov."

"But you can't tell me he's going to ruin the life of his only child out of mere spite. He may not act like it, but I know he loves you. He wouldn't hurt you."

"You don't understand, Felix. You don't know him. He thinks he knows what's best for me, and it doesn't matter what I think. He'll never change his mind."

"But he can't do this. It's *your* life."

"He *can* do it. And he is."

"No. He can't. I'm going to have a talk with him."

"Felix, no. Please, don't do that. He could have you arrested if he wanted."

"Arrested for what? For talking to him?"

"I'm serious. Don't do it. I know him, and I know you. You're both pigheaded, and if the two of you go into a room, probably only one of you will come out."

"Oh come now, Katya. You underestimate me. I'm not violent."

"Just promise me you won't try to talk to him."

"Promise you? First, promise me you'll marry me one day—with, or without, your father's approval."

Katya stared at the ground for several minutes, wringing her hands, before finally answering. "Can't we talk about this some other time?" she asked with an air of resignation.

Felix nodded, and they ambled the remaining few blocks to Katya's third floor apartment in silence. Her neighbor Petya was smoking a cigarette and leaning over the railing looking down on them as they climbed the stairs. "You certainly picked a beauteous day for your picnic, Katya. Any leftovers?"

Felix arched his neck, scrutinizing Petya's portly figure—potbelly hanging over his belt, shoulders slouching forward over his chest, cigarette held limply in his fingers. He had a disfigured right leg and stood with his weight almost entirely on his left leg.

"Hi, Petya," said Katya. "I thought you usually took a nap about now so you could write all night."

"Who could sleep on a day like this?" he said sarcastically.

After reaching the third floor, Felix set the picnic basket down, and Katya rummaged through it. She had some strange connection to Petya that Felix didn't understand. She said she considered him a friend, though Felix wondered if it was out of pity. He didn't care much for Petya, considering him fat, lazy, and conceited. Felix especially hated it when he used big or unusual words. More than anything though, he didn't like the way the twenty-seven-year-old writer leered at Katya.

"Sorry, Petya," Katya said as she closed the picnic basket, "there's nothing left except a couple of boiled potatoes and a pickle."

"That's palatable enough. I'll take them."

Katya dug them out and handed them over.

"So did you go outside and enjoy this *beauteous* day, Petya?" Felix asked.

"I went to the store and bought some paper this morning," he replied. Instead of looking at Felix, he fixed his eyes on Katya as if she'd asked the question.

The entrance to the building creaked open and footsteps echoed in the stairwell. Felix peeked over the railing, but couldn't see who it was.

"It's Dmitry," announced Petya.

"How do you know?" Felix asked.

"I know," he said confidently.

As the person rounded the corner onto the second floor, Felix spotted a familiar small head with short, dark hair and a cowlick and knew Petya was right. It was Dmitry Shostakovich.

"How do you do that?" exclaimed Katya, her face alight.

Petya smiled for the first time and said in a mock humble voice, "It's but one of my innumerous talents."

Shostakovich had likely come to visit his friend, the old painter, Alexander Guzman. Guzman lived next door to Petya and Katya and had a beautiful piano, but couldn't play a note. He admitted to keeping the piano solely because Shostakovich loved it and frequently came over to practice or compose.

"Good evening, Dmitry," called Katya.

"Ah, Katya. How's my favorite poet?"

"Fine. I heard you playing something new yesterday. Have you started on your Seventh Symphony?"

"Oh, those were just some random ideas," he said, wiping his round, black-rimmed glasses on his shirt. He laughed nervously.

"Did you know it's Felix's birthday?" asked Katya. "He's eighteen today."

"Is that so? Happy Birthday, Felix. And to think, only last year I was *twice* your age. Say, why don't you go to the soccer game at Dynamo Stadium with me tomorrow. My treat. I got two tickets today, but I saw my friend just a minute ago and he said he can't make it."

"I'd love to, except I promised my friend I'd help him move tomorrow."

"All right. How about you, Petya? You want to go?"

"No. That would make me too happy. I can't write when I'm happy."

"Did you write today?" asked Shostakovich.

"No."

"Are you happy today?"

"No."

"I think you need a new hypothesis. If either of you change your mind, you know where to find me." Shostakovich walked down the hall to Guzman's apartment, knocked, then slipped inside. Katya kissed Felix on the cheek and wished him happy birthday once more, before she too disappeared into her apartment.

On his way home, Felix enjoyed the cool night air and the sweet, salty fragrance from lilacs and the Neva River. Just as he reached his apartment, a bell chimed twelve times, signifying the end of June 21 and the beginning of June 22. For a reason he couldn't explain, he suddenly felt short of breath, and a disconcerting shiver went up his spine.

Day 2: June 22, 1941

Misha cursed the devil under his breath as he shuffled wearily from the latrine to his barracks. His legs moved so sluggishly, it was as if they were already in bed and asleep. Each and every muscle felt numb with drunkenness, though he'd had nothing whatsoever to drink.

These attacks inflicted him from time-to-time, and he'd never found a defense against them. More than mere tiredness, it was a grogginess so intense that he could barely command his muscles to move, and the sensation could last for eight miserable hours.

He was fortunate this time, because the onset had occurred shortly after midnight and near the end of his duty guarding the planes. It was two a.m., and Misha looked forward to nothing more than deep, thoughtless sleep. His body demanded it. And after only a few minutes of lying on his bed with this lava-like relaxation coursing through his veins, he fell into the sleep of the dead. He did not move. He had no dreams. Time did not exist.

A half hour later he was awakened by a firm grip shaking him by the shoulder.

"Mikhail Borisov?" an impatient, gravelly voice asked.

"Yes, he is," Misha replied, unsure if he was dreaming the whole thing.

"What? I'm speaking to you, asshole. Are you Mikhail Borisov?"

Misha wasn't accustomed to someone using his formal name. "Who? Oh. Yes. That's me." He used his hand to ward off the blinding glare of the flashlight.

"Get dressed then. You're coming with us. You're under arrest."

Misha squinted at the flashlight owner's fat, square face. The man's forehead sloped heavily over his eyes so that they could hardly be seen. Below his head was a grapefruit-shaped body that had outgrown the uniform he wore.

"No. There must be some mistake," said Misha, trying to will himself awake. "Who are you looking for again?"

"Mikhail Borisov! Is that you or not?"

"Yes, that's me. But why would I be under arrest? I haven't done anything."

"You have ninety seconds to get your clothes on. I suggest you get started now."

"But it has to be a mistake! What are you talking about? What's the charge?"

"You're only wasting your own time. You have less than sixty seconds now."

"What? You just said I had ninety seconds!" Misha jumped out of bed and frantically grabbed his uniform and boots from his locker. He saw that another soldier, skinny and pale, had accompanied the fat one.

"What am I being charged with?" Misha asked as he pulled his shirt on.

The fat one ignored him, but the skinny one began to answer, "Comrade, we don't know. We're only following orders, but it's most likely—"

"Shut up!" interrupted the fat one. "Just get your damn clothes on, Borisov, and stop wasting our time."

Misha finished dressing without another word, but couldn't locate his socks and was still barefoot. Socks were a luxury to soldiers in the Red Army as the standard issue were *portyanka*—cheap, square rags that were wrapped around the feet. Misha's mother had given him socks only the month before, and he was especially protective of them. Anything of value left behind probably wouldn't be there when he came back, so he frantically searched inside his locker.

"Your sixty seconds is up," said the fat one. "Let's go."

"But I can't find my socks!"

"Too bad, let's go," he said and grabbed Misha by the arm.

"Let him get his socks for goodness sake," the skinny one said. "Comrade, where do you usually put them?"

"Next to my boots," Misha said. "I always put them next to my boots!"

The skinny guard looked around and then pointed to a small lump of dark clothing in the corner between Misha's locker and the wall. "What's that over there by your locker?"

"Ah yes, that's them," Misha wriggled free from the fat soldier's grip and grabbed his socks.

As he put his boots on, he snatched his last two cigarettes and a couple of matches from the bottom of his locker. They were forbidden in the cells, so he tried to do it discreetly. The skinny soldier watched Misha stuff the cigarettes in his boots, then looked away as if he hadn't noticed.

Misha paced back and forth in the tiny, damp cell—six short steps one way and six short steps the other. At one end of the room was a dingy window with black metal bars. At the other end was a sour-smelling old man leaning against the thick wooden door.

"Be grateful you're not here in the winter," Misha's cellmate said in a raspy voice. "You get ten days here then and it's a death sentence."

Misha could tell from his accent that he was Estonian. "What are you here for?" he asked the old man.

"Don't know. Been five days, and they still won't tell me."

Misha lit one of his cigarettes and continued pacing.

"If you gotta piss, there's a bucket in the corner," the old man said, pointing.

Misha looked at the bucket, then at the old man, trying to decide which of the two was making the room stink.

"Can you read?" the old man asked.

"Can I read what? Estonian?"

"No. It's Russian. I got a Bible my wife brung me, but I can't read."

"I'm not gonna be here long. This is all a big mistake."

"Well, for your sake, I hope so. They don't treat you so nicely here."

"Look, I don't want to talk right now. I need to think."

"All right, I'll be quiet. It's time for me to say my prayers anyway. I can say one for you if you want."

Misha inhaled deeply on his cigarette, hoping it would calm his trembling hands.

"Well?" asked the old man.

"Well, what?" Misha said irritably.

"Do you want me to say a prayer for you or not?"

"No, I don't! If there was a God, I wouldn't be in this mess in the first place! Now leave me alone!"

Misha continued his pacing until the cigarette had burned down to his fingers. Then he stubbed it out and tried to determine what they possibly could have arrested him for. Of course he'd heard of the stupefying number of officers arrested, but he was sure they'd all been imprisoned or shot for good reason. His own arrest had to be a mistake, and it was only a matter of time before they came and apologized.

But after a few more minutes, Misha cast doubt on his own view. As he recalled all those things he'd said to Stepanovich last night, he began to realize he was no different than the thousands of others who'd been arrested. He was in this stinking cell because of his big mouth. If it wasn't Stepanovich, then it was one of the countless, faceless others. Holding his face in his hands, he wept bitterly.

The old man came over and put his arm around Misha. "There, there, my boy. You won't suffer long. They'll be here soon and it'll all be over with."

"*Who* will be here soon?"

" I thought you could hear them. Isn't that why you're crying?"

Misha held his breath, trying to hear anything out of the ordinary, but all he detected was a pair of soldiers chatting in the distance. "I don't hear anything."

The old man knelt below the window, his knees cracking loudly. While making the sign of the cross in an unbroken pattern, he recited the Lord's Prayer.

Misha—still straining to listen—discerned a faint buzzing. After glancing about the cell for a trapped bee, he realized the noise was coming from someplace distant. "What *is* that?" he asked as the eerie sound grew louder, morphing into a deep hum.

"It's the savior! I told my wife he wouldn't forsake us. All you Russians will pay for your sins now!"

"What sins?" Misha said defensively. "I'm only nineteen. I haven't done anything!"

Misha's grandmother had told him stories about the Apocalypse when he was young. It had both terrified and intrigued him then. Now, it only terrified him. He pictured legions of angels descending from the sky with swords drawn.

As the low, distant hum began to be accompanied by far-off thunder, Misha scanned outside in between the bars of the window. He couldn't see much in the dim light, but came to the conclusion that the peculiar humming sound could only be one thing: dozens upon dozens of incoming planes.

"It's the Germans!" he exclaimed. "They're attacking us!"

When the thunder came nearer, the old man clapped. "I knew Hitler would save us!"

"Traitor! I'll tell them what you said!"

Misha caught sight of three panicked soldiers running past. "Why aren't our planes firing up?" he yelled at them. "The pilots should've been ready to go five minutes ago. No, *in the air* five minutes ago!"

As a wave of German planes flew high overhead, not a single gun from the Soviet anti-aircraft artillery fired at them. Even when bombs exploded on the airfield and fighter planes swooped in low raining down bullets like hail—Misha couldn't hear anyone firing back. "Those idiots!" he screamed. "They still won't let us shoot at the Germans!"

While explosions filled the air and shook the ground, Misha glimpsed a nearby building collapse amidst a flash of light and a deafening roar. Figuring his building was next, he ran to the door and pounded on it. "Let us out!"

No sooner had he hollered his words than a blast threw him against the wall. Dust filled the air. His ears rang. Pieces of brick were strewn everywhere. The old man and the wall with the window were both gone.

Misha clambered over the rubble to the outside. Frenetic spotlights searched the murky sky. Fires raged out of control. Smoke stung his eyes. And the unending explosions were so painfully loud, Misha was sure he'd be deaf if he survived.

Spellbound by the devastation, he stared absently at the towering flames all around and the planes crisscrossing the sky. The entire area was lit in haunting shades of red and orange.

Only after the bombing ended and a lone German fighter plane made one last flyby did Misha finally hear anti-aircraft guns firing. They missed. And as the sun peeked above the horizon, Misha spotted—in their same neat rows—all the Soviet planes. Each and every one of them was smashed to pieces and burning.

There were ninety-three planes in all. Ninety-three wrecked planes still chained to the ground.

A scrawny pigeon with ruffled feathers and only one eye stood several feet away from the half-dozen other pigeons feasting on bread crumbs being tossed their way. Each time the one-eyed pigeon attempted to join the gathering near the park bench, it was chased away. When a large crumb was thrown near it, the pigeon snatched the morsel and flew away to the statue of Pushkin, settling on top of the great Russian writer's head.

As a streetcar full of people passed by, a breeze rustled the young leaves of the numerous trees in the park. In a small clearing off to the left of the Pushkin statue, three boys enthusiastically kicked a soccer ball back and forth. And leaning forward on a park bench, tearing crumbs from a loaf of bread, was Felix. It was almost nine a.m., and he'd been sitting on that same park bench for the past three hours.

Across the street from him was the yellow, two-story, city government building where Katya's father worked. It was customary for Katya's father to work late and come home in the early morning hours, even on weekends. The habit had been passed down from Stalin, but 9:00 a.m. was exceptionally late—even for night-owl party officials.

Felix had already decided he'd wait as long as he needed to. He was supposed to help Dima move at noon, but that would have to wait, if necessary.

The experience with the ragged, one-eyed pigeon reminded Felix glumly of his father and how he'd been undermined and ultimately chased away from the university where he'd taught in Ukraine. Those were the darkest days Felix had ever known. His father had started drinking daily, and almost anything would set his temper off. But things had changed so much for the better since then, and all due to the kindness of Ivan Petrovich Pavlov. The Nobel Prize winning scientist admired Felix's father's work in the field of physiology and took him under his wing—bringing him to Leningrad to assist with his experiments. Felix's father had gained enough stature to become a leading scientist in the field, surviving even Pavlov's death in 1936.

Felix spied—at long last—a bear of a man exiting the building. Wearing a wrinkled, white dress shirt and black pants, the man walked briskly down the street, and Felix had to jog to catch up with him.

"Might I have a word with you?" asked Felix.

A stern, arrogant man by nature, Katya's father looked strangely nervous. His shoulders were tensed up toward his ears, and his lips were pursed and void of color. "I don't have time, Felix. I have to get home."

"Then I'll go with you."

Felix walked beside him the rest of the block in silence, trying to figure out how best to broach the topic. After they crossed to the next street, he blurted his question. "Why won't you let your daughter marry me?"

Katya's father cast a dubious, sidelong glance. "Because she's too young."

"She's the same age as her mother—may she rest in peace—when you married her."

"That was different."

"How?"

"It just was. Besides, Felix, it's not a good time right now. The world is on edge these days."

Katya's father was moving exceptionally fast, and Felix found it difficult to keep up. "I'm eighteen," he said. "I'm a man. Tell me the truth."

Katya's father stopped and fixed his eyes on Felix. "All right," he said, "It's because you're a Jew." Then he resumed his frantic pace. "You're a Jew, and nothing in the world is going to change that. Do you think you'll ever be more than a second-class citizen here?"

"In Socialist societies," Felix countered, "there are no classes, no distinctions between—"

Katya's father cut him off. "Don't give me that. You've got two eyes. You see what's going on. Tell me—in your heart—do you really believe that a few decades of communism are enough to wipe out two thousand years of anti-Semitism? You think people will just conveniently forget who killed Christ?"

Felix turned his gaze to the faint moon floating in the blue sky. He tried to comprehend its vast distance from the Earth.

Katya's father halted once more and rested a hand on Felix's shoulder. "I like you, Felix," he said. "I don't care that you're Jewish. But other people *do* care. They may pretend they don't, but I know them. I know what they say behind closed doors. Do you think it would be fair to Katya to be married to you? What kind of a life would she have? If you truly love her, then you'll put her interests above yours and do what's best for her."

Felix dropped his head and stared at Katya's father's brown shoes until he noticed them stepping away. Felix went the opposite direction, his thoughts on the moon. He remembered reading that when meteorites and asteroids enter the Earth's atmosphere, they usually burn themselves into oblivion before ever reaching the surface. The moon, however, doesn't have the luxury of an atmosphere. Its barren surface is dotted with deep craters from the constant bombardment. Scientists speculated that life probably could not exist there. Only the strongest and most resilient of life forms could possibly withstand such harsh conditions.

Felix roamed the streets of Leningrad aimlessly. With a general melancholy weighing on him, he strolled along a particular canal for an hour, then followed the Neva River for another hour. He wandered past the tall, golden-needle spire of the Admiralty, past the Winter Palace, and past the elevated, imposing statue of Peter the Great. With the withering summer sun high overhead, he walked through the expansive city until one image came to dominate his mind: the sculpture of Saint Andrew the Apostle that flanked the huge, bronze doors of the Kazansky Cathedral. He longed to sit in commiseration near the statue's forlorn face.

Like a dying elephant traveling to a designated graveyard it has never been to, so too Felix arrived, without particularly knowing how, at Kazansky's doorstep. A crowd—much larger than usual for 1:10 in the afternoon on a Sunday—had gathered in front of the cathedral. A giant of a man with an unruly beard yelled in anger as tears streamed down his face. Uniform-clad schoolgirls huddled together, looking aghast and consoling one another.

As Felix squeezed through the strange crowd toward the statue of Saint Andrew the Apostle, he heard bits and pieces of conversations confirming his fear that his thoughts were not his own, but open for public mocking and ridicule.

"What did you expect?" exclaimed a pale man with a gaunt face and hollow eyes. "I said all along they couldn't be trusted. They'll pretend like they're your friend, and then stab you in the back."

A young woman with a summer hat pulled low over her head hissed, "The whole thing was just one big lie. They've played us for the fool."

Felix hurried past, not wanting to get near any of them. Fear was alien to him, and its presence now was confusing.

"You know she won't last long. This will be too much for her," muttered an elderly man with wavy, gray hair. "It's probably best to move on. Take what you got and get out."

"Death," an old woman sighed. "That's what will come of this in the end. Maybe not today, maybe not tomorrow, but mark my words, death *will* come."

It was all getting to be too much for Felix. Even when he'd made it through the crowd to the statue, he still couldn't escape the voices.

"With bayonets!" a man shouted. "That's how we'll welcome them."

Since the word bayonet had never entered Felix's mind, this last statement made him stop and consider.

"Welcome who?" Felix asked the man.

"Haven't you heard?"

Felix shook his head.

"The Germans!" the man replied. "They attacked us this morning. Molotov just announced it."

The significance of the man's words was slow to sink in, but Felix eventually understood that it meant war.

He thought of his mother and father, and how they'd be sick with worry by now if they knew. He started to run home along Nevsky Prospekt, catching sight of people with wads of paper rubles in their hands rushing into jam-packed grocery stores. Those leaving the stores had their arms full with sugar, flour, butter, groats, sausage, and canned goods. Felix recognized a Party official's rotund wife. She was balancing over a dozen cans of caviar and four bottles of vodka in her plump arms.

At the State Savings Bank, the line was around the corner and halfway down the block. Everyone in line was pushing, shouting, and demanding their money, "*Immediately!*" A fight between two women broke out near the front, and for a moment it looked like the whole block might erupt in bedlam.

Felix dashed into the street to get by a dozen arguing men cloistered tightly together on the sidewalk. A group of teenagers—mostly boys, a few girls—were marching down the middle of the avenue singing the Internationale. Their voices briefly rose above all the shouting and commotion. "...We peasants, artisans, and others / Enrolled among the sons of toil / Let's change the earth henceforth for brothers ... the last fight let us face / The Internationale / Unites the human race...."

"Comrades," a man with a long beard and black cap roared as Felix approached. "We didn't ask to live through this, but by God we'll make it! They'll see how strong we are!" He waved his cane wildly in the air, and Felix ducked under it as he sprinted past.

Глава Вторая — Chapter Two

A Dream Incomplete

The unhappy clock could tick and it could tock,
  but missing from its life seemed the key to its lock.
High and low it searched in defeat,
  for its logic and reason left it incomplete.
How to fill the void inside, it knew not,
  but secured in that lock was the answer it sought.
The key it so yearned for really did exist,
  but the time on its face could no longer twist.
There is truth in deception, success in defeat,
  but a premature death is always a dream incomplete.

Alfred winced as the pain in his ribs spread outward in all directions with each breath. He'd found only two remedies for the agony: to not breathe, or to not think about it. He chose the latter.

Although his Soviet interrogators let him sleep for only a few hours at a time and fed him day-old black bread and stale water, the only things that really bothered him were his bruised ribs and that he hadn't been able to bathe in so long. The bruises were courtesy of one of the guards after Alfred had turned his head away for the fifth time just as they'd tried to take a photograph of him. From the sheer number of people and the way they were fussing over how it was to be taken, he knew it was going to be used for propaganda purposes and wanted no part of it.

When they finished with the photograph, his suspicions were quickly confirmed. They wanted him to issue a statement calling on German soldiers to overthrow Hitler and his government. They were prepared to inflict further physical punishment, but Alfred shocked them by cooperating on that. He was entirely in favor of banishing that madman from power.

It had been eighteen days since those events, and not much had happened since. The guards would be coming for him soon. They never went longer than four hours between interrogations. *Let them come*, thought Alfred. Let them spend his time however they wished. Stretching his arms over his head, he meandered to the end of his cell. The window there was set unnaturally high, and Alfred had to stand on his tiptoes to peer outside. In between the iron bars, he could see the guard in the wooden tower. He was always there, either pacing back and forth with his rifle resting in his arms or standing stock still and looking down at the people walking below.

Alfred eyed a nearby rose bush, watching a bee drop off the edge of one of the pink flowers and then buzz out of sight over the high brick wall that surrounded the complex. He'd spent hours contemplating the rose bushes. *Why would anyone plant roses in a prison?*

Outside his cell was a dark, windowless hallway that led to two places: the sun and sky outdoors, or to a thick door that opened into a cramped room with just enough space for a desk and three chairs. Alfred had walked down that hallway twenty times the past two weeks, but had yet to be let outside.

He could hear them coming down the hallway now—the unmistakable jingling of keys and the echo of a pair of heavy footsteps. Quickly, but carefully, he spread the green bed sheet over the edge of his bed so that it almost touched the floor. He pulled one side a little higher up from the floor than the other, and then rumpled the parts of the sheet that lay on top of the bed. Stepping over to the doorway, he scrutinized his work. It wasn't perfect, but it did the trick. The drooping sheet hid the loose bricks in the wall. Alfred had started chipping away at the mortar earlier that day after he discovered it practically crumbled with the slightest touch.

Stern Face appeared in the dirty, oval window of the door to Alfred's cell. "Prisoner! Step away from the door," he instructed in broken German. Stern Face said that each and every time he came for Alfred, whether Alfred was in fact near the door, or at the other end of his twelve-foot cell.

The door swung open swiftly, smacking the wall behind it. Alfred watched as more mortar fell to the floor. That was what had given him the idea in the first place, but he didn't like that the door kept doing it. He was afraid it was only a matter of time before the guards had the same thought.

Two men entered Alfred's cell: Stern Face, and a new face. New Face wore small, oval glasses that rested on a thin nose. He had eyes the color of slate, thick dark hair that was combed straight back, and a narrow mustache that barely reached the corners of his mouth. He was short, only coming to Alfred's chin, and his posture was perfect.

"Why does he stink so bad?" New Face asked in Russian.

"He's a Nazi," Stern Face replied matter-of-factly.

"I want him bathed this evening," New Face said. "That smell makes me sick."

Though they'd spoken in Russian, Alfred understood every word. At the thought of a bath, a slight smile crept across his face. As soon as he realized his blunder, he reverted back to his usual stoic expression.

"Does he speak any Russian?" New Face asked suspiciously.

"None," Stern Face answered. "He's an idiot."

"Hey German," New Face said slowly in Russian, "I've come to take you out back and shoot you." He watched Alfred's reaction closely.

Though Alfred again understood what had been said, he only stared blankly. He never let on to anyone that he understood some Russian. There had been a few close calls, like the time his first interrogator asked the translator if he wanted some water, and Alfred said yes and nodded his head because he thought he was the one being asked. He'd gotten out of that one by turning his "yes" into a yawn, and his nod into a neck stretch. Since then, he'd been much more careful—doing his best to look as uninterested as possible in any conversations in Russian, and only responding when something was spoken in German.

New Face surveyed the plaster on the floor where the door had struck it. Then he looked at the bed. "Were you sleeping?"

"No," said Alfred, impressed with the man's impeccable German.

"Then why isn't your bed made?"

Wishing he'd said yes, Alfred made no response. He wondered if the man might be a new translator, but that was doubtful. New Face had an air of authority about him, and translators never visited him in his cell unless an interrogator was present.

"Get your shirt on and come with us," New Face commanded in German. Then he led the way out of the cell and down the hall. Alfred pulled on his smelly, brown t-shirt and followed. Stern Face, with pistol drawn, went last.

At the end of the hallway was an iron gate. New Face called out to the guard on the other side to unlock it so they could pass through. As he waited, Alfred inhaled the scent of freshly polished leather from Stern Face's gun holster.

When New Face turned right after he passed through the gate, Alfred's heart began to race. Could they be letting him outside? But when Alfred reached the intersection, he was directed once again into the small, stuffy room on the left. After slumping into his usual seat, he watched New Face perch himself on the edge of the chair opposite him. New Face rested his arms on the desk, hands clasped together, just like Alfred's previous two interrogators had always done. Only now, the chair for the translator remained unoccupied.

"Private Liskof, can you explain to me why you surrendered yourself to the Soviet Border Guards?"

"I've explained that twenty times already."

"Well, perhaps twenty-one will be your lucky number, because quite frankly, your answers to this question have been unsatisfactory so far."

"You mean the truth is not to your liking?" Alfred said sarcastically.

New Face brought his right hand up and rested his chin on it. "I'd prefer that we don't get off to a bad start. Both of our well-being depends upon a successful outcome."

Alfred arched his eyebrows in astonishment at New Face's frankness. His comment about "well-being" confirmed Alfred's fear that an inauspicious ending awaited him soon.

New Face pulled a cigarette out from a square, tin case and offered it to Alfred. Alfred's first thought was that it might be laced with some sort of chemicals meant to inebriate or asphyxiate him. But then he decided to take the risk. After all, they had more forceful means at their disposal for getting him to ingest something.

The tobacco was harsh, obviously Russian, but tasted good nevertheless. Not having eaten in so long, Alfred became light headed after just a few inhalations.

"When's the last time you had a cigarette?" asked New Face.

"The day I took my leave of the German army and came here."

"Yes? And what day was that?"

"June twenty-first."

"I'm curious. What prompted you to, as you put it, 'take leave of the German army'?"

"I left because I thought they were making a terrible mistake, and I wanted to do something about it."

"How patriotic of you."

Alfred inhaled on his cigarette and meant to reply, but found himself subject to a coughing fit instead.

"You'll have to excuse our Soviet tobacco," New Face said. "I'm afraid it's not very high on our list of priorities. Probably your German tobacco is much more to your liking."

New Face reached into the desk drawer and retrieved a rolled-up poster. "I'd like to show you something," he said as he unrolled the poster and spread it out on the desk.

It was a photograph of Alfred—the one taken right after he'd received the blow to the stomach. He was dressed in his German army fatigues and had a dour expression on his face. At the bottom of the poster were the words: "A mood of depression rules among German soldiers."

"What do you think?" New Face asked.

Alfred shrugged his shoulders. "I don't think it's true."

"But you see, that's where you're wrong, Private Liskof. It *is* true. It is printed quite distinctly on the poster."

Alfred eyed New Face warily, and blew smoke out his nose like he used to as a teenager.

"We need to work together, you and I," said New Face, "so the Soviet people clearly understand your story. It's my job to help you."

Fed up with being in the drab room with its stale air and greenish-gray walls, Alfred leered at New Face, estimating how long it would take to kill him. It wouldn't be difficult. He could just punch his nose up into his face, then jump over the desk and put him in a chokehold.

"You see," New Face continued, "if you were to get up in front of a crowd, we would want to be sure that your message was conveyed correctly. The people of the Soviet Union need to understand that you *deserted*. They need to know that you left because you were treated badly, and that you had no desire to take up arms against your 'brothers in labor.' Soviet citizens must know how desperate the situation is in the German army. Are we beginning to understand one another?"

Alfred cracked his knuckles, then folded his arms in front of his chest. "I understand that I'm a prisoner here," he said, "that you're my interrogator, and that our two countries are at war."

New Face was like a statue—always keeping his gaze on Alfred and never once moving or stretching. "That's precisely why I was sent here," he said calmly. "To help you with your understanding. You are a prisoner here only in the sense that we can't let you simply walk away. I would like us to think of one other as partners, or allies, if you will. If we work together, we can each get something very important to us."

"The only thing I want is an end to this insidious war and to go home."

"There, you see, we have more in common than you think. I too want an end to the war and to go home. And I want you to help me put an end to the bloodshed. Will you help me do that?"

Alfred thought he understood New Face well enough, but hadn't expected this and didn't know how to react.

"That's all right. I didn't expect an answer just yet," said New Face. "We don't have to discuss this anymore right now. I merely wanted us to meet and try to reach an agreement to work together. You think about it for a while and be sure of your answer. Yes?"

After Alfred nodded, New Face stood and opened the door. When Alfred had taken his routine place to return to his cell, New Face surprised him by asking if he'd like to go outside for a brief walk. Puzzled by the generosity, Alfred mumbled in the affirmative, and before he knew it, he found himself outdoors in the slightly humid, yet thoroughly refreshing air of summer. Without a cloud in the sky, the sun was exceptionally bright and hot. Alfred, with his blue eyes, bald head, and fair skin, normally despised weather such as this. The sun was his enemy, he frequently said. But not today. Today, the sun was his childhood friend that he hadn't seen, nor thought about in ages. Today, he was grateful just to be able to breathe the air and walk in the light of day.

Felix had been near the end of the line and when his turn finally came, he had a choice between a shovel, a hand axe, or a hunting knife. Though the shovel wasn't as lethal as the other two, it did have more length, so he could fight from a greater distance. Gripping it with both hands, he thrust it forward like a bayonet. Then he moved his hands closer together on the handle and swung it like a sledgehammer. Next, he picked up the hand axe. It was short—no more than eighteen inches. The hunting knife, dull and rusty, was even shorter.

The ten men waiting behind Felix grew restless and yelled for him to hurry up. Finally, he decided on the shovel, since he could dig a trench when under attack.

He rejoined Dima, who'd been near the front of the line and had received a gun. Dima looked up from inspecting the twenty-five-year-old rifle. "Good choice," he said. "You can dig a trench with that. Those guys who took picks and axes don't know the first thing about modern-day warfare. They think it's going to be like the days of the Vikings doing hand-to-hand combat on open fields?"

Felix glanced at the remaining men waiting for a weapon, noticing they all had the same prominent Jewish nose he did. "Your rifle looks antique," he commented to Dima. "Does it work?"

"It's actually in decent shape. It's the same model my father used in the Civil War."

Dima had several advantages over Felix. For one, he was Russian. And Dima's father, a hero of the Civil War, had drilled Dima from a young age on how to fight and survive in a war.

"You know," Dima said as he scrutinized Felix's shovel, "you could sharpen the handle and make a nice bayonet out of it."

Felix agreed. "Good idea," he said as he retrieved the small knife he always carried with him. He sat on the grass beside Dima and began whittling the end of the wooden handle.

The First Volunteers Division, of which Felix and Dima were part of, was a motley collection of nearly 11,000 men with little or no military background or training. The average age of the men was much higher than the regular army. Some men were approaching fifty, while others, like Felix and Dima, were still in their teens. About a third of the division consisted of Party members or Young Communists.

Felix and Dima had been assigned to a company in the division that consisted almost entirely of men from the same furniture factory. Most all of them knew one another, and instead of using military jargon, those in command would politely say, "I beg of you..." or "Please do so and so...." Only a small percent of the division's officers had any command experience or formal military training. Most, but not all, of the officers wore regular Red Army uniforms, while the vast majority of men wore either their everyday clothes or a relative's old Civil War uniform.

The division had a third of the machine guns they were supposed to have and hardly any artillery. Some of the men, like Felix, had no rifles, and carried only picks, axes, shovels, or knives. More than a few men were armed with nothing but their own courage.

Felix and Dima had joined the People's Volunteers shortly after the war started. They'd gone into training the night of July 3 and used the playgrounds of the Fifth School on Stachek Prospekt as their drill field. Katya came by every evening with tea, a loaf of bread, and a large hunk of cheese.

They were scheduled to receive a month's worth of training, but the rapid advance of the Germans had cut that short, and they were now preparing to head to the front to help hold the Luga line. It was the morning of July 10, and the mood of the men preparing to depart was overtly upbeat. They made black humor jokes about their weapons and readiness, spoke abnormally loud, and mixed a vast array of profanity into every sentence.

In the beginning, Felix joined in, but soon realized the insincerity of it. Their lack of training and adequate weapons was absurd, yet they were being sent to fight.

After the division formed into a column, a man at the front hoisted a red and gold banner presented by the Kirov factory workers. A band assembled behind him, and within a few minutes the division was on its way to the Vitebsk freight station.

The middle-aged veteran marching next to Felix had a thick, white beard that covered all of his neck and most of his face. He wore knee-high leather boots and a gray jacket with five impressive medals pinned to it. In contrast, Felix, with his white dress shirt, black pants, and clean-shaven face, looked like someone who'd just finished visiting a museum.

As they marched along the streets to the band's patriotic songs, families, friends, and onlookers cheered and waved from the sidewalks. Though he tried, Felix couldn't share in the enthusiasm. He saw a now familiar poster plastered on the side of a building they passed. It was a picture of a German soldier with a dour expression, and the caption: "A mood of depression rules among German soldiers."

"Dima, what do you think about these posters all over the city?" Felix asked.

"I think it shows how desperate the situation is in the German army."

"But they're winning. There's talk they may even take Leningrad before autumn."

"They'll *never* take Leningrad!" Dima said sharply. "Not in a million years will a Nazi step on this ground."

"But Dima," Felix protested, "the situation seems rather desperate. Why else would they be sending people like you and me—with only an antique gun and a shovel—to the front?"

"It's only a matter of time before the tide turns. The Red Army was simply taken by surprise. Hitler's treachery caught us unprepared, that's all. Once we regroup, we'll drive the Nazis all the way back to Berlin. The German soldiers are being pushed to their limit by their bourgeois officers. That's why the Party put those posters up, to remind us what's at the root of this aggression. The German soldiers won't put up with much more. They'll rise up against their officers and demand to go back home. And then they'll overthrow Hitler and his sham government and the Revolution will spread. Things may look a little bleak right now, but trust me, it's just a matter of time before the German army falls apart."

Felix felt reassured by Dima's confident words. When he saw the same poster on another building, he wondered how accurate it was. And he wondered too if he would've been able to desert to the enemy lines if the situation had somehow been reversed. The thought of leaving his beloved Katya and Russia filled him with dread.

Back in his cell, Alfred dropped onto his bed like a dead man. He was hungry and tired, and wanted nothing more than to sleep. Still, he couldn't help thinking about his fate. What were his Soviet handlers planning for him? To give a speech denouncing Germany and the capabilities of the German army? If so, what would they do if he declined?

The pungent smell of his sweaty clothes permeated the air, and he stared at the cracked ceiling before finally dozing off. A few minutes later, two sharp raps on the door announced the arrival of the guard who served his late afternoon meal—a combined lunch and dinner.

"Nazi criminal," he called in Russian. "I have brought your dinner."

He was a skinny middle-aged man and did everything at a snail's pace. He liked to ramble on about various topics, often holding complete conversations with himself by asking questions and then providing the answers. His slow, lazy Russian was easy for Alfred to understand, though Alfred was careful to never let on that he did.

As the man shuffled in the door, Alfred examined the contents of the well-worn wooden tray. There was a large bowl of something steaming, the usual stale black bread, and a glass with a small crack that descended like lightning from top to bottom.

After setting the tray down on the bed next to Alfred, the man remarked, "That little commissar has made me bring you beef stew, and—instead of water—English tea. It's better than I eat, and yet you, an enemy of the people, get it." Leaning against the door frame, he leered at Alfred. "But what do I know? I'm an old man putting in my time until they let me die."

He always came unarmed and alone—unlocking the door, bringing in the food, then waiting until Alfred finished so he could take the tray, bowl, and cup back with him. The last several times he'd come, he'd spoken at length about how poorly the war was going for the Soviets. Alfred didn't understand how someone like him could know so many details about the war, but he found himself believing the man and his outlandish stories.

"General P___ complained again that his tanks on the front are all quite old and in need of repair," the man commented dryly. "'And the planes ain't much better!' he griped. They didn't like that none. Complaining don't ever go over too well."

Alfred sat on his bed enjoying the tea, all the while staring at the wall or the dusty floor and pretending as though he didn't comprehend a word being said.

"And what happened to those twenty-five front-line divisions?" the man asked incredulously. "I'll tell you what happened to them. They've been obliterated by the Panzer tanks and the Luftwaffe—those demons from the sky. Tell me, how is it that the great Soviet army is being routed? How is that possible?"

Alfred turned his attention to the food on his tray, noticing the bread wasn't moldy or stale for once. And the stew smelled delicious.

"Perhaps it's all a lie," the man replied to his own question. "Perhaps some of the reports from the front are German propaganda. Or maybe from provocateurs." Then he rejected his own theory, explaining how many of those who had been in command at the start of the war had already been replaced.

While Alfred listened to the man's blather, he glimpsed past him through the open door. It would be so easy to break the man's neck and run down the hallway. But Alfred knew there was nowhere to escape to. In addition to the locked iron gate at the end of the hallway, there was the pistol-clad guard stationed on the other side. If Alfred somehow made it past those two obstacles, there was still no place to go. The entire building was surrounded by a fifteen-foot wall with barbed wire. And of course there was that tower with its restless guard and searchlight.

Alfred doubted the complex was ever meant to be a prison. In fact, he'd never seen another prisoner. He might be the only one. If it was not a prison, then that would explain the rose bushes, the lack of a slot in his cell's door, and the fresh mortar holding the bars in place on his window.

"Hey German, you want in on a little secret?" the man said as Alfred finished a bite of bread and dipped his spoon into the steaming bowl. "That stew's been poisoned."

By the time Alfred translated the word "poisoned" from Russian to German in his head, the spoon was already on its way to his mouth. He had to think fast. Was the man serious? Trying to catch him at understanding Russian? Or maybe he just had a strange sense of humor? If Alfred didn't take the bite of stew, or even if he paused, then he would surely be discovered.

An astute poker player, Alfred glanced at the man's face and decided he was bluffing. Alfred ate the stew, and though it tasted strange to him, he reminded himself that everything tasted strange to him in this country.

"Don't say I didn't warn you," the man remarked.

Alfred savored the stew, finding the taste improved with each bite. If he was wrong about it being poisoned, he decided he may as well enjoy the last meal of his life. Closing his eyes, he ate slowly, focusing all his attention on the aroma and texture of each spoonful. While he ate, the man continued his chatter about anything and everything. Even after Alfred had finished and ventured to the corner of the room to piss in the can, the man rambled on.

"That little commissar is going to eat you up," he said as he shifted his weight from one leg to the other. "He's probably got your trust already. Yes, he's very disarming in his thoughtfulness. Everyone knows about him though. Well, everyone but you, I guess."

"Comrade Surikov," a voice echoed down the hallway. "What is taking you so long?"

"Nothing, comrade," the man replied as he gathered the tray. "I'm leaving now."

After the man's scuffling footsteps faded down the hallway, Alfred quietly moved his bed away from the wall. Then he carefully pulled out the four bricks he'd already loosened. He was halfway done; another four bricks, and he'd be able to squeeze through the opening to the outside.

As he scraped and poked at the brittle mortar with the nail he'd pulled from the bedframe, Alfred thought of his father. He would likely have learned by now that Alfred had deserted to the Soviet lines. And he would likely be enduring scorn from family and friends.

At first, Alfred took pleasure in knowing his actions would bring his father shame and embarrassment. It would be one small retribution for Alfred's anguished childhood. But something was changing in him. A tender sorrow deep within was working its way to the surface, softening his thoughts every once in a while. Like now, when he realized he'd inherited not only his father's rage and despair, but also his love of animals and appreciation of music. For better or worse, Alfred knew that he owed his very life to his father.

After two hours of work, Alfred lay down to rest for a few moments. He felt so tired and groggy that he wondered if they really had poisoned the stew.

From somewhere amidst the crowds of people at the freight station, Felix heard his name being called. Both Felix's and Dima's parents had seen them off at the start of the march, so he doubted it was them. Up and down the platform, friends and family were gathered in circles around a volunteer about to board the train for the front.

Felix searched the faces of the group behind Dima. The volunteer was twice Felix's age, and pressed tight against the man was an old man with a cane, a plump grandma, a tearful wife, and four young boys and girls no taller than Felix's shovel. Turning his attention to a different group, Felix caught out of the corner of his eye Katya hurrying toward him. By her side was her father waving and yelling Felix's name.

Katya bounded up to his Felix, wrapping her arms around him and kissing him on both cheeks. She was wearing a sleeveless dress that bared her thin, slightly tanned arms and shoulders. A few seconds later, her father arrived and shook Felix's hand. With a look of confusion at Felix's shovel, he asked, "Where's your weapon?"

"*This* is my weapon," Felix grinned as he held up the shovel. "And here is my bayonet," he added, pointing to the sharpened end of the handle.

"Are you serious?" Katya's father asked, arching his eyebrows. "They told me we were short on weapons, but I had no idea it was this bad. What are you going to do with a shovel?"

"He'll dig their graves for them, that's what," crowed Dima.

Katya rolled her eyes. "Oh father," she pleaded, "can't you do something? This is sheer insanity."

"Don't worry. They told us we probably won't even see any Germans," Felix said. "And if they do show up," he added with a smirk, "we'll ask them to wait until we finish our training."

Katya grinned at his joke, but didn't laugh. "Aren't you scared of going into battle with only a shovel?"

"We're not afraid of anything," declared Dima. "Least of all the Germans."

"Show me a man without fear, and I'll show you a man without a pulse," Katya's father said gravely.

Taking exception to his words, Dima began arguing with Katya's father. Felix used the opportunity to slip away with Katya, holding her hand as they walked toward the end of the train.

"Your father doesn't look well," Felix commented. "He's so pale. Is he sick?"

"I don't know," Katya replied, her smile receding into concern. "He works non-stop now. Doesn't get any sleep. He's losing weight. And of course the war isn't going well. Every time I see him, he tells me about some new officer or official who's been 'relieved of his duties.' I keep begging him to slow down, to take at least one night a week off to rest. He agrees and promises to do it, but then always comes up with an excuse at the last second."

Felix stopped and took both of Katya's hands in his. "Well, he's always been strong as an ox. He'll be all right," he said, half believing it. "Katya, listen," he continued. "We don't have much time left. They'll be calling us to form ranks any minute and—"

"Don't go," interrupted Katya.

"What?"

"I'm serious," she said. "Don't go. It's not right."

"Katya," Felix said, bringing her hands up to waist level and squeezing them a little tighter, "we've been through this before. If nobody goes to fight, then the Nazis win. We'll be slaves."

"Let the others fight," she said. "You don't have to."

"I do," he said. "I do have to fight."

"Why?"

"To protect people like you," he said, brushing the back of his hand along her cheek.

Her hands started to tremble.

"Now I know that nothing's changed," Felix said, "so I'm not going to ask you to promise to marry me one day." He pulled a ring out of his pocket. It had a small ruby in the middle and a petite diamond on each side. "My mother gave this to me. She said it was my grandmother's ring. I want you to keep it as a promise that you won't forget me—you know, should anything happen." Felix looked into her sad brown eyes and the tears forming there.

"Oh Felix, this world is so crazy," she blurted. "Maybe that's why you fit in so well." Simultaneously laughing and crying, she added, "To hell with your forget-me-not. When you come back, I want to marry you—with or without my father's permission."

"Don't joke about such a thing," he reproached her. "It's not funny to me."

"Who's laughing?"

"You are."

"All right, so maybe I am, but not about that."

Felix's face lit up. "You're serious?"

She nodded.

"Kirov Division of Volunteers! Fall in!" an officer shouted.

Felix gave Katya a big smile and a quick kiss on the lips before departing. After only a few steps, he ran back, pulled her close and kissed her again, this time longer.

"You'll be careful, won't you?" she asked. Her laughter was gone, but the tears still streamed down her nose.

"My Katya, my sunshine, I'll be careful. I promise," he said as he brushed her cheek once more.

Rushing to join his comrades in formation, he remembered he still had the ring. "Katya!" he shouted as he tossed the ring over the young girl walking between them. Katya caught it with both hands.

With a last desirous glance at her slender neck and bare shoulders, Felix turned and fell in line next to Dima and the rest of his division.

Fifteen minutes later, they were aboard the train and heading toward the front. Felix was quiet and gazed out the window at the passing countryside for most of journey. He couldn't stop thinking of Katya and how precious life was. That he could die in battle seemed preposterous. Life had always been fair to him, and God—or whoever was in charge—surely wouldn't allow him to perish at such a young age.

But then he was reminded of that dreaded prophecy. When he was twelve, a kindly fortune-teller had explained to him that the life he'd chosen was fraught with danger. She'd described it as "high risk" and "a fool's gamble."

"If you are not strong enough, not diligent enough," she'd said, "then this life will not turn out as you hoped. You will succumb to a great bitterness, loneliness, and contempt."

"And if I am successful?" Felix had asked.

"If you are successful, then you will undergo a great transformation in your life under the most trying of circumstances. You will unearth a closely guarded secret, available only to a select few."

"And what is that?"

"You will have found the end of sorrow."

A wooden sign had been nailed to a tree for all to read as they disembarked from the train. In hand-painted, red letters, it said: "Our cause is just. The enemy will be beaten. Victory will be ours." Felix—one of the last ones off the train—had just finished reading it when a tremendous blast knocked him to his knees. He'd escaped any shrapnel, but the man behind him hadn't been so fortunate. Dima grabbed Felix by the arm and pulled him to his feet. Dizzy and confused, Felix simply ran along as best he could with this familiar figure who had helped him up.

The train ride to Batetsk had been so uneventful that the chaos they now found themselves in seemed surreal. They'd been unloading from the train when they'd first heard the planes high overhead. A minute later, gunfire and explosions had erupted all around them. German dive-bombers and fighter planes were welcoming the new Soviet troops to the front.

As everyone scattered to find shelter from the lethal rain of shrapnel, Dima led Felix to a small, abandoned cottage where they leaned against the back outside wall. Once Felix caught his breath, he realized where he was and who the former stranger was.

"Dima," he called over the mayhem. "What do we do now?"

"We've got to get to that hill," Dima answered, pointing to a small mound with several trees and bushes.

Felix scrutinized the open field they'd have to cross while Katya's parting words rang in his ears: "*You'll be careful, won't you?*"

"Perhaps we should stay here until the planes leave," Felix suggested. "It'll be dangerous crossing that field."

"We can't stay here," Dima said adamantly. "It's only a matter of time until they start shooting up this house. The trees and bushes on that hill will shield us from the pilots' sight."

Four men rounded the corner of the house and joined them. One was wounded, bleeding profusely from the shoulder. Dima took a piece of cloth from his pocket and handed it to the man. "Here," he said, "put some pressure on the wound."

The man did as he was told. "We've got to get him to a medic fast," Dima announced to the group.

"It's nothing," the wounded man said.

With a second glance at the man's blood-stained shirt, Dima reiterated that they needed to get him to a medic right away. "We'll have to make a run for it," he told the others. "I'm going to count to five, and then you guys go. Be sure to spread out. Don't bunch up and give them a target."

"Are you going with us?" asked Felix.

"No," Dima replied. "I'm going to find a medic."

Felix grabbed his shovel, wondering if he should hold it with both hands like a bayonet or simply with one arm, hanging at his side the way he'd been carrying it.

"One," Dima began to count.

Felix scanned the field with its one hundred yards of open space. There were no houses, trees, bushes, ditches, or anything to hide in or behind.

"Two."

A plane flew high overhead—the roar of its engines building, then fading away.

"Three."

Felix heard a whistling sound, and then a massive explosion that shook the ground they stood on.

"Four."

Thick black smoke drifted their way and briefly engulfed them.

"Five!"

Felix waited for the others to start. Then he sprinted to the far right of them, putting as much distance as possible between himself and the next person. Being the fastest of the group, he reached the midway point first. He could hear planes overhead, but didn't look up, focusing instead on traversing the field as quickly as possible.

When he reached the small hill, he hid behind a tree and watched the others as they came in. The wounded man arrived last, pressing both hands tight to his shoulder. He crumpled to the ground shortly thereafter.

While they waited for Dima to come with the medic, they gaped at the train being methodically demolished. Every time another man joined them on the hill, Felix worried it would alert the pilots and invite an attack.

After the German planes ran out of bombs and bullets, they left the area, stealing away with them all excitement or fervor the volunteers had felt back in Leningrad. The wounded man had long since perished before Dima finally returned.

"Where's the medic?" Felix asked.

"Dead," replied Dima as he collapsed to the ground.

Gnats flew around Felix's head, and to his dismay he found he couldn't block them out. The voice in his head that usually reassured him, instead whispered insistently: "*I don't want to be here.*"

After the chaos subsided, the First Volunteers Division assembled to assess the damage. Over a dozen men had been killed and fifty wounded. The train and the tracks were badly damaged, but that wasn't a major concern for them. Their primary objective was to get to the eighteen-mile section of the Luga line that they were to protect. Once there, they'd be able to finish their training so they'd know what to do the next time they were attacked.

Many didn't fare well on the long march to the front. The division lost nearly twenty percent of its men—not to enemy forces, but to physical exhaustion. Besides being considerably older than regular army troops, most of the men were physically unfit and completely unprepared for such a hike.

When the division arrived at its destination, they had only two days to rest and train before a surprise attack by German infantry and Panzer tanks. Each volunteer had just been given one real hand grenade and one Poor Man's Grenade—a Molotov cocktail. They'd been learning how to throw them when gunfire and explosions in the distance interrupted the lesson. After being informed the Germans were attempting to break through the line near Lake Ilmen, the Volunteers division was dispatched there to repel the advance.

Felix and Dima's company was sent to a small village and instructed to dig in. It was warm, and the sky was clear. A perfect day, Felix thought, for swimming in the Neva River and then lying on the shore to dry off and soak up the sun. Instead, he was getting blisters on his hands from digging a trench.

Their company's commander, an engineer who had never been in a battle before, instructed them to take up positions at the end of the town. When Dima pointed out that the Germans would likely attack from the other end and that it made sense to set up there instead, he was asked to kindly keep his mouth shut and do what he was told.

The village consisted of two dozen small houses and an old church that now served as a combined post office and general government building. When it became clear that some of the houses still had occupants, the company's commander went door-to-door ordering all able-bodied men to come and help fight. The farmers joined the forty-two volunteers grudgingly, carrying axes or old hunting rifles out from their houses.

From their trench next to a row of raspberry bushes, Felix and Dima had a good view down the main road of the town. The lake was to their left, and Dima assured Felix they didn't have to worry about the Germans trying to go through the narrow tract between their position and the lake.

"So where will they attack?" Felix asked.

"If they decide to come this way," Dima answered, "they'll probably come down this road. It's the best terrain for their tanks."

Just as Felix was about to ask what they were supposed to do if they encountered a tank, Dima hushed him and pointed at the other end of town. Emerging from the trees alongside the road were enemy troops. When Felix spotted them, his heart dropped into his stomach and he felt nauseous. A Panzer tank with a skull and crossbones painted on its side came into view a minute later and started rumbling toward them. A few soldiers rode on the back of the tank and several more jogged behind it.

Approximately two dozen Germans scurried low to the ground, swiftly moving in behind houses at the far end of town. The tank continued its trek down the road toward Felix and Dima and the rest of the volunteers.

Felix glanced nervously at the others, feeling slightly relieved to see he wasn't the only one who felt petrified. Pavel, a tall, lanky Siberian, was visibly shaking as he crouched behind an outhouse. Pavel was one of the lucky ones with a gun, but even so, he hadn't yet been taught how to use it.

As the tank drew nearer, their commander ordered them to shoot at it.

"That fool!" Dima muttered under his breath to Felix. "It's a waste of ammunition."

Several volunteers in a nearby trench stood up and shot at the tank. The bullets merely ricocheted off, and a few seconds later the tank pounded their position with its guns. The men were killed instantly amidst a shower of dirt.

A dozen volunteers promptly dropped their weapons and fled into the nearby forest. Felix and Dima watched a comrade with a lit Molotov Cocktail run into the middle of the road. As he hoisted it over his head to throw at the oncoming tank, he was immediately gunned down.

Three volunteers then stepped out from their hiding spot and threw a grenade each at the tank. Two of the men threw the grenades too high and they landed well short of their target. The third man threw his underhand, along the ground, in an apparent attempt to get it to bounce its way underneath the tank. It too landed well short and exploded harmlessly in the middle of the road. Again, the tank fixed its guns on the men's hiding spot—a dilapidated brick fence—and blasted it to pieces.

The battle had barely begun, and already Felix had seen several of his comrades killed and many more wounded. "What do we do about that tank?" he yelled to Dima over the din of battle.

"We've got to flank it," replied Dima.

Felix didn't know what that meant, but he was all for leaving the spot where they were.

"Follow me," Dima hollered to the men around them. Then he leapt from the trench to the back wall of a nearby house.

Felix went next, but the others remained behind. Either they hadn't heard Dima, or they were too scared to move.

Dima and Felix dashed down an adjacent alley toward the main road, stopping at a house on the corner. While Dima readied his Molotov Cocktail, Felix peeked around the corner at the road. They were now behind the tank as it slowly moved away from them toward the end of the village, decimating the volunteers remaining there.

After lighting the cocktail, Dima jumped out and threw it, then quickly returned to the safety of the house. Felix, again peeking around the corner, saw the tank engulfed in flames. A few seconds later, the men inside scrambled out. One of them was on fire and died a few feet from the tank. Another ran to the opposite side of Felix and Dima and disappeared behind some houses.

The gunfire throughout the village was no longer sporadic. It was nearly continuous now.

"Good," commented Dima as he led them back down the alley. "That means we must be fighting back."

Though Felix didn't know where they were going, he followed anyway. He felt safer with Dima. Not only did his friend seem to be the only one who knew what he was doing, he also had a gun.

As they raced around a stone house covered with grape vines, they surprised three German soldiers setting up a machine gun. Two of them were kneeling on the ground assembling the base—their rifles lying on the ground next to them.

The third soldier was standing guard, but he'd been looking the opposite way when Felix and Dima rounded the corner. He swung around, rifle in hand, but it was too late. Dima had already stopped, taken aim, and pulled the trigger. The shot hit the German in the chest, killing him instantly.

While one of the Germans tried to rotate the machine gun toward Felix and Dima, the other lunged for his rifle. Only a few yards away, Dima charged with his bayonet as Felix gripped the handle of his shovel and swung it like a club.

Felix struck the man in the cheek and he collapsed to the ground. Raising the shovel over his head for a final blow, Felix saw the man's terrified expression and couldn't do it. With a glance over his shoulder, he saw Dima thrusting his bayonet into the stomach of the other German. The dying man gasped for air as Dima kicked his rifle away so he couldn't reach it.

"Watch out!" Dima shouted as he turned toward Felix.

Instinctively, Felix took a step back, but not before he felt a sharp pain. He stumbled backward a few steps, then made his way haltingly to the ground. He'd been stabbed with a knife.

Dima darted over and plunged his bayonet into the ribs of the enemy soldier. "Why didn't you finish him off?" he chastised Felix.

Felix, in shock, couldn't reply—not that he knew the answer anyway.

Dima swung the machine gun around, then dragged the three dead Germans in front of it, stacking them one atop the another. Then he fired at several enemy soldiers trying to cross from one side of the road to the other. Of the four making the attempt, only one reached the other side.

Felix, hyperventilating, clutched at his stab wound. It was the most intense pain he'd ever experienced. The blood spurting out compounded his nausea, and he turned his head to the side and vomited.

The voice in his head that had been saying, "*I don't want to be here,*" was through whispering. Now, it just screamed.

It was early morning when Alfred finally awakened. He'd slept for over ten hours and was covered with sweat and mosquito bites. After untwirling the bedsheet from his arms and legs, he threw it irritably across the room.

"Damn this country," he muttered to himself.

He'd come with good intentions, trying to prevent a catastrophe, but no one had heeded his warning. Instead of gratitude—or, at a minimum, respect—they treated him as a common criminal, subjecting him to a hot, stuffy cell and endless interrogations. And what happened to that shower he was supposed to get? Probably just another lie, he told himself.

He felt reinvigorated after breakfast and the English tea they again served him. It strengthened his resolve during the morning interrogation. For the first four hours they discussed Alfred's scheduled speech, and Alfred argued with New Face over every assumption and nuance.

"But, in principle, you agree with me?" New Face asked at one point as he leaned back in his chair and interlaced his fingers behind his head.

"In principle," Alfred replied, "I believe in right and wrong, good and bad, and truth and lies."

New Face arched his eyebrows. "And where has this misguided philosophy got you in life?"

"This *misguided philosophy* has landed me in a Soviet prison where I spend my days either in a tiny cell by myself or in a tiny cell talking to you."

"And do you like spending your days this way?"

"It's great," Alfred said sarcastically, watching New Face for his reaction.

New Face almost smiled, but didn't. "Do you like talking to me for hours on end?"

"Oh yes, it's fascinating." Alfred started to laugh—half out of delirium, half from exasperation.

"Alfred," New Face said sternly, "you need to be honest with yourself. Don't you think it's about time you do something different?"

Alfred held his aching ribs with his hands and shrugged his shoulders.

"You're a soldier," New Face continued. "What would you do if you were going into battle and your gun didn't work?"

"I'd try to fix it."

"And if it still didn't work?"

"I'd get a new one that did work."

"Precisely. So throw away these anachronistic views of yours and adopt some that work. These are not the old times anymore. The truth is what the people need to hear. It's that simple. Here in the Soviet Union, the Party makes the decisions and—"

"The Party doesn't decide for *me*," Alfred interrupted.

New Face frowned, then leaned forward in his chair, bringing his face close to Alfred. His slate-colored eyes took on a duller shade of grey. "I think it's helpful at times like this," he said flatly, "to remind ourselves of why we're here, and why we're both interested in a successful outcome." He sat back in his chair, but kept his gaze fixed on Alfred. "What is it that I want? *I* want to get away from this miserable little outpost and return to Moscow. And *you*—I suppose you would like to continue living, yes?"

Alfred didn't respond. Instead, he focused his attention on how New Face's dark hair was always combed so perfectly straight back. As long as he fixated on that, he wasn't really in this room, wasn't really in this predicament.

New Face, not waiting for an answer, continued. "Now then, let's review once again the important points of what you're going to say and where you'll stand on the stage."

As another futile hour went by, Alfred felt his will slowly breaking. New Face never quit. Even when Alfred succeeded in getting him to acquiesce on a particular point, it would only be a matter of time until New Face returned to the same point and started from the beginning. It infuriated Alfred. He couldn't argue like that. Once a point was won or lost, you had to move on. Those were the rules of debating.

A half-hour later, Alfred was back in his cell. With a sense of resignation, he lay on his bed and contemplated the worth of truth, honesty, and altruism in this day and age. He'd left one country because of its reckless, authoritarian leaders, and somehow ended up in another.

He longed for freedom, for the time when man was unrestricted in speaking his mind and living as he pleased. But when was that time? Had it ever existed? A lifelong student of history, Alfred racked his brain to think of an age when man had truly been free. He scrutinized the ancient Greeks, the Romans, the Egyptians, and realized not a single one had ever allowed true freedom!

He felt like crying, but no tears would come. Where were they? Where were all those tears he never allowed to see the light of day?

Perhaps true freedom, he pondered, is merely acceptance. Acceptance that to live means to suffer and to eventually die. Wasn't that what everyone was fighting for? A vain attempt to decrease their suffering. Hoping that more military victories or more land would somehow make them happy.

But if people accepted suffering—accepted it as a part of life—then wouldn't that change something?

He didn't know. Overcome with despair, he wanted nothing more to do with the world. He was through fighting to ease his suffering. And if death was ready for him, he was certainly ready for death.

"Nazi criminal," announced a voice from the hallway, "your dinner is here."

How Alfred had come to hate the sound of Russian being spoken!

"Well, General P___ was shot last night," the man announced as he entered and set the tray down. "Too many complaints and not enough victories, I guess."

Surprised by a fresh, lone strawberry on the tray, Alfred recollected his prized strawberry patch back home. But the memory incensed him. He knew he'd never see his garden again. It was then that he sprang from the bed and wrapped his arm around the man's throat in a chokehold. Alfred held tight until the man's body went limp, then quietly laid him on the floor.

Alfred removed the unconscious man's Soviet uniform, then dressed himself in it. The clothes were tight, but at least they fit. He slid his bed away from the wall and removed the eight loose bricks. Squeezing through the hole headfirst, he found himself outdoors behind a small, thorny bush.

The sun was high in the sky. White clouds drifted by aimlessly. Everything was remarkably quiet, and, for some strange reason, familiar—as though he'd already seen and done this before.

Through the bush's verdant leaves, Alfred spotted the guard in the tower pacing back and forth as usual. Three Soviet soldiers walked out the door of the building to Alfred's left. They were chatting and stopped to light cigarettes before continuing around the corner. Alfred didn't know what was around the corner of the building, but he hoped the complex's exit was there.

After a brief scan, he jumped out from behind the bush and began walking as casually as he could, his heart beating nearly two hundred times per minute.

He stole a glance at the guard tower and saw the man still pacing. Nearing the corner of the building, he could hear some men having a conversation. They were talking about a long forgotten song and trying to remember the lyrics. "The willow tree whispers my name," one of them hummed, "and the wolf searches for the water, but the stream has dried up—"

"No. It wasn't a willow tree," another man argued.

Alfred pulled his cap down tighter over his head. As he turned the corner, he caught sight of the two men. They were both soldiers, armed with semi-automatic rifles, guarding the complex's entrance.

The old wooden gate behind them was propped open, and beyond it Alfred could see a narrow dirt road and lots of open space. Trucks and motorcycles were parked about fifty yards away, and Alfred hoped to make it there and steal one of the motorcycles.

As he approached the guards, he bowed his head and crossed his right arm in front of his face, pretending to scratch his left eyebrow. He wasn't sure if he'd be questioned, but if so, he could mumble a "yes" or "no" easily enough. If the question demanded more than one word though, Alfred's German accent and limited Russian would surely doom him.

Just as Alfred was a few yards away, an officer came through the gate from the opposite direction. Upon seeing the man, the guards abruptly stopped talking and stood at attention. The officer halted and looked them both up and down. "Are you supposed to be socializing while you're on duty?" he asked sharply.

Alfred recognized New Face's voice.

"No, comrade," the men responded.

Alfred—too close to turn away without drawing attention to himself—passed within a few feet of the three men as he walked through the exit. As he strode toward the motorcycles, he heard one of the men sniffing loudly. "When's the last time you two bathed?" New Face asked.

"Yesterday," the two guards replied in unison.

"Then why do you stink so bad?"

"It's not us. It must be him."

Alfred hoped they weren't pointing at him, but New Face's voice confirmed the worst.

"Comrade," New Face yelled in Alfred's direction, "may I have a word with you."

Alfred kept walking.

"Who was that?" New Face asked the guards.

After saying they didn't know, they shouted at Alfred to stop.

Alfred knew he couldn't turn around, so he pretended not to hear them and kept walking.

New Face ordered a guard to fire a warning shot in the air.

"Halt!" the guards shouted again. A sharp crack echoed through the sky.

Alfred was getting close to the motorcycles—just a few more steps and he could make a run for it.

"I know that smell," Alfred heard New Face say. Then, in German, his Russian interrogator called out, "Stop! Or you will be shot!"

Alfred charged down the road toward the motorcycles.

"Shoot him!" ordered New Face.

Bullets whizzed past Alfred, striking the ground around him and kicking up little puffs of dust. Something stung him in the left leg, and he knew he'd been shot. Nearing his goal, he felt something else penetrate his chest through his back. It didn't hurt, but it was instantly harder to breathe.

His legs giving way from under him, Alfred dove in between two parked motorcycles. The gunfire then ceased, and all was quiet again.

Memories of his father came to Alfred. He recalled himself as a young boy throwing a tantrum: screaming, sobbing, and beating his pillow with his fists. His father barged into the room, warning him to stop crying. "Grow up and be a man," his enraged father had commanded. And that obedient little boy had done just that. Alfred had stuffed his tears and sadness deep inside.

"Alfred!" New Face called. "Come out from there."

But Alfred wasn't coming out. He was dying. He could barely breathe.

In between coughs, he contemplated his father's constant criticism, anger, and indifference toward him. Then, for perhaps the first time in his life, he stopped thinking about himself and what he'd went through, and thought solely about his father. How miserable his father must have been! How unloved he must have felt to have acted the way he did!

In that instant, Alfred released all his bitterness and resentment. As he opened his heart, all the black hate within drained away. Then, he wept and coughed and mourned the loss of his incomplete life. As he began to lose consciousness, he could hear men approaching and New Face urging him to come out with his hands up. But it was too late for that. It was too late for everything. Perhaps in his next lifetime he'd get it right.

With his last breath, Alfred gazed up at the white cottonball clouds drifting in the sky. He felt himself float up and away from his body, and a sentiment emerged from his heart and rose along with him. It was three words—Forgive Me Father—and they drifted higher and higher until they coalesced into a small bright star in an infinite black sky.

Глава Третья — Chapter Three

THE GREENFINCH'S SONG

I am caviar and fireworks,
   and music too loud for your ears.
I am your opiate,
   the master of your hopes and fears.
You'll know me when I enter you.
   you'll moan with the deception deep inside of you.
Feels so good, between your thighs,
   feel the meaning of life explode in lies.

From the edge of the forest, Misha gazed at the dark green coaches of the train as they crept around the bend in the tracks. Children stood or sat with their faces pressed up against the windows and waved at Misha and Igor. Misha waved back—holding his arm up high and swinging it slowly back and forth.

"Where are they going?" asked Igor. He was a twelve-year-old boy with big ears, a pug nose, and in desperate need of a bath and haircut. He'd begun traveling at Misha's side two days ago, much to Misha's dismay.

"I heard they're evacuating Leningrad and sending children to live on the other side of the Ural Mountains until the war is over," Misha answered.

Some of the children on the train were quite young, no more than three or four years old. A few appeared to be Igor's age, but the vast majority were between five and ten years old. A group of older boys yelled out the window to Misha and Igor asking where the Germans were. Misha pointed behind himself. "How far?" they asked. "A long way," Misha yelled.

Eventually, the whole train passed by and there was nothing but the clack-clack of the rails as the caboose vanished into the forest.

"Why would they leave the city? My father says the war will be short. A few weeks or months at the most," said Igor.

Misha felt uncomfortable whenever the boy talked about his father in the present tense. "The only way the war will be that short is if the Germans win," he replied.

"You're a liar!" accused Igor. "My father says Stalin will lead the Red Army to victory. He's not a coward."

Misha didn't know if the last statement was meant to refer to the boy's father or Stalin. It didn't really matter though. Misha wasn't going to argue with him. The boy had been through enough already.

Plopping on the ground to give his tired legs a rest, Misha took a drink from his canteen then passed it on to Igor.

The boy and his parents had been living in a rural area not far from the border when the Germans came. Igor's father had recounted to Misha how they were forced to stand by while the soldiers stole their animals and looted their home. When finished burning their crops, they turned their flame thrower on the house. Igor's father had tried to stop them, only to be laughed at and beaten. That seemed to be the hardest part for the boy to take, Misha had noticed—the German soldiers taunting Igor's formerly invincible father.

Igor and his parents made their way to the nearest village after that, only to find that it too had been burned to the ground. They then resigned themselves to joining the mass of refugees on the roads east, not knowing where they were going nor how long it would take to get there. That's where Misha had met them.

Three days ago, Igor's father had suffered a fatal heart attack, and a mere three miles further up the road, Igor's mother had been crushed by a truck that veered off the road. Before taking her last breath, she begged Misha to take her son to his uncle in Leningrad.

Pulling his pack around his shoulders, Misha called to Igor, "Break's over. Let's get going."

It wasn't long after they'd started walking again that Igor tugged on Misha's arm, asking another of his annoying questions. "How many Nazis have you killed?"

"Enough," replied Misha, ducking under a low-hanging branch.

Igor ducked as well, but then grabbed the branch and bent it back until it broke. "You can *never* kill enough Nazis," he said resolutely.

Misha was seven years older than Igor, and the two of them had nothing in common except their hatred of the Nazi invaders.

"When we get to Leningrad, I'm going to join the Red Army and kill a thousand of 'em," Igor boasted. "Stalin will give me the Order of Lenin."

Misha gave a weary sigh. "Let's just hope we make it to Leningrad before the Nazis do." He wasn't going to Leningrad solely for Igor's sake. Misha's mother also lived in Leningrad, and he wanted to get her out before the Germans overtook the city.

"Look! Mushrooms!" Igor announced as he bounded to a nearby fallen tree.

"They're probably poisonous," declared Misha. A city-dweller since birth, he had no idea how to tell which mushrooms were edible.

"No, they're not. Some Russian you are!"

Misha took the opportunity to survey their surroundings. Atop a treeless hill surrounded by fields and forests, he spied a grove of birch trees ahead and looked forward to walking through them. He'd decided not to travel on the roads anymore. Besides being clogged with soldiers and refugees, they also put Misha at increased risk of being caught again. He'd left his posting at the airbase after it had been obliterated by the German Luftwaffe. Then he'd been rounded up with other lost soldiers and forced to fight with another division. He'd narrowly escaped death yet again when his division was annihilated by hundreds of Panzer tanks.

A decree issued by Zhdanov on July 14 stated that anyone leaving the front, regardless of rank or responsibility, would go before a field tribunal and be shot. Misha wasn't entirely sure it applied to him since the front had been moving right along with him every step of the way toward Leningrad.

The sound of two planes overhead brought Igor back to Misha's side. "Are those our planes?"

"No," Misha answered, having already spotted their black iron crosses.

"What are they doing out here? Are we near a military base?"

Misha shrugged. "None that I know of."

As the sound of the planes' machine guns filled the air, Misha guessed they'd broken off from their formation to search for targets of opportunity. He watched them loop around for another strike, wondering what they'd found.

"I bet they're shooting up that train," commented Igor.

"That's ridiculous," Misha replied. "Why would they attack a train full of children?" But then, with a pit in his stomach, he conceded to himself that Igor was probably right. The German pilots would have no idea what or who was on that train.

"You have to do something," Igor pleaded. "They'll kill all those kids."

"Shut up!" snapped Misha. "What the hell can I do?"

"Shoot the planes!"

Misha put his odds of hitting the plane at one in a hundred. And if he did hit it, he estimated even greater odds of his shot causing any significant damage. Despite the improbability, he aimed his rifle at one of the planes as it approached for its second attack. When he squeezed the trigger, the bang startled Igor and he stumbled backward a step. Misha fired three more times, but nothing happened. Both planes completed their attack and began to circle around for another strike.

"You missed them," Igor said in a whine.

"Igor, you're an imbecile," Misha scolded. He hated the boy and his ridiculous big ears just as much as the Germans at that moment. "It's nearly impossible to hit a plane from this distance."

"My father could do it. He could shoot a rabbit from over two hundred yards away."

Misha cussed under his breath and leveled his rifle on his left arm. When the planes descended, he fired four more shots, but the planes again completed their strafing run and began to circle around. Then the plane on the right—the one Misha had *not* shot at—started spewing black smoke from its engine.

"Hoorah!" shouted Igor as he jumped up and down.

"Not bad, huh?" Misha grinned.

"How did you do it?"

"I shot its engine," he boasted, reasoning the harmless lie was worth it to put a smile on the boy's face for once.

They watched the damaged plane spew more black smoke by the second, and before long it lost altitude and the pilot ejected. As his parachute opened, his plane disappeared from sight and crashed with a loud thud in a far-off field. The other plane flew away.

Misha removed his cap and held it up to shield his eyes as he tracked the German pilot drifting down like an early autumn leaf. Misha had swiped the cap from a fallen comrade several weeks earlier. In addition to protecting his head from the sun and rain, the lieutenant's insignia on it had come in handy a few times.

As a gust of wind caught the pilot's parachute, it pushed him closer to Misha and Igor. In the distance, gray and white clouds of smoke arose from the damaged train.

Misha began running toward the descending pilot, pausing every once in a while to glimpse at the parachute and adjust his direction. When the pilot dropped from sight behind the pine trees over the next hill, Misha and Igor were less than a hundred yards away. They arrived to find him struggling to free himself from the branches of the large oak tree he'd landed in. Misha thought to shoot him, but decided it would be too difficult to search him while he was stuck in the tree.

Pine cones and brown needles covered the forest floor, and the whole area was infused with the sweet, fresh scent of pine. As Misha waited for the pilot to untangle himself and make it down to the ground, Igor yanked on Misha's rifle. "Let me shoot him," he begged. "Let me shoot him for my pa."

Misha pushed the boy to the ground. "Don't you ever grab my rifle!"

The pilot swung from the last branch down to the ground, then said something in German as he feigned a smile and held his hands above his shoulders. He wore a brown leather jacket and had a pair of goggles hanging from his neck. A head shorter than Misha, he was probably twice Misha's age.

"You know that train you just attacked was full of children," Misha announced.

The pilot shook his head uncomprehendingly. He had thin, blonde eyebrows that were barely visible against his pale white skin, and his face had a natural sereneness that Misha found galling.

"Shoot him in the knee first," urged Igor. "My pa told me it hurts real bad, but won't kill a man. He said that's what they used to do to the rich farmers during the Civil War."

Misha—itching for a reason to pull the trigger—jerked the tip of his rifle upward, hoping the pilot wouldn't obey the order to raise his arms higher. When he did, Misha then made him lie on the ground. While Misha pointed the rifle from a few feet away, he instructed Igor to search the pilot's pockets. Igor found a pistol, a half-eaten slab of bread, and a photograph of the pilot with his family. His wife was beautiful, his son still a baby, and his daughter a smiling two-year-old with big dimples and curly blonde hair.

Eyeing the smoke in the distance getting thicker and blacker, Misha sadly recalled the friendly boys on the train who'd waved to him and asked where the Germans were. That they might all be dead infuriated him. Stepping closer and pressing his boot to the German's neck, Misha placed the tip of his rifle against the man's skull.

"Yeah, shoot him!" exhorted Igor.

But Misha didn't pull the trigger. Not yet. He wanted the pilot to see what he'd done first.

After forcing the German to his feet, the three of them marched along the railroad tracks toward the smoke around the next bend. The closer they got, the more audible the yelling and screaming became. Misha could make out some of the words from the adult voices: "fire," "evacuate," "children," "hurry," "dead."

When they could at last see the train, Misha's heart sank. He'd hoped that the damage would be small and injuries few, but could already see several motionless bodies strewn about. One of the coaches was on fire, with smoke pouring out its smashed windows. A short distance away, dozens of children huddled together, hugging and holding hands.

The pilot—walking in front with his hands up—whimpered, crossed himself, and started reciting a phrase over and over. He turned his head toward Misha, his arms trembling and eyes full of tears, then took off in a sprint. Misha yelled at him to stop and considered shooting him, but the pilot wasn't fleeing the scene. He was racing toward the train.

After charging into the coach that was on fire, the pilot was already carrying out a small boy by the time Misha and Igor caught up. When the German dashed back in to save another, Misha followed. Together, they rescued six children.

Misha hoped they were done when a young girl with a pink bow in her hair tugged on his shirt. "My brother is still in there," she cried, pointing at the burning car.

"Are you sure?"

She nodded.

"He's probably already out here somewhere. Ask the others," Misha said. "I'll go in and check one last time."

Flames were roaring out the back of the car, and Misha didn't want to enter it again, but he did anyway. Unable to see through the thick smoke that stung his eyes, he stretched his arm over and under every seat to feel for any bodies. Under the fourth seat, he came upon a bare leg and pulled it toward himself. He didn't know if it was a boy or girl, dead or alive. He carried the child out and laid it on the ground.

After an extended bout of coughing and rubbing his red eyes, Misha saw he'd retrieved a lifeless little girl with long brown hair and a small doll tucked inside her dress—the head of it peeking out by her shoulder. There was no blood on her, but she wasn't breathing all the same.

A giant of a man in a Red Army uniform barreled toward the burning car, almost stumbling headfirst into it with his enormous, lumbering feet. He was out of breath, and, for some reason, had only one ear on the right side of his head. "We must separate cars or they all burn," he called to Misha in a heavy peasant accent.

"We can unhook it," replied Misha, "but we'll never be able to move it. Those cars weigh fifty tons."

When One Ear began detaching the burning coach anyway, Misha shook his head disdainfully. "Idiot," he muttered under his breath. Peasants had such thick heads.

Then, to Misha's utter disbelief, the giant dug his heels in, grunted, groaned, and pushed the coach ten feet down the tracks. As One Ear bent at the waist recuperating from his strenuous effort, the pilot jumped out of the burning car carrying yet another child. Catching sight of the German, One Ear gawked at him with a dumbfounded expression.

Misha recognized the limp body in the pilot's arms. It was one of the boys who'd waved to him earlier. The pilot—eyebrows and hair singed from the flames—laid the boy down, then checked his pulse and breathing. While Igor, One Ear, and Misha gathered round, the pilot began pushing rhythmically on the boy's chest.

"Were you the only guard on the train?" Misha asked One Ear.

"No. One other. But he is dead," came the reply.

Misha saw two young women and a *babushka*—an elderly woman with a kerchief tied around her head—treating the injured children. They were tearing strips of cloth from bed sheets and using them as gauze to wrap around wounds. Misha counted over a dozen bodies on the ground with white sheets covering them and another two dozen or so children who were wounded.

With his eyes on the pilot, One Ear asked, "Is he the one that jumped out of plane?" He spoke slowly and enunciated each syllable, as if he was a child still learning the language.

Misha nodded.

The wounded boy was unresponsive to any of the pilot's efforts. In fact, every push on his chest just caused more blood around his midsection. Eventually, the pilot gave up and sat on his heels, moaning and coughing.

With a look of contempt at the German, Misha muttered under his breath, "Murderer."

"What we do with him?" asked One Ear.

Out of the corner of his eye, Misha glimpsed the little girl with the pink bow and wondered if she'd found her brother.

"Let's cut his stomach open and pull his guts out like they did in the old days," suggested Igor.

"Are *you* going to do it?" Misha asked sharply.

Igor dropped his gaze to the ground and shook his head dejectedly.

"I know," Misha blurted. "Let's tie him to a tree and each give him a pop to the nose!"

"Yeah," exclaimed Igor, echoing Misha's excitedness. "Let's bloody him up and then leave him out here for the bears to find! We could even smear him with honey!"

Misha laughed a brief, derisive "ha," then told Igor to shut up. He heard the little girl with the pink bow calling out her brother's name: "Seryozha! Seryozha!"

"We should turn him over to authorities," proposed One Ear.

"The authorities?" Misha said incredulously. "Like who? You want us to track down General Zhukov? He'd just shoot the Nazi on the spot."

"It is right thing to do," One Ear said firmly. "It is not our place to judge and sentence him."

Misha studied One Ear's broad, flat face, trying to figure out if he'd been born with only one ear or if it was the result of an accident. "Are you blind? Don't you see what he's done? He deserves to die for what he did."

"It is not for us to decide," One Ear repeated, stuttering a few times on the last word.

"Then whose right is it?"

One Ear opened his mouth, but hesitated, staring dumbly at Misha with his mouth agape.

"Russ-ian," Misha said, sarcastically pronouncing each syllable. "I - am - speak-ing - Russ-ian. Do - you - un-der-stand - me?"

Igor erupted in scornful laughter. "Do you un-der-stand Russ-ian?" he mocked as Misha had.

One Ear pursed his lips as his face turned crimson red. "It is not for us to decide," he stammered again.

"Then whose right is it? God's?" Misha said it as a taunt. To profess belief in God in the Soviet Union was tantamount to heresy.

"He's a Jew!" accused Igor.

"I am no Jew."

"Then what are you? A *Christian*?" Misha asked insolently. "You're certainly no Soviet!"

"I," he said haltingly. "I ... am ... a—"

"What?" Misha asked impatiently. "What are you?"

"A man!" One Ear proclaimed with a stomp of his foot.

"He's a coward!" yelled Igor.

One Ear turned toward Igor with an angry stare, and Igor hid behind Misha.

"As Soviet soldiers, we have an obligation to the Motherland to defend our country," Misha said.

"German risked his life to save child," said One Ear as he pointed to the boy on the ground.

"That boy would still be alive if it weren't for him shooting up the train!" Misha shouted.

"He did not know train was full of children," argued One Ear. "Look. He cries."

Misha had already seen the tears streaming down the pilot's face. "That's just from the smoke," he argued. "It got in my eyes too."

One Ear offered the German his handkerchief, which he accepted and used to dry his eyes. The little girl with the pink bow was only a few yards away now, still calling for her brother.

"It's all an act," declared Misha, feeling reassured by his own words.

"He made mistake and knows it," One Ear said. "Give him to me. I take him to prison in next town. They serve justice there."

The little girl's call for her brother changed abruptly from a plea to a wretched scream. She rushed to the dead boy lying in front of the pilot. "Seryozha!" she cried.

Misha took a deep breath, trying to calm his mounting rage. "We're going to serve justice *here*," he said as calmly as he could. "Right here, and right now." With a shove, Misha commanded Igor to take the little girl over to the women who were treating the wounded.

"In fact," Misha said with a glare at One Ear, "you're going to help us." Pulling a rope from his pack, he held it out to the giant. "Help Igor tie the German to that tree over there."

When One Ear didn't budge, Misha purposefully adjusted his cap with the lieutenant's insignia. "That's an order," he asserted.

One Ear took a step closer to Misha, towering over him. But Misha wasn't about to be intimidated by a half-brain peasant. Pointing his rifle at the pilot, he shouted to Igor. "Hey, show Half Brain how to tie a knot."

"I know how to tie knot," One Ear said indignantly as he clenched his fists.

"Then what are you waiting for?" Misha answered. "Does it take that long for your brain to tell your legs to move? Get over there and tie him up."

The air was hot and sticky, and drops of sweat rolled down Misha's forehead to his eyebrows. The leaves of the trees were a dark and somber shade of green against the bright July sun. As Igor and One Ear tied the pilot's arms and legs to the tree, he didn't resist in any way. He gazed straight ahead at nothing in particular, that same harmless expression on his face that aggravated Misha to no end. When they were nearly finished, he asked something in German.

"What did he say?" Igor asked, turning toward Misha.

Misha shrugged his shoulders. "Who cares," he said, "just finish up."

The German repeated himself, emphasizing the last word: "tah-bak."

"I think he wants cigarette," One Ear said.

"Shut up," said Misha. "You don't know that."

But then the pilot looked at One Ear, nodding his head and repeating the same word: "cigarette."

"I do not smoke," One Ear said, peering at Misha. "You have cigarette?"

"Of course I have a cigarette," Misha said. "I'm a man." Pulling out a half-smoked cigarette, he lit it and took a long drag. "I ain't giving it to him though."

The crackle of flames filled the air, and Misha wiped sweat from his forehead and retreated to the shade.

"We got him tied up, Misha," announced Igor. "He can't get away. Are you going to hit him now?"

Misha leaned his rifle against the tree and approached the pilot. He stretched his arm over his head, then swung it around in circles to loosen it up. After inhaling the last of his cigarette, he blew the smoke in the pilot's face.

Igor giggled. "Break his nose, Misha!"

Having never actually been in a fight before, Misha wrapped his fingers around his thumb and flung his fist wildly. He struck the pilot half on the nose and half on cheekbone.

"Goddamn it!" he cussed, shaking his hand in agony. He was sure he'd broken his thumb. But at least the pilot's face—grimacing, nose bleeding—was no longer so annoyingly placid.

Catching sight of the group of boys and girls who were watching, Misha called to them. "Children, would you like to get some revenge against the Nazi pilot who attacked your train?"

None of the them said yes, nor did any say no. They just gaped with big eyes.

"It's time you older boys became men," said Misha. "Who wants to be a Soviet soldier and defend the Motherland? Raise your hand."

A short, cross-eyed girl with pigtails raised her hand high. Nine boys followed suit.

"He said 'boys,' Masha," scolded the eldest boy. "Put your hand down."

"No, that's all right," injected Misha. "She was the first to put her hand up. She can keep it up. Now, which of you who raised your hand is brave? Step forward."

Again the girl was the first to take a step. She wore a plain brown dress and held a piece of driftwood she'd fashioned into a toy pistol.

"Excellent," said Misha after they'd all stepped forward. "That was your first test. Only the brave can be soldiers in Stalin's Red Army." Misha paused to look each of them in the eye for emphasis. "Now, by the power vested in me as a lieutenant in the Red Army of the Union of Soviet Socialist Republics, I hereby designate each of you a volunteer soldier. Raise your right arm and repeat after me."

Standing tall, faces solemn, the children lifted their arms.

"I, a citizen of the USSR, stepping forth in the ranks of the Armed Forces," Misha said and waited while the children repeated it, "take the oath and solemnly vow to be an honorable, brave, disciplined, diligent fighter, strictly guarding military and state secrets." He only knew part of the actual oath, so he made up the rest as he went along, "... and defend the Motherland—the glorious birthplace of socialism—with every drop of my blood."

One Ear stood off to the side frowning with his thick arms folded in front of his chest. From time to time he would shake his immense head side to side.

"Now line up here," Misha ordered the children. "Your first duty as Red Army soldiers is to serve justice against this enemy soldier."

Misha glanced at One Ear kicking at the dirt. "Good idea, huh Half Brain?" he taunted.

A boy with bleach-blonde hair and glasses that kept sliding down his nose ended up at the front of the line. He tried to move further back, but the others wouldn't let him.

"Step forward," Misha commanded. He felt pleased with himself for having everything under control: the pilot was about to get his due, the boys were learning how to be men, he was the undisputed leader, and Igor revered him.

"Comrade, I beg of you," implored One Ear, "stop this."

"Shut up," Misha snapped as he kicked an apple-sized rock away from where he was standing.

The boy in line inched forward, more by the pushing of the boys behind him than his own volition. His skin was pale, like the pilot's, with light freckles dotting his cheeks, and he picked up the rock Misha had kicked.

"Good idea," said Misha. "That's how they punished people in the old days. We'll stone him."

The boy gawked at Misha uncomprehendingly, as though Misha had made his pronouncement in a foreign language. With a grunt and a scowl, One Ear marched off toward the front of the train.

Misha, afraid of losing momentum, called to the hesitant boy, "Let's go!"

"Come on," Igor joined in. "Don't be a sissy."

The boy cocked his arm back, holding the rock behind his head, but then left it there.

"Throw it," Misha yelled. "What's the matter with you? He killed your friends!"

Instead of heeding Misha's advice, the boy dropped the rock and ran away in tears to the older lady who was tending the wounded.

"I want to go next!" Igor yelled. "Misha, let me go."

Disgusted by the bad example that had been set, Misha replied, "All right, Igor. You go now. Hurry up."

As several of the smaller children who'd been watching began leaving, Igor picked up the rock and threw it awkwardly. It missed the pilot and the tree by a good ten feet.

The boys all laughed. "You throw like a girl," they jeered.

Igor's big ears turned beet red. "Shut up!" he yelled at them.

The woman with the kerchief hastened to the scene, demanding, "What's going on here?" After a glance at the pilot with his bloody nose tied to the tree, she gasped. "You monsters," she chided Misha and Igor.

"Old woman," Misha said contemptuously. "Go back and tend to the wounded."

One Ear was returning from the front of the train, holding his right hand in his pocket. "Borya!" the woman called to him. "Borya, do you know what's going on here? Come stop this madness." Hearing her, he quickened his pace.

"Half Brain isn't in charge here. *I* am," said Misha. He turned to Igor, snickering at the boy's face contorted in fury and indignation. "Are you going to let them tease you like that?" he said with a smirk.

Igor ran at the pilot, pulling a knife from his belt. "This is for my pa!" he shouted and plunged the blade into the side of the German's neck. Bright red blood gushed forth as the pilot bent his head over the deadly wound, trying to stem the flow.

Several girls screamed and ran off. One Ear raced to the pilot and pushed Igor away. "That is enough!" he yelled.

"Children, stay here! The Nazi isn't dead yet," Misha hollered, though he could tell from the pilot's wound that he would be in a short while.

Spying One Ear pull a pistol out of his pocket, Misha dove to the ground. When the gun had fired and Misha didn't feel anything, he knew the oaf must have missed him. Rolling on the ground to grab his rifle, he turned and prepared to return fire. But One Ear had already put the pistol down and was walking away. Behind him, the German pilot slumped from the tree—a gunshot wound to his chest.

"Borya!" the woman screamed, covering her mouth with her hands.

Head bowed, hulking arms hanging at his sides, Borya trudged over to her. Dropping to his knees, he leaned forward into her arms. She held his large head to her bosom, stroking his bushy brown hair, and exclaiming, "Dear God, Borya, what has happened? I don't understand anything anymore. I just don't understand."

Misha's mind went blank momentarily, then his malice melted into bewilderment. The German pilot looked like a gory scarecrow, his head lying limp and bloody over his right shoulder. Closing his eyes, Misha heard the wounded children whimpering softly, the crackle of the flames, and the old woman whispering, "Oh Borya. My Borya. This is madness. What have we done? What have we done?"

Katya set her notebook and pencil aside and lay flat on her back. It was sometime between two and three in the morning, and she was on the roof of her apartment building on guard for fires from German incendiary bombs. Peering up at the night sky, she smiled at the thought of God looking back at her from across the cosmos. She'd been writing poetry for the last three hours, working and reworking lines until they couldn't be improved.

Much of her poetry was optimistic and poignant, because that's who she wanted to be. To her classmates, she was idealistic, and to her father, naive. But that was their loss. Katya regarded life as something meant to be loved, and she actively cultivated her childlike qualities: whether it be skipping down the sidewalk, doing arts and crafts, humming nursery rhymes, or just being silly and laughing at what a strange world it is.

It was her grandmother who had nurtured that in her. When Katya was nine years old, her mother had died and her father took her to live with her grandmother in the countryside. He came and visited often, but as the years went by, Katya began to view him more as a generous stranger, then her father. He was someone who stopped by and chatted over tea, brought food and gifts, and then disappeared the next day.

Though her father clearly loved and respected his mother, the two of them had a strained relationship and bickered often in front of Katya. They argued mostly about God and religion and what Katya should and should not be taught. Her grandmother, Katya came to understand, was a rebel. That was why her son, a Party official, made her live in a cottage in the woods by herself, rather than in the city with the two of them. Her grandmother not only believed in but lived her life on a daily basis according to some very dangerous ideas. She was a Mennonite. The last one in the whole of Russia, she claimed. All the rest had emigrated to Canada as soon as it became obvious the Bolsheviks would be victorious in the Civil War.

She'd become a member of the historic Christian church at age sixty-seven by undergoing adult baptism. She had taught Katya all the group's essential teachings: that one's loyalty was ultimately to God and not the State, that people should be voluntarily baptized as adults rather than involuntarily as infants, and—most heretical of all—pacifism. Mennonites, Katya learned, maintained that Jesus taught peace, as epitomized in his instruction to "love your enemies."

It wasn't until Katya got older that she realized just how revolutionary the teachings were. Since the war with Germany had started, she frequently found herself in conflict, either outright with other people, or internally. She was discovering that living what you believe is not always easy. And sometimes it was downright dangerous.

Katya's stay with her grandmother lasted until a week after her thirteenth birthday when her grandmother passed away. Katya's father brought her back to Leningrad to live with him. Despite how much he adored and spoiled Katya, the two of them bickered often. It became painfully clear that Katya's grandmother's teachings could not be easily undone. He repeatedly explained to Katya that her views could get her in trouble, and cautioned her to be careful in what she said in front of others.

With a satisfying inhalation of the warm night air, she watched the fat anti-aircraft blimps as they hovered high above the buildings. They looked like oblong meatballs, and their floating in the sky would catch her off guard sometimes and she'd wonder momentarily if she was in a dream.

It had been six days since Felix left for the front, and she had no idea if he was dead or alive. She deemed worrying a waste of time and energy, but couldn't help herself when it came to him. Life without him was unimaginable.

The door to the stairwell creaked open, and in the dim light, Katya saw her neighbor, Petya, appear next to the fire-fighting equipment. He accidentally kicked one of shovels, and it knocked over an ax which then fell between the water buckets and sand pails. He limped toward her, his bad leg scuffing a pile of spilled sand. A moth fluttered inside the stairwell door before it slammed shut.

"What a prodigious evening," he announced.

"Yes, it's gorgeous," she agreed, grateful to have some company. She wasn't interested in Petya romantically, but she did consider him a friend and someone she wanted to get to know better. He seemed to know a lot about the world, and he had a dark side that intrigued her.

Sitting close by her side, he tilted his head back at the stars. "It's always so peaceful," he commented. "I used to come up here for inspiration all the time—just take in the stars and listen to the sounds of the city. But now, of course, it's so quiet. No cars. No people. Nothing."

"Why did you stop?"

"Not sure. There are so many quiet activities in our lives that we love to do and give us pleasure, but we don't do them. Or rarely do them. It's strange. We decry all these busy activities we claim we *have* to do every day. But the truth is, we *choose* to do them. We choose them over the quiet activities."

He sighed and his arm brushed against Katya's as he stretched. The hairs of his arm tickled her skin and gave her a pleasant shiver.

"It's all because of Original Sin," remarked Katya.

"I knew religion had to play some role in it," he said with a sneer. "Tell me more."

"The whole concept of Original Sin is that we're inherently flawed beings. Adam and Eve were kicked out of the Garden of Eden for failing to control their urges, their curious nature. They were made to feel guilt and shame for who they were. Ever since then, we've been out to prove that we *are* good enough, and deserve to be allowed back into the Garden of Eden."

"Interesting," said Petya. "So you're saying we do all these things we don't like because we think they're the way to prove our self-worth? That's probably why the Germans are trying to take over the world—out to prove to everyone they're not the culprits they were made out to be after the first world war."

"I hadn't thought of that," Katya said. "But I think you're right."

"And what about you, Katerina Selenaya? What do you expend your precious energy on?"

"On silly, bourgeois things, like worrying about my Felix," she half-joked.

"Oh yes, he went to the front, didn't he? Have you heard from him?"

"No, and it's driving me crazy." As she ran her fingers through her hair, she thought she smelled cologne.

"Well, certainly it's no fun being in love with a soldier. You shouldn't get too attached to him."

Katya turned to him, and even before she said anything, Petya backtracked his last statement. "What I mean is you shouldn't get too attached to him being around much. I've said it crudely, but I mean that as a friend. He's a great guy, and war is a difficult time for lovers. I just want you to know that if you ever get lonely and want someone to talk to, I'm available. I'm always around you."

His last sentence made her a little uncomfortable, but she brushed it aside. "Thanks."

They sat in silence for a while and stared up at the sky.

"They say the Germans will use gas," Petya said.

"Yes, and they also say Leningrad will be taken in a month. These rumors fly all around the city like pigeons. I've learned not to put too much faith in any of them, except for the ones about a potential famine."

"You mean you don't believe our diligent, honorable officials and their assurances of massive food supplies?" Petya said sarcastically.

"I remember my father telling me about the food shortages here in the 1920's," said Katya. "I hope we don't have to live through anything like that."

"Did you also hear the Germans are planning a paratroop attack on our fair city?"

"Yes. The Supreme Command announced it just last week, right?" Katya brushed a mosquito away from her bare arm. "Do you think we'll wake one morning and see Nazis falling from the sky like hail?"

"I hope so," Petya said. "Maybe that would enkindle my creativity."

Katya didn't laugh.

"I'm only kidding," he said.

"I know. I guess I'm just not in a joking mood. It feels inappropriate to laugh when our men are dying on the front defending us."

Katya smelled cologne once again and stole a glance at Petya. His chubby face was clean-shaven. He was wearing a fashionable shirt she'd never seen before, and his dark hair was freshly washed and neatly combed.

"Your shift is about over, isn't it?" Petya asked.

She nodded.

"Who gets the glorious job of defending our building from those cursed Nazi planes next?"

"Guzman."

"Really? I saw Shostakovich going to visit him earlier," Petya said. "He was telling me how he and other musicians were sent to dig trenches beyond the Forelli Hospital. He said one pianist came in a new suit and was later covered in mud up to his thighs. Another one came with a briefcase and kept slipping off to a shady bush to read some thick volume of musical history every few minutes."

"You can't expect musicians to be very proficient at those kinds of things," Katya said. "Did you know Shostakovich is applying for the Volunteers?"

"Yes. Dmitry's quite the patriot, and after all he's been through too."

"I doubt he'll be accepted," said Katya. "Even he seems to think they'll probably assign him to air-raid duty."

Petya ran his hand over his hair, patting down a spot that was apparently sticking out of place. "I've never understood why they haven't arrested him—that evil 'formalist.' They brand him an enemy of the people, and yet he's allowed to walk around and write new symphonies as if everything's fine."

"I certainly don't envy him," Katya said. "He told me he keeps a bag packed and ready to go should they come and arrest him in the middle of the night. He said he's been expecting that knock on the door every night for several years now. It must be tremendously stressful living like that."

Petya slapped a mosquito on his arm. "What do you think of the charges? That he's a formalist," he said. "Some of my friends say that Stalin himself wrote the articles in Pravda condemning his work."

Katya heard her father's voice in her head telling her to be careful of what she said on contentious political matters, and her first reaction was to not answer. But she was tired of doing that. Silence felt dishonest. Besides, she trusted Petya.

"I think calling him a formalist," she said, "is just another useless label that we seem to be so fond of these days. 'He's a counter-revolutionary.' 'She's a Trotskyite.' 'He's a formalist.' It's just a way of dumbing down complex issues so that you don't have to examine the complexities or nuances of anything."

Petya smiled. "Well put," he said. "And here I thought honesty had gone out of style." He stretched his neck around in a slow circle. "Do you ever feel intimidated around him? Shostakovich?"

"Intimidated? Why?"

"Why? He wrote his first symphony when he was just eighteen. And he's a celebrity, not only here, but throughout Europe and America. They've played his symphonies in Rome and London and—"

"I'm happy for him," Katya interrupted. "His music is so moving."

When Petya made no reply, Katya sensed she had erred in her response. "Do you feel jealous because you'd like the attention and recognition he's getting?" she asked.

"Absolutely," he said. "I know I could be just as successful as him if only I worked a little harder at my writing. I wish some of his productivity would wear off on me."

"You need to be patient."

"No," Petya said sharply. "That's one thing I don't need. Things have been expected from me for a long time now. You're still young, and there's no pressure on you to make something out of your life yet. When you get to be my age in another eight years, you'll understand."

She looked up at the countless stars in the sky, recalling the things Petya had told her about his childhood in the orphanage. She shuddered at some of them. If they'd happened to her, she was sure she would have been crushed by the cruelty of it all. "How's your novel coming?" she asked. "Last we spoke, you were on the third chapter."

She often learned more about Petya through his writing than by talking to him. He let her read drafts of his stories in exchange for feedback. She admired his writing—the rawness and sincerity of it. With a little encouragement, she was sure he could overcome all the onerous circumstances of his life and become one of the country's top writers.

Petya began to sigh, but then cut himself off. "It's ... it's nearly finished," he said haltingly. "I mean it *is* finished. Well no, it's got a ways to go." Finishing his abandoned sigh, he said intently, "It will be done this week."

"That's good news," exclaimed Katya, squeezing his arm reassuringly. "When can I read it?"

"Soon. Soon."

"You've said that for the past two months."

"Yes, I know," he said peevishly.

Katya gazed into outer space again, trying to connect the points of the constellation Ursula Major. When she was halfway finished, a shooting star streaked across the black sky. "Petya, did you see that?"

"Yes," he said. "Pure resplendence."

"We get to make a wish now," said Katya. She closed her eyes, reciting a heartfelt prayer for Felix's safety, then smiled at the thought of him—his curly hair, his iron-grey eyes, how courageous he'd been at the train station when he had only a shovel to defend himself on the front. Turning to Petya, she asked if he'd made a wish.

"Yes," he answered.

As a light breeze massaged the hair on the back of her neck, she noticed for the first time how close they were sitting next to one another.

"I wished for your happiness," Petya said.

She gave him a playful punch on the arm. "You're not supposed to tell! Now it won't come true."

"Oh. Then we'll just pretend I didn't say anything." He stretched his arm around Katya's shoulder, squeezed her toward him, then let go.

The door started to creak open again, and Katya made her way to her feet. Dmitry Shostakovich walked toward them in careful, measured steps.

"Katya?" he said in his tenor voice. "Is that you?"

"Yes, Dmitry. It's me."

"Your father just called Guzman's place. He's been trying to reach you."

Katya felt alarmed. Her father never called for her at home. "What is it? What happened?"

"He informed me Felix was wounded at the front."

She gasped.

"He's on a train on his way to a hospital here in Leningrad."

Petya made his way to his feet and stood next to her. "How bad is it?" he asked.

"I don't know. I don't think her father knows either or else he would've told me." He took a few steps toward Katya. "Your father said he'd be home in three hours to take you to the hospital."

Clasping her hands in front of herself, she nestled into Shostakovich's outstretched arms.

Petya mumbled something and lit a cigarette as the anti-aircraft blimps continued sailing silently through the warm Leningrad night.

Глава Четвёртая — Chapter Four

THE LAST LINE

Once there was nothing,
        no thought could be found;
But things soon changed
        when "life" was unbound.
Along came logic,
        shortly after time
Something from nothing
        has no right to define
Out of touch
        but in control,
Who are they
        to sell my soul?
Thinking is dangerous
        for we all just might find
Not the answers we seek,
        but a void in the mind.

Petya Soyonovich slouched at his tiny desk, elbows propping his head up, and stared at a sheet of paper with one sentence written on it. It read: *Ivan chimed the bell three more times than he was supposed to, and he knew there would be hell to pay from the other monks.*

It had been forty-five minutes since he'd written it, during which he'd stared out the window for five minutes, organized his small library of books by title, then again by author, made a grocery list, shaved, and written his friend in Moscow a long-overdue letter. For such a supposedly gifted writer, he reflected bitterly, he wasn't the least bit productive with his time.

His small, overcrowded room—intimate in a claustrophobic way—had a bulky wardrobe closet that hogged the corner opposite the door while his desk was wedged between his bed and the wall. Overlooking a filthy brick wall was a lone window which neither breezes nor the sun's rays ever passed through.

Tapping a pencil against the side of his head, Petya reflected for the thousandth time on his curse: try as he might, he couldn't live up to the standards of success that had been set in his childhood. At the tender age of eleven, he'd written an immensely popular parody of Pushkin's famous poem, "Eugene Onegin." Petya had been informed at that time that he was on the path to being the next acclaimed Russian writer, a mere step away from genius. Fifteen years later, he was still struggling to take that step.

On many days—today for instance—Petya felt that he had actually taken a step, or *two,* backward. His excuses were endless: not enough time, too much time, no inspiration, too tired, too alert. Each day that he couldn't write, he believed more and more that he was an impostor.

Throwing down his pencil in disgust, he went to the stairwell to smoke. He shared the apartment with two other people: Boris, a plumber originally from Novosibirsk whose wife and two-year-old daughter had already evacuated the city, and Oksana Petrovna, an older lady with a psychotic cat. Oksana detested cigarettes and forbade Petya and Boris from smoking in the apartment.

The stairwell, dim even though it was daytime, was pitch black at night because someone kept stealing the lightbulbs. Today the hallway was full of flies and reeked of rotting food. It wasn't usually like that. It was a nice building, but someone had spilled some food scraps—potato peels, onion scraps, fish heads—and for some reason neither they, nor anyone else, had cleaned it up.

After finishing his cigarette and returning to the apartment, Petya contemplated venturing out to buy some tea. He was running low, and everyone told him the stores were running out of everything. He cursed Hitler for taking so long to capture the city. With the methodical Germans in command, he was sure order would be restored and that the city would never run out of crucial items like tea.

When someone knocked at the front door, Petya found himself unable to discern who it was. To improve his writing skills, he'd trained himself to pay attention to ordinary details, such as the way people knock on doors. He knew everyone's knock, from the *takity tak tak* of Guzman, to the *duk duk* of his artist friend, Vladimir. The current knock—*tump tump ta-tump*—didn't fit anyone he knew.

Before deciding whether to open the door, he stood and listened to the voices on the other side.

"Damn, it stinks out here," a sardonic male voice said. "You'll fit in perfectly if this is the right place."

"Shut up," a younger male whined in response. "I don't think anybody's home. Let's go get some food."

"We just ate a few hours ago."

"It's *my* money. Give it to me. I'm hungry."

"We spent all the money your parents gave you a long time ago."

Opening the door a crack, Petya beheld a young soldier in army fatigues and a big-eared, adolescent boy with his finger up his nose. Before he could ask what they wanted, Oksana's cat bolted out the door.

"Get that cat," exclaimed Petya. "It's not supposed to be out."

The young man in army fatigues quickly maneuvered to pin the cat against the wall with his leg. Then he grabbed it by the back of the neck and threw it inside the apartment. The cat landed on its feet, shook its head, then licked its paw as if nothing had happened.

"Thanks," said Petya. "That asinine cat is truly vexing."

"No problem, comrade. I'm Misha, and this is Igor. We're looking for Grigori Selenii. Does he live here?"

Petya gazed at them suspiciously, wondering what they wanted with Katya's Party official father. "Do you have an appointment to see him?"

"He's my uncle," announced the boy.

"His parents died," Misha added, jerking his head toward Igor. "Before his mom died, she asked me to take him to her brother in Leningrad."

Petya recalled Katya mentioning her aunt who lived way out in the country. "Did you knock on the door down there?" He pointed toward Katya's apartment.

They nodded.

"Katya is probably busy at the hospital," said Petya, "but she should be back in an hour or two. Check back then."

"Who's Katya?" asked Misha.

"Grigori Selenii's daughter."

"Oh," Misha replied as he peeked over Petya's shoulder into his apartment. "Are you going somewhere?"

"Why?"

"I was thinking that maybe Igor could stay with you until they return."

Having lost his own parents—shot before his eyes by the Bolsheviks during the Civil War—Petya felt sorry for the boy. Still, he didn't like kids and didn't know how to handle them.

"Don't worry. He'll be quiet and won't bother you," Misha said with an elbow to the boy's ribs. "Right, Igor?"

Igor shrugged, staring at the floor.

"All right," Petya agreed. "He can stay with me until Katya returns."

"Great! Stay out of trouble," Misha said to Igor as he patted him on the head like a dog. After nudging the boy toward Petya, he turned and walked down the hallway.

Igor watched Misha descending the staircase, then thrust his hands in his pockets and frowned. "Didn't even say goodbye," he mumbled.

Petya directed the boy to his room inside the apartment. "You can relax on my bed until Katya gets back."

Igor jumped on the mattress and scooted over to the mirror on the wall where he began inspecting his face.

Petya sat at his desk to write, but was distracted by the boy picking at the numerous pimples on his nose, forehead, and chin. "Would you like to take a bath or a shower?" Petya asked, desperately hoping the smelly boy would say yes.

"Nah," replied Igor. "I don't like baths." Holding his face inches away from the mirror, he was popping one pimple after the other.

Petya, noticing his right cheek beginning to twitch, gritted his teeth to try to stop it. "I'd prefer you don't get the mirror dirty."

"I won't."

Turning in his chair so he couldn't see the boy, Petya tried focusing on his writing once more. As he alternately chewed on his pencil and twirled it with his fingers, Igor started humming—softly at first, but then progressively louder.

"Stop that, please," Petya said, his cheek twitching even more. He tossed a newspaper on the bed. "Here. You can read that."

"There's no pictures in it."

Petya's friend, Vladimir, had somehow got his hands on a French magazine a few years back. It was full of advertisements and pictures of stuff to buy. Petya dug it out of his desk drawer and handed it to Igor. Then he returned to contemplating the next line of his novel.

After ten minutes of futility, he began daydreaming of a career as a street sweeper. Then, much to his surprise, something came to him:

> But the Lord had confided his wishes to Ivan. And who was he to argue? God had explicitly stated that he was a chosen one, and Ivan, though humbled, accepted his fate.
>
> He retreated to the green onion-domed church and knelt before a painting of John the Baptist. It showed the man's disembodied head on a silver platter, and Ivan felt a capacious void in his bosom. As he recited the Lord's prayer...

"I'm hungry," Igor interrupted.

With a growl, Petya limped to the kitchen, then returned with a bowl of black sunflower seeds. "Here," he said. "Now could you please not bother me for a while? I like to work in quietude."

"You like to work in what?"

"Just don't talk or make any noise for a while. All right?"

Before Petya resumed his writing, he heard footsteps coming up the stairs. With a groan, he realized they belonged to his roommate, Oksana, and not to Katya. He continued writing:

> ... a young woman entered the chapel wearing a short dress and a veil over her face. She knelt beside Ivan, her arm lightly brushing against his, and whispered, "I want you."
>
> It was the first time she'd admitted it, and Ivan slid his hand under her dress, stroking the soft, smooth skin of her thighs. "Oh Katya," he said. "Why must we torment ourselves..."

"Damn it!" Petya yelled, thrusting his face in his hands. Wadding the paper into a ball, he hurled it across the room. "Damn it. Damn it. Damn it."

"I was being quiet," protested Igor.

"It wasn't you," Petya said as he uncorked the bottle of vodka on his desk. After two long swigs, he put on his black beret and grabbed his apartment keys. "Come on," he said.

"Where are we going?"

"To get some tea."

Igor hopped off the bed. "Tea? You should buy food before it's all gone. Misha told me the city will run out if the Nazis surround it."

Petya sighed, disappointed the alcohol hadn't taken effect yet. "I can live without food," he said as they departed. "I can't live without tea."

"If that's true, how come you're so fat?"

Petya grimaced and decided to ignore the boy's insolence. As they descended the stairs, Igor ventured another question. "So what's my cousin like?"

"Katya? Well, she smells considerably better than you, but other than that, you two have a lot in common."

"Really?" said Igor excitedly.

"Yes. She has this certain quality about her—just like you—that makes one wish he were somebody else."

Felix pushed himself up in bed and peeked underneath the bandage on his leg. The wound—still covered with a scaly, dark red scab—looked disappointedly unchanged from the last time he'd checked. In his first ever combat experience, he'd been stabbed between the thigh and groin, and not a day went by when he didn't lament his mistake.

Without warning, a wave of pain thrust from his leg, through his lower back, past his shoulders, up his neck, and into the base of his skull. It pulsated and pounded and tied his body into one massive knot of tension. Then the pain receded. He was alone in his room, the sun shining faintly through the windows, a fly buzzing on the ceiling.

He prepared for a formerly mundane task: getting out of bed. His swollen thigh was black and blue, and he could only bend his knee with difficulty. To get out of bed, he had to place his right foot under his left leg and lift it over the edge of the bed, and then swing his torso up quickly before too much pressure weighed on the knee. Accomplishing it all in one swift motion, Felix then hobbled to the kitchen and retrieved the newspaper from the table— careful all the while not to wake his napping father.

Back in his room, Felix scanned the headlines skeptically. Dima kept him updated on the real situation at the front, and Felix marveled at the half-truths and exaggerations he read in the newspapers. Everyone in the city seemed to know the war was going badly, and while the press wasn't necessarily printing lies, neither was it giving citizens an accurate picture. A heroic handful of factory workers holding off an entire German company for two days was a feel-good story, an inspiration, but Felix felt it misled people.

If that was an indication of how the war was going, then how was it that Leningraders heard the shelling getting closer and closer every day?

It had been ten weeks since his birthday celebration with his friends, and the entire month of August was nearly over. Before Felix had been released from the hospital, he'd started making inquiries about a different position that would keep him closer to Katya. But every job seemed to require extensive standing or walking, and Felix couldn't do that with his injured leg. He knew if he waited until his leg was healed, they'd send him back to the front.

As a result of Katya's relentless pestering of her father, Felix had been granted an interview for a clerical position that was opening. However, Katya's father had failed to mention that it required a typing test. When Felix found out, he'd spent twenty hours straight teaching himself how to type. Out of the six people they'd interviewed, Felix had typed the least number of words per minute, but was the only one who hadn't made a single mistake. Impressed with Felix's meticulousness, the commanding officer selected him for the job.

In addition to what Dima told him, Felix learned a great deal in his capacity as a clerk typing orders to frontline commanders. He felt he knew more than most about how the war was really going.

In a few more days, it would be September and the Harvest Moon would return to bathe the city in its peculiar orange tint. Setting the newspaper down, he gazed out the window to the east. There was a tall apartment building blocking the view beyond, but he frequently saw the moon rise behind it. It was always a mystical sight. When Felix lived in Ukraine, autumn had been a time for rest and gratitude. The harvest rush would be over, food plentiful, and people enjoying the remnants of summer. But here in Leningrad at war, Felix felt nothing but anxiety. He knew all too well what came after the Leningrad autumn: the Leningrad winter.

Unable to bear the thought of Katya in the city if the Germans surrounded it, he deliberated how to get her out. There was only so much he could do to protect her.

When the front door of the apartment creaked open, Felix listened intently for who had arrived. Then his father's voice sounded from the hallway, uttering those three words he'd been eagerly awaiting all day: "Felix, Katya's here!"

He stumbled out of bed and made his way down the hall. His father was engaged in conversation with Katya, gesticulating wildly the way he often did when excited. He worked so much these days that he rarely ever saw Katya. "Ah, you're a sight for sore eyes," his father was exclaiming.

Katya, short brown hair curled up at the ends, was dressed in a sleeveless black and gold striped blouse that fully bared her slender, graceful neck. Felix thought she looked like a model from one of the smuggled Western magazines his friends showed him. "Father's been working a lot of hours lately," he called out as he approached. "Staring at beakers and vials for days on end."

"Oh, you can't imagine," his father added. "Every time the anti-aircraft guns start firing, those dogs howl like there's no tomorrow, and Tolya curses them like an old sailor. But that's beside the point, Felix. Isn't she the most beautiful thing you've ever seen?"

"Without a doubt, father." He kissed Katya on the lips and wrapped his arms around her. "Hello, gorgeous," he whispered in her ear.

"I'll leave you two lovebirds alone," his father said, departing down the hall.

Felix led Katya by the hand to his bedroom. It was a warm day, and Felix swung open the large windows at the foot of his bed. Katya loved to sit in the windowsill and read, draw, or just look out over the city. On a clear day like today, you could see the Neva River and even the Spire of the Admiralty in the Peter and Paul Fortress.

"How's your leg?" she asked.

"Much better now that you're here." He kissed her on the cheek, a big grin on his face. He saw her nearly every day, but it didn't make a dent in his affection for her.

"You're so adorable," she said. "Everybody thinks you're so tough and strong, but I know the truth. You're a puppy dog."

"Only for you."

"Is Dima coming by for lunch?"

"Yes," Felix replied. "He should be here soon."

"You must be excited. You haven't seen him since you were wounded, right?"

Felix nodded. "Did I tell you he was made a commander shortly after that?"

"Our Dima? A commander? I guess it was only a matter of time."

"Apparently the first one was deemed incompetent—I can certainly vouch for that—and then the second one was killed only a week later."

Katya went over to the open windows, propping her arms on the windowsill and leaning out. Felix admired the delicate curves of her body and her smooth, tan skin. He wished they had more time to be alone together. "Did you remember to bring yesterday's newspaper?" he asked.

"Yes, I have your *precious newspaper*," she teased, retrieving it from her bag and handing it to him. "How did you manage to miss yesterday's news?"

"Father gave the paper away before I had a chance to read it."

As Katya grabbed a pencil and pad of paper and situated herself, catlike, in the windowsill, Felix wondered if she'd write poetry or draw the city's skyline. The sun, which had been behind one cloud after another for the entire day, finally broke free and shined directly on her. Felix wasn't surprised. She had that effect on most people. Why should Mother Nature be an exception?

Before reading the newspaper, he resolved to talk to her about leaving the city. Taking a deep breath, he cleared his throat and blurted, "I want you to evacuate Leningrad."

Her closed eyes opened with a start, her pencil and paper falling to the floor.

"I think it's for the best," he continued. "You'll be safer someplace else."

Katya peered at him, then turned and looked out the window. "So you want me to leave too."

"Well, it seems like the best decision at this point and time," he said.

"But we may never see each other again if I go."

"We can't think that way. We have to trust and believe. It is our faith that will keep us together."

"I do believe," she said softly.

"I think it makes the most sense for you to go live—"

"In Moscow," she said, finishing his sentence.

"Sure," agreed Felix. "Maybe your father could pull some strings."

"He already has."

Felix remembered the "too" she'd said earlier, then put the pieces together. "Your father has already arranged for you to be evacuated, hasn't he?"

She nodded. "I was going to tell you after lunch," she said. "The train leaves tomorrow afternoon."

Felix felt a sinking feeling in his stomach, but also a sense of relief. "I want you to be safe," he said. "I'm terrified of something happening to you."

She came over to the bed. "And *I'm* terrified of something happening to you," she said, squeezing in next to him.

He stretched his arms around her, holding her tight, and they stayed that way—wordlessly—for a long time.

Felix's father's voice eventually broke the silence. "Dima's here," he announced.

With a kiss to the top of Katya's head, Felix started to leave to greet his friend.

"Wait," she called. Pulling the ring he'd given her off her finger, she held it in her hand. "I don't want—" she said and stopped, then slid the ring back on. "What I mean is, let's get married tomorrow before I leave. I know we've been making all these plans for our wedding, but let's just the two of us go to the bureau tomorrow morning and get a marriage license."

She lifted her face toward him, and for the first time he could recall, the sorrow in her chestnut-brown eyes disappeared completely. Meeting her gaze, he felt as if he held the entire world inside his heart. "Konyeshna"—of course—

he whispered. Lingering in the doorway smiling at her, he wished the moment could go on forever.

As he made his way down the hall, optimism coursed through his veins. One of his dreams was now a step closer to becoming reality.

His father was standing at the front door with Felix's best friend, inquiring about the sling that held Dima's left arm.

"It's nothing," Dima said dismissively. "The German fascists tried to take me out with their cannons. They got lucky and a piece of shrapnel hit me in the wrist. I'll be back in action soon enough."

"Then the Nazis will be sorry," exclaimed Felix's father.

Dima laughed. "Definitely."

Felix was taken aback at how different his friend looked. Though it had been a mere two months since they'd last seen one another, Felix recognized how much straighter Dima stood and how hard his body looked under his uniform. He seemed to be all muscle now. Felix, having been confined to bed for weeks, had no doubt who would win a pushup contest held today.

"You're limping still," called Dima.

Felix shrugged. "The healing hasn't been so smooth, but it's a hundred times better than just a few days ago. Once I walk for a minute or two, it's all right. It's just when I've been sitting or lying for a while that it gets so stiff. Another week and I should be back to normal."

They embraced heartily, and then Dima patted Felix's stomach. "I see your mother has fattened you up like a goose," he said with a grin.

"Yes. And it seems you're as strong and lean as a tiger." Felix laughed and slapped Dima on the back.

"Food isn't something at the front of your mind in battle," reflected Dima. "I completely forget about it until the end of the day. But by then I'm so exhausted that I take a few bites and fall asleep before I finish."

"Well, I hope you're hungry today," Felix's father said warmly as he departed for the kitchen. "I'll finish getting lunch ready."

"Where's your wonderful wife?" Dima called after him. "I was hoping for some of her delicious borscht."

"A friend of hers phoned saying that a store on Vasilevski Island was selling butter. So the two of them are going there to see if there's any truth to it."

"Yes, I've heard the food situation has gotten quite out of hand," said Dima. "It's all these panic-mongers and hoarders that cause so much trouble."

"Certain items are definitely hard to come by, but there's no shortage of rumors!" Felix's father joked over his shoulder. "Or—for today at least—borscht! She knew you were coming and made some beforehand."

Katya emerged from the Felix's bedroom and gave Dima a hug and kiss on the cheek. "So how's our commander?" she asked, staring at his pistol and leather holster.

"A little tired," he said, "but no worse for the wear." He retrieved a small booklet from his pocket and handed it to Katya.

Katya looked it over, thumbing through a few pages. "It's in German."

Dima nodded. "It's a Leningrad guidebook. I found it in the pocket of a dead Nazi."

Katya handed it to Felix. "Why can't they just leave us alone?" she asked. "This war makes no sense to me. They come to our country and bomb our roads, bridges, and cities, killing young and old alike. And for what? No matter how many times it's explained to me, I'll never understand it. I mean the Germans are human too. They—"

"They're not human," injected Dima. "They're Imperialists. And that's all you need to understand."

Felix set the booklet down and winked at Katya. "They're not only Imperialists," he said with a sly smile, "they're *efficient* Imperialists. The worst kind."

Katya laughed, but Dima did not. Instead, he scowled.

Felix prodded his friend toward the kitchen, where his father was busy slicing a loaf of dark bread. "Sit. Sit," his father requested. "It'll be ready in a minute."

The small, light-filled room smelled of fresh dill. While Dima took a seat at the end of the table, Felix and Katya retrieved spoons and bowls.

"Katya, Felix tells me you have a new roommate," remarked Dima.

"You mean Igor? Yes, he's quite a handful—always getting into things, curious as a cat. But my neighbor, Petya, has been wonderful. He helps me keep him occupied."

"Igor is your cousin?" Dima asked. "Is that right?

"Yes," she answered, setting four white soup bowls on the table. "I'd never met him before, though. He's from the country, and my father and his mother never talked. Igor told me the Germans burned their house and bombed the neighboring village, so he and his parents were refugees for a while. When his parents died, a Soviet soldier brought Igor all the way here to Leningrad and found us."

Felix set a spoon next to each person, then sat down himself. The windows next to the modest square table were open, and a slight breeze carried in the sound of children playing in the courtyard below.

"How old is he?" asked Dima.

"Twelve."

"Then he should be helping out on the front or at least doing something here in the city."

"Believe me, he wants to," said Katya. "The problem is he has the maturity of a ten-year-old. Whenever he tries to help, he usually makes things worse."

Felix's father began filling each person's bowl with a cold, pomegranate-colored soup. Katya used a match to light a burner on the stove, then set a tea kettle on it.

"Dima, you've no doubt heard about the retreat from Tallinn," Felix's father said. "Practically the entire fleet's been sunk. It's such a crime the way the whole affair was handled."

"What do you mean it's a crime?" asked Dima.

"It's a crime there was never a plan to evacuate. So many lives and so many ships could have been saved. My friend—one of the few to survive—told me all about it. They were trying to navigate the harbor with its thousands of Nazi mines while being bombed by Nazi guns from the shore and swarms of Nazi planes in the air."

"The real crime is those Estonians taking up arms with the Germans," Dima said, clenching his fist. "We must all get behind the Party and be united with a single focus. If we're divided, the Germans will beat us. We *never* should have retreated from Tallinn."

"But, Dima," Felix's father said, "the rules of war dictate that sometimes you attack and sometimes you retreat. To never retreat when you've been beaten is suicide. Surely you understand that?"

"Retreating is something I hope to never understand," Dima said. "Tallinn would have kept the Germans busy for a long time. Now all those Nazi troops will be joining the battle for Leningrad."

"Father, do we have sour cream?" Felix asked.

"No, I'm afraid not. Your mother hasn't been able to find any. I have some dill though." He retrieved a small bowl overflowing with the pungent herb and put it on the table.

"Dima, do you remember Katya's neighbor, Petya?" Felix asked. "Katya said he told her he doesn't think it's necessary to stock up on food because the city will have to surrender soon."

Katya grinned and poked Felix with her elbow. Felix glanced at her and winked, awaiting Dima's tirade.

"He's a traitor," Dima said resolutely. "If the Party weren't so busy preparing for the defense of the city, then people like him would be dealt with. Anyone who thinks of surrender should be shot."

Felix's father was oblivious to his son's mischief until he noticed Katya having difficulty suppressing a giggle. "If we had a whole army of people like you, Dima," he said, joining in, "we'd never lose a battle."

"Well, I don't know about *every* battle," Dima said earnestly.

Katya burst out laughing, and Dima gaped at her quizzically.

"I'm sorry," she said. "I just remembered a joke someone told me."

Felix turned to her, a glint in his eye. "We could all use a little humor. Why don't you tell us the joke?"

She raised her bottom lip, directing a pretend scowl at Felix. "No. I'm terrible at telling jokes," she said. "Let's eat. I'm sure Dima's starving."

"Yes, let's eat," Felix's father said as he sprinkled dill on his soup.

A small bee flew in the window and buzzed around the table until Katya shooed it back outside again.

"Slow down, Dima," she commented upon returning to the table.

Felix, normally a fast eater himself, was surprised at how much quicker Dima was now.

"Sorry. You don't have much time for meals at the front," explained Dima.

Felix's father passed around a saucer with raw garlic. "Katya, how is the work at the hospital going?" he asked.

"Oh, I don't want to talk about it," she answered, dropping her shoulders. "These poor old men and young boys keep pouring in. It's awful, just awful."

"I agree. Let's not talk about that," Dima said. "We mustn't concentrate on the negative: the retreats, the traitors, the wounded, the food situation. We need to focus on the positive—on the news and stories that inspire us. We should be talking about the Colonel Podlutskys of the war."

"Podlutsky," Katya repeated. "I know him. He's in our hospital. All the men speak so highly of him. What did he do?"

"He was in the artillery unit of the Seventieth Division," Dima said. "They fought the Germans with everything they had, but were badly outnumbered and ultimately encircled. With the division in shambles, Podlutsky led his detachment out of encirclement one hundred twenty-five miles behind enemy lines."

"Yes. I heard about that," said Felix. "But don't you think the Soviet people deserve to know the truth about how the war is going? The newspapers often hide disappointing news, and it only feeds the rumormongers."

"The truth is what history writes," Dima responded as he took another thick slice of black bread. "If the Party is wrong, then it will be so judged. But the Party is not wrong. You'll see. Speaking of which, how is your father, Katya?"

"Overworked as usual. I think he suffered a minor heart attack two weeks ago, but he won't admit it. He was having difficulty breathing and kept holding his hand to his chest complaining of pain and tightness. I couldn't get him to go see a doctor though. He said, 'The doctors are busy with the wounded. I won't have them wasting their time on an old man with indigestion.' I fear he'll do himself in before the Germans ever do."

Felix's father used a piece of bread to soak up the remaining soup in his bowl. "I tell you what I'd like to ask him," he said while eating the bread. "I'd like to know about these rumors of people being evacuated—particularly children—right into the path of the Nazis."

"I'm afraid you'll have to wait to ask him that," Katya said. "He's in Moscow now."

"Moscow? When did this happen?"

"He left on the train yesterday morning."

"So the city's not surrounded yet? That's one less rumor to believe," Felix's father said.

"Father," Felix said in an exasperated tone, "I told you the Northern Railroad was open and that trains were still going to Moscow. You trust Katya, but not me?"

"Don't be cross, son. I'm a fool for a beautiful woman." He held his hands over his heart and gazed across the table at Katya. "If Katya told me the sky was green, I'd believe her."

"Why can't you listen to me like your father does?" Katya said, playfully pinching Felix on the arm. "Actually, Igor and I will be joining my father in Moscow tomorrow."

"So you'll all live in Moscow?" asked Felix's father.

"No. Father's supposed to return the first of September. Igor and I will stay in Moscow until this madness is over with."

Felix sensed both his father and Dima looking at him, waiting for an answer to a question that hadn't been asked.

"Yes. My father's set it all up," Katya continued. "And Felix quite agrees with him."

"I think it's for the best at this time," Felix said flatly. He was wary of Dima's reaction and didn't have to wait long.

"I don't think anybody who can help should leave," announced Dima. "Now, more than ever, it's important for us to stick together. United, we can win, but if able-bodied people evacuate the city, we're digging our own graves."

"Don't try using your twisted logic with this, Dima," Felix said, no longer amused by his friend's intransigence and arrogance. "It's the Germans who are digging our graves, and you know it. It's not right to blame the people of Leningrad for needing some safety, for wanting to protect their loved ones."

"It's precisely that kind of thinking that will doom us," responded Dima. "That's the most dangerous type of thinking there is, because it hides behind those antiquated notions of the individual having more importance than the collective whole. That's sentimentality masquerading as logic."

While Felix simmered in indignation, Dima continued eating as though there had been no tension in the conversation. "Felix, don't be angry," he said. "I don't hold your misguided thinking against you. You just need more time for the Party's teachings to sink in. That's why I'm so patient with you, and you should be patient with yourself as well. It takes time and courage to change these beliefs that have been ingrained in us for so long."

Clenching his fists, Felix was about to tell Dima what a conceited, presumptuous ass he was when Katya put her hand over his and squeezed. Seeing Katya smiling so calmly soothed his nerves. He could tell by the expression on her face that she wanted him to concede the argument, because it was pointless to argue with Dima. Taking a long, slow breath, Felix said, "Thanks, Dima. And I'll do my best to be patient with you as well."

Dima looked puzzled for a moment, but then continued eating.

After lunch, Dima, Felix, and Katya decided to go for a stroll. It was another warm, sunny day, and the air was thick with the scent of turning leaves. Fall was fast approaching.

Once at the Kazansky Cathedral with its elegant dome set against a tepid blue sky, they walked under the shade of a row of linden trees whose leaves had turned yellow. While Felix told a joke, Katya picked a leaf from the ground, admired it up close, then stuck it in Felix's hair.

They turned down a small street that was blocked off to traffic and encountered a burly man staggering toward them. Unable to keep his balance, the man stumbled, fell to the ground, then haltingly made his way back to his feet. He cursed at the people passing him by, and though his speech was slurred, much of his blasphemous rant was quite clear.

"The Germans are coming!" he shouted. "They're going to take over. And the Soviets can't stop them. Nobody can! They'll slaughter all the commissars. Every last one of them. Do you hear me?"

Those within earshot veered away from him to the far side of the street. His face was red and puffy, and he wore badly tattered Red Army fatigues.

"Down with the Soviets! Down with the Commissars! Down with Socialism!" he called.

Upon seeing Dima reach for his pistol, Felix hurried ahead, moving as fast as his gimpy leg would allow him. "Comrade," he called to the man as calmly as he could. "You need to stop with that talk."

"I ain't your *comrade*," the man replied. A fresh scrape on his forehead trickled blood down his left cheek.

"Please," Felix implored, standing directly between him and the approaching Dima. "It's for your own good."

"I ain't *nobody's* comrade," the man continued loudly. "I'm autonomous. Nobody tells me what to do!" Catching sight of the uniform-clad, pistol-bearing Dima, the intoxicated man hollered in his direction, "I'm autonomous, I said!"

An exceptional student of the Russian martial art, sambo, Felix wrapped the much bigger man in a bear hug, commanding, "Look at me!"

The man couldn't focus, setting his eyes everywhere except on Felix. He gawked at Dima, Katya, and the people starting to gather around.

"Look me in the eyes," Felix demanded. The man reeked of alcohol, and Felix could tell by his breath that he was drunk on cologne. "You need to be quiet now," Felix said in a soothing voice. "You've had too much to drink, and you're going to get in big trouble if you keep talking. Do you understand me?"

Dima had now arrived, standing ten yards away, pistol in hand.

"It's all right, Dima," Felix said. "He didn't know what he was saying. He's done now."

The man glared at Dima. "You bastard," he said. "I ain't afraid of you."

"Stop," Felix whispered, placing his hand over the man's mouth. "Stop talking."

"You're just like the bastard who shot Vitya in the back!" the man roared at Dima as he struggled to free himself from Felix's grasp.

"Felix, move away!" Dima ordered.

"Dima, he's drunk," Katya pleaded. "Don't do this. Please."

"I don't care," Dima replied as he pointed his pistol.

"The Germans are coming!" the man roared to the crowd of half a dozen people. "They're going to slaughter every commissar and communist they find. Down with the Soviets!" Breaking free of Felix's hold, he took two steps toward Dima before a shot rang out. The bullet struck him in the chest, sending him immediately to the pavement.

Katya let out a high-pitched scream. "Oh God!" she cried. "You didn't have to do that, Dima. You didn't have to do that!" Rushing to the fallen man's side, she inspected the wound and checked his breathing.

"Leave him be," Dima called as two policemen ran out of a nearby alley. "Let the traitor die."

Ignoring him, Katya told Felix she needed something to stop the bleeding. Felix removed his shirt and handed it to her. "If we can get him to a hospital right away," said Katya, "I think he has a chance."

While one policeman questioned Dima, the other talked to the people in the crowd. After only a few seconds, they converged on Felix and Katya and told them to move away from the wounded man.

"We can't. We need to keep pressure on the wound," Felix argued.

"Move away," the taller of the two policemen repeated menacingly.

"I'm a nurse," Katya explained. "Help us get him to a hospital."

While one of the policemen pulled Katya away by the arm, the other moved in on Felix. "Unless you want to get arrested," he threatened, "I suggest you move away *now*."

"He's dying, you idiot," Felix said angrily. "Can't you see that?"

The policeman tried yanking Felix away, but Felix executed a nimble move that instead sent the policeman to the ground. As the other policeman withdrew a small black club from his belt, Dima jumped into the fray, locking his arms around Felix and convincing him to move away.

When Felix calmed down, he felt something in his hair and brushed it away. The yellow linden leaf Katya had placed there floated to the pavement.

The dying man had long since taken his last breath by the time Dima persuaded the two policemen not to arrest Felix. During this time, Felix and Katya had done their best to convince a shaken, crying girl who'd witnessed the scene that the dead man was a German spy disguised as a Soviet soldier. The girl's father was in the army, and she couldn't comprehend how a Soviet soldier could kill another Soviet soldier when the Germans were the enemy.

When finally allowed to leave, Dima, Felix, and Katya trudged back to Nevsky Prospekt without a word between them.

The stately Nevsky was filled with a curious mix of citizens and soldiers. Two young boys carried gas masks while a company of infantry marched in tight formation, half of them stealing glances at a young woman in her summer dress. Despite all the talk of a food shortage, a mother and her three children sat on the curb enjoying Eskimo pies.

Dima was the first to break the uncomfortable silence. "Felix, let me give you a word of advice," he said, narrowing his eyes as he grabbed his friend by the arm. "You better decide who's side you're on, and you better decide damn soon."

Felix jerked his arm out of Dima's grip. "I know what side I'm on," he declared. "The side that knows right from wrong."

"That's your problem," asserted Dima. "You think you're somehow *qualified* to decide. But it's Moscow that determines what's right and what's wrong. The Party is the one with the knowledge of history. The Party is the collective wisdom of the Proletariat. Who are you to think you know better?"

Felix forced a deep breath. "We've been best friends ever since we were kids," he said. "So let me say as a friend—"

"We are *not* friends," interrupted Dima. He held his hand in front of him, pointing a finger in Felix's face. "There's no room in these times for quaint things like friendship. We are *comrades,* nothing more, nothing less."

Felix pursed his lips, holding his tongue.

"Let me give you one last piece of advice," said Dima. "You have this habit of crossing lines that shouldn't be crossed, and one of these days you're going to be very sorry. One of these days, you're going to cross the last line." Without saying goodbye, he turned away and walked to the other side of the street.

Felix recalled the times he'd spent with his closest friend. As kids, they'd shared dreams of becoming pilots, explorers, and Olympic athletes. When they were nine-year-olds, Felix had saved Dima from drowning, and Dima had made a blood-vow to return the favor one day. In those simpler times, no matter how mad they got at each other, they were always able to forgive and forget.

A sharp pain shot up Felix's leg. He was so sick of the war. It was insatiable—taking and taking, and never giving.

And now it had taken his best friend.

Katya cussed aloud after tripping on the uneven sidewalk. She managed to stay on her feet, but startled both herself and Igor with her profanity. Each step was torture, and it had taken tremendous effort to force her reluctant legs this far. She didn't want to leave her beloved Leningrad, didn't want to leave Felix, didn't want to go to Moscow. Yet here she was—suitcase in hand—heading to the train station.

That morning, she and Felix had gone to the bureau for a marriage license. On their way in, they'd congratulated a departing couple, hoping they too would soon be just as happy. Filled with anticipation, Felix and Katya had barely announced their intention to the clerk when he replied indifferently that they needed two witnesses. Undeterred, Felix asked if they had to know the witnesses. When the clerk said no, Felix went outside and persuaded two strangers to take a few minutes out of their day. Next, the clerk reviewed their papers and disappeared into another room, only to return a few minutes later with a cold reply that the office had run out of forms and he could not process their request. Refusing to answer any further questions, he demanded they leave and locked the door behind them.

Katya felt suspicious about the whole situation, but what could she do? Nothing made sense anymore. She was convinced the entire world had gone mad.

Igor, walking a pace ahead now, was doing his best to impress her by carrying three of their bags. Katya normally thought it adorable when he tried to act twice his age around her, but she was too preoccupied to pay him much attention.

"I bet Felix couldn't carry all three of these," Igor declared.

Felix was on duty, but had a lunch break in fifteen minutes and would be meeting them at the train station to say goodbye.

After Igor repeated himself a little louder, Katya said curtly, "We'll test him later."

Ahead of them a long military column shuffled haphazardly through an intersection. They were a stark contrast to the upbeat and boisterous troops at the start of the war. Felix had told Katya that most of the men you saw moving through the city like this were the remnants of forces that had survived some battle and had been hastily regrouped for redeployment. The Soviet commanders were constantly moving troops around trying to plug holes in the tenuous line protecting Leningrad from the Nazi assault.

The sun was bright and high overhead, and the scuffing of the soldiers' boots on the pavement reminded Katya of a funeral procession. Once clear of the dispirited men, Katya and Igor rounded a corner and beheld a new mass of people blocking their way. This time it was women, children, and old men standing in a queue. Katya looked for the front of the line to see what they were waiting for, but it snaked all the way around the corner of the next block.

"What are you in line for?" Igor asked an elderly man standing at the end.

"I don't know," he answered. "Hopefully something good." A woman further up in line added, "I heard they're selling sugar."

Katya hastily squeezed past the people and decided to cut through a park. It was filled with trenches, but unlike the other parks you could still walk through this one with ease.

"There's a few benches over there in the shade," Igor said. "Do you want to take a break from the sun for a minute?"

Katya glanced at the trees with their jumble of red, gold, and green leaves, then shook her head. A pair of squirrels chased one another into the empty trenches and then back out again.

Halfway through the park, Igor set the bags down and panted for a few seconds. "You must be getting a little tired by now," he suggested. "Would you like me to stop so you can rest?"

"No. I'm fine," Katya replied and kept walking.

After a few more minutes, Igor dropped the bags yet again. "It's no problem for me to wait a minute if you want to rest," he said, leaning over with his hands on his knees.

Wanting to get to the station quickly so she could spend as much time with Felix as possible, Katya gave a definitive "no," then added, "I already told you, I'm fine."

"Come back," called Igor. "You've got to see this."

"What is it?" she asked. "Are you all right?"

"Look," he said, pointing at the ground under a nearby tree.

Katya surveyed the tree's crimson leaves and the carpet of mushrooms under its thick, knotty branches. It was more mushrooms than she'd ever seen under one tree. "Igor, we don't have time to pick mushrooms."

"No. It's not that," he said. "Those aren't edible anyway."

"Then what?"

"It's a bad omen. The old people in my village had a saying: 'Many mushrooms; many deaths.' They said it's a warning about the coming winter. That it will be hard."

Katya studied Igor's face, hoping he might be joking. "There's lots of old sayings," she remarked. "That doesn't mean there's any truth to them." But her own words didn't reassure her. She wasn't superstitious, but did have great respect for folk wisdom. She'd always been amazed at how some of the old timers could predict the weather or how well the crops would do that year or what gender an unborn baby would be.

Lifting her suitcase once more, she also took one of the bags Igor had been carrying. "Come on," she said.

Igor protested that the bag she took from him was too heavy for her, but when she offered to give it back, he complained his shoulder hurt—an old injury, he claimed, from taming a wild horse.

When they arrived at the train station, it was overflowing with evacuees. Anxious mothers and uneasy children gathered around mounds of boxes, suitcases, and bags spread out on the walkways. After leading the way through the crowds to their train's platform, Katya carved out a space for their bags, then stood atop one as she searched for Felix. Their train had not yet arrived, and she was five minutes ahead of the schedule she'd set for herself.

"Let me know if you see Felix anywhere," she said.

"I will," replied Igor as he plucked a piece of paper from the brown leaves of a scraggly bush and began reading it aloud. "Beat ... the ... Jews." He read haltingly, unsure of each word he pronounced. "Beat ... the ...." He held the leaflet in front of Katya, asking, "What's this word?"

"Commissars," she answered.

"Beat ... the ... Commissars," he continued. "Their mugs beg to be bashed in. Wait for the full moon. Bayonets in the Earth! Surrender!"

Igor, mouth agape, curled his furry eyebrows toward his pug nose. "Does this mean we're giving up?"

"No," said Katya. "The Germans dropped those leaflets from a plane. They're trying to scare us."

Igor wadded the paper up and threw it back in the bush. "I'm not scared," he said, his voice sounding more nasal than usual. "I was just worried about you."

A long train with dark green passenger cars began slowly backing in, and Katya knew they'd begin boarding in a few more minutes.

"How come Felix isn't here yet?" asked Igor.

"I don't know," she said, scanning the crowds and wondering the same thing.

"Is he a Jew?" blurted Igor.

"Who? Felix?"

"Yes. My father always told me to stay away from people with names like Iosif or Felix. He said people with those names were always Jews."

"And what did you father tell you about Jews?"

"He said they have big noses and beady eyes, and that they're bad people."

"Well, you've known Felix for a while. What do you think? Is he a Jew?"

Igor wrinkled his forehead. "I don't know," he whined. "That's why I asked you."

When Katya didn't respond, he added, "He seems like a Russian. He's always nice to me—even bought me an Eskimo pie once. But his nose is kind of big."

"If I told you he was Jewish, would you hate him?"

Igor shrugged, then asked, "Does he make human sacrifices to the devil?"

Katya took him by the hand and drew him close to her. It saddened her that her cousin had never known their grandmother and her teachings on peace and tolerance. Since Igor was still young and impressionable, she decided she would be the one to pass them on to him.

"I bet your father was a very wise and knowledgeable man," she said. "He probably taught you a lot of things, right?"

He nodded.

"But I think your father had a bad experience with someone who happened to be Jewish, and then thought all Jews were like that. Igor, Jews are no different than you or I. We all experience joy and sadness. We all make mistakes. We all get mad sometimes and say things we regret. We're all humans."

Igor gazed thoughtfully at her, but then crossed his arms in front of his chest, asking, "So why do the Nazis hate the Jews so much?"

"I don't know for sure," she answered honestly. "I think many have been taught by Hitler to hate Jews. He wants to use them as a scapegoat—someone to blame all their problems on."

"I hate Hitler," Igor said proudly. "I'd kill him if I could."

Evacuees were now boarding the train. Officials had to check each person's papers, then check them again, then argue for a minute, and finally check them one last time before allowing the person on.

Holding her stomach anxiously, Katya continued looking for Felix. "Igor, could you walk to the end of the train and see if you can find Felix? Don't take too long though."

No sooner had Igor disappeared into the crowd than Katya spotted a man the same height and build as Felix. He was on the other side of the platform and walking the opposite direction Igor had gone. When she spied curly dark hair sticking out from under his hat, she wrung her hands and took a step toward him.

"Felix!" she shouted. As he turned his head toward her, she saw a forty-year-old man with sunken cheeks and a thin black mustache.

The intensity of her disappointment startled her. She felt bewildered at how she'd become so deeply attached to Felix. It was as though she could not live without him.

The line to board the train was now empty, and the only people left on the platform were those who had come to say goodbye. The large clock behind Katya told her she had six minutes before the train departed.

Holding back a flood of tears that threatened to overwhelm her, Katya squeezed her eyes tight and pictured her grandmother humming a Bible verse as she tended her little garden with its cucumbers, tomatoes, carrots, and dill. Katya had never seen her grandmother weep or lash out in anger, and that was what she aspired to. But it was so hard. Every time Katya opened the newspaper or listened to the radio, she'd be confronted with the latest Nazi atrocity and would feel her chest tighten. She used to be so sure that she understood her grandmother's Mennonite teachings, but living them was another matter altogether.

An elderly man with a brown cap and a nervous smile asked Katya if she needed help with her bags. She shook her head, then spotted Igor on his way back.

With a deep inhale, she tried to fill herself with her grandmother's strength and faith. She knew what she had to do.

"Igor, help me with the bags, please," she called. "The train's about to leave."

"But Felix isn't here yet."

Lugging their bags forward, she replied flatly, "I can see that."

After finding their seats, Katya pressed her face to the window, resuming her search for Felix. Igor put his arm awkwardly around her shoulder, saying, "Don't worry. I'll take care of you."

Katya shuddered at the thought of never seeing her beloved again. She wanted *his* arm around her shoulder, and *his* voice telling her not to worry. She longed to run her fingers through his hair, put her lips to his skin, feel his strong hands on the small of her back. When the tears finally came, she felt no relief. What good were they anyway? They couldn't change anything.

"It's Felix!" Igor shouted, pointing out the window.

Felix was running along the platform toward them, jumping up every few steps and yelling to the passengers on each car: "Katya! Katya!"

Sticking her head out the window, she called to him, then fled down the aisle. "You can't get off," Igor said as he followed. "The train's about to leave."

When she got to the exit, Felix was already there, and she leapt from the stairs into his outstretched arms. Clutching her in his arms, he swung her in circles, her feet never touching the ground. "I'm so sorry, Katya," he said, his voice cracking. "I couldn't find you. I just couldn't find you."

Burying her face in the side of his neck, her tears flowed in a torrent. "I can't do this," she choked in between sobs. "I can't leave you."

He pulled his head back and showered her cheeks and forehead with kisses.

With a loud rusty groan, the train lurched forward and started inching down the tracks.

"Katya!" exclaimed Igor, pulling on her arm. "The train's leaving! Hurry, let's get on!"

Katya heard the train, as well as Igor. But nothing was going to break her embrace. Holding her lover as tightly as ever, she watched the train pull away—overjoyed she wasn't on it.

Caught in a nightmare from which he couldn't awaken, Misha tried to yell, but only managed to eke out a feeble noise similar to the bleat of a baby goat calling for its mother. When a bloody German pilot crawled out of the ground and tried to strangle him, Misha was frightened back into consciousness and awoke gasping for air.

He was alone, swaying slightly from side to side, sitting atop a wooden seat that folded out from a wall. He had trouble catching his breath and convincing himself that it had all been a dream.

A rifle leaned against his left leg. Through the window to his right, he could see houses and trees passing by. Slowly recollecting his plight, he remembered taking a seat on the train as it traveled between stations. That's when he must have fallen asleep.

With a sense of relief, he tried to put more of the pieces of the puzzle together. He had to do this a lot lately. It was as though a part of him wanted to forget—to deny his situation and the things he'd done in his life.

It was August 30, and he was a guard on a train on the Northern Railroad. After dropping off Igor in Leningrad, Misha had tried to find his mother, but had been arrested for lack of papers. Along with the rest of the deserters, refugees, and the merely lost, he'd been herded before a tribunal where each person was either sent to a firing squad, a construction battalion, or reassigned to another infantry unit.

Condemned to the deserters group, Misha knew he was destined for the firing squad, but a high-ranking officer had interrupted the proceedings, stating he needed twenty-four men to be guards on the trains evacuating citizens from the city. As the tribunal pulled men from every group but his, Misha lost hope. But it was a small, overcrowded room, and in the brief disarray of men switching from one group to another, Misha slyly slipped out of his and into the group of men being selected.

He was proud of his ability to survive, but also felt fate had destined him for something. If the officer had walked in five minutes later, Misha would've already been marched off to the firing squad.

Opening the door of the coach, the wind blasted him with the scent of smoke and buckwheat. The sun was bright, and they were passing by a blackened forest that was still smoldering. Bomb craters with brown water dotted the landscape, and four smashed train cars lay helplessly on their side next to the tracks.

Returning to his seat, Misha wondered how many more times he could cheat death. The way to outlive others, he reasoned, was to do whatever you had to: lie, steal, or cheat. Those with moral dilemmas or remorse were bound for a quick demise in this war.

When the door from the next train car opened, Misha jumped to his feet.

It was Olga, the woman who collected passengers' tickets and checked their papers. She held no military rank, but there was no doubt as to who was in charge on the train.

With a scowl at the open door in front of her, she said, "Comrade, I see you have disobeyed me once again by opening the door." Sunlight shined on her broad face, and her gold tooth glinted when she spoke.

Misha saw no point in responding. He'd been caught red-handed and awaited the usual venom from her lips. She was a forty-five-year-old mother of three grown sons who were in the navy. Hailing from a small village in the north, she had an accent to match and a boxlike frame that was not unlike the T-26 tanks that defended Leningrad. With her on the train, Misha often pondered why guards like him were even necessary. He'd heard many accounts, and also personally witnessed her push, kick, and punch people—men, women, and once even a child—who dared cross her.

As she stepped closer to him, Misha was certain he was about to be the next one on the receiving end of her blows.

Baring her menacing gold tooth, she hissed, "You little weasel. You're going to get what's coming to you." Her breath smelled like moldy tea.

With a grating squeal, the train's brakes suddenly engaged, jerking both Misha and Olga forward.

"Why the hell are we stopping?" asked Olga. "We can't be at Obukhovo yet."

Obukhovo was their first scheduled stop, and Misha could tell from the scenery that they were indeed not there yet. Leaning out the doorway, he spied three men on the station platform ahead. "There's an officer and two soldiers waving for us to halt," he announced. The name of the station was written on white-painted stones nestled among red and white petunias. Misha read it aloud: "Mga."

"Let me see," Olga said, shoving him out of the way.

Mga was a small station about twenty-five miles southeast of Leningrad. It was the last of the numerous, sleepy little stations in between Moscow and Leningrad, and they didn't usually stop there.

When the train at last came to a standstill, Olga, Misha, and the eleven other guards on the train jumped down and started toward the Red Army officer signaling impatiently for them to gather round. Anti-aircraft guns thumped in the distance, and judging from the loudness, Misha guessed they were only a few more miles up the tracks. Walking a few paces behind Olga, he gripped his rifle tightly, expecting to see German warplanes any second.

A few of the guards had already assembled in front of the officer, and he was gesturing at the sky a mile ahead of the train. Misha instantly saw what he was pointing at: more than three dozen paratroopers were gliding through the sky.

"Comrades, I am Major Leshchev," the officer announced. "We are in a very dire situation. As you can see, the Germans are attacking. We have very few men here to fight back. What do you have on this train? Any weapons?"

Olga spoke up. "We have nothing of use, comrade. We've been evacuating citizens from the city, and were returning to get more."

Leshchev shook his head and cussed. "I need all the men I can get. How many soldiers do you have?"

"Just these men here," she said. "They're the guards for the train, but they will stay and fight."

Leshchev paused a minute, looking pensively over the men, before saying, "Bring every weapon and cartridge you have. We have to prevent the Germans from taking this station."

"You heard him," Olga yelled. "Get going."

Misha wandered over to the shade. He didn't have anything else to get, so he kicked at the dry earth with his boots. When a breeze came, it picked up clouds of dust and rolled them along the ground.

"Comrade Major," Misha overheard Olga say. "I wish to stay and fight as well."

Leshchev didn't even raise an eyebrow. "Can you handle a rifle?" he asked.

"Yes. I've had training."

"Very well," he said. Then, turning to one of his men, he ordered, "Lisovsky, go tell the conductor the tracks ahead have been bombed. He'll have to go back to Volkhov."

With a lethargic salute, the man left for the front of the train. "And one other thing," the Major said to Olga. "Tell your men to bring all the food, water, and blankets you have on the train." Then, leaning in and whispering just loud enough so that Misha heard, he added, "We've been fighting the Germans all the way from Novgorod. We have no artillery, very few cartridges, and my men are exhausted."

Misha watched as Olga hesitated. He wondered if she grasped the full meaning of what Leshchev had told her—that the situation was futile, and that an additional twelve men and one woman weren't going to make a difference.

"I will stay and fight," Olga responded firmly. "And so will my men."

He nodded his head somberly. "Someone told me this is the last railroad in and out of Leningrad. Is that true?"

"Yes," confirmed Olga. "This is the last line."

Leshchev glanced in the direction of Leningrad and sighed. "These are dark days, comrade," he said. "Long, dark days."

Misha warily regarded the German paratroopers taking up positions in the distance. If they took this station, Leningrad would be cut off from the rest of Russia.

The train reversed course and pulled away from the station. The breeze picked up again, and a solitary crimson leaf twirled by Misha. He tried to keep track of it as it scurried along the ground—past the hurried footsteps of his fellow guards, past the retreating train, and eventually past the tiny station of Mga that had quite unexpectedly become the key to the battle for Leningrad.

ДВА — Part II

We two form a multitude. — **Ovid**

Hitler's war plan for the Soviet Union, code named Operation Barbarossa after the Holy Roman Emperor who marched east in 1190, had as a general objective the destruction of the Soviet Union's military capability and control of the country's vast agricultural, oil, and raw-material resources. With a total of three million German troops, Operation Barbarossa was to culminate in an assault on Moscow. German forces were to attack from the north and the west in a giant pincer movement. The capture of Leningrad was critical to Hitler's plan. Only after Leningrad was taken could the forces from the north march on Moscow.

Field Marshal Ritter von Leeb, the sixty-five-year-old commander who had triumphed over the Maginot Line in France, was in charge of the forces from the north. His army, Group Nord, was to have taken Leningrad by July 21—a mere month from when the invasion of the Soviet Union began.

Now, in early September, von Leeb's forces consisted of about twenty divisions, including Panzer and mechanized corps. They numbered around 500,000 men. The fall of Mga had effectively closed the circle around Leningrad, and the only remaining connection with the "Russian mainland" was by air or over Lake Ladoga to the east.

Men, women, and children still living in Leningrad at this time were estimated at three million. Though the Soviet forces facing the German troops were nearly equal in numbers, they were anything but equal in terms of artillery, rifles, machine guns, ammunition, and organization. The German forces had every advantage, including two tank divisions to the Soviet's none. In addition, the German Luftwaffe controlled the skies.

After winning the battle for Mga, von Leeb consolidated his forces in preparation for a new offensive to take place on September 9. It was designed to be the final blow that would break the spirit of the Russians and lead to Leningrad's surrender. If the ground assault did not succeed, then Leningrad would be annihilated by air and artillery bombardment just like Warsaw and Rotterdam had been. Von Leeb and the German Supreme Command anticipated a quick victory over Leningrad, so they could then move on to Moscow and perhaps end the war in October—only slightly behind schedule.

Глава Пятая — Chapter Five

ALL THAT MATTERS

Dragged,
  by well-fed ignorance
Down,
  into subtle lies
That can't disguise
  this ruse,
  this fuse,
  that goes
Tick-tock, tick-tock, tick…
Meet me down by the railroad
  where the tracks curve west.
Meet me before the realists
  steal the youth from my chest.
Meet me while this righteousness
  still burns on my breath.

Petya held the envelope a few inches above the whistling teapot. He was a self-taught professional at opening letters and then resealing them so that recipients never suspected. Already finished unsealing the first envelope, he was now working on the second one.

He'd actually stopped reading other people's mail a year ago because he found their letters—as well as their lives—boring. But he was quite eager to view the two letters he had now. Katya's father, Grigori, had asked Petya for a favor before he'd left for Moscow. Knowing there was a chance the Germans might cut off his return route to the city, he'd asked Petya to be on the lookout for a letter from the Bureau of Archives and Records. If one came, Petya was to then mail a letter that Grigori had already sealed and addressed. To ensure Petya's compliance in not reading either letter, and also to keep everything a secret from Katya, Grigori had hinted to Petya not so subtly that a certain region in the far north was still terribly short of workers for its mining operations.

Considering how badly the war had been going, Petya wondered if Grigori would even have the chance to return from Moscow. He knew that when senior Party leaders were called to the capital these days, it wasn't to congratulate them on their achievements. There were two groups for those deemed guilty in the Party's blame game: the lucky ones, who were reassigned to new positions in different, less desirable regions of the country; and the unlucky ones, who were shot after they deplaned.

With the precision of a surgeon, Petya pushed his special not-too-sharp, not-too-dull knife under the seal and carefully slid it the length of the envelope. Then he removed the letter, postmarked yesterday, September 3, and read:

> *Comrade Grigori Selenii,*
> *As you requested, this is a notification that the specified individuals, Felix Varilensky and Katya Selenaya, visited our office. They arrived in the morning on August 29, 1941 and requested a marriage license. Per your instructions, they were denied.*
>
> *- Stepan Rostovich*
>   *Bureau of Archives and Records*

As Petya retrieved the letter from the second envelope, Oksana Petrovna's weary voice rang out. "Petya, are you making tea?" She was in her room, calling through the closed door.

Petya tucked the letters and envelopes under his shirt. "Yes," he replied, waiting to see if her door was going to open. "But I just used all the water," he lied. "I'll put some more on." He was stunned that she was home, as she was usually at her job at this time of day. She worked at the Mariinsky Opera Theater as a technician on the set. Since the war had started, all the technicians had been reassigned to making artillery guns and tanks out of canvas and plywood. They scattered the props around the city to fool the Germans.

"No. Don't bother," she said.

Petya went to his room, locked the door behind him, and read the letter Katya's father had written.

Dear Nikolai Semyonovich,

I know you are busy fighting the war and I apologize for taking your time. But if you are reading this, then my fears have come true and I have been separated from my daughter, Katya. You know from our many late night talks that she has been seeing a certain Jew originally from Ukraine—Felix Varilensky. It has always been my belief that their misguided courtship would be short-lived, that it was merely a phase she was passing through. I have tried to be patient, waiting for their eventual break up, but I fear the war may have brought them closer together for the time being. I am greatly concerned that she may make a terrible mistake in my absence and so I would like to speed up the process, so to speak, of their going their separate ways. I know you too would be alarmed if your daughter was seeing a Jew. So from one parent to another, I ask for your help in seeing that F. Varilensky is reassigned from his clerical duties back to the front, where we desperately need more men anyway. If you can do me this favor, I will forever be in your debt.

Your friend and comrade,
- Grigori Selenii

Petya grinned as he put the letter back in the envelope and resealed it. What a pleasant surprise to learn that Felix would be leaving for the front again. He combed his hair straight back, put on a clean shirt, and set out to mail the letter that very afternoon.

He glided down the stairs, whistling a whimsical tune he'd picked up from his roommate, Boris. As he exited the building and felt the sun on his face, he whistled even louder. Seeing Katya and Igor in the distance, he walked toward them. They were examining an apartment building that had been struck by a German shell. The side of the building had crumbled, exposing the interiors of several apartments—yellow wallpaper, hanging pictures, toys on the floor....

"Bon jour, mademoiselle," he said to Katya, bowing regally.

"What did he say?" Igor asked.

"He said hello in French," Katya replied. "Hi, Petya."

"Lovely to see you this afternoon," Petya continued. "You look absolutely ravishing, as usual." He admired the low-cut neckline of her dress and the glimpse of the top of her breasts it offered.

"In this outfit," she said, examining her faded dress. "You must be kidding."

"Au contraire," he responded. "You wear it very nicely. Those comely flowers on your dress must be terribly envious though. They simply pale in comparison."

Katya blushed and gave him a sidelong glance. "You're a sly one, Petya Soyonovich," she said with a grin.

"Why are you in such a good mood?" Igor asked Petya.

"Well, my little lummox," answered Petya, "I suppose war makes one cogitate on the meaning of life and appreciate it more. I'm just grateful to be alive today. And thankful that you and Katya are as well. And besides, the sun is shining!"

Katya audibly exhaled. "Thanks for the reminder. I've done nothing but worry lately."

"Happy to return the favor," replied Petya, unable to take his eyes off her. She was like an exquisite work of art in the Hermitage, and no matter how long he looked, he never got tired or bored.

"What's a lummox?" asked Igor.

Petya ignored him and studied Katya's adorable ears, delicious pink lips, and the thin brown eyebrows that arched gracefully over her chestnut-brown eyes.

"Did you hear Shostakovich on the radio on Monday?" Katya asked.

"Yes," said Petya, "he's quite the worker-bee, isn't he? Completing new scores, serving as a fireman during air raids—"

"My favorite part was when he said, 'Remember that our art is threatened with great danger. We will defend our music. We will work with honesty and self-sacrifice that no one may destroy it.'"

Petya didn't want to talk about how great Shostakovich was. "Were you able to read any of my novel yet?"

"Yes. It's really good! I finished it this morning. It's so unlike any of the other stuff you've given me. I'm amazed at your diversity. I think this one is going to make you famous for sure."

Katya's last sentence was like a balm for his jealous heart. If only others could know how great he was, then life would be worthwhile. "I'll take you on my publicity tours to Paris and America one day," he said with a laugh.

"I'm going to hold you to that, you know." She pinched him playfully.

Petya felt so happy just to be near her. "Well, I'm pleased you like it."

"Oh—before I forget—I wanted to ask if you'd be willing to have Igor stay with you on the night of the eighth. That's this coming Monday. Felix is coming over that night."

"Certainly, certainly. It would be my pleasure to have Igor's company again," Petya lied.

"Thank you so much. I really appreciate all the time you spend with him. I think it's important for Igor to be around other men, especially someone as educated as yourself."

"Perhaps I'll teach him a few words of French," Petya said. "Parle vous Francais, Igor?"

"I don't need to learn no stupid French," Igor huffed.

Petya laughed, then caught Katya peering at his two envelopes. Shifting them as naturally as he could to his other hand, he ensured the blank side of the envelopes was facing her.

"What are those letters?" she asked.

"Oh, nothing special," he answered. "Just on my way to mail them."

Katya kept her eyes on the envelopes. "The handwriting on that one envelope looked just like my father's."

"Oh really?" Petya said, holding up the envelope so he, but not Katya, could see the address. "No. That one's from Oksana. She asked me to mail it for her. Actually, I better get going. Need to get these out before the Germans take over the city." He laughed again and stepped away, doing his best to move his large frame rapidly without limping too much. "Bye," he called awkwardly over his shoulder.

Katya perched on the edge of her chair, alternately taking tiny sips of tea and then trying to smooth some of the thousand wrinkles in the white tablecloth. On the other side of the table, Felix slouched and poked at his food as he stared out the window.

"How are the potatoes?" asked Katya. "I fried them with lots of garlic, just the way you like."

"Good," he said flatly. Forcing a smile and a glance at her, he added, "They're very good."

Katya sipped her tea. "The weather's been so nice. It hardly feels like autumn. I guess summer is making up for its late start."

Felix made no reply. He continued gazing out the window, though at what, Katya had no idea. It was 6:40 p.m., and the sun wouldn't be setting for another two hours. She'd been trying to make her tea last as long as possible, but was now, sadly, at the bottom of her cup. Turning her attention to the wrinkles in the tablecloth again, she pressed on them even harder, but it made no difference.

After listening to the unbearable sounds of Felix chewing his food and his fork clinking against the plate, she asked, "Would you like more potatoes? It's no problem for me to make more."

Felix gave a look as though he didn't understand the question, but then mumbled something and shook his head.

"How about some tea, then?" asked Katya. She stood up, wringing her hands, anxiously awaiting his answer.

"I don't want any tea," he said.

To fight the maddening silence, she tapped her fingernails against her empty teacup. "Maybe I'll have some more." But instead of putting the kettle on, she returned to her seat and joined Felix in staring out the window.

"Why don't you just not go?" she blurted.

"If I don't go," he said distantly, putting his fork down, "they'll shoot me."

"But your clerical duties are very important to the war effort," insisted Katya. "You told me your superiors think very highly of you and your work."

"They don't want to see me go. The decision is out of their hands."

Katya reached over the table and put her hand on top of his. "I'll ask my father to pull some strings and see if you can stay in your current position."

"You haven't heard from your father since he left. You don't know where he is and you have no way of getting in touch with him. And besides, I don't think he'd lift a finger to help me," Felix said frankly.

"That's not true," she quibbled. "Someone left that note a few days ago, saying my father wanted to let me know he was all right and still in Moscow. I think it's just a matter of time before he comes back."

"Time," Felix said, "is something we don't have."

"Oh, don't say that! I can't stand it when you talk like that—like it's the end!"

"Katya, we need to face reality," he said calmly. "There's no use hiding from it. We're going to be separated for a while." He squeezed Katya's hand and finished his last bite of fried potatoes.

"Then if you're going to the front, so am I," declared Katya. "The hospital director is always saying how they're short of nurses there."

Felix sighed. "I'd prefer you don't do that," he said. "I've heard nurses on the front suffer higher casualties than the men fighting." He leaned toward her, brushing the back of his fingers along her cheek. "Katya, stay here. I'll get leave to come and visit once in a while. And we'll write."

Though his tender touch and words calmed her, she was still seething about the unfairness of it all. She hated the Germans for laying siege to her city, and she hated the Soviets for taking Felix from her. A Bible verse her grandmother loved ran through her mind: "Love your enemies, do good to those who hate you, bless those who curse you, pray for those who abuse you." But Katya couldn't make any sense of it right now. How could she possibly love those she hated?

With his hand, Felix tilted her chin up so their eyes met. "Yes? You'll stay?"

She abruptly stood, brushed crumbs off her dress, and nodded. Staying was the least bad out of all the wretched options she had. "Let's not talk about it anymore tonight," she said. "We're together now, and that's all that matters."

Felix rose from the table, then kissed her on the forehead and leaned into her arms. They held one another, swaying back and forth for a long time, then headed to the balcony. Her apartment was on the third floor, and though the sun was hidden behind neighboring buildings, there was a nice view of the wide avenue below. Katya often spent hours watching the people and cars go by, but the street was quiet and empty now—as was the case everywhere in the city these days. The usual traffic had been replaced by soldiers, policemen, and barricades. The citizens of her block had erected an ugly wall of sandbags at the far end of the street. Whenever Katya saw it, she was reminded of how there was nothing to fall back on, nowhere to retreat to.

"Petya told me this morning the Germans have been dropping flyers giving an ultimatum to the city to surrender by September 9," said Katya.

"Tomorrow?"

"Yes. They—"

She was interrupted by the wailing of air raid sirens.

They both looked up, but saw nothing out of the ordinary, just the usual deep blue sky of autumn, with an occasional pale, borderless cloud.

"Should we go down to the shelter?" asked Katya.

"Let's wait a minute. It might be another false alarm."

Katya thought she saw a shiny object in the sky, but then it disappeared. A few breaths later, they heard the firing of anti-aircraft guns and then tremendous explosions. Massive clouds of gray dust billowed into the sky, and with each passing second, the blasts drew nearer.

Before fleeing the balcony, Katya glanced below and saw a familiar figure hunched over a cane shuffling down the street. Her name was Evgenia Pitskova, once a feared informant for the secret police, and personally responsible for sending twenty-three people from this block to gulags, torture chambers, or early graves through her insinuations and, sometimes, outright lies. Since her fall from favor with both the secret police and the Party, people now hated her openly, unafraid of her threats of reprisals.

"Hurry!" Katya yelled to her. "The bombs are coming this way. You have to get off the street."

"Don't you tell me what to do!" she hollered back, shaking her cane at Katya.

Across the street, two adolescent boys and their mother were hurrying into their apartment building. Evgenia tried to squeeze in with them only to be kicked out the door and pushed to the ground by the boys. She fell hard and didn't get back up. "You kikes won't get away with this!" she cursed at them.

Katya watched the surging clouds of dust and debris moving toward them like a massive tidal wave forcing its way farther and farther inland.

"I'm going to get her," Felix said, hurrying out of the apartment.

"No. It's too late," protested Katya.

"Meet me in the basement," he called from the hallway.

Katya fled down the stairs after him, but then ran back to the apartment to close the curtains. If the explosions shattered the windows, she didn't want tiny shards of glass all over the place.

Before closing the first curtain, she saw Felix emerge into the street below. As she pulled the second curtain closed, a thunderous explosion and extensive trembling nearly knocked her over. She glimpsed the end of her street disappear in a thick fog that swallowed the old woman lying on the ground and the valiant young man running to save her.

Racing out of the apartment and down the two flights of stairs, Katya thrust open the door to the outside. Through the impenetrable dust, she called out Felix's name, then another explosion shook the earth, sending her stumbling forward.

Evgenia's scornful voice rang out. "What are you doing? Put me down!" Then Felix appeared through the fog, carrying the old woman in his arms as she struggled against him.

Katya held the door open, and the three of them made their way to the basement, Evgenia uttering threats and curses all the while.

The air of the dimly lit and cramped shelter was cool and smelled of tobacco smoke. A baby let out a high-pitched scream as they entered.

"Make some room please," Felix said as he set Evgenia down on one of the long benches lining the walls. The old woman cussed at Felix one last time, then demanded he go back out and get her cane.

Katya's neighbor, Oksana Petrovna, moved away from the bench. "Why did you bring her here?" she asked in a scornful tone.

"You should have left her where you found her," said another.

As everyone jostled for space, anti-aircraft guns pounded relentlessly and the ground continued to shake with each bomb that fell. It was the first time Katya had been in the shelter, and she thought it little safer than her apartment. There was nowhere left for her and Felix to sit. Children outnumbered adults two to one, and they cried relentlessly as they clung to their mothers.

"Hello, Katya," a voice called from the darkness.

She turned and saw Petya and Igor sitting in the corner. Igor was hugging his knees to his chest and rocking back and forth. Petya, looking calm and relaxed, was smoking a cigarette.

"This is quite the revelry, isn't it?" said Petya.

"I'm glad to see you two are all right," Katya replied.

Petya blew smoke over his left shoulder. You and Felix certainly took your time getting down here," he said. "You must have been busy."

"Petya!" Oksana scolded. "I'm warning you for the last time. You better put that damn cigarette out!"

Petya took a long drag, then snubbed out the cigarette on the wall. Tucking the butt in the crease of his rolled-up left pant leg, he called to Felix. "How's the clerical work for the army going?" he asked with a smug smile. "That is what you do, isn't it?"

"I've been reassigned," Felix said irritably. "I'll be going back to the front tomorrow."

"No. You don't say," commented Petya, dropping his head forward and revealing his double chin. "What a shame."

A large explosion rattled the entire building, shaking dust from the ceiling of the shelter.

"This is hell!" Oksana shouted. "Damn those Germans! I hope we pay them back—make them suffer twice as much!"

Katya caught several of the women crossing themselves and reciting prayers, even the ones she knew to be members of the Communist Party.

"They kept telling us Leningrad was impregnable," a woman mourned.

"They were all lies," responded Oksana. "They told us our anti-aircraft defenses were a giant wall. They said our borders were secure, that the Red Army was unbeatable. Then they said the Nazi soldiers would revolt against their commanders. Lies. Lies. Lies!"

Katya waited for someone to argue or reproach her, but nobody did.

After lighting a small candle, Felix poured vodka into two yellow teacups. They were chipped on the outside and stained brown on the inside from countless years of holding scalding black tea, but they were Katya's favorites nonetheless. It was nearly 10:30 p.m., and he gazed out Katya's bedroom window while he waited for her to finish her shower. Of all the apartments in the building, hers was the only one whose windows hadn't been shattered by the bombardment earlier that day, and Felix found it curious that Katya's windows had been the only ones taped in the form of a cross, rather than the usual—safely secular—X. With no glass available to replace broken windows, the other apartments would unfortunately have to install plywood.

Every once in a while, Felix spotted a vague blue light on one of the streets below signifying a moving military vehicle. In the apartment buildings across the street, everything was dark. It seemed the city was deserted, but Felix knew better. There were innumerable people behind those dark walls. Tired, scared, and filled with dread about what the next day might bring. Those same people were also brave, resilient, and intensely protective of their cherished city. They'd rather see it wiped from the face of the earth than let Nazis occupy it.

Felix took a drink of the vodka, savoring the burn on the inside of his throat and taking a deep breath to extend the feeling. Hearing the bathroom door open and then Katya laughing at something, he smiled to himself. He adored the way she laughed so suddenly and unexpectedly at little things, the way a child does. When she did that, it brought out the child in him as well, and that's what he appreciated most about her. She had an uncanny ability to take them both back to the basic goodness of childhood, to feel the joy that is always there inside, but so often clouded over in adulthood. He never imagined loving someone so much, nor had he thought it possible to be so afraid of losing someone.

Katya—mischievous grin on her face—arrived in an alluring yellow dress. Felix ogled how nicely it conformed to the seductive curves of her body. Opening her hand, she revealed two dark chocolates. "My father was hiding these in the tea jar for a month. I think he must have forgotten about them." She started to say something else, but the air raid sirens stopped her.

As she wrapped her arms in front of herself, Felix peeked out the window at the searchlights crisscrossing the sky.

"Oh, bother," Katya exclaimed. "Should we go back down to the—"

Felix didn't let her finish her sentence. Pulling her close, he pressed his lips to hers and ran his hands gently from her hips up past her waist, then back down again. Then he whispered in her ear, "I love you, Katerina Selenaya."

She laughed elatedly, her brown eyes luminous in the candlelight, then jumped on him and wrapped her legs around his waist.

"And do you love me?" Felix asked jokingly. He frowned and emulated a sad puppy.

"Comrade, you should be ashamed of yourself," said Katya, doing her best imitation of a pretentious Dima. "That's sentimentality masquerading as logic."

Felix chuckled. "Surprisingly, I'm not mad at him," he said. "Despite everything that happened and what he said, I don't hate him. He's *wrong*, but I think in my heart I understand what he's after."

"My grandmother always said that's the most important place to have an understanding of anything," replied Katya. "To have an understanding in your head means nothing."

Felix could hear explosions now, but they were muted and distant. "Seems like you've got everything figured out," he said as he kissed the underside of her wrist.

"Absolutely," she giggled. "Go ahead, ask me anything."

Inhaling the irresistible scent of her skin, Felix gave a contented sigh. Then he looked at her fondly, asking, "What's the square root of one hundred forty-three?"

"That's too easy," she said. "You sure you don't want to know something a little harder—like the meaning of life?"

He turned her hand over and kissed her fingers. "Who cares about the meaning of life when there's chocolate and vodka?"

She laughed, and Felix held out one of the chipped, yellow tea cups.

"Comrade," she said in mock seriousness, "pledge to me we'll be contractually obligated under law one day."

Felix grinned and shook her hand earnestly. "Yes," he answered, "I promise we'll be married one day." Then he fed her the chocolate, and she chased it with vodka.

The light from the candle cast shadows on the playful designs of the wallpaper, and Katya purred like a cat as she bent her head to the side so Felix could kiss more of her neck. Through the thin walls they could hear Guzman's piano, which meant Shostakovich must be visiting and that they too had decided against going down to the shelter.

Felix had never heard the music Shostakovich was playing and wondered if the composer was writing another of his popular marches. Or perhaps it was part of the new seventh symphony he was working on. Whatever it was, it was extraordinary—both uplifting and righteous, and sorrowful and melancholy all at the same time. It was hypnotic in its sudden key changes, mounting tension, and unexpected pauses. The distant explosions and anti-aircraft fire provided a kind of perverse percussion to the piece.

Sitting on the edge of the bed, Felix pulled Katya onto his lap. As he brushed his lips across the tiny hairs on the back of her neck, he wished he could stay in this moment forever. Let the candle flicker, but keep burning. Let the music falter, but keep playing. Let time come to a stop right now, and he would be eternally happy.

The lovers kissed and embraced and trembled with each touch. Outside, air raid sirens echoed endlessly, and German planes dropped payloads of death and destruction on a besieged city filled with determined people who refused to give up.

Some were so determined that they even refused to stop loving.

Felix awoke before the sun had risen. Katya's arm was draped across his chest, and he gently lifted it and placed it by her side. Then he dressed in the dark, careful not to wake her.

Before leaving, he watched her for a while as she slept: curled up on her side, right hand under her head, bangs hanging over her face, chest peacefully rising and falling. He preferred to remember her this way, rather than with a bunch of bumbling words between the two of them. After pressing his lips lightly to her forehead, he slipped out the door and down the hall.

After climbing the stairs to the roof where he and Katya had spent many a spring and summer morning watching the sun rise, he peered in every direction. The city was shrouded in darkness, but Felix could still see a great deal due to his exceptional nighttime vision, and also because of the light from a great fire in the distance. When he exhaled, he could see his breath. And when he inhaled, he smelled the faint scent of caramelized sugar for some reason. He gazed at the bright orange fire, wondering what the Germans could have bombed that would burn for so long.

When he went down to the street, the light was low and crept surreptitiously around buildings and the dark figures walking about. Shadows were indistinguishable from one another, all blending together to create an impossibly inky collage. Pulling his collar up, he set off down the sidewalk. People and buildings appeared and disappeared like ghosts— images of a time and place he'd seen many times before but might never again.

As Felix reached the Neva River, the sun started peeking over the horizon. On the other side of the river's calm water, he could see the golden spire of the Admiralty glittering in dawn's early light. The buildings on the far shore of Vasilevski Island were black and murky, and the complex looked more like a giant castle of a foreign kingdom than another sector of Leningrad. He wondered if Lenin ever appreciated what a beautiful city it was. Or if he'd been so caught up in his politics that all he ever saw were "repressed masses" and "bourgeois excess."

Blue-gray clouds hovered over the rooftops and river, and the vast sky seemed to extend forever. Felix felt boundless and free traversing Leningrad's wide avenues. Catching the scent of the sea, he watched the ripples of the Neva River make their way from one distant side to the other. The sweeping vistas reminded him of the countryside in Ukraine, only he was in the middle of a large, cosmopolitan city. To him, it was the best of both worlds.

He walked and walked, letting his heart guide him to the grandiose Winter Palace, the Hermitage museum, the eloquent Palace Bridge, and ultimately the statue of Peter the Great on his rearing stallion. It was Peter who had carved this great city out of the woods and stone and swamp. It was he who had built the imposing Peter and Paul Fortress and the massive Kronstadt naval base. It was Peter's inspiration for a lavish capital, second to none, that had lived on through the years as the city grew and matured. Saint Petersburg, as it was originally called, was his window to the West, his showcase of the mighty Russian Empire. It was regal, elaborate, stately; even in its current crisis, Felix still believed in it. He believed in its music, its ideas, its arts, and its vision. It wasn't just the city's inhabitants the Germans were up against. It was the city itself, and it had a soul of its own.

Grimacing at the piles of sandbags surrounding Peter the Great's statue, Felix was tempted to tear them off and let the "bronze horseman" ride again, to have him lead his countrymen out of the hopelessness and siege they found themselves in. They needed Peter's iron will more than anything. To make it through this crisis, they'd have to believe in themselves unconditionally. Only stubborn souls and firm convictions would enable them to withstand the hardships to come.

Heeding the call of his beloved Kazansky Cathedral, Felix turned back toward Nevsky Prospekt. When he saw the cathedral from afar, he felt comforted. It hadn't changed like the rest of the city. As he strode under its immense left wing and amidst its giant stone columns, he remembered that Kutuzov, the great field marshal who was so instrumental in the Russian victory against Napoleon, was buried on these hallowed grounds. "Who will be the Kutuzov of this war?" Felix asked aloud.

At the forlorn statue of Saint Andrew the Apostle, Felix thought back to that fateful day—June 22—when he'd last visited it. It was then that the Germans had begun their invasion and irrevocably interrupted his life. He swallowed hard, accepting that things could never be the same again. Pulling himself away from the cathedral, he took a deep breath and decided he was through resisting the way things were. He'd been preparing himself, mentally and physically, for the rigors of battle.

It was time to report to the front.

Streetcar No 9, fitted with a front-mounted machine gun, lumbered along the tracks past countless damaged buildings. The suspicious motorman nearly went right by Felix and two others, before abruptly stopping to let them on. Even at this early hour, the car was packed with soldiers and civilians. Two young officers sat in the back, casting dubious glances at everyone and whispering back and forth to one another.

While the red trolley moved slowly down the wide expanse of Stachek Prospekt, Felix took in the scenery. The street was littered with cars, some simply parked along the side, some in pieces and burned out, and some still burning. The entire city had been transformed since the early days of the war. Sandbags lined the ground floor windows of many buildings. Windows on upper floors were boarded over or taped with large X's. There were bunkers, firing points, and anti-aircraft guns everywhere. Huge silver balloons nested on the ground, ready to go up each night to stave off low-flying German planes. Manholes and sewer openings had "extermination" points for firing at German tanks should they break through. Corner buildings had reinforced concrete "pillboxes" that were designed to withstand the floors above collapsing so soldiers could keep firing. Huge steel anti-tank "hedgehogs" and sandbag barricades with barbed wire blocked many streets from motorized entry. In the distance, Felix could hear the warships of the Baltic Fleet firing their tremendous guns endlessly into the German lines.

Felix made his way to the back of the streetcar, pleased his injured leg felt strong and healthy once again. As they passed by a charred corpse in the middle of the street and an idling sixty-ton KV tank, Felix eavesdropped on the two officers speaking in hushed tones about the previous night's bombing. "You've no doubt heard about the Badayev warehouses?" said one to the other.

"I know there were some enormous fires in that sector. They bombed Badayev?"

"Yes, with incendiary bombs."

"And the food reserves? The flour, sugar, canned meat—"

"It's still burning now. They haven't been able to put it out."

"You mean it's *all* gone?"

"Yes," he replied, nodding gravely.

Felix felt outraged at the news. How could the authorities be so negligent as to put all the food for the city in one place? It was either treason or stupidity. Everyone in Leningrad knew about the Badayev food warehouses, and with all the German spies in the city, no doubt the pilots knew exactly where to drop their bombs.

He thought of Katya and was overcome with regret at not forcing her to get on that train out of Leningrad, especially when he found out later that it had been the last one to leave the city. He had helped ensure an adequate food supply for her, but that was before Igor started living with her.

Spotting the Kirov works up ahead, Felix knew he'd be at the front soon. He'd been reassigned to the Second Regiment of the First Volunteers Division, or what was left of it. The First Volunteers had lost nearly two-thirds of their strength and had very little of the arms and equipment they'd started out with. He wasn't keen on rejoining his former comrades, and was particularly anxious he might be put in a platoon under Dima's command. Though Dima was probably one of the more competent commanders, that didn't necessarily mean his men would be safer. Dima, more than anyone Felix knew, was the most likely to sacrifice himself—along with others—if that's what it took to accomplish some goal.

There was a steady stream of soldiers and workers heading toward the Kirov works. As the largest engineering sector in all of Russia, it had hundreds of shops and thousands of laborers. On the other side of it was the enemy. The Germans were only two-and-a-half miles away at this point, a mere ten miles from Leningrad's Palace Square.

A disorganized, haggard stream of people also moved in the opposite direction—away from the Kirov works. Women and children carrying bedding, clothes, bags, and milk tins were evacuating to safer parts of the city, such as the Petrograd and Vasilevski Island districts.

When the trolley reached the Kotlyarov streetcar barns, the motorman announced, "Last stop. Everyone off. This is the front."

Unsure where to go, Felix jumped off with the others and followed them. No one seemed to know exactly where the Second Regiment was, only that the First Volunteers had been in Pushkin a week ago and had likely fallen back.

As he hiked ever closer to the front and its ominous sounds, he queried people, but no one could help him. After an hour of passing by military trucks, barricades, tank traps, dugouts, and machine-gun nests, he took a break to wipe the sweat from his face and adjust his pack. Finally, a pair of stretcher-bearers carrying a wounded man told him where to go. "The trenches just beyond that cemetery," the man said, motioning over his right shoulder.

After locating the First Volunteers, a baby-faced officer assigned Felix to the First Platoon of the Second Regiment. In search of the First Platoon, Felix had already checked several trenches and was on his way to the next one when he stopped for a drink of water from his canteen. High in the sky was a dogfight between a Soviet and German fighter plane. Felix watched the Soviet plane evade pursuit by making a sharp turn to the left and diving toward the ground. At the last second, it pulled up and barely avoided crashing into the earth. It was a desperate attempt, Felix thought, but that was what it would take to defeat the Germans.

The fighting was heavy in this area, and there was a constant din of machine-gun fire, exploding mortars, and occasional screams of agony. Houses stood in ruin. Trees burnt. The stench of rotting flesh filled the air.

Despite all the signs of combat, Felix couldn't locate the enemy. They were somewhere up ahead: behind houses, or camouflage, or in trenches of their own. Every now and then, he would spy a soldier clad in green race from one spot to another, crouching all the while and taking a few shots at the Russian lines as he did so.

Felix jumped into the next trench he came to, certain it would be empty since he hadn't seen anyone firing back at the Germans. But there were twelve men sitting there, all with their backs to the incoming fire. Each of them had a rifle, but it was either lying harmlessly at their feet or resting against the wall. On Felix's right, at the far end of the trench, was a dead Soviet soldier. Dark red blood encrusted his right side from the neck down, and his face was sunk into the orange-colored earth.

Only two of the men turned their heads to look at the stranger who'd just dropped into their trench. The rest of them continued staring blankly at the dirt they sat on. Their strong body odor and thick stubble on their cheeks testified that they hadn't showered in over a week. The men's incomprehensible apathy in the midst of battle made Felix wonder if they'd even *slept* in a week.

A mortar round exploded in front of the trench, and dirt fell like rain over top of them. Startled by the deafening sound of the blast, Felix pulled his helmet down as low as it would go. The other men hadn't even flinched.

Once he confirmed this was the First Platoon, Felix pulled out the pack of cigarettes he'd brought. He didn't smoke himself, but figured they'd make a nice gift for his new comrades. He'd heard that cigarettes were sometimes hard to come by on the front. As the pack made its way down the line of men, each of them took one and nodded appreciatively to Felix.

The sun was hot, and Felix took another drink from his canteen. Catching their envious eyes on him, Felix guessed they'd all run out of water, so he passed his canteen down the line. Again, they all partook and nodded gratefully to him. One even summoned the strength to speak. "Thank you, comrade," he said hoarsely.

When someone suddenly dove into the trench, Felix nearly leapt to his feet in alarm. Turning to face the stranger, he was dumbfounded to see Dima gaping at him. "Ah, Varilensky, so nice of you to finally join us," Dima said in a sarcastic tone.

Felix was taken aback, both by the unexpected sight of his friend and by the fact that Dima had called him by his last name.

"We expected you yesterday," Dima griped. Though he had the same stubble on his chin as the others, his overall demeanor was nothing like theirs. His words and movements were quick and sharp. The scowling expression on his face was anything but vacant.

"My orders were to report today," explained Felix.

Dima scoffed aloud. "That's not what I was told. I don't want to waste time arguing though. Where's the ammo? We need to get it distributed."

"Where's the what?"

"The bullets," Dima said irritably. "They said you'd be bringing a crate of ammunition with you. We're nearly out."

Another mortar exploded nearby, and again none of the men—except Felix—reacted. "I had no such orders," he said to Dima. "And I have no ammunition to give you."

"Devil take it!" Dima muttered. "Do you even have a rifle?"

Felix shook his head. "I was told I'd be assigned one when I reported."

Dima opened his mouth, but said nothing, then turned to the rest of the men in the trench. "Comrades!" he called. "We're going on the offensive again. We're going to retake the area south of the school."

None of the men moved, nor even showed any sign they'd heard him.

"Dima, I realize I just got here," Felix said hesitantly, "but your men don't look like they're in any shape to mount an offensive."

"First of all," Dima said, glowering. "You will address me as Comrade Lieutenant. Secondly, if I want your opinion, I'll ask for it." He checked how many rounds he had left in his rifle, then added, "My orders are to attack. The enemy must not have a moment's rest."

"Do we have any artillery?" Felix asked.

Dima didn't respond. He was peeking his head over the shallow clay ditch at the German lines.

"Any machine guns?"

Again, Dima didn't respond. Instead, he hollered to the other men in the trench, asking how many grenades they had left.

"Comrade Lieutenant, do you have a weapon for me?" asked Felix. "Or will I be sent out with a shovel again?"

"Enough of your provocations!" Dima yelled. "You'll get your weapon from the enemy or when one of us has fallen." He turned to the others, commanding,

"Men! Be ready to move out when I give the signal. Kazinsky and I will take out the machine-gun nest on the left flank first, then we'll move up that side."

Felix scanned the men's faces, noting their complete lack of emotion, and wondered how far their "offensive" would make it.

"Where's Kazinsky?" Dima shouted over a series of thundering explosions.

One of the men pointed at the end of the trench. After glancing at the corpse with its face pressed against the dirt, Dima addressed Felix. "Grab his gun. You and I will take out the machine gun."

"He just got here," one of the men said. "You trying to kill him already, Lieutenant?" He said the last word contemptuously.

"Perhaps you would like to go in his place?" retorted Dima.

"It's all right," Felix assured the others. "I'll go." He made his way down the trench and slid the gun out of the dead man's hands. It was a nice rifle with a scope, but it seemed strange for some reason. Dima yanked it away, quickly inspected it, then handed it back. After noticing some markings on the rifle, Felix realized why it seemed strange. It was German.

"Let's go," Dima shouted to Felix.

They bolted from the trench amid the venomous spitting of the machine gun and bullets slicing through the air around them. Before reaching the safety of an old brick schoolhouse, Felix caught a glimpse of their target. The German machine gun was surrounded by sandbags and situated next to the corner of a building where the gunners had an excellent angle to fire on a wide expanse of the Soviet lines. Felix spied only a narrow gap where the nest was vulnerable.

The school's playground was filled with bomb craters and unexploded shells. Two swings moved from side to side in the light breeze. Felix saw one of the classrooms through a window. Child-sized desks were scattered about, most of them tipped on their sides. On the chalkboard was a crude map of the area, a swastika, and the Latin words: Veni. Vidi. Vici. In the far corner, a German soldier lay sprawled on a group of desks. His head and neck were wrapped in bloody gauze, and his right arm hung limply over the edge. Felix tugged on the back of Dima's shirt and pointed to the classroom.

"They took it last night," remarked Dima, "but we drove them back again this morning." Then he nodded to his right. "You see that bomb crater on the side of that slope, in between those small bushes?"

"Yes."

"When I run from here to that next building, you go for the crater and dive in."

Felix scrutinized the distance to the building Dima was referring to. "That area is wide open," he said. "The machine gun will cut you down before you get there."

"That's the idea," replied Dima. "I'll draw their fire so you can make it to the crater. You should be able to get off a good shot from there and take the gunner out. They've only got one guy manning it for some reason, so that'll make things a little easier."

Felix wasn't sure Dima was correct about being able to get off a shot from the bomb crater. If Felix couldn't manage it, he'd be a sitting duck once they spotted him. The plan seemed absurdly risky to Felix. One, or even both of them, could be killed before they even got close to accomplishing their objective.

Creeping to the edge of the wall, Dima squatted low and prepared to sprint. "Varilensky," he called. "Make them count. There's only two bullets left in that gun." Then he dashed away, the machine gun following his every footstep.

Felix took off for the crater, making it there in just a few seconds. Squinting through the scope, he recognized immediately that he couldn't get a shot off from here. He'd have to move further to his right, although there was no cover there. When he darted from the crater, another German soldier arrived at the machine-gun nest. He was carrying ammunition, and alerted the gunner to Felix's position. Knowing he only had a second or two before the machine gun swung around and started spitting its lethal slugs his way, Felix took aim at the gunner's head and fired.

The bullet went high, striking the man's helmet just above the eyes. He was stunned for a second, but then quickly finished swinging the gun Felix's way.

As the machine gun began firing at him, Felix blocked everything out, carefully aiming two inches lower than last time, then squeezed the trigger. The bullet smashed through the man's right cheek, and he slumped forward.

The other soldier immediately pulled his dead colleague away so that he could fire the machine gun. Felix—out of bullets—had no choice but to try scrambling back to the schoolhouse. Out of the corner of his eye, he saw someone running straight at the machine gun. It was Dima. He had a grenade in his hand and lofted it high in the air and then dove to the ground. The grenade landed just behind the machine-gun nest and exploded. The German soldier crumpled into the sandbags just as he fired his first round at Felix.

Dima hopped over the sandbags, fired an additional bullet into each of the fallen Germans, then picked up a rifle and some ammo, and ran to Felix. "Here," he said, handing the rifle to Felix, "those German guns seem to suit you."

At first, Felix thought Dima's remark a provocation, but then he saw him wink.

"Let's get the others and move out," said Dima, already heading for the trenches that held the rest of their platoon.

When the two of them were within shouting distance, Dima yelled, "Comrades! Let's go!"

Nobody responded.

"Fedushkin! Ivanovich! Let's go!" Dima repeated.

Still no response.

Felix ran to the trench and peered in, expecting them all to be gone or dead. But they were still there in the same positions as when he'd left.

Dima shouted at them from a few yards away. "Come on, men! For the Motherland! For Leningrad!"

Two of the men started to move, but the others remained motionless, seemingly half asleep. Dima withdrew his pistol and pointed it at them. "Cowardice is no different than treason," he announced. "Those of you wishing to remain here will be joining Kazinsky—in *permanent slumber*."

The ultimatum had no effect, and Felix thought Dima had erred by threatening them with eternal sleep. That probably sounded quite appealing to most of them.

"Listen to me," Felix said to the men as a mortar whistled overhead and exploded fifty yards behind them. "You're exhausted. You want some rest and water and food. You didn't ask for any of this and you don't want to be here." They turned their heads to look at him. "But we are *not* going to die in this miserable trench from a German shell launched a mile away!" Felix had to shout to be heard above the din of battle. "If we are to die today," he continued, "then let our deaths have meaning! Let us die defending our wives, our children, our parents." He looked each man in the eye. "Don't fight for the generals. Or for the Party. Fight for yourselves and your family, for your right to exist!"

At first, none of them stirred, but then one by one they grudgingly picked up their rifles and tumbled out of the trench. Dima was out in front, leading the charge, but the men stayed close to Felix. There were no shouts of "hurrah!"

In three hours of heavy fighting, the combined Soviet offensive drove the Germans from their second line of trenches. For Dima's men, the price had been steep. Of the forty volunteers under his command at the start, only eighteen remained. The fighting had been like that of 1916: inch by inch, trench by trench. With very little ammo, Dima and his men had to work their way in close to the German lines, fasten their bayonets, then charge. The ensuing hand-to-hand combat was bloody and intense.

The platoon was now resting in a large warehouse that the Germans had occupied only a short time ago. There were cigarette butts, tin cans with German labels, and pages from a German newspaper scattered across the floor. It was mid-afternoon, and most of the men were sprawled out on the bare floor catching an hour of sleep. Felix and Dima were preparing to begin their shift as lookouts on the roof.

"We have an average of nine bullets per man left," lamented Dima.

"I thought you said we were going to be resupplied with more ammo and grenades," said Felix.

"In a perfect war, we would've been," replied Dima with a sigh. "I was promised additional troops too."

"If we don't get that ammo soon, we *have* to pull back," Felix said adamantly. "It's only a matter of time before the Nazis re-arm and bring in some reinforcements."

"We're not going anywhere," remarked Dima as he rummaged through crates of mineral water searching for an unopened bottle.

"Are we to fight the enemy and their tanks with our bare hands?" Felix asked sarcastically.

"What are you complaining about? You've got a rifle and plenty of bullets."

Felix slung his German rifle around his shoulder and joined Dima in searching through the crates.

Dima pulled one of the crates toward the wall and sat on top of it. "Don't you understand, Varilensky?" he asked as he lit a cigarette. "We can't let them rest. We can't let them plan, strategize, and regroup. We have to fight them with everything we have right here, right now, or else we're finished. By going on the offensive, we've tricked them into thinking we're stronger than we are. We can't let them know we're hanging on by a thread. Every battle counts now, no matter how big or small. We've got to hold on one hour at a time. We've got to destroy their tanks one at a time, and kill each fascist one by one. There's no other way." He paused to take a long drag on his cigarette. "Every platoon's in the same shape we are. I know it's bleak, but I would rather die than see the Nazis take Leningrad. Do you understand that?"

Felix found an unopened glass bottle, poured half of it into his canteen, and gave the rest to Dima. "I want to beat the Germans just as much as you. We only disagree on how to go about it. Sacrificing ourselves isn't going to defeat the enemy or make Leningrad any safer. Heroes and martyrs don't win wars; only those who stay alive win wars. The smarter one—the more cunning one—stands the better chance of coming out the victor. It's not glamorous, but that's how you win."

"When you're in charge one day, you can decide the best way to go about it," said Dima. "For now, I'm in charge, and we're staying here." He exhaled a cloud of smoke, then started walking away. "Come on. Let's get up to the roof."

After relieving Fedushkin and Ivanovich, Dima panned back and forth with his binoculars. "I know you Nazis are there," he grumbled. "Where are you?"

Felix followed him across the flat roof and sat on the three-foot wall that prevented people from falling off. The roof provided an excellent vantage point.

With no buildings or trees blocking their view, they could see nearly a mile in front and behind.

"What do you suppose they're doing?" Felix asked.

"I wish I knew," said Dima. "We used to be able to see them just over that long, rolling hill, but they seemed to have disappeared."

Gunfire and explosions continued to echo in the distance. Felix had gotten used to it already, and was starting to find it comforting. Only when it stopped and silence took over did he get nervous. Using the scope on his rifle, he checked on the other Soviet forces next to them. Dima's platoon had been part of a broad offensive and had moved up to this location with the help of other, better equipped regiments. Unable to locate any of them now, Felix got a bad feeling their platoon was out here all alone.

After scanning further to the right, he discovered a dozen distant tanks moving across the horizon. He felt relieved that their reinforcements included tanks, since they were in woefully short supply. But when he steadied his arm and focused again, he spotted a black and white Death's Head emblem painted on the side of one of them. His gut told him to turn and look in the other direction. When he did, he found the same thing—German tanks pushing their way past the Soviet lines. They were using their favorite means of encirclement: the pincer movement. "Look over there," he directed Dima. "And they're on the other side as well."

Dima looked to the right, then to the left with his binoculars.

"I don't see any of our comrades. They must have fallen back already," Felix said nervously. "We need to get moving ourselves. We don't have much time."

With no hint of alarm, Dima lit another cigarette. "We're not going anywhere," he said casually.

Felix felt his ears turn bright red. "We have no ammo!" he shouted.

"Doesn't matter." Dima tilted his head back and blew smoke into the air. "We're not retreating."

"Damn you!" Felix cursed, clenching his fists. "Either we retreat or this warehouse will be our grave."

"This warehouse," Dima replied, scratching his chin, "is just as good a place as anywhere to die." He fixed his eyes on Felix, then added sarcastically, "Perhaps our deaths will have meaning here."

Felix lunged at him, swinging a fist at Dima's face. With no chance to get out of the way, the punch hit him squarely in the jaw. His head snapped back, then he wiped blood from his bottom lip with the back of his hand. "That's good," he said. "*That* is what we need to win this war—a little more hate and fear, and a little less desire to *understand*."

Felix stared past him, at the bombed-out Soviet army truck below.

"Consider this your final warning," added Dima. "Any further insubordination and you'll find yourself in front of a firing squad." He spit off to the side, and a bloody tooth fell out and bounced on the roof. "Even if I'm the only man left to do it."

Word of their platoon's impending doom spread quickly. When Dima was elsewhere, a tall Siberian with bloodshot eyes from lack of sleep incited the men. "Who is he to decide we should all die like rats?" he asked. "Why should we be sacrificed to appease a madman?" When some of the men nodded their heads in agreement, he became even bolder. "We need a change of command!" he roared, clenching his fist and driving it into his other hand. "The Lieutenant isn't going to stop until each and every one of us is dead!"

Mutiny seemed imminent as nearly all of the men murmured their agreement. Felix, who had been trying to rest, now gave up on that idea and listened to the discussion.

"Comrade," someone addressed the Siberian, "you should keep your voice down. Sound travels a long way in a warehouse."

"I don't care if he hears me!" he shot back. "He's threatened me for the last time. I'm leaving. If he tries to stop me, he'll get a bullet in the face."

"What do you mean, you're leaving?" asked someone else.

The man paused from cramming items into his pack and seemed perplexed at the question. "I'm getting out of here," he said, regaining his composure. "That's what I mean. I'm going back to our side of the line. If any of you have half a brain, you'll come with me." He stood up, towering over the men near him, and slung his rifle over his shoulder.

"I'm going too," another man said.

"Me too," said yet another.

Felix sat up and faced them. "Comrades, don't be foolish," he called. "We have to stay together. It's the only way we have a chance."

One of the more quiet and reserved men turned to Felix. "I'll stay if you take over," he said. "I trust you. I don't trust the Lieutenant."

Others echoed the man's sentiment.

"Dima is the commander," Felix responded without hesitation. "We follow him."

"But he's lost his senses," a man countered. "We could easily arrange for the Lieutenant to have a little *accident* and for you to take over command. I'd stay then. If not, I'm leaving. I won't sacrifice myself."

"Neither a mutiny nor a sacrifice will accomplish anything," said Felix, trying to reason with the men. "Staying here right now is the best chance there is of getting out of this alive. We're already surrounded, and it's safer here than out in the open. Our forces might repel the German attack. The reinforcements and ammo might still arrive. Any number of things could happen. Let's at least wait until nightfall before trying to sneak back. To go at this hour—in broad daylight—is suicide."

"Staying *here* is suicide! At least we have a chance out there," the Siberian argued. "It'll be too late if we wait until nightfall. We have to go now!" He marched to the door and opened it. The din of distant battles and bright yellow sunlight burst into the warehouse. "We're sitting ducks here. Now, who's with me?"

After much hesitation, one man joined him, then another, and then several more. In the end, ten men gathered around the door when footsteps echoed through the large chamber. Everyone turned and watched as Dima strode toward them from the other end of the warehouse. The deserters—clutching their rifles tight—fixed their eyes on their emerging commander.

"Comrades," said Dima calmly, "could you tell me what's going on here?"

The Siberian closed the door and stepped forward. "We ... we're ..." he stuttered, "going." Then he cleared his throat and stuck out his chest. "We're leaving, Comrade Lieutenant."

"Is that so?" Dima answered. He had a look of astonishment on his face, though Felix knew him too well to believe it.

"Yes," the Siberian said, "and you're not going to stop us."

"Well, you're all smart men," said Dima. "I'm sure you've thought this over and are aware of the risks. You've no doubt already figured out how you're going to get past a few thousand Nazi soldiers, and how you're going to make it to our lines without your own comrades shooting at you. And I'm certain you've already rehearsed the story you'll tell the commissars explaining why you're falling back toward the city you've sworn to defend."

The deserters exchanged nervous glances with one another.

"What an interesting conversation that will be," Dima added.

"We'll tell them the truth," said the Siberian, "that our commander went out of his mind."

"I see. So you'll tell them that your commander—following his superior's orders—ordered you not to retreat, not to cede an inch of ground to the enemy?"

Felix watched the deserters shrink before his very eyes. Their necks twisted one way to peer at Dima and then the other way at the Siberian.

Dima addressed Felix and the other non-deserters. "We have lots of work to do. Our first priority is to strengthen our firing points. After that—" He stopped and glanced at the men near the door, calling, "You might as well be on your way."

None of them budged, but then the Siberian opened the door again and stepped outside.

"Or," Dima said loudly, "if any of you have changed your mind about this treason to your country, you're welcome to stay and fight. If we die, we at least die with glory and honor, instead of shame and cowardice. But mark my words, once you step through that door, you will have become traitors, enemies of the people."

"It's better than certain death," the Siberian countered. Five others joined him. Four remained inside.

As Fedushkin held open the door for anyone else wishing to join them, Felix studied the deserters—their faces dusty and pale, heads hung low. He got a strange premonition that Fedushkin was going to die that day. Felix had nothing to base it on. Each of them had absurdly high odds of dying on any given day at any given hour. Yet he couldn't shake the sense that Fedushkin would not live to see tomorrow.

After the door slammed shut with a loud, reverberating thud, Dima addressed the men who remained. "I want you two manning the southern firing points. We'll have four men serving as lookouts on the roof. We'll rotate every three hours. Those on the...."

Felix waited patiently for Dima to finish giving his orders, then approached. "Comrade Lieutenant," he said dispassionately, "permission to look around the warehouse? Perhaps there's some weapons stashed somewhere or—"

"Permission denied," Dima interrupted without looking at him. "I just went through the entire warehouse. I need you on the roof with your scope. We don't know which direction they'll be coming from, so we have to ensure we've got them all covered."

"But if I could—"

"Enough!" Dima yelled. "Shut the hell up, and do what you're told for a change."

Felix glared in response. "As you wish, *Dima*," he said provocatively and walked away.

He never made it to the roof. Instead, he gave his rifle and scope to Ivanovich and then wandered through the enormous warehouse searching for things that might be of use.

The warehouse was mostly empty, as nearly everything had already been evacuated by the Russians or plundered by the Germans. Felix focused on an oblong room that used to be a workshop. Scraps of rusty metal were piled in a corner and a long workbench held a vice, boxes of nails, and an antique drill press. In another corner sat half-a-dozen unmarked, black barrels. Two of them blocked a small door, and Felix went over and kicked them. They were empty.

After moving three more empty ones out of the way, Felix found one that was still half full. Opening the plug at the top, he sniffed. It was turpentine.

Lowering his shoulder, he rammed the small door behind the barrels open. Inside was an ancient generator covered with dust and cobwebs. He checked its tank for diesel fuel, but there wasn't any.

After finding nothing further of note, he climbed to the roof to mull things over. They could use the turpentine to make Molotov Cocktails, but they didn't have any glass containers. Then he remembered the empty cases of mineral water. And what about those boxes of nails? Those would make excellent bullets, if only they could fire them somehow.

While he pondered, the men on the roof convened around him. Ivanovich was the first to speak. "We stayed because you said you'd lead us back to our lines come nightfall."

Felix opened his mouth to reply that he'd made no such promise, that he wasn't their commander, and that it was just an idea anyway. But he stopped himself, because he realized morale was tenuous, and the slightest misstep might just start a downward spiral of hopelessness that would condemn them all.

"We can expect a German attack before then," he said. "We'll have to be prepared."

"How can we fight? We barely have any ammunition and only a couple of grenades."

"We'll make our own weapons," answered Felix. "I found some turpentine and dozens of glass bottles. We'll make Molotov Cocktails."

"What good are a few Poor Man's Grenades going to do?" one of them scoffed.

"We'll make bombs too," Felix said.

"Out of what?"

"I saw several boxes of nails," answered Felix. "We can use those."

"What are we going to do? Throw them with our hands?"

"No," Felix said excitedly, suddenly comprehending how they could use the nails. "I counted at least five unexploded artillery shells outside—some German, some Soviet. Ivanovich, you told me you worked in a factory that made shells, right? So you can tell us how to get the gunpowder out. Then we'll make homemade bombs with the nails."

The men liked the idea. "That would be quite a bomb, huh?" they said to one another. "Those nails would fly in a hundred different directions. The Nazis wouldn't know what hit 'em."

When everyone else heard Felix's plan, they were eager to help out. Those who weren't on duty as lookouts or at firing points helped build the improvised weapons. They worked feverishly on the Molotov Cocktails—

filling the mineral water bottles with turpentine, then using gauze from their medical supplies to serve as fuses.

Making the nail bombs was more complicated. Ivanovich wasn't entirely sure his plan to get the gunpowder out would work and kept repeating that German shells might not be the same as the Soviet ones he built. To drill into the shell, they had to get electricity to the old drill press, which meant firing up the ancient generator. Though the gas tank of the bombed-out truck appeared empty, Felix was persistent and able to siphon out nearly a gallon from the bottom.

He was pleasantly surprised when the generator started easily and the drill press still worked, but the good fortune didn't last. They'd just started drilling a hole in the first shell when the drill press quit working. They traced the problem to the generator, whose well-worn, long belt had broken in two.

After a frantic search for a replacement belt yielded no results, Felix suggested they check if the bombed-out truck had one that might work. It did. But it wasn't a good fit, and the smell of burning rubber told them it wouldn't last long. Working as quickly as possible, Ivanovich drilled holes in the shells while the rest stayed as far away as possible in case one exploded by accident.

All during this time, no one could find Dima. Felix twice went through the warehouse calling his name, but received no response. Eventually, the men started speculating that their commander had snuck out, and that he'd had a secret plan of escape all along.

In Dima's absence, everyone began taking orders from Felix, though Felix didn't pose them as orders. He asked questions, then hinted at the solutions until the men themselves came up with the answer and volunteered to do it. Not every man was needed to help make weapons, but Felix arranged for everyone to play some role, no matter how minor. He believed the men regaining their confidence was just as important as constructing the improvised weapons. As they worked, he could sense the gradual shift. The despair at their situation lessened, and was replaced by a newfound determination to survive.

When they were nearly finished, Ivanovich fretted that the length of the fuses on the nail bombs was too long. Felix assured him they could shorten them quite easily on the spot. Then Ivanovich feared the turpentine had somehow gone bad and wouldn't light. He wanted to test one, but Felix talked him out of it, both because he feared the Germans might see the smoke and because they couldn't afford to waste one.

While the men completed the last two nail bombs, Felix again went to look for Dima. Hearing a recurring thump every twenty seconds or so, he followed the sound to an out-of-the-way room where he discovered Dima throwing his knife into the soft wood of a big bulletin board. Dima—smoking a cigarette and staring out the window—called out to him, "What is it Varilensky? Are the Nazis here yet?"

"No. Not yet," Felix said. "Is everything all right, Comrade Lieutenant? We've been trying to find you for the past two hours."

Felix knew the answer to his own question. The only time Dima ever practiced throwing his knife was when he was particularly agitated.

Dima tilted his head back and blew smoke into the air.

"I found some turpentine," Felix announced. "We used the mineral water bottles to make Molotov Cocktails."

"How did you find it if you were on the roof?" asked Dima without turning or looking at him.

Felix bit his tongue. He didn't want this to turn into another confrontation.

"So you disobeyed a direct order?" Dima added. "Are you testing the warning I gave you earlier?"

"We've made some other things too," Felix commented, wiping dust off his pants. "Would you like to come and see?"

Dima dropped his head and sighed. "Why not," he said. He folded his knife, hid it inside his boot, and checked the time on the pocket watch his father had given him. "Show me all your *glorious* weapons."

Felix led him to the front of the warehouse where the men were finishing up.

"It's a nail bomb, Comrade Lieutenant," declared Ivanovich, beaming like a young boy who'd just caught his first frog. "We got the gunpowder from some unexploded shells, and now we're packing it together with the nails."

"We made Molotov Cocktails too," another man said proudly. "We have thirty-six of them—three per person."

They watched Dima's face for his reaction. Felix saw the fire in their eyes, and hoped Dima would be pleased, but he seemed indifferent.

"The only problem is," Dima said flatly. "They'll surely come in with their tanks first. The nail bombs won't do any good against a tank, and how are you going to get near enough to throw a Cocktail at them? They'll cut you down before you get close."

The men fixed their eyes on Felix, awaiting his rebuttal, but he had none. In previous encounters with tanks, there had always been things to hide behind, ways to sneak up on them, but there was nothing around the warehouse except open space.

The downward spiral began. There was no hope after all.

From time to time Felix glanced over the short wall encircling the roof, but mostly he sat ruminating over how the Germans were now between him and

Katya. His emotions swung wildly, and he hated fate for putting him in this impossible situation.

Filled with fury and indignation, he vowed to himself that neither the Germans, nor the Soviets—nor fate itself—was going to stop him from getting back to Katya. He'd do whatever he had to do. German soldiers were no longer fellow humans to him, but obstacles to be overcome. When he aimed his rifle at them, he no longer saw a father, a brother, or a son. He saw a uniform that needed to stop moving, a uniform keeping him from all that he loved.

He raised his head over the wall again, but saw no enemy approaching—only the same old bombed-out truck with three of its tires in tatters. Dima—still pensive and distant—sat nearby chain-smoking cigarettes and gazing into the cloudless sky. "I'm out of tobacco," he said. "Do you have any?"

Puzzled by the question since Dima knew he didn't smoke, Felix shook his head slowly.

Dima put his knees together and leaned forward until his forehead rested on them. After a minute, he lifted his head, asking, "Do you remember Vera?"

"Vera," Felix repeated, hoping the name would spur his memory. "No. I don't remember any Vera."

"Sure you do," said Dima. "She was in our class. Short, with brown curly hair. Shy."

"Vera Nadakov?"

Dima nodded.

"What about her?"

"I can't stop thinking about her," he said, his voice flat and hoarse. "It's driving me crazy."

Felix remembered Vera as a nice girl who was pretty enough, but much too timid to be popular with the boys.

"She had a crush on me in seventh grade," Dima said.

"Vera? I had no idea. You two were such opposites."

"She used to write me love letters and apologize for being so shy. They were the nicest letters anyone's ever written me," explained Dima. "I remember I even cried once reading one."

"So what happened?"

"Nothing really. She was so quiet and thoughtful and courteous and praised me so much that I felt uncomfortable around her. She was so *good*, and she kept insisting that I was good too. I couldn't stand it. I wanted her to cheat on a test or call me an idiot occasionally, but she wouldn't. All she ever did was tell me what a good person I was."

"Didn't you hit her with your slingshot once?"

Dima nodded, his eyes glistening. "I hit her with a little stone in the side of the head, trying to make her mad at me. I wanted to hear her curse and call me names. She was bleeding, and they took her to the nurse's station. I was suspended from school for three days."

"You'd always told me that was an accident," said Felix, "that you didn't mean to hit her."

"That's what I told everyone, but I did it on purpose. When I returned to school, she wrote me a letter saying she still loved me. Can you believe it?"

"No," Felix exclaimed, "you never told me any of this before."

"The next year she moved away, and I've never seen her since. I've hardly even *thought* about her since. And now, for some reason, I can't stop thinking about her." He put his head down again, trying to stifle a few sobs.

Resisting the urge to ruin things by offering advice or relaying some similar experience of his own, Felix instead took a drink from his canteen. Then he patted Dima on the shoulder and scanned the horizon for signs of the approaching Germans. A light breeze picked up and felt good against his sweaty skin.

"Too bad I don't have that slingshot anymore," Dima joked as he wiped his eyes. "We could use it now."

Felix laughed as he put his scope down. The dilapidated Soviet army truck caught his attention again, and then a crazy idea came to him. "We can *make* a slingshot," he said excitedly. "A *giant* one that could launch the Molotov Cocktails at the German tanks!"

"What are you talking about?"

"That truck still has one good tire on it," Felix explained. "We can use the inner tube as the rubber band."

"I don't know," Dima said skeptically. "We'd need a winch to draw it back, and a massive fork to hold the inner tube. Trying to aim it would be futile, and who knows how far it could launch anything."

Felix wasn't willing to give up so easily. "Didn't you tell me you made your slingshot with your dad? And you were a hell of an aim, I recall. We'll put it on the roof to increase its firing distance, and the Germans won't be able to see it as they approach."

"But we don't even know which direction they'll come from."

"We can make it mobile," Felix countered. "We'll construct it so we can aim in any direction and move it backwards or forwards if needed."

Dima rested his chin on his hand and furrowed his eyebrows. "It's worth a shot at least," he relented.

They set to work immediately, Felix conveying the idea to the others and getting everyone involved once more. Making it mobile ended up being the most difficult part. After considering several options, they decided on large steel rods from the scrap metal heap, attaching them to the roof on each side of the building. They mounted them in such a way that they could adjust their aim, but mobility was limited to manually taking the inner tube and winch to whatever side the Germans were approaching from.

Once finished constructing their giant slingshot, they filled empty tin cans with dirt until they weighed the same as the Molotov Cocktails. Then they test fired the cans to refine their aim. To everyone's surprise, they were able to launch projectiles nearly ninety yards, although hitting a target at that distance was a different story.

"Don't worry," Felix assured the men. "When we were kids, the Lieutenant was the best shot in the whole neighborhood."

"You men do exactly what I tell you," Dima said resolutely, "and I'll hit those bastards."

"Maybe the giant slingshot will be our next secret weapon," someone joked.

Everyone laughed, except Felix, who was contemplating how ninety yards wasn't much when it came to combating tanks, whose firing range was much greater. But it was about sixty yards farther, he surmised, than anyone could throw a Cocktail by hand.

Felix watched warily as Ivanovich raced from the north side of the roof over to him and Dima. "Comrade Lieutenant," he announced breathlessly, "we've spotted something."

Dima stretched, then placed both hands on his head and twisted until his neck cracked. "Tanks?"

"No. Just one man."

"One man?" Felix repeated, unsure he'd heard correctly.

Ivanovich nodded.

Dima used his binoculars, and Felix his scope.

"Over there," directed Ivanovich, pointing to a cluster of green bushes.

When Felix focused on the area, he saw a German soldier leap out and start toward the warehouse at a full run.

"It's an enemy soldier," remarked Felix. But then, strangely enough, he recognized him. "No! It's not a German, it's—"

"Fedushkin!" Dima shouted, finishing Felix's sentence. "Shoot that son of a bitch!"

Relieved that his earlier premonition about Fedushkin dying hadn't come true, Felix put his rifle down.

"I said shoot that traitor!" repeated Dima.

"He might be able to tell us something," argued Felix.

Dima put his binoculars down and took aim with his own rifle. Felix recalled Dima's threat to send him to the firing squad for any further insubordination, but laid a hand on the barrel of Dima's rifle anyway, forcing it down toward the roof.

"Damn you," cussed Dima. It was too late for him to take aim again as Fedushkin was only a few yards from the front door now.

Felix dashed toward the stairs to go down, Dima's voice calling angrily from behind.

"I warned you, Varilensky," he shouted. "God dammit, I warned you!"

When Felix arrived, Fedushkin was inside the warehouse, gulping water from a canteen one of the men gathered round had given him.

"Where's everyone else?" the men asked eagerly.

"Dead," replied Fedushkin. "We'd run out of ammo and decided to make a run for our lines. Halfway there the Nazis spotted us and started firing." He paused to take another drink of water. "We kept running, but then our own comrades started firing at us!"

"They thought you were Germans?" someone asked.

"I don't know," said Fedushkin. "We dropped our guns and held up our hands as we ran, but they still kept shooting at us! They hit Andrei in the chest and killed him. We had to turn back or else we would've all been killed. But damn, we were so close!" He shook his head and growled.

"We ran back to the same spot we'd started from—a shallow, muddy trench," he continued. "We were bombarded with mortars and machine-gun fire by the Nazis. With no weapons, we decided we had to surrender. I wrapped my white t-shirt on the end of a stick and waved it in the air. When they stopped firing, we put our hands up and walked toward them. But when we got close to their trench, they started shooting us! I was the only one to get away alive."

Felix heard Dima's familiar footsteps coming from the other end of the warehouse. "Then what did you do?"

"I ran to a building and found a dead Nazi, then got the idea to put his uniform on and try to make my way back here."

"What's the fighting like there? Who's winning?" asked Felix.

"Tough to tell," answered Fedushkin. "But as I made my way back here, I could see the Nazis starting to fall back."

"They're retreating?"

Fedushkin nodded.

The men grinned and slapped each other on the back. "Very good," they said. "Felix, you were right!"

"That's the good news," added Fedushkin.

Everyone grew quiet. Felix turned his head over his shoulder at Dima.

"And the bad news?" Dima asked, pistol in hand.

"They're headed right for us, Comrade Lieutenant," he said with trembling hands.

"How many?"

He shrugged. "Ten. A hundred. A thousand. Who knows?"

Felix tried to discern if Dima's pistol was pointing at him or at Fedushkin.

"How much time do we have?" asked Dima.

Fedushkin shrugged again.

All eyes fell on Dima and his pistol. "I'll deal with you later," he said, returning the weapon to its holster.

Felix didn't know who Dima was referring to, but that was a concern for the future.

Dima took a big breath and addressed all the men. "Tell everyone manning a firing point on the south side to come to the north. We'll need to reposition the slingshot as well. Let's get ready!"

It was only a few minutes after they'd moved the slingshot and readied Molotov Cocktails that Felix spotted the approaching Germans. With his scope, he sighted three tanks, a car, and two motorcycles. Half-a-dozen troops rode on top of each tank.

The sun was low in the sky and cast long shadows on the advancing convoy.

"I'm surprised they haven't started firing on the warehouse yet," Dima commented as they drew near.

"They're probably hoping to check back into their hotel and get some sleep," joked Felix.

The men laughed nervously.

Along with Dima, Felix peeked over the wall at the first tank, spying the upper half of a German soldier leaning out an open hatch and casually smoking a cigarette. "They don't seem too concerned about us," he remarked dryly.

"I'll be damned," said Dima, putting his binoculars down.

"What?" Felix asked.

"Well, I'm not sure," Dima said, then paused. "But I don't think they know we're here." He snuck another glimpse over the wall. "The way they're approaching so lackadaisically ... it's like they think this whole area has already been cleared."

As the convoy neared their range of fire, the men became still and quiet. "Remember what we discussed earlier," Dima called softly to those near him. "Let them come in like there's no one here. We have to be in close range, so wait until I give the word."

A few of the men crossed themselves when Dima wasn't looking.

As the tanks began to slow, one of the drivers popped his head out and looked through a pair of binoculars at the warehouse. Felix and the rest of the men on the roof sunk low behind the wall.

"Come on, you bastards," Dima whispered impatiently. "Just a little closer."

Peering through one of the firing holes he'd chiseled in the wall earlier, Felix watched breathlessly as the tank driver with the binoculars made a hand signal and the convoy came to a halt. They were about twenty yards out of reach of the slingshot.

"What's going on?" Felix whispered. "Did they spot someone?"

The German car—gray with a black iron cross on the side—pulled ahead of the tanks. The driver stepped out of the vehicle, yelling and gesticulating with his hands.

"That looks like a general's car," said Ivanovich.

Felix had his doubts, but kept them to himself. "Probably," he said. "That would explain why there's three tanks and two motorcycles providing an escort."

The news spread quickly around the rooftop. "It's a Nazi general!" they whispered to one another.

After a minute, the first tank pulled in front of the car. The second tank took the right flank, and the third the left. The two motorcycles sped past all of them and would reach the warehouse in a matter of seconds.

When the tanks began to roll forward, Dima signaled for Ivanovich to pull the winch back, then Felix placed a Cocktail in the pouch of the inner tube.

A shot rang out unexpectedly, and one of the motorcyclists fell to the ground.

"Damn it," Dima cussed as he tightened the tension on the slingshot. "Who the hell fired?"

"It must have been someone from below," said Felix.

Another shot echoed, and the second motorcyclist fell to the ground.

The convoy came to a stop again.

"All right, let's give 'em hell," said Dima.

Felix lit the Cocktail while Dima made one last adjustment to the aim. Then Ivanovich disengaged the clasp, and the flaming bottle streaked through the sky like a miniature rocket.

The convoy never saw it coming. The deadly bottle splattered across the top of the first tank, setting it, and the six men riding there, on fire. The soldiers jumped off and rolled on the ground, trying to extinguish the flames. A few seconds later, the tank's crew stumbled out, screaming and on fire as well.

The men riding atop the other two tanks hurriedly climbed down and dove to the ground. While one tank began firing on the warehouse, the other turned sharply to the left.

"Hurry! Load another one," ordered Dima.

But with the building being rocked by shells from the tank, Ivanovich couldn't reset the slingshot. Felix pushed him out of the way and quickly loaded another Cocktail. Dima aimed it and gave the order to launch.

The bottle sailed just over the tank firing at them.

As Felix reloaded the winch, the tank began reversing away, continuing to pound the warehouse with its shells and machine gun.

The building trembled in its foundations, and it seemed like an eternity before Dima finally gave the signal to launch.

But the wait was worth it—another hit! The left side of the retreating tank was engulfed in flames, and its crew scrambled out. When one of them tried dousing the flames with a fire extinguisher, Felix took aim and stopped the uniform from any further movement.

Although there was still one more tank and plenty of German soldiers on the ground, Dima's men were targeting the retreating car.

"No," Dima hollered at them, "the car can't hurt us. Get that other tank!"

They loaded another Cocktail, but Felix feared the tank might already be out of range. He watched the bottle fly through the air and explode on the ground next to the car. The startled driver cranked the wheel to the right, smashing into the side of the reversing tank. The collision mangled the front of the car, rendering it undriveable, but it didn't slow down the tank in the least.

Dima had Ivanovich pull the winch back as far as it would go. The tank was already out of the range they'd practiced for. Soon enough, the tank driver would realize he could stop and fire on the warehouse without fear of being hit by the deadly, flaming bottles.

Felix crossed his fingers as the Cocktail streaked toward its target, but it missed. The distance had been good enough, but not the aim.

"Load another one!" commanded Dima.

"But the tank's well out of range," protested Ivanovich.

"Load it, damn it!" Dima said. "We'll hit the car."

The car's driver had helped a wounded man out of the back seat, and they were hiding behind the vehicle. Dima and Ivanovich launched two Cocktails at them. Although they missed, the resulting oblong fires were close enough to convince the Germans they couldn't stay there. They made it no more than a few steps from the vehicle before being struck by bullets.

Felix and the others were firing on the German infantry, while Dima and Ivanovich switched to hurling nail bombs from their giant slingshot. The tank that had escaped now began its retribution, shelling the front of the warehouse and the rooftop mercilessly. A large section of the wall in front of Felix was obliterated, and chunks of concrete rained down on top of him. Once he recovered, he rolled to another position and resumed firing—picking off German uniforms meticulously one by one.

The nail bombs proved to be extremely lethal, and the remaining German troops made a desperate run for the west side of the warehouse. But there was nowhere for them to hide, and they were methodically cut down.

After a while, the gunfire came to an end and the unbeatable tank stopped its shelling and retreated. Felix guessed it had run out of ammunition.

"You did it, Felix!" his exultant comrades shouted.

"*We* did it," Felix corrected them.

"Let's see if they're stupid enough to come back for another thrashing!" the men boasted, slapping one another on the back. "Hell, a few more battles like that, and we'll be the ones encircling Berlin!"

Felix used his scope to check on the bloody uniforms splayed on the ground. None of them moved, not even in the slightest. Except one. It was the wounded man from the back seat of the car. Judging by his age and the epaulets on his fine uniform, Felix felt certain the man was a senior officer. When he announced the information to the others, even Dima smiled.

The man staggered to his feet, put his hands in the air, and started toward the warehouse. Dark red blood covered the side of his wrinkled, leathery face. Felix couldn't tell what rank he was, but the invasion of grey on his otherwise black head of hair told him that he likely wasn't a mere lieutenant. No matter his rank though, he would be a valuable source of information, and a powerful bargaining chip should the Germans attempt another attack.

Felix and Dima had made their way down from the roof and were walking toward their new prisoner when a lone shot resounded. The wounded German collapsed to the ground. Felix turned to see Fedushkin still aiming his rifle.

"You idiot!" Dima screamed as he charged and knocked him to the ground.

"That's what the Nazis did to us when *we* tried to surrender!" griped Fedushkin.

"*We* are not Nazis!" Felix hollered. He rushed to the German officer, but it was clear he was already dead. A large chunk of the right side of his forehead was missing.

Dima pulled his pistol from its holster, pointed it at Fedushkin and fired. Another shot. Another man with part of his head missing.

This isn't war, thought Felix. *War implies a kind of organized means of two enemies fighting one another. This is madness.*

Felix wasn't sure he believed in heaven, but he did believe in hell, and was convinced they were creating it for themselves right here, right now. They were building the walls and stoking the fires that would burn them and all those not yet born. And who was to blame? Who exactly was the enemy?

He looked to the sky, and the sun burned his face.

After seizing the guns and grenades from the dead Germans, Dima and his tattered platoon retired to the warehouse to tend to their wounded. Three more men had been killed in the fighting, and another four had minor lacerations.

Felix was pleased with Dima's decision to let everyone rest before they discussed their next move. He and Dima withdrew to a corner of the warehouse and collapsed to the floor, not even bothering with improvised pillows or something to lie on.

Before drifting off to sleep, Felix yawned and stretched his arms. For the first time since the war started, he felt cautiously optimistic about his side's chances. They'd only won one small battle, but he'd seen a determination and resourcefulness that encouraged him. The men hadn't prepared and fought so hard because they'd been ordered to. They did it because they wanted to. Perhaps they were tired of being beaten time and again. Or perhaps it was sheer vengeance. Whatever the reason, Felix started to believe their situation wasn't so futile after all. As Dima had pointed out, they didn't necessarily need to turn the tide on the Germans. All they needed to do for now was stop them from advancing on Leningrad. *That* was their goal. *That* would be a victory.

As the setting sun dipped below the horizon, the deep buzz of approaching planes could be heard, but no one paid it any attention. Not until the ground around them erupted like a volcano and the warehouse burst into flames did anyone think of the possibility of a German airstrike.

The warehouse became a flaming inferno in a matter of seconds. Those who weren't killed by exploding shrapnel were rapidly consumed by smoke and flames. Felix and Dima struggled together toward the outside, but only Felix made it. When he realized Dima wasn't with him, he ran back into the warehouse. The last thing he remembered was tripping over Dima's motionless body and the suffocating smell of the thick, acrid smoke.

Глава Шестая — Chapter Six

Rats in a Whirlpool

Hate drips from my ego,
  that vertigo,
  that somehow eludes me.
That which cannot be destroyed,
  that which cannot be enjoyed.
This affliction,
  this condition,
  that confounds me,
  surrounds me,
  until early dawn
Of each and every day.
The harder I try,
  the farther I fall.
The louder I scream,
  the softer you call.
I see your lips move,
  but hear nothing at all.

Katya pivoted in the chair to better see her coworker behind her. He was pacing back and forth again, treading over the same well-worn area on the red and tan rug. She was fairly certain she'd heard him correctly, but was so shocked that she wanted to be positive. "I'm sorry, Lev. What did you just say?"

"I called you an idiot," he repeated, his eyes looking like little black sunflower seeds behind his thick glasses. "You're stupid."

Katya fixed her eyes on the portrait of Lenin hanging next to the door, trying to figure out why Lev would say something like that to her. She'd merely made a suggestion that they sweep out the warehouses and railroad cars to try to reclaim the flour left in the cracks and corners and such.

"We can't waste our time on dumb ideas that lead nowhere," Lev said irritably.

Katya's first instinct was to belittle him in return. Her second instinct was to defend herself and her idea. But she decided against either of those, because she'd recently learned a very useful trick from Petya. She'd noticed he often took a second, sometimes several, before answering someone. He'd explained to her how he'd developed the 'one-breath rule,' as he called it, while living in the orphanage. Before replying to anything confrontational, he would make himself take one complete breath, which almost always resulted in him changing his response.

Inhaling slowly, she closed her eyes, then released any tension she noticed as she exhaled. It was one thing to not be able to love her enemies who were destroying and starving her city, it was quite another to have no compassion for her fellow Leningraders. In her mind, she pictured her grandmother, then Jesus, and tried to respond as she thought they might.

"Lev, it's important to me that we treat one another with respect," she said, trying to calm her rapidly beating heart. "If you don't like one of my ideas, then I would prefer you criticize the idea, and not me personally. It makes me feel anxious."

"I don't care how you feel," he said bluntly. "I don't give a damn about your emotions. My job is to keep Leningrad from famine, not pamper a spoiled debutante."

Katya was hungry and tired, but had already decided how she was going to react. She stubbornly refused to hear Lev's analysis of her. To respond with compassion, her grandmother had taught her, you need to take yourself out of the equation. "Are you frustrated with the difficulties of your job and the demands on you and your time?" she guessed.

"Yes. This job is impossible. How do you feed a city when you have no food?" He gesticulated wildly with his hands. "What does the director expect from me? To wave a magic wand and create a million loaves of bread out of thin air?"

Katya breathed a little easier. "Lev, you work very hard. I know, because I see you every day. You've been putting in long hours, and like everyone else, you're probably not getting enough to eat. You haven't seen your son since he left for the front, and you're under an immense amount of stress. You're trying to do, as you said, the impossible—keep the people of Leningrad from starving. I imagine you're feeling overwhelmed."

Lev slumped into a chair, his face softening.

"Why don't we call it a day?" suggested Katya.

After removing his glasses and pressing the palms of his hands to his eyes, he yawned and squinted at the clock on the wall, mumbling, "Where on earth does the time go?" Putting his glasses back on, he peered at Katya over top of them. "No. Let's finish up," he said, a slight frown forming at the corners of his mouth. "I'm sorry about those comments I made. Please accept my apologies. You're correct—I have been on edge lately. But it's not right for me to take it out on you. You work just as hard and deserve to be treated better."

"Apology accepted," she said with a pleased smile. Noticing his red face, she added, "Are you feeling embarrassed because you'd like to have talked to me more courteously?"

"Absolutely," he exclaimed. "It's ridiculous the way I treat people these days. I hate it. But I have no patience. My temper erupts at the drop of a hat. I'm always hungry, and the weather's turning colder. But it's no excuse! I have to get control of myself!" Resuming his pacing, he leaned forward and held his hands behind his back before stopping abruptly. "All right, I'm done," he said.

"Done with what?" asked Katya.

"Feeling sorry for myself. Leningrad needs me. She needs all of us to be strong. Now let's get back to work. We'll implement your idea to sweep out the warehouses and railroad cars and hopefully reclaim some more flour. I doubt it'll be much, but every little bit helps." He grabbed his pencil from the table. "Let me add that to the list before I forget."

While Lev jotted in his notebook, Katya excused herself to refill her glass. Only by drinking endless cups of water could she make it through each day. The trick fooled her stomach into thinking it was full. It frightened her to think that her hunger, and everyone else's, was only going to get worse.

When she returned to the room, she asked Lev if they were on track for the new rules and ration cards that were to take effect the first of October.

"Yes. We'll be ready," he answered as he went to the window and opened the drapes. It was pitch black outside. All the street lights had been turned off. Anything at all indicating there were still people living and working in the vast city had been concealed lest the German bombers see something to aim for. "I can't believe next week will be October already. Before you know it, winter will be here."

Katya's thoughts drifted to Igor, wondering how he'd coped today. Since he was a growing boy on the verge of puberty, she worried that the lack of food might stunt his growth. "So nonworkers and children will be reduced to one-third of a loaf of bread a day, and a pound of meat for the month. Is that right?"

Lev muttered something inaudible, then said, "I'm afraid so. The rules are draconian, but as the director says, we have to do it to even give the city a chance of survival. There'll be some cereals, macaroni, pastries, and butter for them too, but not much—hardly enough for an adolescent boy. How old did you say Igor is?"

"He's going on thirteen."

"Do you have any extra food on hand?"

"Some," replied Katya. "But it's going rather quickly. Igor eats like a horse, and I'm afraid I'll have to start locking the food up while I'm gone." Katya waited for Lev to turn back toward her. "The director is a wonderful, energetic man, and he's doing a tremendous job."

"But?" asked Lev.

"But I wish he'd realize a twelve-year-old needs twice as much food as a five-year-old. He puts them on the same ration, and it doesn't make any sense to me. Could you speak with him? He respects your opinion. He'll listen to you."

While scribbling in his notebook again, Lev answered, "I've already talked to him about it. He stresses the food must go first to those making a direct contribution to the war effort. I can't see him changing his mind on any of the regulations." He tapped his pencil on the table and gazed up at the ceiling. "Why don't you find Igor a job? Then his ration will be increased."

"I've tried," Katya said wearily. She ran her fingers through her hair and stretched her neck to each side. "Can't seem to find anything."

"I just thought of something," Lev announced. "We should check the breweries. They've all been closed down, but might still have some grain left in storage."

"Good idea," replied Katya. She took a drink of water and contemplated the dismal numbers she'd written down earlier. Leningrad had 2.9 million citizens and an additional 500,000 troops defending the city, but they only had enough food on hand to adequately feed half that number. "Is there absolutely no way to get supplies from the outside?" she asked.

"For now, no," Lev said firmly. "The only open route to the mainland is across Lake Ladoga, and there's no ships, piers, highways, or warehouses that can handle the amount of food we need. If any ships make it across the lake without being sunk by the Germans, then that's a bonus. But we shouldn't count on anything from there."

The kerosene lamp cast dark shadows across the room. Katya held back a yawn and pinched herself to try to wake up. So many people's lives depended on the job she, Lev, and the director did. It was a tremendous weight—oppressive at times—but Katya was determined like she'd never been before. She loved Leningrad with all her heart and soul, and vowed to do her part to assure its survival. She and Lev worked late into the evening, leaving Katya thoroughly exhausted by the time she left. Wrapping a scarf tightly around her head and neck to combat the chilly wind that had started blowing from the north, she set off on the long walk home. The sun was now setting before 8:00 p.m. each night, and the days would only get shorter and colder from here on out.

With each new block, she tried to come up with a new strategy for either finding more food and making their existing supplies go further. She dwelled on the food situation both day and night. It haunted her dreams—people as thin and brittle as corn stalks in autumn, people dying by the hundreds each day in the bitter cold of winter. She couldn't let it happen. Not here. Not in Leningrad.

The streets were all deserted, and she made the trip home with nothing but the leafless, skeletal trees and the howling autumn wind to keep her company. There was no shelling now, and the quiet felt strange. But she knew their enemy would begin again—with Germanic precision—at 7:00 a.m. the next morning. Katya hoped that would be their downfall—that the Germans' obsession with order, precision, and rationality would doom them in this chaos that had become her home.

She said another prayer for the siege to be lifted, for the winter to be mild, and for Felix and her father to return home safe and sound. She didn't know if her prayers would be answered, but that wasn't the point. Prayer wasn't a means to an end for her. She prayed simply to reaffirm her own faith in the universe.

The wind picked up, and she shivered with cold as it blew right through her light jacket. She'd have to start wearing her fur coat soon if this kept up. Passing near the hospital, she decided to skip volunteering there that night. It was late and she still needed to make dinner and wash clothes once she got home.

It was all very peculiar to her—how and why she'd been reassigned from her work at the hospital to assisting the city's food supply official. She was convinced her father had something to do with it, despite the fact that she hadn't heard from him since he left for Moscow nearly a month ago.

She walked past a massive streetcar lying on its side, a victim of one of the Luftwaffe's never-ending bombing runs. On the other side of the street, a scruffy white horse pulled an overloaded wooden cart as two soldiers marched alongside, lugging machine guns over their shoulders. Katya had to look away, because the younger soldier reminded her too much of Felix.

As difficult as life was, she was not entirely unhappy. She surprised even herself with her disposition. There was death and destruction all around her, very little to eat each day, long hours with Lev and volunteering at the hospital, and arriving home every night to a cold apartment and her neighbors' endless grievances. Yet through it all, she managed to find moments when she was grateful to be alive, thankful she had two legs to walk on, two arms to work with, and a beating heart that kept fighting to remain open.

She nearly passed her block because they'd recently whitewashed all the street signs. If the Nazis broke into the city, it was hoped they would get lost in a maze of nameless streets and avenues. Even the number of her apartment building had been whitewashed.

Inside the dark stairwell of her building, she climbed up with extreme caution, testing each step before she shifted her weight to it. Under the conditions Leningrad survived in, she knew the slightest injury could easily lead to one's demise. To break a leg or catch the flu these days meant almost certain death.

As she ascended the stairs, she heard a man pounding on a door and yelling, "Guzman! Guzman!" Upon reaching her floor, the man called out to her in the darkness. "Is that you, Guzman?"

Recognizing Shostakovich's voice, she answered, "No, Dmitry. It's me, Katya." Then she knocked on her apartment door and summoned Igor.

"Oh, thank goodness you're here, Katya," said Shostakovich. "Where's Guzman? Have you seen him? He's not in his apartment, and I don't know where he could be."

Igor opened the door, and light streamed into the hallway illuminating Shostakovich's anxious, round face. "Calm down, Dmitry," said Katya, smelling alcohol on his breath. "I'm sure he's fine. Igor, have you seen Guzman today?"

"I saw him a couple hours ago," Igor said. "He was going to the market."

"The market?" Shostakovich repeated, examining Igor over his black-rimmed glasses. "So late in the day? Why would he be going to the market?"

"Dmitry, would you like to come in and have a cup of tea?" asked Katya. "You seem rather agitated."

"Yes, actually, I wouldn't mind that."

Shostakovich scurried into the kitchen, sat down, and began rubbing his glasses on his shirt while Katya put a kettle on the stove.

Igor followed them in, adding, "Guzman said he was going to sell his fur cap."

Shostakovich leapt out of his chair. "What? His fur cap? He's going to need that for the winter. Has he lost his mind?"

"He said he had two of them," said Igor.

"Oh, he said that? He has two?" Shostakovich sat down again, sighing.

Pulling up a chair next to him, Katya laid her hands on top of his. "What's wrong, Dmitry?"

Shostakovich fidgeted with the bottom button of his shirt. "It's just that winter is coming on," he said softly. "And who's going to look after an old Jew? He's such a dear old man. He doesn't realize the degree of anti-Semitism out there."

"Yes. He's just like Felix," said Katya. "Both of them choose not to see it."

"It would be good if Jews could live peacefully and happily in Russia, where they were born," Shostakovich continued, slurring a few of the words. He took a deep breath, sat up straighter, and added, "We need to remind everyone that the dangers of anti-Semitism are real. The infection is still very much alive."

Katya went to a cupboard and returned with three tea cups. "Guzman and Felix are both very passionate people. I don't think either one of them would ever leave Leningrad voluntarily." She placed three small spoons next to each tea cup. "We still have a little sugar left. Would you like some in your tea, Dmitry?"

"Please," he answered, crossing his legs, only to uncross them again a few seconds later. "I've found that most all Jews are passionate. That's why I love Jewish folk music. It's happy and tragic at the same time—laughing through the tears."

Igor had left the kitchen and hadn't returned, so Katya only poured tea for herself and Shostakovich. "Felix told me once he heard a Jewish influence in your music," she said.

Shostakovich nodded. "Yes, that's true."

"I always find such wonderful things in your music, Dmitry," Katya said as she sat beside him again. "I wish more people heard your beautiful ideas and discussed them."

Shostakovich took a sip of tea. "Art destroys silence," he said. "Some think art is all about beauty and the such, but I don't buy it. Art to me is the pursuit of truth." In setting his cup down, his trembling hands spilled tea all over the table. "I'm so sorry," he apologized, rising hastily from his chair. "Let me wipe this up."

Katya stood and took his quivering hands in hers. "Dmitry, don't worry. Guzman is going to be fine," she said, trying to reassure him. "You and I will see to it. We'll take care of him."

"No. No. No," Shostakovich fretted. "I'm afraid not."

Katya pulled back to get a better look at his face. "Why not?"

"Because they're making me leave the city," he blurted. "I've held them off as long as I could. They're evacuating me to Moscow, and then who knows where."

"Evacuating you? But I thought all the rail lines had been severed."

"Not by rail. By plane over Lake Ladoga. They're making Akhmatova go too."

"Anna's leaving too?" Katya nearly choked on her own words. "I heard her reading poetry over the radio just the other day. She's such an inspiration to everyone. I can't believe you're *both* leaving."

"I think it's absolute cowardice to leave the city, but they're forcing us out," he said.

Shaken by the news about Shostakovich and Akhmatova leaving the city, Katya felt like crying. It seemed like *everyone* was leaving her.

"Let's not talk about it anymore," said Shostakovich. "What's done is done." He crossed his legs again, asking, "How's Felix getting along?"

Katya shrugged. "I don't know," she answered, her voice trailing off. "Haven't heard from him."

"Yes, well the communication system has really broken down. I wouldn't worry too much if I were you. Mail to and from the front is tenuous at best. What about your father? Is he back from Moscow yet?"

Katya shook her head and sighed. "I haven't heard from him either. Perhaps you could make some calls for me? See what you can find out?"

Shostakovich arched his eyebrows over the thin black frames of his glasses. "I'll see what I can do, but I make no promises." Finished with his tea, he made his way toward the front door, Katya following behind. In the dark hallway, he gave her a brief embrace. "I feel much better now. Thank you for the tea and for listening," he said. "If I don't see you again before I leave, take care of yourself, Katya. Remember, we *will* win this fight. I'll finish my Seventh Symphony and we'll perform it here in Leningrad—whether the Germans are still sitting outside or not. You'll see."

"But what price will we pay for victory?" asked Katya apprehensively.

Shostakovich was already heading down the stairs. He responded by reciting one of the more popular sayings going around these days. "Leningrad is not afraid of death," he sang, his voice echoing through the empty hallways, "death is afraid of Leningrad."

After closing and locking the door, Katya leaned against a wall and wrapped her arms around herself. Both inside and out it was getting colder, and she was finding it harder and harder to keep warm. A solitary explosion echoed in the distance, but it was nothing more than noise to her anymore. Back in the kitchen, she peered out the window searching for the stars, but none were to be found. It seemed they too were abandoning her.

It wasn't long after the aroma of the fried potatoes drifted through the rest of the apartment that Igor appeared in the kitchen. He slouched in a chair at the table while Katya spooned some onto his plate. It wasn't much. Katya planned each meal in advance, and this was all she had allotted for tonight's dinner.

"You're awfully quiet tonight," she commented after several minutes of silence. "Everything all right?"

She'd noticed a shift in Igor of late. He rarely spoke, and he moved less and less each day, preferring instead to lie curled up in his bed under several blankets. As she started pondering again how to increase his ration, a knock came at the front door. After a glance at the lethargic Igor, she decided to answer it herself.

It was Petya. He followed her back to the kitchen, stopping at the doorway and leaning against a wall. "Sorry," he said, staring at the food on their plates. "I didn't know you were eating."

Katya sat at the table, feeling more tired than hungry. "Did you make it out to the countryside today?" she asked. "Any luck?"

"I went," said Petya, "but it was a waste of time. Those damn peasants are so edacious. They've got all these beets and potatoes and cabbage in their cellars, but they won't trade any of it. They have closets full of fur coats and expensive jewelry now. The only thing they'll trade for anymore is vodka."

"Sorry it didn't work out," Katya replied. "You really need to find a job that's directly involved in the war effort, then your ration would be increased."

"Don't you think I know that?" Petya said irritably. "You've told me that ten times already. Every day, I look, but there's nothing available for a cripple like me. Everyone's biased against someone with a handicap."

Katya suppressed a jaded sigh. Everyone seemed to be on the edge of quarrel these days. "Petya, I'm really tired. It's been a long day," she said. "I was only trying to help. I understand it's been difficult for you to find a job, and you're probably resentful about it."

"It's humiliating," he admitted. "I'm hungry, have no energy, and have to hobble all over the city begging people for a job. They take one look at my leg and then make up some bullshit excuse why they can't take me." He sat down beside Katya at the table. "Those doltish Germans make me so furious. They should either take the city or leave. What do they plan to do? Sit in their trenches outside the city and starve us all to death?"

"That's what I heard," said Igor.

Petya sneered at him. "What did you hear?"

"I heard the Nazis were digging in, that they'd given up on taking the city."

"That's a bunch of lies," Petya said hotly. "They're not going to sit out there in the Leningrad winter and wait for us to wave a white flag. They'll freeze to death the same as us."

"Well, that's what I heard," Igor said through a mouth full of food. "They're going to blockade the city so no food or supplies get in, and bomb us every day until we surrender."

"Who told you this?" asked Katya.

"Guzman," Igor answered.

Petya put his elbows on the table, propping his head up while he gazed at Katya eating. "Damn Germans," he said flatly. "They said they were coming to 'cleanse the world of communism.' I hardly see how blockading Leningrad is going to accomplish that."

Katya put her fork down. "Petya, I feel uncomfortable eating in front of you like this when I know you're hungry."

"If you gave me some, you wouldn't be uncomfortable anymore," he said with an awkward, forced laugh.

Katya lowered her eyes. She thought highly of Petya. He took care of Igor when she wasn't around and was always available to help her out with anything. That she considered him a good friend made what she was about to do all the more difficult.

"I think it would be best if you left," she said. "I need to ensure Igor and I have enough food to survive, and I'm not sure that we do."

Petya—eyebrows arched in astonishment—stood and bowed dramatically. "I am sorry to have disturbed you this evening. That was not my intention. Please forgive me." He didn't wait for a reply before limping down the hallway.

Although what she'd done was necessary, Katya nevertheless felt frightened about it. "Petya, wait," she said, hurrying after him.

"You're right," he said, turning to face her. "I can't be asking you to share your food with me. I understand the situation. We all need to fend for ourselves now."

Whether he meant it or not, his words cut Katya deeply. She remembered him using those same words to describe the time in his childhood after they'd shot his parents. She reached out for his hand, giving his fingers a sympathetic squeeze. With his horrendous time in the orphanage and a lifelong disability, she was certain he'd been 'fending for himself' his entire life.

Petya faked a smile and added, "I'll go back to those peasants tomorrow and trade my bottle of vodka. And I'll find a position that'll increase my ration. You don't have to worry about me."

As she watched him hobble out the door, she called softly, "I will anyway."

Her prayers that evening were particularly desperate. In addition to asking God to keep her father and Felix safe from harm, she begged for the strength to uphold her values, because that was getting more difficult with each passing day. One of her biggest fears was that her compassion and humanity would crumble under the weight of the daily deprivation of Leningrad under siege.

Franz eyed the six shivering prisoners with contempt. "Those two at the end?" he asked the fellow German soldier who was transferring the prisoners to Franz. "Why didn't you just shoot them?"

"Because they were already dead," he replied. Pursing his lips and flicking his cigarette butt to the ground, he handed a form to Franz. "Well, obviously they weren't. But there were bodies all over the place: Soviet, German, and of course Falkenhorst himself. Those two," he said, pointing at the men on the far right of the line, "we found lying just outside the warehouse—which was still burning. They weren't moving, so we assumed they were dead."

Franz found it hard to believe the scrawny, pitiful Russians he saw before him were the ones responsible for taking out Major Falkenhorst and all his men. "You should always put an extra bullet in their heads just to be sure," he advised. "They're tricky bastards."

After signing and returning the form, Franz leered at the prisoner with the big nose, convinced he was a Jew. "So these are the only two to have survived?"

The German soldier nodded his head, then walked inside the battered brick building and closed the door behind him. A large truck made its way noisily into the courtyard, coming to a stop in front of the prisoners lined up against the wall. Franz and two other soldiers would be transporting the prisoners in the truck to a camp farther behind the German lines.

Franz abhorred that the German army expended its food, time, and effort on these sub-humans. He believed it would be better to execute and bury them in shallow graves.

Before Franz and another soldier could herd the six Soviet soldiers into the back of the truck, an officer approached asking to be shown the two men responsible for killing Falkenhorst. Everyone wanted to see the two Russians who had managed to kill the formerly invincible warrior. Major Falkenhorst, or Old Leather Face as he was called behind his back, had been famous for his ruthlessness with the enemy. He'd never lost a battle, and had always escaped unscathed from every skirmish. Franz had idolized him for his toughness and uncompromising nature. If he were still alive, all these Russian prisoners would have been dead already. Falkenhorst had been a man who knew what it took to win a war., unlike the choirboy lieutenant in charge of Franz's platoon who had somehow been duped into regarding Russians as actual human beings. They weren't. They were animals, and the choirboy would learn that soon enough.

After a third soldier hopped in the cab to drive, Franz and his partner, Otto, joined the prisoners in the back. As the truck drove to their destination, Otto rested his rifle on his lap while Franz kept his pointed at all times. Franz knew better than to let his guard down with the sneaky sons-of-bitches. What amazed him about the Russians was that no matter how many they killed, they just kept coming. They wouldn't give up. It reminded Franz of a childhood vacation when he'd caught rats in traps just so he could throw them in a whirlpool and watch them drown. That's what the Russians were like—rats caught in a whirlpool. It was inevitable that they were going to drown, yet still they fought, refusing to accept their fate.

Franz was steadfast in his faith in the Fuhrer and his directives. Hitler had led them to unimaginable victory thus far, and it was preposterous to question his judgment. Still, his decision to move the entire Forty-First Panzer Corps and several Motorized Divisions to the Moscow front had taken Franz by surprise, since Leningrad had yet to fall. But he trusted the strategy of relentless bombing and cutting off all supplies would eventually force the city to surrender. Already, their spies gave accounts of citizens dying of hunger.

The truck bounced and shifted its occupants relentlessly from side to side. Clouds of dust made the air nearly unbreathable, and the wooden benches they sat on were hard and cold.

"Are we even on the damn road?" Franz called to Otto, although he didn't expect an answer. Otto kept to himself most of the time. The young soldier reminded Franz of that lunatic, Alfred Liskof, who had tied him to a tree and left him for dead. They both thought too much and tolerated Jews and communists more than they should.

"What do you think, Otto?" Franz hollered over the truck's loud engine and incessant squeaking. "Did the Jews make this road?"

Otto ignored him, but Franz was used to it. They'd made this lengthy, tedious trip together countless times. It was always boring—despite Franz's attempts to enliven things, which usually consisted of him provoking Otto to the point that he would actually say something.

"Hey Otto, what do you call one Jew drowning in the sea?"

Otto gave a little look of dismay and turned his head away.

"Pollution!" Franz shouted and guffawed. "But wait, it gets better. What do you call ten-million Jews drowning in the sea?" He paused a few seconds for the punch line. "The solution!"

Otto had no reaction, but Franz laughed heartily—his high, nasal chuckles filling the back of the truck.

The prisoner with the dark, curly hair and grey eyes made a remark aloud while gazing at Franz.

Franz tapped Otto on the knee. "What did that rat say?" he asked. In addition to his native German, Otto also spoke Russian, Italian, and French.

When Otto didn't answer, Franz repeated his question and shook Otto by the shoulder.

"He said you laugh like a pig being slaughtered," Otto replied.

"Is that so?" Franz said, pointing his rifle at the man. "What's his name?"

Otto asked, then relayed the man's name. "Felix."

"Tell Felix that he *is* going to be slaughtered like a pig," said Franz, smirking.

Before Otto could say anything, the prisoner spoke again, and Otto translated for Franz. "He says we're doomed to repeat Napoleon's fate."

Franz recalled the dumb stories Alfred had told him about Napoleon's ill-fated invasion of Russia. "Explain to him that *we* are not the French," he said emphatically. "Nobody has beat us, and nobody will. You tell these stupid rats what I said."

Otto addressed the men in Russian for nearly a minute, but when he finished, they all started laughing.

"Why are they laughing?" demanded Franz as a thick blue vein on the side of his forehead started to bulge. "You son-of-a-bitch. What did you say to them?"

"Just what you told me to," Otto answered.

Franz sneered at the prisoners. "There was absolutely nothing funny in what I said."

"Certainly not," said Otto. "They should be paralyzed with fear. I have no idea why they would find it funny." He then said something else to the Russians, and they all laughed again.

Catching Otto in a brief grin, Franz concluded Otto was having fun with the Russians at his expense. Waiting a few minutes until the time was right, Franz remarked in a casual tone that he'd been talking to Major Halder a short while back.

The resulting grimace on Otto's face was a good start. "The Major wanted to know how the men were doing—what morale was like," Franz continued.

Otto sat up straight and gripped his rifle. "Yes, well, he's a brilliant commander. Of course, he'd want to know about those things. He's the best there is." Rummaging through his pockets, Otto hastily pulled out a pack of cigarettes. He didn't take one for himself, but did offer one to Franz.

Though Franz had plenty of cigarettes, he took one anyway, tucking it in his pocket. "He asked specifically about you," Franz added smugly.

Otto's upper lip started to quiver.

"I told him you were doing well," said Franz, "but that you seemed to have a certain *fondness* for Jews."

"That's a lie," blurted Otto unequivocally.

Franz continued as if Otto hadn't said anything. "He seemed rather displeased about that."

"I'm no lover of Jews," Otto replied in a weary, businesslike tone. "I understand just as much as the next German the problems they're responsible for." As though sensing how unenthusiastic and rehearsed his words sounded, he then added with conviction, "In fact, I think we could solve a lot of the world's problems by getting rid of the Jews."

Franz licked his lips, then smiled slyly, baring his small, yellow teeth. "Well, there's Jews right here in this truck," he said, pointing his rifle at the prisoners. "What should we do about it?"

Otto scowled. "You don't know that."

"I'm positive that one there with the big nose is a Jew," said Franz. "What did you say his name was? Felix?"

"You're going to determine whether someone is a Jew based on the size of their nose? That's asinine."

"It's what?" asked Franz with a look of confusion. "Never mind. I have a surefire way to tell a Jew from a Russian. If they fail the test, then we'll get rid of 'em. Just as you said we should."

Otto began blinking incessantly. "We were instructed to take these prisoners to a specific destination," he said. "If we don't deliver them, then—"

"If anybody asks any questions," Franz interrupted, "we'll just say they tried to escape." He yelled at the driver to stop the truck.

"This is ludicrous," said Otto, his eyes darting to and fro. "They're all Russians. We're wasting time."

"We'll know for sure in just two minutes," remarked Franz as he signaled to the prisoners to get out of the truck. "Why don't we make it interesting? Since you're so sure there's no Jews in this bunch, I'll bet you my meat ration for the next week that at least one of them fails the test. And if I win, you give me that bottle of schnapps your father sent you."

They had the prisoners line up on the side of the long, flat road. It was a treeless area, surrounded by blackened fields that had been recently burned.

"What exactly is this surefire test you're going to give them?" Otto asked skeptically.

"First, we have to blindfold them," said Franz. "You know these pricks will cheat every chance you give 'em."

While Franz pointed his rifle, Otto and the driver had the prisoners kneel while they blindfolded them. When they were done, Franz searched through his German-Russian dictionary. He didn't trust Otto to translate the right thing.

Once he found the phrase he wanted, he instructed Otto and the driver to untie the prisoners' hands. Then, starting at the beginning of the line, he said in broken Russian, "Make cross." Franz waited a few seconds, then nudged the man with the butt of his rifle and repeated his demand for him to make the sign of the cross.

"I don't think he understands what you're trying to say," said Otto. "I'm not even sure *I* understand what you're trying to say."

"He understands well enough," Franz said. "He simply doesn't know how to do it. Here's your first Jew." Franz aimed his rifle at the man's head, but before he squeezed the trigger, Otto repeated the command to make the sign of the cross. With correct pronunciation, the prisoner moved a shaky hand to his face, touching his index finger to the bridge of his nose, then to his right shoulder. He'd done it wrong already.

Franz gave a mocking "Nyet" and executed the man.

Before the shot had finished echoing through the dull autumn sky, Franz moved on to the next prisoner, poking him with the barrel of his rifle and repeating the phrase for him to make the sign of the cross.

The man did it perfectly and without hesitation: moving his thumb and his first two fingers in an exaggerated fashion from his forehead to his stomach, and then to his right and left shoulder.

But Franz again asserted "Nyet" and pulled the trigger.

"You idiot!" yelled Otto. "What are you doing? He did it correctly."

"No, he didn't. He went from right to left. I saw him."

"Imbecile! You're a Catholic. Of course you do it from left to right. Russians are Orthodox, like the Greeks. They do it the opposite way—from right to left."

Franz glanced beyond Otto at two bedraggled refugees coming down the road—a chubby woman pushing an overladen cart and an old man with a cane hobbling alongside her. "What is he talking about?" Franz asked the driver.

"I think he's right," the driver replied meekly.

Before Franz even got to the next prisoner, the man sat back on his heels and shouted something defiantly.

Otto gave a snort in response.

"What did he say?" asked Franz.

Otto hesitated. "He said ... um ... How shall I put it politely? He invited you to go have sex with yourself."

The prisoner then spat blindly in front of him and tried to get to his feet and charge, but Franz shot him first.

"You see?" exclaimed Franz. "They're animals. Complete animals." The third dead man lay sprawled on the road, his left arm awkwardly tucked under his torso.

The two refugees were still coming closer, strangely enough. Usually they steered clear of situations with gunfire. But all Russian were senseless to Franz. "Don't worry about them," he called to Otto and the driver. "They don't have anyone to tell."

Franz was particularly eager to shoot the next man, Felix, but was concerned he might actually make the sign of the cross correctly. "You know, there's only three left," Franz commented matter-of-factly. "Why not shoot them and be done with it? Three less communists in the world."

The driver shrugged his shoulders. "If we did, we could be back in time for dinner. Maybe get some meat instead of leftover beans and bread."

"No. The deal was only for Jews," objected Otto. "You've won the bet. Let's put these three back on the truck and get going."

"You want to be on that miserable bumpy road for another two and a half hours?" asked Franz.

"Yeah, I'm already hungry," the driver said. "We'll just say they all tried to escape. Nobody's going to care about a bunch of prisoners anyway."

The high-pitched squeak from the wheels of the woman's cart hurt Franz's ears. "Tell them to get the hell out of here," he said irritably to Otto.

Since Otto couldn't very well report on Franz without implicating himself, Franz decided to proceed with his plan to execute the remaining prisoners. Wanting the two who'd killed Falkenhorst to see it coming, he ordered the driver to remove their blindfolds.

Otto was still conversing with the refugees, who—instead of passing by—were actually crossing the road toward them. "I told you to get rid of them," yelled Franz.

"I did, but they're insistent on trading us something for food," explained Otto.

Stupid, senseless Russians. Franz would shoot them too if he had to. Turning their way, he waved his rifle at them as a warning, but they kept approaching. The woman—thick as a tank—pushed her rickety cart toward Franz, all the while endlessly butchering the German word for "trade". The old man, covered in dingy blankets from head to toe, had stopped to speak with Otto.

Franz shouted crossly the Russian phrase for "go away". In response, the woman gave a maniacal grin, the sun glinting off her gold tooth. She then pulled back the tarp covering the contents of her cart, revealing a man with a submachine gun.

Rat-tat-tat!

All three bullets struck Franz in the chest, and he fell to the ground feeling his life slipping away. After several more gunshots, Otto and the driver joined him on the dusty road.

Dima stretched his cold hands toward the smoldering fire, but it had ceased giving off any heat twenty minutes ago. Countless, thick gray clouds filled the sky, and a fine mist that continually switched to light rain and back saturated the air. Felix had gone off with three of the partisans to gather more firewood. As to where the rest of them had gone, Dima didn't know. Nor did he care.

He'd been sitting there for three hours thinking—brooding over so many unpleasant facts. Most of all, he dwelled on the numerous things he'd lost in such a short period of time: his pride, dignity, confidence, and—with the exception of Felix—every man under his command.

Pinching his nose, Dima shoveled the last bite of stale bread and rancid grilled horse meat into his mouth. He chewed five times, then swallowed and hoped he could keep it all down. The Germans hadn't fed them much for the two weeks Felix and he were in their POW camp, and Dima's stomach was weak and sickly now.

His teeth chattered as a cold shiver ran up his spine, and he wondered how could you be a commander if you had no one to command? You couldn't, he decided. That was the depressing answer. His career was dead, and he wouldn't be surprised if he faced a court martial for getting every one of his men killed.

And for what? What had he accomplished?

Leaning his head back to feel the mist on his face, he let out a bone-tired sigh.

The Nazi interrogators had pummeled him mercilessly. Nearly every day, they'd strapped him to a chair in a smoky room with an extremely bright light. If they didn't like his answers, they let him know it with a swift whack from a club or by burning a hole in his skin with a cigar. He'd never experienced so much pain in his life, and each time he took a deep breath now, he felt a sharp, stabbing pain above his stomach.

It was during his ninth interrogation that Dima had broken down—when the pain and lack of food, sleep, and warmth pushed him to do the unthinkable. They'd promised not only to end the physical punishment, but to also give him a bowl of hot stew with bread and coffee. To entice him, they'd set the three items on a nearby tray, allowing him to smell but not reach them. Then they'd continued shining the light in his eyes, badgering him with questions, and whacking him with their hard little stick. "We're not asking you to tell us where General Zhukov's bunker is," they kept saying. "We just want one little thing that might be of use to us. Then you can eat and sleep."

And Dima had given in. He'd told them about the poor distribution and shortage of ammunition. When they replied that was common knowledge, he told them other things until they were finally satisfied. Then he joylessly ate the food, drank the coffee, and slept for twelve hours. When he woke up, he hated himself thoroughly, particularly his body for betraying him. Even now, as his hands and feet went numb from the cold, he wouldn't do anything about it.

Felix and the others returned carrying armloads of firewood and began stacking them under a large pine tree where it was still dry. Dima only knew the names of two of the partisans so far. The tall, skinny one who had hidden under the tarp with the submachine gun, and who was helping Felix stack the wood, was Misha. The stout woman with the gold tooth was Olga, who was apparently in charge of the rag-tag group.

She and the others had been involved in the battle for Mga, and after being thoroughly routed by the Germans, had fled to the woods where they'd remained ever since. They fought behind the lines as partisans—destroying German ammo dumps, attacking supply convoys, blowing up roads and bridges, and severing telephone and telegraph wires. There were ten—eight men and two women—but their numbers kept growing as more and more ordinary citizens became disgusted with the brutality of the German occupation.

According to Olga, Felix and Dima were now a part of this group. Dima was indifferent to the news. He had nothing to go back to, but Felix didn't like it, and was presently protesting to Olga about how he wanted to return to the Leningrad front.

Her response left no room for compromise. "Don't cross me, kike," she threatened. "You do what you're told or I'll have you shot. I'm in command here, and the sooner you get that through your thick kike skull, the better." She then marched away to her tent.

As the mist turned into light rain again, Dima got up and followed her. At the entrance to her tent, he pulled the canvas door aside and saw her leaning over a map, a kerosene lamp hanging from the ceiling. "Comrade, might I have a word with you?"

"No. I'm busy," she said, not even looking up. The map, crudely drawn, showed the locations of forests, streams, villages, roads, and trails. German positions were indicated with swastikas.

Dima came in anyway. "I've noticed," he said, "that you seem to have some problems with Comrade Varilensky."

Olga wrinkled her short, fat nose and snorted. "That's none of your business," she snarled. "Now get out, before I throw you out."

Despite Misha's warning to be wary of her, Dima pushed Olga's hat off a stool and sat down. "I'm making it my business," he said dispassionately.

Rather than more animosity, she seemed intrigued by his challenge. "I'm in charge around here," she explained, "and I suggest you don't get on my bad side, because I can be very *unpleasant*."

"I'm not questioning your authority," replied Dima, crossing his legs in front of him and wrapping his hands around his top knee. "As for getting on your bad side, I don't really care."

Olga raised her eyebrows. "I don't have a problem with you," she said. "You're a Russian. I only have a problem with that Jew."

"Good. I'm glad we're clear on that," said Dima. "I came to inform you that if you've got a problem with Varilensky, then you've got a problem with me too. If anything happens to him—either by you or because of you—you'll have to answer to me. Are we clear on that as well?"

Olga stepped toward him, forming her hand into a fist. "Are you threatening me?"

"Absolutely."

"I could give the word and have you killed right now," she said.

"You could," Dima agreed. "But I want you to know that I can slice your throat faster than you can utter another obscenity-laden order."

She retreated a step, and Dima knew he'd gotten to her.

"Either you're really crazy or really stupid," she said.

"That's for you to decide," he replied. "But lay off Felix and do your best to keep him out of harm's way. You do that, and you don't have to worry about me plunging a knife into your throat while you sleep."

"I already regret we rescued the two of you," said Olga.

Dima opened the tent flap to leave. "Me too," he muttered.

"Don't think for a minute that you've won," called Olga before he slipped outside.

"I don't," answered Dima. "That's why I came to speak to you in the first place."

He walked heavily back to the campfire where Misha had taken his seat. Felix was stoking the fire on the other side, and Dima slumped on the log behind him.

Misha retrieved a flask from inside his brown tattered coat, took a swig, then offered it to Dima. Taking a big gulp, Dima relished the painful burn down his throat. When he gasped at the end, Misha grinned and laughed.

"Good stuff, huh?" said Misha. "Got it from an old farmer. Makes it himself." After taking back the flask, he took another swig. "It's the only thing that keeps me going out here. Not only does it keep the bears away, it gives you some really interesting dreams at night." He chuckled again and passed the flask to Felix, who gasped as well after taking a drink. Catching Dima eyeing his coat, Misha ran his arm down the ratty sleeves. "Pretty stylish, huh?" he joked.

"It looks warm at least," replied Dima. He'd noticed that most of the other partisans were dressed in similar shabby clothes. None of them wore uniforms.

"Don't worry," Misha said. "We'll get you guys some warmer clothes. We'll head into the village tomorrow evening and see what we can find."

Felix continued poking a stick at the logs and coals, arranging them so that the fire came back to life.

"So what did you think of our little rescue yesterday?" asked Misha. "Those Nazis guarding you didn't know what hit 'em when Olga pulled that blanket off!" He imitated firing the submachine gun, then giggled like a schoolboy. "That was the second time we've tried that ruse—worked like a charm the first time too."

Felix and Dima stared at the fire, neither responding.

Misha glanced at them both, then took another sip from the flask. "It was a hell of a lot more fun than what we've been doing lately," he said. "For the past few days, we've been hauling farm machinery out here to the woods to hide it from the Germans. Talk about boring."

As Misha passed around the flask again, Dima choked down a second gulp. He could feel his body warming as the fire came back to life and the alcohol took effect.

"Where you two from?" Misha asked. "Me, I'm from Moscow. Don't know if I'd want to be back there now though. I hear the Nazis are closing in, and that it's complete chaos there." He guffawed, then added, "Not like here!"

When neither Felix nor Dima answered his question, Misha peered at them both, then guessed, "Leningrad? Am I right?"

Felix nodded.

"I knew it!" proclaimed Misha. "I can always tell if someone's from the country or the city, and when I saw you guys, I just knew you were from the city." He fetched a pouch of tobacco and piece of newspaper from his pocket and offered to roll a cigarette for them.

"He doesn't smoke," Dima said, referring to Felix, "but I'll take one."

"Doesn't smoke?" Misha said incredulously. "How do you make it from day to day?"

As Misha handed Dima a freshly rolled cigarette, Dima passed the flask to Felix. The fire was now burning bright and hot.

"So what was it like to be a German prisoner?" blurted Misha.

With no intention of answering, Dima gazed at Felix, hoping he'd say something. But Felix just took another drink from the flask and continued tending the fire.

Dima was certain the Germans had beaten Felix just as badly as they had him. He'd seen the burn marks on Felix's hands and neck, but every time Dima asked him about it, Felix only replied that it was over and he didn't want to revisit it—that nothing positive could come from rehashing what they'd done to him. Dima wondered if he too had broken down and told the Germans some classified information. Since Felix used to do clerical work for the army, he probably knew quite a few secrets the Germans would find interesting.

But somehow Dima knew that Felix hadn't capitulated. He'd noticed a change in Felix since those days of long ago at the beginning of the war. Felix was no longer hesitant, and with each passing day he seemed more determined and less unsure of himself.

"I understand," Misha said when no one responded. "You guys are probably exhausted. It's been a long day. I think I'll turn in myself." He stood up and stretched his arms over his head.

Dima held out the flask for him, but Misha waved it off. "You guys keep it. I've got more," he said as he left.

The camp was deep in the woods, and without Misha's chattering, the quiet was unbearable for Dima. There was only an owl hooting in the distance, the crackle of the fire, and the booze sloshing in the flask as they took turns drinking.

Dima reflected on when the Luftwaffe bombers set the warehouse ablaze two weeks earlier. He thought about that day a lot lately, how Felix endangered himself by returning to the inferno to rescue him. Felix claimed they'd made it out together, each helping the other find the way outside. But Dima knew better. He remembered struggling toward the exit through the thick, blinding smoke that was choking him, and he recalled seeing Felix a few steps in front—his broad back pointing the way for him to follow. Then Dima had fallen, and crawled on his hands and knees before collapsing completely. Before losing consciousness, he'd heard Felix calling out to him, but Dima had blacked out as he tried to answer.

The next thing he recollected was a dusty German boot kicking him in the side. He was twenty yards from the burned-out shell of the warehouse, and Felix, still unconscious, was sprawled out next to him.

In spite of everything Dima had said and done to Felix—even threatening him with the firing squad—Felix had risked his life to go back into the burning warehouse to save him. Dima could neither comprehend it nor get over it.

As the homemade liquor pulled him further under its influence, Dima leered at his former best friend. He felt so much raw hate at the moment that he detested him even more than the Nazis. Felix was a naive, obsolescent imbecile to have done what he did. Was he so out of touch that he didn't understand anything of this world? Anything at all?

Felix was sitting across from him staring into the fire. Dima was convinced he was thinking about Katya, worrying about her wellbeing despite his own bleak circumstances. How could they have ever been friends? They were nothing alike.

After Dima's next drink, Felix blurred and split in two. Dima refocused his eyes and called to him, "I know what you did."

Felix looked up. "You do?"

"Yes."

"They told you?"

Dima furrowed his eyebrows. "Who?"

"The Germans, of course."

Dima shook his head sharply to try to make sense of what Felix said, but it only made everything spin infuriatingly. "Don't play games with me," he said, slurring his words. "I know you ran back into the warehouse for me."

Felix motioned for the flask, and then took a swig. "Oh," he said flatly.

"Why did you lie to me about it?" asked Dima. "Why did you say we made it out together? That without me, we wouldn't have made it?"

Felix shrugged his shoulders. "Mostly because I don't remember everything. The last thing I recall is the two of us still inside the warehouse."

Dima gaped at him suspiciously. Even if Felix didn't specifically remember pulling Dima's unconscious body to safety, he must have figured it out later. "It was a stupid thing you did," Dima said adamantly.

"No. It wasn't," Felix responded. "It wasn't stupid at all."

"Bullshit!" Dima exclaimed emotionally. "You could have been killed."

"You would've done the same thing if our positions had been reversed."

Dima tipped the flask upside down, draining the last few drops into his mouth, then said, "You're a bigger fool than I thought if you believe that."

"No. I know you," countered Felix. "If you were in my shoes, you would have done the same thing."

"You don't know me at all," Dima said, his voice rising. "You knew me when we were kids, but that was a long time ago. We're very different now."

"You're still that same kid I grew up with," asserted Felix.

Dima hung his head. "I wish."

The mist, having grown more and more dense, finally turned into light rain once again.

"Things were simple back then," Dima added wistfully. "Not like now."

"It doesn't matter if you see it or not," insisted Felix. "I do. You're still that same kid who wants to change the world. The same kid who cried for days after your pet mouse died. The same kid who wants to save everyone and everything."

Dima held his head in his hands. "That kid," he replied haltingly, "died a long time ago."

The fire popped and hissed, faltering in the steady drizzle.

Closing his eyes, Dima focused on the fluttering pain in the middle of his chest. "Tell me the truth," he said, "because I really want to understand. I want to know why you so foolishly went back in to the burning warehouse."

"All right," Felix said. "I'll tell you the truth. I did it because I'm selfish."

Dima nodded knowingly and breathed a deep sigh of relief. Selfishness was something he understood all too well. It was what he was accustomed to seeing in those around him.

But Felix wasn't finished. "I did it," he continued, "because I wanted you to continue living. I wanted you to survive to see the end of this war, and to fall in love, get married, have children, and grow old, fat, and happy. I risked my life for you, because I consider you my friend. Despite all that's happened between us, when I look at you, I still see my best friend—the same one I grew up with, had so much fun with, admired and rooted for—"

"Shut up!" screamed Dima. All his accumulated rage through untold years of denying himself in the name of pleasing others, of striving to receive their accolades while avoiding their criticism, of constantly trying to live up to his father—the great engineer and decorated Civil War hero—came rushing forth like a summer thunderstorm. He leapt from his seat with glossy eyes and a lump in his throat. "Just shut the hell up!"

But Felix wouldn't heed his warning. Instead, he added unwaveringly, "I did it, because you—Dima—are worth saving."

Dima charged at him. "Shut up, you son-of-a-bitch!" He knocked Felix off his seat to the ground. "You don't understand shit about this world!" But Dima's voice betrayed him, and he could no longer keep the salty water in his eyes from streaming down his face. Fleeing into the woods, he cussed and broke off low-hanging branches in his way.

"You asked for the truth!" Felix called after him.

Dima ran and ran until he tripped to the ground and didn't get back up. He stayed there, crying in shame, until the light rain turned into a downpour, mixing with his tears and washing them into the earth, where they were accepted unconditionally.

Глава Седъмая — Chapter Seven

FOREVER HUNGRY GHOSTS

Senses alight,
    walking at night;
I feel what God had in mind,
    when he was bored,
    on that dreary day long ago.
But he was at his peak.
And in his own image,
    to a fault,
    to today,
    am I.
God's creation,
    from his imagination.
I see Him,
    from time to time,
    in glimpses,
    when I'm not thinking,
    when I'm at my peak,
    I am He.
And He is me.

"It's coming your way!" Petya shouted. His plodding footsteps and the sound of claws attempting to grip a polished wood floor filled the apartment.

A second later, the black cat came racing around the corner, slipping and rolling on its side, but then regaining its footing and racing toward Igor. Igor spread his feet wide and sunk low to the ground to block the hallway, but the cat still managed to squeeze by him. Lunging after it, Igor caught it by the hind legs, but it scratched him viciously until he let go.

"Damn it," lamented Petya. "We almost had it." They'd been chasing the cat for the last fifteen minutes.

Igor slowly got to his feet, inspecting the bloody scratches on his hands. "Where did it go?"

"In my room," Petya replied. "I'll go get it. You stay out here and keep a lookout for Oksana. She shouldn't be back for another three hours, but you never know with her."

Igor nodded and licked the blood from his hands.

After closing the door of his room behind him, Petya sat on his bed to rest for a minute. It took tremendous effort to move his body, and he was so intensely hungry.

He bent down and saw the skinny feline hiding under his bed. It hissed when it saw him and wedged itself further into a corner. It was quite possibly the last pet left in their building. Petya used to see and hear cats and dogs wherever he went, but not anymore. As hunger became more dire, all the cats, dogs, and birds in the city had started to disappear.

Retrieving a pair of thick leather gloves from a drawer, he pulled them on and kneeled by the bed. It was a terrible thing he was about to do, but he'd convinced himself it was the lesser of two evils. His accomplice, Igor, hadn't needed any convincing.

Petya crawled under the bed until he could reach the cat. Then he grabbed it by the tail and pulled it toward him. It made its terrible, high-pitched screeching sound again and retaliated with its claws, but Petya's dense gloves were like impenetrable armor. A half minute later, the cat was dead—strangled by the same desperate hands.

As Petya gazed into its lifeless eyes, he realized it was the first thing he'd ever killed in his life, and he felt both wretchedly guilty and all powerful at the same time. So many times he'd wanted to kill that cat for waking him up at night, for stinking up the apartment, for pissing in his shoes, and now that he'd finally done it, he didn't know whether to jump for joy or pray for forgiveness.

Igor opened the door, saw the lifeless cat, and asked matter-of-factly, "You know how to skin it?"

Petya shook his head, still trying to convince himself that it had been an act of mercy. After all, the cat was old, half-blind, and had been slowly starving to death. "I'm sure I can figure it out," Petya answered.

"My pa made me skin a squirrel once," said Igor. "It was really hard. I hated it."

As miserably as Petya was handling the sudden decrease in food, Igor was in even worse shape. He moped around the apartment all day, rarely ever going outside.

Petya removed his gloves and picked up the cat. "I'll skin it," he said. "You make sure we've got some hot coals. I put that little stove up on the roof."

While Igor left for the roof, Petya carried the cat into the kitchen and took out the sharpest knife they had. He had just cut the head off when a devilish voice whispered, "You snake. You're going to burn in hell."

Petya spun around quickly, his eyes searching frantically for the voice's owner. Gripping the knife in his hand, he held it out defensively. "Who's there?" he called.

When no one answered and his inspections down the hallway and under the kitchen table came up empty, he wondered if the voices from long ago were coming back to play tricks on his mind.

For much of his life, Petya felt like an impostor—a fraud who only looked like everyone else. *They* didn't hear voices without owners. *They* took sanity for granted. Petya didn't. He couldn't. Sanity to him was the ice of a frozen lake. Most of the time, the ice was thick, and Petya stood firmly on top. But there were hours or days when the ice was thin and cracked loudly as he walked over it. This was his advanced notice that not every face he saw or voice he heard was real. And those isolated instances when the ice gave way and he fell in had resulted in the most terrifying chapters of his life: not being able to tell right from wrong, dreams from reality, genuine voices from imaginary. It was like being caught between two worlds, unable to be fully in one or the other—simultaneously looking in from the outside and out from the inside.

So far, he'd been able to pull himself out of those occasions fairly quickly. But his greatest fear was that one day he'd fall so far through the ice that he'd be stuck underneath—looking up to where he'd once been, longing to be the man he used to be, forever trapped on the wrong side of the ice.

Deciding the voice calling him a snake hadn't been real, Petya calmly returned to skinning the cat. If the voices were indeed coming back, it was vitally important he maintain his composure. He already felt as though his life was only one misstep away from spinning out of control. It was October 8, and he still hadn't been able to find a position that would increase his rations. Except for the small bag of sunflower seeds he'd stolen from Oksana, he was completely out of food. He'd lost twenty-eight pounds in the last six weeks, going from a weight of 206 down to 178. If he hadn't been so overweight before the war started, he might have already starved to death.

Igor trudged into the kitchen with two wooden skewers, and Petya split the chunks of meat and slid them on. Under a gray sky on the roof, they roasted the meat over the stove's orange coals. When it was done, they returned to the kitchen and sprinkled their kabobs with salt and the only seasoning they had left: dried parsley.

Sitting at the kitchen table, Petya chewed each bite thoroughly, pretending it was chicken and not cat. Igor took his skewer and retreated to a far corner, where he ate with darting eyes and intermittent growls.

Petya decided to save his daily bread ration for later. The hard and heavy bread tasted terrible. Filled with barely edible ingredients, it gave him a stomachache every time. Hearing another voice, he deliberated whether it was real or not. "Did you say something?" he asked Igor cautiously.

"Yeah," replied Igor. "You didn't hear me? I asked why God hates us."

"Why does God hate us?" Petya repeated. It was an odd question, especially coming from Igor.

"If he didn't hate us, he'd rescue us. Right?"

Though Petya considered himself an atheist, he had often thought that God was eerily similar to an abandoned adolescent, like Igor. His words and actions resembled not so much a wise, compassionate deity, than a resentful youth with a child's mentality of good and evil, love and vengeance, judgment and eternity.

"Since when did you develop an interest in theology?" asked Petya. It felt strange to him to talk about God and religion so much these days. Before the war, the subject was taboo, but now everywhere he turned were old ladies making the sign of the cross, children saying prayers, and now Igor initiating a discussion on the moral principle of God's actions. It all reminded Petya, agonizingly, of that part of his childhood spent with his aunt—a closeted Baptist who beat him mercilessly for every sin he committed, and even some he didn't.

"What's theology?" asked Igor, wrinkling his pug nose.

"Religion."

Igor swallowed his last bite of food. "Katya talks about it all the time," he said. "She says there's nothing to be afraid of as long as we keep our faith in God." He licked his fingers. "But I don't believe her."

"Maybe God hates us because we haven't praised him enough," Petya said sarcastically. "Or perhaps he's dead, as the philosopher Nietzsche says."

"He's not dead," remarked Igor. "He's just not coming back."

"What?" Petya exclaimed, surprised to hear such a shrewd notion coming from Igor's lips.

"I don't think He's coming back," repeated Igor, "because He's seen what's happened here and He can't face it."

Petya couldn't believe his ears. Did Igor just say what he thought he did, or were the voices conspiring against him once more? Either way, he felt lost. He was accustomed to viewing Igor as a witless juvenile, but could no longer regard him in those terms after what he'd just said.

Gritting his teeth, Petya scowled out the window. He had so much hate for religion. It had poisoned so many people, and they, in turn, had passed that poison on to their children. The whole world was infected. Even here in the Soviet Union, where religion had been banished as a relic from the past, people still worshiped and believed. If he could, Petya would burn every holy book, every church, every synagogue and mosque in the world. People needed to be educated. They needed to understand how cruel and detrimental religion really was.

Though the air raid sirens began their unearthly wailing again, echoing through the cavernous streets and lifeless ruins of collapsed buildings, Petya chose to keep walking. There was a time when he would have run to the nearest shelter, a time when he valued safety above all else, but he was beyond that now.

He was dying. Little by little, day by day, cell by cell. Not an hour passed when he didn't think about that. Let the German planes come and drop a bomb on him. That wouldn't be such a bad way to die. Quick and painless. And symbolic too. What more could a writer ask for?

He was returning from another attempt to get a position that would increase his rations. Although he'd failed, he wasn't bitter about it. He'd learned to lower his expectations to avert having to face the sting of rejection.

There were a lot of lessons he'd learned about protecting himself, like not getting too close to anyone, because they'd eventually be taken away. His parents had been taken from him in the Civil War. Then his aunt had been taken away— arrested for her religious beliefs by the communists and exiled to a remote labor camp. In the orphanage, it seemed that any friend he'd made was sure to be adopted and taken from him. Petya's only saving grace through it all had been his intelligence, and he'd learned to wear it like a coat of armor.

He stopped and glanced at the sky above, then burst out laughing without knowing why. Each day seemed to bring something new and unexplainable into his world. Like now, any direction he turned he saw everything saturated in a strange, purplish tint: the dark, bombed-out buildings, the wet pavement, the streetcars passing slowly and quietly down the tracks. He felt like a ghost walking up the stark streets of a deserted city. Even when others crossed his path, they seemed surreal, as though a backdrop to his exclusive dream.

Sometimes Petya wondered if he really did exist. Perhaps he'd already died and was a lost spirit condemned to haunt the streets of the city he'd loved, but never truly enjoyed while he was alive.

If he thought about it too much, he started to feel terrified since he couldn't prove that anything was real. He didn't know that it wasn't all just a dream, but he did know that, whatever it was, it was beautiful. It was mayhem and despair and destruction, and it was also beautiful beyond words.

When he arrived at his favorite statue in all of Leningrad—one of the few that wasn't surrounded by planks and sandbags—he shivered with cold as the wind gusted. Gazing up at Pushkin, the greatest Russian writer ever, Petya reflected on how he'd live his life differently if given the chance. He decided he'd laugh more at himself, rather than others. He'd take more walks with no destination in mind. He'd be more vulnerable, and less guarded. He'd sleep in on Saturdays and not feel guilty about it. He'd read more poetry, and less news. He'd listen to more music, and less gossip. He'd notice more often when people smiled, and less when they frowned. If he could live his life over again, he'd regularly appreciate the noble scent of the ocean, and the sheer perfection and simplicity of a wave crashing to shore and dissolving into nothingness.

Peeking his head above the rocks, Felix spied Misha walking toward him over the winding dirt road. After seeing Misha wave his right arm high in the air, Felix prepared to light the match. But then Misha unexpectedly fell to the ground. Felix stopped and listened intently, but there was no gunfire or anything else out of the ordinary, just a squirrel chattering in the large oak tree nearby. He glanced at the dynamite he'd wedged into a crack in the rock, deliberating whether to light the fuse and run or go check on Misha, who was lying face down on the road. Since Misha had been drinking heavily that day, Felix suspected he'd merely passed out.

Upon seeing Misha move his arms, then shake his head and slowly climb to his feet, Felix struck the match, lit the dynamite, and scrambled down the slope, jumping the last six feet to the road below.

Misha was still brushing himself off when Felix reached him. "What happened?" asked Felix.

"I don't know," Misha replied. "It was weird. Everything just blacked out all of a sudden."

"You and Dima need to stop drinking that rotgut all day long," chastised Felix.

"No. It wasn't from the alcohol," Misha said. "It was something else."

Felix waited to hear what else it was, but Misha didn't elaborate. They hurried over to the cluster of trees where Dima and another partisan, Yuri, were waiting. Yuri, a bear of a man with wide shoulders, thick forearms, and a massive beard, was the first to meet them.

"What took you so long?" he asked. "I could have done that in half the time."

Felix ignored him and searched for Dima, finding him still sitting on the same fallen tree as when he'd left. Dima was smoking another cigarette and had no reaction whatsoever when the dynamite exploded and filled the air with its deafening boom. He hardly had a reaction to anything anymore. Felix was troubled not only by that, but the apathy, and sometimes downright animosity, that ruled Dima's life these days. Lately, Dima and Misha got drunk together nearly every day.

Yuri forged his way through the thicket of trees to inspect the road, and Felix followed behind. Felix could see right away that they'd been successful. The dynamite had smashed the immense rock and caused a mini avalanche that now blocked the road, making it impossible for German trucks, tanks, or other vehicles to pass.

The four men gathered their things and began marching to the little village of Lestovo where they were to meet up with the rest of the partisans. Several inches of snow covered the ground, and when they stepped, their boots would make either a sucking sound as they sank into the mud, or a crunching sound as they stomped over dead leaves. It was cold and the sun was hidden behind thick clouds, but at least they were all dressed for the weather. With their heavy coats, hats, wool scarves, and insulated leather mittens, they kept warm easily.

Felix walked in front next to Yuri, who was quiet for a change. Yuri had spent the last eight years of his life in a Siberian gulag, and not a day went by when he didn't remind others about it.

After a mile, Felix glanced over his shoulder and saw Misha and Dima lagging behind yet again. He tugged on Yuri's coat, and the two of them stopped to allow their comrades to catch up.

"I'm getting tired of those two drunkards," Yuri complained as he lit a cigarette.

Felix understood his sentiment. He didn't know about Misha's past, but Dima hadn't been the same since the fire at the warehouse. Dima seemed to be lost in his own world, continually muttering unintelligible thoughts and ideas that only he could hear.

"For eight whole years I suffered injustices you can't even imagine," Yuri ranted. "But not once, I tell you, did I ever lose conviction in my country. I knew there would come a day when I would be called upon to serve her." He spat on the ground as he watched Misha and Dima step gingerly around a muddy area. Dima seemed to be the more drunk of the two and appeared to be focusing exclusively on putting one foot in front of the other. "Not like those fools," continued Yuri. "They have no honor. They have no shame!" He shouted the last sentence in their direction, but neither of them acknowledged it.

Felix reflected on his own time spent as a prisoner, but his captors had been Nazis, not Soviets, and he wondered how similar his experience had been to Yuri's. Felix's interrogators had beaten him regularly—sometimes two or three times a day. But Felix had told them nothing. He simply went within himself, blocked out the pain, and instead thought of Katya. When they'd finally got to him was when they'd sat him outside the closed door of the room where Dima was being interrogated. After forcing him to listen to his friend scream and plead for an end to the punishment, they offered to stop torturing Dima—and even let his comrade eat and sleep—if Felix told them some piece of useful information.

"Perhaps you should walk a mile in their shoes before you judge them so harshly," Felix said to Yuri. "You know Dima was captured by the Nazis, and they—"

"What could be worse than *eight* years in Siberia?" injected Yuri. "Nothing. That's what! Did I tell you how in the winter the frost would be three inches thick on the *inside* of the windows? It was so cold in those barns they kept us in that you could see your breath. And we had to work outside all day long where it was twenty degrees below zero. You *never* got warm. A quarter of the men froze to death every winter. You don't know how good you have it here. You get hot food and fresh bread—"

"And booze too," Misha added as he and Dima finally caught up. "Don't forget about that."

Yuri finished his cigarette and flicked the butt at Misha and Dima. It bounced off Dima's coat, but he didn't even notice. A few steps later, Dima tripped and fell to the ground.

"Leave him there," Yuri said. "Serves him right."

Dima made it to his knees, but the prospects of him making it all the way up to his feet looked doubtful.

"Alcohol is the biggest poison man ever invented," Yuri said. "And you two fools are living proof."

Misha started toward Dima, but aborted offering assistance when he saw Felix heading over to his friend. "What on earth possessed them to ever let you out of Siberia?" Misha asked facetiously.

Having heard this story half-a-dozen times, Felix shook his head wearily.

"They set me free to defend my country from the enemy," Yuri answered and launched into his tiresome explanation of how he'd ended up here with the partisans.

Misha winked at Felix when they passed by each other, and Felix understood that Misha was patronizing Yuri. He did it for entertainment.

As Misha strode alongside Yuri, Felix pulled Dima up, then put his arm around him to help him walk.

After half-a-mile in silence, Felix turned to Dima, advising, "You can't go on like this. You're killing yourself. You're going to go blind drinking that concoction the old farmer makes."

"So what if I'm killing myself," Dima said, slurring the words. "What's it to you?"

"I want to help in some way," Felix answered, then paused. "But I don't know what to do."

"You can leave me the hell alone," stammered Dima. "That's what you can do."

"No," Felix said resolutely. "That's the one thing I can't do. I can't just stand by and watch you drown yourself. We're too young for that. You may have given up on yourself, but I haven't."

"Who said I gave up?" Dima replied in an indignant tone. "Just because Misha and I drink a little bit to keep warm, you think I've given up?"

Pleased that Dima was even talking to him, Felix tried provoking him into continuing. He hoped to learn what exactly was eating away at his friend. "Hell yes, you've given up," Felix accused. "Look at you. You're a drunk. You can't even walk by yourself."

Dima pulled away from Felix and began walking on his own, staggering from side to side, but managing to stay on his feet.

"You think you're so damn perfect, don't you?" Dima sneered.

Not wanting the conversation to switch to him, Felix said, "I'm not perfect. But at least I'm not a drunkard. I don't deny what's bothering me. I face it head on, rather than trying to drown it with liquor."

"I don't do that," Dima said defensively. "I'm only trying to ... I mean I want to ... Hell, just leave me alone, will you!" He marched ahead—stumbling and wavering—until he was in front of everyone.

Felix hiked behind Yuri and Misha. Hearing Yuri explain how the Panzers had broken through their lines, Felix knew Yuri was approaching the end of his lengthy story.

"We simply weren't prepared to fight against tanks," said Yuri. "Our entire regiment was in complete chaos only thirty minutes into battle, if you can even call it a battle. I don't think we inflicted a single casualty on them. Anyway, after we were encircled, all the men wanted to surrender, but I wouldn't do it. I said they could be cowards if they wanted, but I wasn't joining them. I took an oath to protect my country, and I was going to make sure I lived to fight another day! I snuck past the German lines and...."

Knowing there was still another five painfully long minutes to the story—boring details about how Yuri made it through a minefield and swamp—Felix tried to cut it short. "So that's how you ended up as a partisan?"

"Yep, that's how it happened," answered Yuri, puffing his chest out. "Been fighting those Nazi pigs behind the lines ever since."

They came to the now familiar village of Lestovo with its two dozen, small, clay houses and the stone church that had been turned into a horse stable by the communists. Felix had already learned about the precarious life of those in villages like Lestovo, and how difficult it was for the partisans to know who to trust. When the partisans weren't there asking for something, then the Nazis were there plundering the villagers' meager possessions and threatening their lives over information on the partisans.

"Weren't there some goats there when we came this way last week?" Misha asked, pointing at a small, empty pen.

"Yes. I remember them too," Felix said. "The Germans probably took them."

The village used to be full of cows, pigs, chickens, and goats, but every time a group of Germans came through, they helped themselves to some livestock. Fortunately, the villagers had enough potatoes, cabbage, beets, and canned raspberries and tomatoes stored away in various hiding places to get them through the winter. They even had enough food to sometimes give to the partisans.

"The Germans are such fools to treat the villagers so badly," commented Misha.

"I agree," Felix said. "For all their proficiency at invasions, they're clueless about how to make friends out of former enemies. It's like their plans of conquest covered every detail, except what to do once they won."

"They haven't won yet," said Yuri, switching his rifle from his left hand to his right.

"I know," Felix replied, "and they're not going to either."

They all stopped and looked at a crude wooden cross marking a new grave. A bouquet of dried flowers rested on top of the freshly-dug dirt.

"The worse they treat the villagers, the more our numbers grow," remarked Yuri. "I'm glad the Nazis are so brutal with them. People are getting a taste of what life under their rule would be like."

Felix studied Yuri's face for signs of 'the look,' as he now called it. Felix had seen it three more times since first spying it on Fedushkin's face. And each time, the man had died before the sun rose the next day. Why he saw this foreshadowing of imminent death, Felix had no idea. It happened when he least expected it, usually during a meaningless conversation or when their eyes met briefly as they passed by one another.

Seeing nothing on Yuri's face, Felix breathed a sigh of relief and turned his attention to the gathering villagers up ahead. As he drew nearer, he concluded Olga must have ordered one of the villagers to be taken into custody. The man's wife, who wore a thin, white apron and had been peeling potatoes on their porch, peered nervously at the two partisans holding her husband by the arms. Men in tattered old coats like the partisans wore, women with scarves wrapped around their heads, and a handful of wide-eyed children were listening to Olga's diatribe.

"The Nazis have started a war of extermination!" she hollered. "They want to destroy Russians, annihilate us from the face of the planet. The only way to survive is if we all fight them to the death. And here," she said, pointing to the man in custody, "is a traitor, who, instead of fighting the Nazis, has chosen to help them."

"Vladimir, what did you do?" one of the men in the crowd asked.

"I'll tell you what he did," Olga responded. "He told the Germans where the farm machinery was hidden."

Vladimir, a bony man with long arms that hung nearly to his knees, hung his head, all but confirming the accusation's veracity.

"We have no choice, but to win this war against the fascist aggressors," Olga said. She motioned to Yuri, who stepped forward and aimed his rifle at the man. "And this is what happens to German collaborators. Let this be a lesson to everyone." Olga then nodded to Yuri, but Felix pulled the barrel of Yuri's rifle down before he could shoot.

"Why not give him a chance to redeem himself?" asked Felix. He hated speaking up, but neither could he stand by and watch this.

The villagers turned their attention to him while Olga's face turned beet-red.

"There's no room for compromise," Olga yelled. "The only way we'll smash the Nazis is with an iron fist."

Felix felt nauseous and tense, but took a deep breath and continued. "Give him a second chance," he said to the villagers. "He's made a mistake—as we all do. Give him an opportunity to make up for it. Perhaps we could use him as a double agent and set a trap for the Germans."

"There are no second chances in war," alleged Olga. She then fixed her eyes on Yuri and said, "I order you to shoot."

"There are always second chances," contended Felix, resting a hand on Yuri's shoulder. "This man was in a Soviet prison not long ago for crimes against the state. He was given a second chance, and here he is, defending his country by fighting the Nazis behind the lines every day."

A few of the villagers nodded their heads. "And if he betrays us again?" one of them asked. "What then?"

Another villager answered him. "If he snitches again," he said, "we'll carry out justice ourselves—the old fashioned way, with a rope and a tree."

"Yes. He's not going anywhere," Vladimir's wife called from the porch. "Give him a second chance."

The crowd looked to Vladimir. "The Germans offered me money to tell them," he said, raising his weathered face to them. "But I wouldn't do it. Then they threatened to burn down our house, and I didn't know what to do. Where would we live? How would we make it through the winter without a house?" He gaped expectantly at the faces of his neighbors. "If you give me another chance, I will make up for it."

The partisans and villagers all turned toward Olga now. She pulled her dark wool hat from her head, spat on the ground, then wiped her mouth with the back of her hand. "Of course, we'll give you another chance, comrade," she said reservedly. Then she signaled to the two men holding Vladimir's arms to let go. "And if the Germans burn down your village because of this traitor," she announced to the crowd, "you'll have Comrade Varilensky here to thank."

Felix caught her sneering at him—the rapidly fading sunlight glinting off her gold tooth. He was relieved the confrontation was over. No doubt Olga hated him, but he couldn't let that stop him from being who he was. He answered to no one but his own guiding conscience, that voice inside him that saw everything so clearly.

"Let's move out!" commanded Olga. As the motley group of partisans began departing the village, she waited for Felix, then pulled him aside.

"You think you're pretty smart, don't you kike?" she whispered in his ear.

"What I *think*," Felix said, ripping his arm from her grasp, "is that we're all in this together—you, me, the villagers, everyone. And we're not going to win this war until we start acting like it."

"I've brought down many a man sneakier than you," she replied. "Be happy with your little victory here today, because it was your first and your last."

The partisans trudged the mile-and-a-half to their camp in silence. The clouds had dispersed, allowing Felix to spot the crescent moon low on the horizon. Yuri had told him that in the village he grew up in, they called it a Blood Moon during the month of October. Felix thought it appropriate given the number of lives being lost across Russia recently.

Earlier that day, he'd heard that Kiev had fallen and that as many as 600,000 Red Army troops had been taken prisoner there. Kiev, in Felix's native Ukraine, was the mother of all Russian cities, making the news particularly devastating.

The whole world was watching Leningrad now. If the city couldn't hold out, then Hitler would move all the troops stationed there to the battle for Moscow. With Moscow barely holding on as it was, a couple hundred thousand additional German troops would surely tip the balance. And if Moscow fell, then all of Russia would likely fall.

Felix contemplated how only a sliver of the moon could be seen, as though it had shrunk and would soon be extinguished. But the entire moon was still there, he knew, even if one couldn't see any trace of it. It was a matter of faith.

"Guzman!" Petya shouted irritably and banged on the door again. "Open up. It's me, Petya. Are you there?"

Petya waited a few seconds, then kicked the bottom of the door. He was cold and hungry and didn't like having to stand in the hallway any longer than he had to. "Guzman, we're all moving into Katya's apartment today. I've come to help you. Open the door."

Katya had invited everyone on the floor—Petya, Oksana, and Guzman—to move into her apartment so they could conserve their scarce firewood. Katya's apartment was also the only one on the floor that still had windows. All the rest had sheets of plywood and were as dark as night no matter if the sun was shining or not.

No one would be expected to share their food, but they could help one another out in other ways to make it through these difficult times. Katya was particularly worried about the listless Guzman, who seemed to both move and speak less each passing day. Oksana and Petya's roommate, Boris, hadn't been heard from in a month, and Oksana speculated he was either dead or had found a way out of the city to rejoin his wife and daughter. Petya had already searched Boris's room for food, tea, vodka, or cigarettes, and had come up empty.

"Guzman! I'm leaving if you don't answer the door," Petya called. He knew Guzman was there. The old man was too weak to go anywhere.

Just as Petya was starting to wonder if the old painter might be dead, he heard some shuffling and a few weak coughs from inside the apartment. As Guzman opened the door, Petya complained, "I've been knocking on your door for five minutes."

Guzman, covered from head to toe in dark blankets, said nothing in response. His face was pale and ghostly. His eyes bulged.

Frightened by his haggard appearance, Petya took a step back. "How are you feeling?" he asked uneasily.

"Like a sprinn chiign," Guzman mumbled.

Petya cupped his hand to his ear. "Like a what?"

"Like a spring chicken," repeated Guzman.

It took him a second, but Petya realized the old man was making a joke. Petya laughed, then added, "Yeah, like a spring chicken in a wolf's den."

Guzman managed a weak smile, then invited Petya in.

"What do you need to take to Katya's?" Petya asked as he inspected the cluttered apartment.

It was obvious Shostakovich hadn't been there to play the piano in a long time. It was covered with newspapers and dirty clothes, and the bench was lying on its side.

"My pillow, sheets, and blankets," answered Guzman in between labored breaths. The hair from his long nose had started to blend into his newly grown beard, and his thin lips could barely be seen behind the curly black and gray hair that now covered his face. "My hat and coat too."

Petya considered arguing with him about that, because the next time Guzman was going to make it outside would likely be when they took his body to the cemetery. His health had declined significantly in the past two weeks.

The apartment smelled like urine, and Petya traced it to a bedpan in the corner of the hallway. He emptied the bowl out the window, as everyone did these days, then collected the items Guzman wanted and lugged them to Katya's apartment. When he returned, Guzman was still standing in the same place. Leaning against a wall for support, he was staring at an oil-on-canvas painting hanging opposite him. "I painted that when I was twenty-seven," he announced.

Petya glanced at the painting of the Winter Palace, but wasn't sure what to say about it. All the colors were very dark—the sky almost black—and the palace itself wasn't much brighter.

"Isn't it the ugliest thing you ever saw?" said Guzman.

Catching the slight smirk on Guzman's gaunt face, Petya chuckled. "It is, actually."

"Good. Good. There's hope for you yet, my boy," replied Guzman, patting Petya on the shoulder.

"Do you want to take it to Katya's?"

"No. It's better left here—where it's always been."

"What else do you want me to get?"

Guzman scratched his chin as he mulled Petya's question. "My boots," he finally answered.

"What about food? You want me to get it? Or do you want to do that yourself?"

"Food?" Guzman said. "What's that?"

Petya laughed again, but wasn't sure whether or not to believe he had no food. "All right. You make your way over there, and I'll get your boots and gather up your firewood."

Guzman dragged his feet down the hallway of his apartment, keeping close to the wall and coughing every few feet. When he reached the door, he turned and called, "Vanya!"

Petya gave him a puzzled look, but before he could say anything, Guzman continued.

"Don't forget to feed my parakeet while I'm gone. Promise me you won't forget, Vanya."

Petya thought he might be joking again, but Guzman's hollow stare said otherwise. "I won't forget," said Petya. "I promise." Losing one's mind was something Petya could sympathize with.

"Thank you, Vanya. I know I can count on you," Guzman mumbled as he continued on his way to Katya's apartment.

When Petya finished transferring Guzman's things, he found the old man rambling incoherently on Katya's couch.

"We'll meet again one day, Marfusha. I promise," said Guzman. "Life is so very long and we're so very young. Vanya! Let's not be late this time. Have them get the sleigh ready."

Igor was curled up in a thick, cushioned chair on the other side of the room. "Who's he talking to?" he asked Petya.

"Ghosts," replied Petya.

Returning to Guzman's apartment, Petya scoured the kitchen for food. He didn't find any, but did come across something splendid—a tiny glass container of black tea. Petya hadn't had tea in a month and missed it even more than food. Deciding to take advantage of Guzman's apartment's peace and quiet, as well as the piping hot ceramic stove, Petya made a cup of tea and settled in to write.

Convinced that great works of art were birthed through suffering, he persisted at his writing despite the cold and the slow, daily starvation. He didn't fear death so much as being a failure. Petya was convinced he was destined to write something profound that would have an impact on society. All the suffering he'd underwent in his life, including the current calamity of Leningrad under siege, was but preparation for this work of genius. All the pain and sorrow in his life was for educational purposes only. His success was assured—as long as he stayed on the right side of the ice of sanity.

When inspiration didn't strike, Petya randomly selected one of Guzman's books and tossed it on top of the coals. Then he held his frigid hands over top of the stove and gazed at an orange pot that had been home to a plant that had long since died. Sticking out from underneath the pot was a piece of paper, and after retrieving it, Petya discovered it was Guzman's ration card.

Tucking the card in his pocket, Petya went to investigate a knock at one of the doors on the floor. In the dim light of the hallway, he spied a uniform-clad courier in front of Katya's apartment.

"Can I help you?" asked Petya as he eyed the package the man held under his arm.

"I'm looking for Katerina Selenaya," the man replied. "Do you know if she's home?"

Petya limped over and unlocked the door, then held his finger to his lips. "Shh," he said. "The boy is sleeping." He didn't know if Igor, or Guzman for that matter, were actually sleeping, but he didn't want them to overhear. "You have a package for her? I can give it to her for you."

The man stiffened and shifted the package to his other arm. "I have explicit instructions to give it only to Katerina Selenaya," he said. "I ask you again, comrade, is she home?"

"No. She won't be home until late this evening," said Petya. "I'm her brother. Can't you just give it to me, and I'll give it to her when she returns?"

The man licked his chapped lips as he studied Petya.

"Surely you don't want to have to come back here again this evening," added Petya.

"You're her brother?"

Petya nodded. "You see," he said, pointing at the number on the apartment door, "we even live in the same apartment."

"Then why did you just come from that other apartment?"

"I was over there helping our neighbor," Petya said, trying to sound congenial. "He's ill and not doing so well." Petya tried to get a look at the writing on the top of the box. "Who is the package from? Is it from our father?"

"No. It's from a ..." The man tilted the package toward the light coming from the apartment. "It's from a Comrade Shostakovich."

"Ahh, it's from Dmitry," exclaimed Petya. "We've been expecting it for some time now. We'd nearly given up on it."

Petya held out his arms, and the man hesitantly handed it over.

"Don't worry, comrade," Petya assured him. "I'll make sure my sister gets it." He quickly closed the door and locked it, then listened for the hopeful sounds of the man's footsteps. But instead came another knock on the door.

Gripping the package tight, Petya held his breath and remained quiet. After a few seconds, he heard the man mutter, "Ah, to hell with it," and walk down the hall.

When the footsteps were long gone, Petya returned to Guzman's apartment with the package. His hands trembled, both from weakness and from excitement, as he tore open the box and read the letter lying on top:

Dear Katya,

I made some calls as you requested and found out what happened to your father. I'm sorry to have to be the one to tell you this, but I was informed that he died of a heart attack while in Moscow. Such is life that all our best men are taken from us when we need them most. He will be sorely missed.

I've pulled a few strings to send you this little package, because I worry terribly about you and Guzman getting enough to eat. I hope this finds you in good health and spirits. I'm sure Guzman has been telling you how things were better "in the old days." But don't listen to him. The times are rough now. There's no arguing that. But the more Russia suffers, the more her soul shines bright. It does no good to reminisce about the good old days, because there were none. Times were rough before the Germans invaded, and times were rough before the revolution. The tsar was a butcher, and the people of Russia were poor and hungry. Russia was in constant turmoil and the vast majority of people were miserable while the fat bourgeois pissed on the backs of the workers and peasants. How conveniently the great Western humanists forget this! They'll never understand the people of Russia. They don't want to understand, because we're different than they. Our skin may be the same color, but we're nothing like them and they can't accept that. But I'm through thinking about them. Devil take them and their smug lives contemplating how they're always right!

My apologies for the tirade. I've been a nervous wreck lately. I hope this letter and package get to you as it has been no small feat. I am in Kuibyshev now, and I was able to buy three cans of caviar, a bottle of vodka, and some cigarettes here. The vodka is the real thing, not that lethal stuff the peasants make and then pour into empty vodka bottles. I've included the vodka and cigarettes because I know they're in high demand there and you should be able to trade for something you really need, be it food or whatever. The caviar I leave at your discretion. You can probably trade it for more food, but if it's not worth it, then eat it yourself. These items are meant for you and

Guzman equally, though I beg of you not to show him the vodka or cigarettes, for I know he'll want them. Please trade for them first. I don't know if I'll be able to get any more packages to you, but I'll try.

I miss my dear Leningrad. I hope she's holding up well. Take care of her for me.

- Dmitry

PS I've finished putting the final touches on my Seventh Symphony. I hope to have it performed soon—in honor of you brave Leningraders.

Petya set the letter aside and dug through the wadded-up newspaper in the box until he found the treasure. It was a beautiful sight: that brand new bottle of vodka, those cigarettes, and those cans of caviar. He nearly wept at the sight of them.

"Look at them," decried Yuri, nodding toward some people behind Felix.

Felix didn't need to turn and look. He knew who Yuri was referring to and what they were doing.

"It's not even noon yet, and the two of them are already drunk," Yuri continued. "I think it's past time our leader stops tending to her rats and puts an end to this." He scowled and left Felix for Olga's tent.

The rats Yuri referred to were actually five baby mice that Olga had found in the woods and kept as pets. Felix scanned the sky, wondering if the sun would be successful today in its never-ending struggle to break through the dreary clouds of autumn. As he made his way through the muddy snow toward the fire to warm his hands, Misha noticed him.

"Hey there, Varilensky," called Misha, slurring a few words.

Dima had his eyes closed and was holding his head in his hands.

"I told you that stuff would make you go blind, Dima," Felix said righteously.

"Go to the devil," replied Dima.

Felix poured hot water into a tin can to make tea. "No. I think I'd rather just sit here," he said, finding a seat between Dima and Misha.

"Yes, stay," encouraged Misha with a hiccup. "You're just in time. I had an epiphany about God and was about to enlighten Dima."

Misha offered Felix the flask he and Dima had been passing back and forth, but Felix waved it away.

"I say before you that God was—without a doubt—drunk when he created man," announced Misha.

"That's not an epiphany," said Felix. "That's lunacy."

"I'll explain," continued Misha, his head swaying slightly back and forth. "He'd been drinking a lot of his most recent creation, wine, and was feeling all this love and peace and joy. He was overflowing with it, and that's when he created man. He thought man was the best thing he'd ever created, but he sobered up later on and realized what a mistake he'd made."

"So what's your point?" Felix asked.

"My point, dear comrade, is that the only way to know God is by attaining the same inebriated state He was in when He created us."

"So that's why you're always getting drunk?"

"You got it," replied Misha, taking another sip from the flask. "It's the only time this world makes sense."

Dima lifted his head from his hands and spoke up. "No. You're wrong. God was completely sober when he created man."

Felix peered at Dima's bloodshot eyes and unshaven face. He was surprised to hear Dima comment on God. Dima usually chided others for their infantile beliefs in an omnipotent deity or else argued with them that evolution had already proved God did not exist.

"He knew what he was doing," Dima continued. "That's how He is."

Misha raised his eyebrows, looking puzzled. "How is He?"

"Spiteful," Dima said bitterly.

Nobody spoke after that. Felix poured more hot water into his tin cup while Misha rolled a cigarette. Dima leaned in toward the fire with his arms on his knees, studying the flask in his hand. After taking a drink, he stood and wavered in place, then shook his fist at the sky, yelling, "Damn you, God!"

Afraid Dima was so drunk he might fall into the fire, Felix readied himself to prevent it. He wanted to shake some sense into his friend, but knew it wouldn't help. Whatever dark place Dima was caught in, it was his hurdle alone to overcome.

Muttering that he needed to piss, Dima turned to the woods, but not before Felix caught a glimpse of Dima's face and saw, to his great horror, 'the look.'

Felix denied it at first, convincing himself it had been a mistake, but then he gave in to the crushing realization that—like Fedushkin and the others—Dima would not live to see the sun of a new day. Unable to bear the thought, Felix vowed to protect his friend. He would personally ensure that no harm came to Dima for the rest of the day.

Yuri stormed out of Olga's tent, marched to the campfire, and snatched the flask from Misha. "The party's over, you miserable drunkards," he declared.

Unfazed, Misha pulled a twig out of the fire and lit his cigarette. As Yuri emptied the flask on the muddy ground, Dima returned from the woods, yelling angrily, "What the hell do you think you're doing?"

"Something that should have been done a long time ago," Yuri answered. "I'm through standing around watching you two contaminate this group."

"Then perhaps you'd like to sit," Dima said heatedly. He clenched his hands into fists and took a wild swing at Yuri's face. The punch landed squarely on Yuri's cheek, and he retaliated with a kick to Dima's groin that sent him wincing to the ground in pain.

While other partisans gathered at a distance to watch the fight, Felix rushed in to the middle of it. "Stop it!" he shouted, but Dima, back on his feet, was already rushing at Yuri.

Utilizing the skills he'd mastered in the Russian martial art form, sambo, he caught Dima as he went by, using his own force against him to force him to the ground. Dima—muddied, but undaunted—staggered to his feet while Felix restrained the much larger Yuri. "Just let it go, you two," Felix warned, but neither man heeded him. Dima charged again, and Felix, in trying to simultaneously protect Dima and stop the fight, was struck by two hard blows: one to the middle of the back, and another that landed on his jaw. He couldn't tell who had thrown which punch, but it didn't matter. He wrapped his right leg behind Yuri's legs, then in one swift push, sent him to the ground. Then he slipped around behind Dima and locked his arms up.

Olga arrived on the scene, shoving people out of her way. "What the devil is going on here?" she demanded. Spotting Yuri with blood trickling from a cut on his face, and Dima struggling to free himself from Felix's hold, she growled at Felix, "You again? I warned you!"

A young woman spoke up. "It wasn't him," she called out. "He was trying to break up the fight."

"Silence!" chided Olga.

As Yuri fled to his tent, Felix released his hold on Dima's arms.

"Consider this your last warning," Olga said menacingly. "Next time you get the shack."

The shack was a tiny, crude shed with neither plumbing nor heat. The last man to serve the standard three-day, three-night sentence there had died of pneumonia a week after his release.

Dima stomped away into the woods. Felix noticed blood in his mouth, and that a tooth was now loose.

"Varilensky, you've earned yourself double-guard duty for the next week," said Olga. Then she grunted, spat over her shoulder, and walked away.

As the crowd dispersed, Felix remained by the campfire, stretching his aching back from side to side. The young woman who had spoken up in his defense approached and asked, "Why didn't you say anything? I saw what happened."

Felix had seen her for the first time only a few days ago. He didn't even know her name yet. "You wouldn't understand," he answered flatly.

"Try me," she said with a smile.

Felix gave up on trying to ease the discomfort in his back and glanced at her. She was cute, with short brown hair that curled inward at the ends and eyes the color of emeralds. He liked how she scrunched up her nose when she smiled.

"Comrade Leminskaya," Olga yelled from the entrance of her tent. "Come here, please."

Felix was jarred by Olga's use of the word "please." He couldn't recall her ever using that term before.

Before departing, the petite woman put her hands on her hips and addressed Felix once more. "If you want me to walk on your back later, let me know. I've been told I'm pretty good at walking over men," she said with a wink.

When she reached Olga's tent, Felix overheard Olga warn her, "Stay away from that troublemaker."

Misha—who hadn't budged from his place by the fire during the entire melee—took a drag from his cigarette and remarked, "I think Natasha likes you."

"Who?" asked Felix.

"Natasha. That little temptress you just talked to. She joined last week. The Nazis burned down her house."

Misha offered Felix his cigarette, but Felix waved it away. "Oh, that's right," said Misha. "I forgot you don't smoke. Anyway, Olga seems to have taken a liking to her."

"To who?"

"To *Natasha*. What's wrong with you?"

"Nothing," lied Felix. The truth was he couldn't stop thinking about seeing 'the look' on Dima's face.

"Well, a roll in the hay with her will clear your mind. She's really charming— not to mention a great body." Finished with his cigarette, Misha flicked it into the fire. "Exactly the way I like 'em," he continued. "Except every time I get her alone, she just asks me about you—where you're from, why you're so quiet. You should let her give you that backrub sometime."

"I don't think a backrub is going to do any good," said Felix. "Something feels out of place in my spine."

"That's not the point," Misha groaned. "It doesn't matter if your back is really hurt or not. The point is getting her in bed, and a nice backrub is a great way to start. Boy, I've got so much to teach you."

Felix found his can of tea and took a sip. "I already have a girl."

"So? What's that got to do with anything?" Misha ran his fingers along his upper lip, then blurted, "Wait. You're not talking about Anna, I hope. Listen to me, you don't want anything to do with her. I learned that the hard way."

"No. Not Anna."

"Well, who then?"

"She's in Leningrad still."

"Your girl's in Leningrad?" Misha said incredulously. "Well, you've got to move on then. This is war. Who knows if you'll even be alive tomorrow? You might as well have some fun while you can. That's what booze and women are for—to make life bearable. When's the last time you saw her?"

"The ninth of September."

"Are you serious? It's the middle of October now. You have to get on with your life. I'm sure she's moved on by now." Misha tapped the side of his head with his index finger. "If there's one thing I know, it's women. When the rooster's away, the hens will play."

The fire crackled and popped, and Felix finished the last of his tea. "I'm going back to Leningrad as soon as I can," he announced. "We'll be together again soon."

"You want to get *in* to Leningrad? Are you crazy? The Germans have it blockaded and the whole city is starving. You're much better off here. We've got food, alcohol, and even pretty women to keep you warm at night. What more could you ask for?"

Felix stood and turned to go.

"Let me introduce you to Natasha later," suggested Misha. "A night with her will lift your spirits and make you forget all about this girl from Leningrad."

"No, thanks," Felix said over his shoulder. "I don't want anyone else."

Back in his tent, Felix found Dima fast asleep and snoring loudly. Felix removed his muddy boots and lay down on his own bunk. After several minutes, he closed his eyes, and in that space where one is no longer awake nor asleep, he saw Katya. Under a gray winter sky, she was strolling in the park. In a white fur coat and hat, she was as beautiful as he'd ever seen her. When big fluffy snowflakes glided lazily down to earth, she stopped and caught one on her tongue.

There was a dark, ominous figure approaching from behind. Neither man nor beast, it grew in size as it crept closer. Felix called out to Katya, but she couldn't hear his warning, and as the phantom overtook her, Felix tried to scream, but instead woke up.

He stared at the ceiling of the tent, then attempted to return to the park with Katya, longing to feel the touch of her skin, hear her childlike laugh, taste her lips on his. Failing at that, he began scheming how to get back to Leningrad. He had to know if she was alright.

First, everyone told him to wait because the Germans were going to overtake the city any day. When that didn't transpire, they told him to wait because the Red Army inside the city would be breaking out soon. That hadn't happened either, and Felix was tired of waiting. Katya's birthday was tomorrow, and it was going to be a long day knowing he had to spend it without her.

Hearing some movement, Felix turned his head just in time to see Dima taking his pocket watch from his hiding place under his bunk. As Dima looked about the tent suspiciously, Felix pretended to be asleep.

Once Dima slipped outside, Felix put his boots back on and followed. In addition to wanting to protect his friend, Felix wanted to know where exactly Dima was going with his most precious possession.

Felix trailed him all the way to the village of Lestovo, where he watched Dima disappear into the house of the old farmer who sold the homemade booze. When Dima came back out, he was smoking a cigarette and had a large glass bottle in his hand.

Dima never saw the fallen branch which was to play such an instrumental role in his life. On his way back to camp, he'd stepped on it awkwardly, crashing hip first to the forest floor. He'd had to bite his coat sleeve afterward to keep from crying out in agony.

Now that the throbbing had subsided somewhat, he checked his bottle of booze to ensure it hadn't broken. Satisfied it wasn't leaking, he lay on the ground, holding up his ankle and deliberating what to do next. He was roughly halfway between Lestovo and camp—about a mile each way—and doubted he could hobble to either.

To get rid of the pine cone poking him in the back, he slid over a few inches on the thin blanket of snow. Besides a woodpecker battering a tree in the distance, it was quiet, but after only a minute or two, he heard someone walking his way. Straining to see if they were friend or foe, Dima caught a glimpse of the man and concluded he was both. It was Felix.

"What happened?" Felix asked as he drew near.

"I twisted my ankle on that branch," replied Dima, pointing at the moss-covered stick partially hidden in the snow.

Felix shook his head disappointedly. "It's going to be dark soon," he said. "If it's going to take longer than usual, we'd better get a start now. Let me help you up."

Dima refused Felix's outstretched hand. "No. I think I broke something. It's never hurt this bad before."

"Then let me see if I can carry you." Felix tried to lift Dima over his shoulder, but groaned in misery and nearly collapsed to the earth himself. "I can't carry you. That blow to my back earlier today messed up my spine."

"How ironic," muttered Dima.

Felix glanced at the sun low on the horizon. "What time is it?"

Dima shrugged.

"Don't have your pocket watch, huh?" Felix pursed his lips and shook his head again.

"No," said Dima.

"I didn't think so."

Noticing Felix leering at the full bottle of liquor lying next to him, Dima asked sarcastically, "You want some?"

"I'm surprised you haven't opened it yet and started drinking," Felix said in an equally derisive tone.

"I'm through drinking."

"Ha," scoffed Felix.

Dima carefully stood up on one leg, then began slowly shifting his weight to his leg with the injured ankle. Before getting halfway, he shrank back to the ground with a whimper. "Damn, that hurts," he said dejectedly. "I can't put any weight at all on it. Guess I'll be sleeping here tonight."

Felix glared at him. "What the hell is wrong with you? You think this is some kind of game? You'll freeze to death if you have to spend the night out here."

Dima shrugged. "Probably."

Felix crossed his arms across his chest and kicked at the ground with his boots.

"What?" asked Dima.

"Nothing."

"Don't give me that. I've known you too long. You only do that when there's something you want to say. What is it?"

"It's *you*," Felix replied. "What happened to you? Where's the Dima I once knew? The one who refused to give up? The one who laughed and danced and told jokes? The one with those big ideas and big ambitions?"

It was a fair question. Felix had a right to know. "I'll tell you what happened," Dima said as he pulled out a cigarette and stuck it in his mouth.

"All my life I've been waiting for that time when I would have everything together—when all the pieces of my life would fall into place." He struck a match and lit the cigarette. "And they did. Everything came together when the war started. I felt both competent and confident. I knew my place in the world."

"And so?" asked Felix.

"*So,*" Dima continued. "Then everything fell apart again. I always thought that once you got everything together, it was supposed to stay together."

Felix squatted next to him. "You know what my dad would say to me when I was feeling like you are now? He'd say, 'The dog who always feels sorry for itself will try like hell, but never catch a fox.'"

"What the devil does that mean?"

"He'd never tell me," Felix said with a laugh. "He'd just say, 'Don't you forget that.' And I haven't!"

Dima chuckled.

"But I've thought about it for years now," added Felix, "and I think it means that having pity for your situation in life is self-defeating. We can't control certain things. If we dwell on our shortcomings or failures, we'll never accomplish what we most desire."

Dima inhaled deeply on his cigarette and then blew the smoke over his head. "I wish my father had given me that advice. You know what he told me when he gave me the pocket watch on my sixteenth birthday?"

Felix shook his head.

"He told me, 'You're a man now. Go make a name for yourself.'"

Felix took a drink of water from his canteen and looked at the setting sun once more. "That was all your father knew. There's no rule that says we have to repeat the mistakes of our parents."

"Too late for that," Dima said with a sigh. He finished his cigarette and shoved the butt into the snow. "I think you should go."

"Where?"

"Anywhere," Dima said. "You should just leave."

"Why?"

"Because I'm already dead—that's why."

The sun set another inch on the horizon, and the wind scattered snow flurries around the forest. Felix stood and kicked at the ground again, then marched away without another word. The sound of his departing footsteps burned Dima's ears.

Energetic squirrels with thick, cinnamon-brown fur leapt from branch to branch, tree to tree. A nearby owl eyed them intently, but didn't move from its perch. Dima inspected his swollen ankle, surprised at how big it was. It no longer hurt, but that was because both of his legs were now numb from the cold.

Leaning his back against the tree, he propped up his injured leg on a nearby rock and gazed at the snowflakes' exotic dance down to the earth. He hadn't paid so much attention to falling snow since he was a kid. Ever since he'd come to the understanding that what was important in life was what other people thought of you, he'd forgotten how magnificent snowflakes were. He caught a few with his gloves and was mesmerized by their geometric intricacy.

When the lone cloud birthing the snowflakes moved on, Dima turned his attention to the stars. He'd forgotten about them too. Able to see millions of tiny lights overhead, he was astounded at the sky's vastness. He doubted he'd ever seen so many stars in his life. His grandmother had told him that each star was a guardian angel for someone, and he tried now to determine which one was his. Was it the bright one in the Ursula Major constellation? No, he decided, it had to be that faint one in the thick fog of the Milky Way—the star whose light appeared to still be shining, even though it had probably burned out a thousand years ago.

Hearing the unmistakable sound of twigs being snapped and dead leaves being crunched under the snow, Dima was relieved that Felix had come back for him. "Over here," Dima called.

But there was no reply and the sounds stopped. Dima peered through the snow-covered forest, but couldn't make out anything in the scarce light. "Felix? Is that you?"

Again there was no response, but the movement began again. And Dima heard not one, but two, sets of footsteps. As they drew nearer, they were accompanied by whispers, but not the poetic way that Russians whispered, but instead gruff and stilted. Then he distinctly heard the German word, "slowly." Dima knew that word well from his days as a German prisoner of war. His interrogator always said "slowly" when commanding a subordinate to burn Dima's skin with a cigar.

Dima's rifle lay by his side, but he didn't pick it up. In his haste to leave camp, he'd neglected to ensure it had ammunition. He strained to hear every noise the forest made. *Snap*, came a sound from his right. *Crunch*, came a sound from his left. The Germans were converging on him from opposite directions. He could see a faint outline of one of them hiding behind tree. Then the one on Dima's right sprinted from out of the dark to within twenty-five yards.

Convinced he was about to die, Dima never imagined it would be like this—so lacking in glory, so all alone.

Though he didn't know all the words, he thought to recite the Lord's Prayer, but then decided against it. He didn't believe in heaven. If he was going to die, he was going to that place where one was neither dreaming nor awake, the place where nothing existed, not even himself.

The two shadows now conversed openly in German, and Dima expected any second to hear a grenade rolling through the leaves. But instead, they kept moving from tree to tree, getting closer and closer, until they were no more than ten yards away. Then the German on the left announced in badly broken Russian, "Soviet soldier, surrender."

With neither gun nor grenade to defend himself, Dima raised his hands above his head and replied in Russian, "I surrender."

"Coming. Coming," Petya sang as he hurried down the hallway to answer the door. Expecting Katya's voice, he asked cheerfully, "Who is it?" Today was her birthday, and he'd invited her over for a celebratory dinner in his old apartment.

"It's Igor," came the response.

Petya's good mood, enhanced by a shot of vodka and the anticipation of spending time with Katya, was immediately imperiled. Grudgingly opening the door, he scowled down at Igor's grimy face. He was sure the boy hadn't taken a bath in at least a month and a half now. "She's not coming over, is she?" Petya asked with an air of resignation.

Igor furrowed his eyebrows and pulled his dingy blankets tighter around himself. "*Who's* not coming over?"

"Katya."

"How should I know if she's coming over? She ain't home yet."

"What do you mean? She told me she'd be home by seven thirty tonight." Hearing a squeaky drawer open and close, he glanced down the hall at Katya's apartment. "You little devil," he exclaimed. "She's there. You're just playing games with me."

"No. That's Oksana," said Igor.

Petya scratched the back of his neck, then held his hand to his cheek in thought. "Well, then what do you want?" he asked irritably.

"Oksana says she knows we killed her cat, and—"

"Shh! Not so loud." Petya pulled Igor inside his apartment and listened for more noises coming from Katya's apartment. "You never mind what that crazy old nag says," he whispered. "She can't prove anything."

"But she says she knows ways of getting even," Igor whined, "and that I'm not going to like it. She said if I tell her what I know that I won't get in trouble, only you will."

Petya gripped Igor's blankets and pulled him to within a few inches of his face. "You rat on me," he threatened, "and you'll be sorry. You better just keep your mouth shut."

Hearing someone coming up the stairs, Petya tried to determine who it was based on their footsteps. But everyone went up and down the stairs so slowly and carefully these days that he couldn't differentiate them from one another. When the person got to the third floor, Petya leaned out his doorway and saw by the dim light that it was Katya. "Good evening, Katya," he called out. "Are you ready for your birthday surprise?"

"Hi, Petya. Yes. I'm very excited. I was thinking about it the whole trip home." She peered down the hall at Petya and added, "Oh my, you look so nice. I can't come over wearing this. Let me change and I'll be right over."

After Katya ducked into her apartment, Petya patted Igor on the head and shoved him out to the cold hall. "We'll be fine. We just need to stick together. All right?" He didn't wait for Igor's response before closing the door.

While combing his hair again in front of the mirror, Petya rehearsed his plans one last time. An evening alone with Katya was a golden opportunity that he'd been planning for the entire week. He rubbed the last few drops of his cologne on his face and neck, brushed lint off his sweater, then crammed the items on top of his desk into a drawer. As he was smoothing out wrinkles in his bedspread, he heard a knock and then Katya's voice.

Whistling as he limped to the apartment door, he opened it and invited her in. Then he bowed regally, took her hand, pressed his lips to it and said, "Bon jour, mademoiselle."

She grinned. "Oh, you Frenchmen are so debonair," she said with a giggle. She was wearing a black sweater with knitted red and yellow flowers on the front and tiny blue ones on the sleeves. She'd been letting her hair grow longer of late, and it now reached the middle of her neck. Two earrings with sparkling, rose-colored gems dangled from her ears.

What Petya was drawn to more than anything, though, were her long black eyelashes and chestnut-brown eyes. He could look into those eyes forever and never tire of it.

After escorting her to his room, he closed the door behind them.

"Mmm," she said. "It's warm in here. I'd almost forgotten what heat feels like."

Petya had appropriated Guzman's small ceramic stove for the occasion, and was also burning some of Guzman's picture frames. Firewood was getting next to impossible to find lately.

"That's the first of many pleasant surprises," proclaimed Petya. With no chairs, he invited her to sit on the edge of his bed, then handed her a half-full glass.

Katya sniffed the contents and exclaimed, "Real vodka! How did you get that?" She closed her eyes and inhaled it again. "I could get drunk just from smelling it. I haven't had anything to eat since breakfast."

Petya held his glass up for a toast. "Happy birthday. May you live a long and healthy life, and may all your wishes come true."

She smiled warmly. "To good friends," she called and clinked his glass.

Petya frowned at the word *friend*. He knew that's how Katya thought of him, but he was out to change that tonight.

They each downed the hefty shot in one gulp, exhaling satisfactorily at the end.

"You are definitely full of surprises," remarked Katya. "If there's one thing I appreciate in people, it's unpredictability. It's much more fun not knowing what someone will say or do."

"On that note, close your eyes," said Petya playfully.

When she had done so, he uncovered a tray he'd prepared beforehand. On it were two teacups with loose tea leaves, courtesy of Guzman, a can of caviar, courtesy of Shostakovich, and four slices of bread, courtesy of Guzman's ration card.

"You can open your eyes now."

Katya stared wide-eyed at the tray. "Oh my goodness! Where did you get all this?"

"That is a secret," Petya said proudly as he slid over on the bed and pulled the tray between them. "Suffice it to say, I'm a lot poorer now," he lied. "Let's have a slice of bread with caviar, then we'll have the second one a little later. For dessert, we'll have tea."

"Sounds good to me," said Katya. "I think I lost two pounds today alone. You can't imagine how hungry I am." After a pause, she added, "I take that back. I'm sure you *can* imagine how I hungry I am."

He laughed.

"Maybe I'm dreaming," said Katya, still gaping at the caviar. "Pinch me."

Petya pinched her lightly on the arm.

"I'm must be drunk already," she said. "I didn't even feel that."

He pinched her again, but harder.

"Ouch." she blurted, slapping his hand but giggling at the same time. She tried to pinch him back, but he grabbed her arm and wouldn't let her. "That's all right," she said with a grin. "I'll get you later."

They caught each other's eye, neither looking away until Katya broke the silence. "You look quite handsome tonight."

"Mercí," he replied in French, then spread the orange caviar on two slices of bread. When he finished, he noticed Katya still gazing at him.

"Don't take this the wrong way," she said. "But you look so different since you've lost so much weight. You look ... healthier."

Petya chuckled. "It's this new starvation diet I'm on," he joked. "It does wonders. My skin has completely cleared up—no acne at all—and my double chin has been reduced to one."

They both laughed for a long time.

"It feels so good to laugh again," said Katya, placing her hand on his and squeezing tenderly. "It's something you take for granted when things are going your way."

Petya held out a slice of bread with caviar. "Enough talk," he declared. "Let's do something else we used to take for granted: eat." Sinking his teeth into the slice of bread, he moaned as the tiny orange eggs popped in his mouth.

Before Katya took a bite, she bowed her head in prayer.

Seeing people pray or make the sign of the cross usually irked Petya, but not with Katya. "What did you pray for?"

"Just the usual," she answered. "That every man, woman, and child might find peace within themselves. I believe it's the only way we'll ever have peace in the world."

Petya looked past her at the bluish-gray wall and the drawing he'd hung there of a witch about to be burned at the stake. "Humanity scares me," he said distantly.

"How so?"

"Its capacity for cruelty. Its bloodthirsty vengeance. Its delight in seeing others trip and stumble."

She put her bread down. "Do you feel disheartened, because you'd like there to be more kindness in the world?"

"Yes. I mean no." He wrinkled his forehead. "I guess I'm not sure. You don't expect us to be nice to the Nazis, do you?"

"I struggle with that one, but I do believe kindness to the devil still brings more kindness into the world."

Petya nearly guffawed, but saw she was serious. "That's easy for you to say. Things like this," he said, pointing to the drawing of the witch about to be burned, "don't affect you."

"That's not true," she protested. "I know exactly what you mean. Sometimes I get so afraid I'm going to be crushed by the senselessness of this war. All this malice and destruction is breaking my heart. I see people starving to death or being killed by bombs, and I wonder why the world has to be like this, why God allows innocent children to suffer so."

There was an explosion in the distance, followed by a crackle of gunfire. "Katya, if there is a God," said Petya, "I hate Him."

"Petya, don't say that! You can't hate God."

"No. It's true. I've never told anyone before, but I'm telling you now. What kind of a God would let His creation languish the way He does?" The fire made a sudden hissing sound, and one of the candles flickered in a draft. "Does God want to stop evil, but isn't able? Then he's impotent. Is He able to stop evil, but not willing? Then He's malevolent. If He's both willing and able to stop evil, then why is there evil?"

Katya looked across the room pensively. "Voltaire's argument," she said with a nod. "But what if evil didn't exist? That whole argument falls apart then."

"Certainly, but who could deny evil exists? This war and the Nazi atrocities are proof enough. Did you hear what they're doing in the villages now? They're—"

"I know what's happening," Katya interrupted. "But what if evil is just a label people put on actions they don't understand? What if evil is merely the tragic consequence of ordinary people making horrible decisions trying to get something they want?"

"For example?"

"For example," Katya repeated. "I heard the German newspapers said Germany needed security, and that's why they invaded our country—to prevent any future assaults to their peace and wellbeing. But surely there were other, less violent, options."

"They were lying when they said that," Petya contended. "They never viewed us as a threat to their security. What they've wanted all along is to kill us and take our land. If that's not evil, then what is?"

Katya pulled her feet up to the bed and hugged her knees. "But to me, if you look underneath their strategy, you see that what they're really needing is peace, safety, and perhaps respect," she said. "They want to be strong enough so that no one else will ever be able to do to them what was done after The Great War. There's nothing evil about wanting to be safe. The problem is with the strategy they chose—preemptive war."

"I didn't know you thought that way," remarked Petya.

"Neither did I," she said with a laugh. "It just came to me."

Petya poured them each another shot of vodka. "I have no idea how we got onto this subject," he said.

Katya hiccupped. "I remember. We were talking about God. Speaking of whom, you know it was His son, Jesus, who taught that peace and understanding is the best route—not the easiest—but the best. It's unfortunate that so many supposed Christians don't follow his teachings."

Petya handed her the refilled glass, then held his up in preparation for another toast. "To hypocrites," he said.

"To hypocrites," Katya laughed, holding her glass up high. "Ourselves included."

"Here, here!" said Petya.

After clinking glasses and downing the second shot, Katya ate more of her bread with caviar while Petya tried to stare at her without being noticed. He loved her face, body, laugh, and fascinating thoughts. He could sit there for eternity listening to her talk about God, philosophy, art, and poetry. "I've never met anyone quite like you," he said. "You're so open to new ideas and so unattached to your existing ones."

She blushed. "I enjoy talking to you too. My conversations only go so far with Igor," she said, then chortled.

Petya laughed along with her.

"It's so warm in here. Not that I'm complaining, mind you." She pulled her sweater off over her head, reducing her to only two more layers of clothes. "You don't mind do you?"

"Feel free to take off as many clothes as you like," Petya said, grinning.

Katya didn't laugh, and Petya knew he'd blundered. He busied himself spreading the last two slices of bread with caviar, all the while chastising himself for his crude remark. After a minute or two, the tea kettle boiled and Petya got up and tended to it. When he turned back around, he found Katya lying flat on the bed.

"Your ceiling is spinning around in circles," she said, slurring a few words.

"I'm so pleased you noticed," he replied. "That was your next surprise. It took me two days to set that up."

She giggled uncontrollably at that, covering her mouth with her hands and rolling from side to side. "You're so funny," she said once she calmed down. "I never would've guessed it. I remember when my father and I first moved into the building, I thought you were this dark and mysterious figure. You always seemed to be deep in thought and tormented by something."

"You got the tormented part right," he quipped.

"Seriously," said Katya, "what's it like to be Petya Soyonovich?"

"Well, before you moved in, my life was very simple," Petya replied. "I was alone, bitter, forlorn, and disconsolate. It was great fun."

"And now? After I moved in?"

"Now," he said with an exaggerated sigh. "My life is even more lamentable, because you've given me hope of one day finding someone as enchanting as you to share my life with." He stretched out beside her on the bed, and she pinched him on the back of the hand.

"Told you I'd get you," she said mischievously.

He tickled her on the side in response, then heard a voice say, "You miserable, lying snake. She's too good for you."

"Sorry, did you just say something?" he asked.

"How could I?" she answered. "I was too busy laughing. I'm ridiculously ticklish."

Petya took a deep breath. *Not now*, he pleaded silently. *Please don't let the voices come right now.*

"But I *was* just about to ask you something," she said, twisting a strand of her hair around a finger. "I want to hear more about the tormented part."

Petya was desperate to tell somebody about the unusual things going on in his head, but decided he couldn't come right out and tell Katya about the voices. That would scare her away for sure. He could, however, talk about it in a roundabout way. "Well, I feel discombobulated more often than I'd like," he said. "Torrents of ridiculous memories come to me, and I can't seem to stop them. I speculate sometimes that it's delirium, and that I've lost control over the thoughts that enter my mind."

"What kind of thoughts?"

"For instance," he said, "I'll be walking down the street and—for no discernible reason whatsoever—remember when I was a child in a school play and forgot my line in front of everyone. Or I'll be preparing dinner and suddenly recall the time I told an inappropriate joke to people I didn't know that well." He fidgeted with his hands and turned on his side to face Katya. "I don't know what's worse: this chronic remorse or losing control of when and what I want to recall. Isn't that what happens to lunatics and maniacs? They have completely random thoughts—things they would just as soon forget, like drowning a puppy because it wouldn't shut up, or being molested as a child." He wiped his moist eyes. "I'm so afraid of ending up like that, of letting them win."

Katya slid her fingers between Petya's. It was something so simple, so basic, and yet he nearly wept with gratitude at the gesture. Instead of being judged, as he feared, she had compassion for him.

The candles cast dark shadows on the wall, and Petya was fascinated by the edge where the darkness disappeared so suddenly and completely. He shifted farther up the bed so his head was beyond Katya's and he could feel her hair touch his face. It was all so magical. "Who would've thought that amidst this travesty there could be joy?" he commented.

Katya brushed her bangs from her eyes, then let go of Petya's hand to make shadow puppets on the wall.

"What's that?" asked Petya. "A dog?"

"No, silly," she said. "It's a horse. See how it's rearing its head."

"That's not a horse," he jested. "That's a hairless poodle who has only one ear for some reason."

Katya fell into a fit of laughter, and Petya wanted time to stop so he could stay in that moment forever. If there was a heaven, he was sure it was something like this.

When Petya poured their third shot, Katya proposed the toast.

"To love," she said.

"Of course," replied Petya. By tradition, the third toast was always to love.

After downing only half the vodka, Katya announced dreamily, "I *love* love. Don't you?"

"Loving someone?" asked Petya. "Or being loved?"

"Hmm," she hummed in contemplation. "Being loved."

"To *be* loved means nothing to the unhappy," stated Petya. "But to love! To love means to live. It means there's something in the world for you, and gives you a reason to get out of bed in the morning." They were lying next to one another again, and he ran his fingers through her hair. He so wanted to kiss her. "I want to both love and be loved."

Katya propped herself up and finished the rest of her vodka. When attempting to set her glass back on the tray, she missed and it fell on the floor and rolled under the bed.

"Sorry about that," she said, slurring her words badly.

"Don't worry about it," Petya said absently. He was pondering how love had always been the villain in his life, never the hero. Summoning his courage, he asked, "Do you think you could ever love me?"

He listened to the fire crack and pop as Katya hesitated in responding.

"I'm not sure how to answer that," she finally said. "I always feel constrained with the number of words we have to express this thing called love. We have one word, but it refers to so many different things—from the way you feel about a pet, to the way you feel about your parents, to how you feel about your boyfriend. On the one hand, I think it's deep never-ending love that makes the world go round. But on the other hand, I don't think of love as something that's static, something that never changes. I can love someone one minute, but not the next. And then of course...."

She's evading the question, thought Petya. "Of course she is," he heard a voice answer. "She doesn't want to answer. She hates you."

Petya hoped if he ignored the voice, it would go away. "What about this minute?" he asked Katya after she finished.

"In this minute?" Katya said, pausing.

Petya took a deep breath and exhaled slowly as if he was smoking a cigarette. "She'll never love you," he heard the voice say. "Why should she? You're a snake." Petya saw everything begin to spiral downward. The voice was so convincing.

"What are you grimacing about?" asked Katya.

"Oh, nothing," Petya said. "Nothing I can't handle."

"Is it something painful?"

"You could say that." He closed his eyes briefly and begged the voice to leave him alone, then said, "But you're evading my question, Katya."

"What question?" she asked with a hiccup. "Oh wait, I remember. In this minute ... I am in love with the whole world. So yes," she said, adjusting herself so their faces were in front of one another, "I do love you."

"She's lying!" the voice screamed.

"No!" Petya cried aloud. "Shut up!"

Katya pulled back, her face pale and frightened.

"No. Not you. I'm sorry, Katya," he apologized, stroking the side of her face. "I didn't mean you."

"Then who were you talking to? As far as I know," she said, looking guardedly about the room, "I'm the only one here."

"I heard someone outside," he lied. "You didn't hear them?"

"No." She sat up and grabbed her sweater. There was no sign on her face of the gaiety they'd shared only a few moments ago. "I'm tired," she said. "Tired and drunk. I should probably get going."

"No," begged Petya. "Please stay. We'll have tea next. I just have really good hearing, that's all. I'm sorry about that. Really, I am." Picking up one of the candles, he excused himself to go to the bathroom. "I'll be right back and we'll have tea," he said. "Wait for me."

In front of the bathroom mirror, he seethed with rage. Here he was so close to getting what he dreamt about every night, and now it was probably out of reach. He banged his head against the wall—determined to inflict some pain on the malicious voices.

After a few minutes, he hurried back to his room, hoping to still salvage the evening, and reminding himself that she'd said she loved him. Upon opening the door to his room, he discovered Katya curled up on the bed weeping.

"What's wrong?" he asked, rushing to her side. "It's not because of what I said earlier, is it? I told you I wasn't talking to you. I was—"

"No. It's not that," she said between sobs. "It's probably because I've drank too much. The room started spinning again, and I felt so lonely after you left. Why does everyone always leave me? My mother left me when I was a child. My grandmother left me when I was a teenager. My father left a few months ago, and I haven't heard from him since. Felix left me. Shostakovich left me. Everyone's left me. Everyone!"

Petya put his arms around her, pulling her close. "My dear sweet Katya," he said, kissing the top of her head. "Not everyone has left you. I'm still here, and I'm not going anywhere."

As she buried her face in his chest and wept, Petya felt an incredible space open up within him. He suddenly felt whole, as though a missing part of him had been found and put back into place. He tried to kiss her on the lips, but she pulled away.

"No," she protested. "Friends don't do that."

"But we can be so much more than friends," he declared.

"I don't want to. I like our relationship as it is. Felix is my lover."

Petya cringed at the mention of Felix's name. He pulled her close again and kissed the side of her neck, but she pushed him away—more forcefully this time.

"Stop it," she said, getting to her feet.

Petya pulled her back toward the bed, and she collapsed into his arms. "That's better," he said, helping her lie down.

He rose from the bed, blew out a wildly flickering candle, then pulled his sweater off over his head. When he returned to the bed, he kissed her arms from the wrist to the elbow and then climbed on top of her. She didn't resist.

"Katya?" he said, running his hand along her cheek.

She didn't reply. She'd passed out.

He knew he could have his way with her, but he didn't want it to be like this. Maybe because he loved her. Maybe because he respected her. Maybe because he knew it was wrong.

Lifting her head, he stuck a pillow underneath and spread a blanket over top of her. Then he lit a cigarette and poured himself another shot of vodka. He wanted to get even more drunk—to curtail his thoughts, to silence the damn voices. When all else failed, he liked to feel numb.

What he would have preferred more than anything was for Katya to be madly in love with him and be his alone. But reality had never cared much about his preferences.

The two German soldiers sat on a fallen tree across from Dima. They were eating smoked meat, drinking from their canteens, and eyeing their prisoner uneasily.

Dima, with his hands and feet tied together, wondered why they hadn't already killed him. He suspected there was something else going on—that the two Nazis weren't alone out here in the woods.

The shorter German came close and asked Dima something in Russian, but Dima, not understanding the man's badly broken Russian, replied in the form of a riddle: "Twelve pears hanging high. Twelve men passing by. Each took a pear and left eleven hanging there. How can that be?"

Dima maintained a somber look the whole while, and the German frowned and returned to his seat on the dead and rotting tree.

When faint sounds in the distance announced more arrivals, the shorter German went and hid in the woods, while the other sat close to Dima, holding a knife tight to Dima's throat.

Unlike last time, the newcomers—two figures side by side in the pale moonlight—hastened openly toward Dima. They spoke in Russian, but Dima dare not warn them lest his throat be cut.

The German had his face right next to Dima's, and Dima could smell the sweet, peppery scent of the smoked meat he'd eaten. The soldier wasn't much older than Dima and had yet to outgrow the chubby cheeks of his boyhood. His small eyes darted nervously back and forth from the figures in the distance to the spot where his partner was hidden.

The newcomers approached rapidly, and Dima recognized the broad chest and determined gait of the one on the left. It was Felix, and he was carrying a pair of crutches.

The unsuspecting duo walked past the shorter German hiding in a thicket, and he stepped out, behind them now, pointing his weapon and speaking in his horrible Russian for them to surrender.

The three prisoners—Felix, Dima, and the third man—sat next to one another, each with their hands and feet tied. Their two German captors stood several yards away discussing something, but always keeping a close eye on them. An owl sat on a branch, hooting from time to time as Felix whispered to Dima the story of what had happened. The man he'd arrived with was Vladimir—the same Vladimir that Olga had wanted to shoot earlier that day.

When Felix had knocked on the door of Vladimir's house, his nervous wife had explained how the Germans had just been there and had taken her husband against his will. Known for his intimate knowledge of the forest, they'd coerced him into leading them to the partisans' camp. After obtaining a pair of crutches from another household, Felix had then started racing back to Dima. On his way, he'd run into Vladimir, who had managed to slip away from the Germans and was hurrying to warn the partisans of the impending attack.

The shorter German came over now, pointing his rifle and shushing the three of them to be quiet. Then he went back and stood with his partner, who had his arms folded across his chest and was shaking his head. Dima speculated that they were waiting for the rest of their platoon to catch up before they did anything with their prisoners. It was clear that they recognized Vladimir, but since they couldn't communicate with him, they'd have to wait for their platoon's translator to explain why Vladimir was caught walking through the woods—not with the German platoon—but with an armed Russian.

Vladimir explained in a soft voice that he'd seen two groups of German soldiers with forty to fifty men each. One group was coming from the north; the other from the south.

"Our comrades are as good as dead," Dima whispered to Felix. "There's no way they can fight off two full platoons."

The taller German soldier came over and shushed them this time—raising his chin and crossing his right index finger under it, in imitation of slicing someone's throat.

After he left, Vladimir suggested they stop talking.

"Or else what?" asked Dima.

"Or else they'll kill us," Vladimir replied.

"They're going to kill us anyway," said Dima. "They're just waiting until the rest of their platoon arrives. All they're going to do for now is make threats."

As Dima squirmed to move a few inches from his position, Vladimir asked nervously, "What are you doing?"

"Trying to get comfortable. I think I'm sitting on some squirrel's acorn," he said. "Might as well enjoy the last few minutes of our lives."

"I agree," added Felix, "but it's impossible to get comfortable like this. You'd think they'd at least give us a blanket to sit on so our asses don't get so cold."

Dima snickered quietly. His own lack of fear astounded him, and that Felix could poke fun at their current predicament impressed him too. He never imagined the end of his life would be spent joking lightheartedly. "Maybe if we ask them nicely, they'll tie us up to a tree instead. Then we'd at least have something to lean on," he jested.

"Yeah, is that too much to ask? This position is killing my back," said Felix.

Dima chuckled, feeling grateful to be spending this time with his friend. "I'm sorry about that incident earlier today. I don't know if I was the one who hit you in the back or not, but it never should've gotten to that."

One of the German soldiers again got out a piece of smoked meat and started eating it.

"He's making me hungry," Dima said. "He took my bottle of booze. The least he could do is give me a bite of that sausage."

Felix laughed. "Perhaps you'd like a cricket instead?"

"A cricket?"

"You don't remember? When we were eleven, I bet that you couldn't eat a live cricket every day for a week."

"Huh," said Dima. "I'd forgotten all about that."

"You had this magnifying glass I wanted, and I got you to bet it," continued Felix. "I remember counting the days until it would be mine."

Dima gave Felix a sidelong glance and grinned.

"And I almost won on the very first day," Felix said. "You nearly puked three times before you got the cricket down."

"Those things tasted so nasty," remarked Dima.

"I was so mad when you won."

"You bet your brand new soccer ball that you got for your birthday," Dima said.

"Yeah, and you never let me forget it. Every time we would play soccer, you'd say, 'Guess how I got this great ball?'"

Dima laughed. "I still have it."

"After I was done being mad," Felix said, "I remember being so impressed that you were able to do it."

"I did it because you and everyone else told me that I couldn't, and I was going to prove you all wrong."

"That's the Dima I admired," Felix said. "You loved to prove people wrong about you."

"Yeah, but I never stopped."

"What do you mean?"

"I mean all my life I've been trying to prove myself."

"Prove yourself to who?"

Dima sighed. "To *everyone*."

Felix studied the two guards, then the ropes around their wrists and ankles. "Never thought we'd be in this situation for real one day," he said. "We must have played out this situation a hundred times when we were kids. How did we get out of it then?"

Dima reflected for a second. "I remember," he said. "They'd have you tied up, and I'd jump out of that old willow tree and wrestle them to the ground."

"Yeah, but you always died when you did that. You'd rescue me, but get shot while doing it and have this big, dramatic death. For ten minutes, you'd flop all over the place, grunting and groaning and telling me to go on without you. Your last words would always be in this strained whisper, saying, 'Felix, promise me you'll never give up. Promise me.'"

"Yeah, I remember that," Dima said, softly chuckling.

There was a sound in the distance, and both of the Germans stood up to look. It was the first time they both took their eyes off their prisoners, and Dima strained against his ropes, using the opportunity to pull his pantleg out of his boot, undo a few laces, and retrieve a small folding knife.

"Where did you get that?" asked Felix.

"From the old farmer who sells the booze."

"He gave it to you?"

"No. I traded my pocket watch for it."

"Oh," Felix said in an astonished tone. "Then I owe you an apology. I thought you'd traded your watch for the booze."

"I told you I was through drinking. I thought about some of the stuff you said about me being too young to give up and decided you were right. The farmer liked the watch so much, he just gave me the booze. I took it for Misha."

While their captors turned their backs, Dima managed to get the knife to Vladimir who was now cutting through the ropes that bound Dima's hands together.

"It must be the rest of their platoon from the north," commented Felix.

Dima strained to pull his hands apart, and the last bit of rope snapped in two. He took the knife from Vladimir and began sawing furiously at the rope binding his feet.

"Hurry," whispered Vladimir.

Both of the Germans—still gazing into the distance—lowered their rifles and relaxed. The taller one began walking in the direction the sounds were coming from.

"Give me the knife when you're done, then make a run for it," Felix said.

"That won't work and you know it," replied Dima. "We've only got one chance of getting out of this." Finished freeing his legs, he crouched in preparation to stand.

"Dima, wait," Felix said breathlessly.

Dima turned to him.

"I saw 'the look' on your face earlier today."

"You mean the look that says that person's going to die that day?"

Felix nodded.

Dima fixed his eyes on him. "Well then, give my best to Katya. You've been a good friend, Felix." Gripping the blade of the knife between his thumb and index finger, he added, "And I promise, no big, dramatic death this time." He grinned and winked, looking just like the kid who'd won the cricket bet.

As he jumped to his feet, the two Germans immediately noticed and raised their weapons. Dima threw his knife at the closest one, and it plunged into the man's shoulder. Then Dima charged with a crazed scream, unleashing all the pain and anger he'd ever held inside.

The shorter German was stunned from the knife wound and by Dima's ungodly shriek, but the other soldier—ten yards farther away—took aim and shot Dima twice in the torso.

"No!" cried Felix.

But the bullets didn't slow Dima down. He kept charging until he tackled the shorter German to the ground. Then he pulled the knife from the man's shoulder and plunged it into his throat, killing him instantly. Dima grabbed the man's rifle, but was shot three more times as he did so—once in the leg, and twice in the belly. But again the bullets didn't stop him. He returned fire and his second shot struck his enemy in the center of the chest, sending him sprawling to the ground.

The rest of the German platoon was advancing rapidly. Dima could hear them shouting orders and rushing through the woods. After retrieving his knife, Dima staggered to Vladimir and handed it to him. As Vladimir cut the rope around Felix's wrists, Dima fired a few rounds at the approaching Germans. He could see at least thirty, maybe more, in the distance. Blood was pouring from his torso, and he felt like he was going to faint.

"Felix," he called out as black splotches started cascading in front of his eyes. "You have to get back to camp and warn the others."

The last thing Dima saw was Felix sawing through the ropes around Vladimir's legs. He could feel himself lying on the ground and wanted to get back up, but couldn't do it. He'd command his arms and legs to move, but they wouldn't respond. He could hear the Germans yelling and shooting, and Vladimir and Felix arguing.

"He's dead!" said Vladimir. "Let's go, before we are too."

"No!" Felix yelled. "We're taking him."

Dima could sense a figure over top of him shouting his name and knew it had to be Felix. Dima wanted to tell him not to worry, that everything had already been decided, that it was useless to struggle against fate. His death was meant to be that day. More than anything though, Dima wanted his last words to be humorous. If he could still speak, he'd quip, "Felix, promise me you'll never give up."

As he felt his body being lifted, he understood that Felix had won the argument. He sensed extreme tightness in his chest and hollowness in his stomach. Then he couldn't feel anything, and his mind started racing—searching for something to think about, something to distract him. But there was no running away this time. Everything slowed down. Thoughts and images moved through his mind like a lazy river on a warm, summer day. He saw himself as a young teenager helping a man in a wheelchair cross a busy street. Then he saw himself as a young boy, laying under an apple tree with Felix on a gorgeous fall day. He didn't know what they were talking about, but he felt a tremendous sense of gratitude and connection flowing between the two of them.

Then Dima saw his mother, father, and older sister sitting around the modest, oval table in the apartment he'd grown up in. They were all so young. Dima was seated at the table too, and everyone was looking at him, telling him to do something. But he couldn't understand what they wanted.

Then the image became more focused, and Dima was no longer a young man being carried through a forest, but a small boy sitting at a dinner table with his family surrounding him. He peeked down and saw he had the hands of an infant.

His family continued their animated encouragement. There was his sister with her short blonde hair and pink dress, his father with his favorite tan sweater, and his mother with her bright blue eyes and long hair exquisitely wrapped atop her head. What did they want of him?

On the table in front of him was some kind of food. He didn't know what it was, but it smelled good and everyone else had an identical serving on a plate in front of them. The food was dark and rectangular, and the top of it was covered with creamy white stuff. As he seized a handful and held it close for a better look, his family cheered him on even more. They were all smiling and laughing. His father was holding up the first finger of his right hand and pointing at Dima with his left hand. His mother and sister were pretending to chew and pointing at the food in Dima's hand.

He tried putting it in his mouth, but was only partially successful. Most of it ended up smeared across his cheek. As he ate this delicious new food, he gazed around the table at his exuberant family clapping for him. He thought it was the most wonderful feeling in the whole world and hoped his entire life would be like this.

And then the light gradually faded to dark. He wanted to cry and plead with his family not to leave him, but there was nothing. Not even the breath in his chest.

ТРИ — Part III

What anger wants it buys at the price of the soul. — **Heraclitus**

A lie told often enough becomes the truth. — **Lenin**

When darkness settled over the sea between Peterhof and Leningrad, a million stars were visible high in the night sky. They were tiny points of light that never moved and never changed. They were there before the city existed, when it was flat and cold and populated only with bears, birds, and squirrels. They were there on May 16, 1703, when Peter the Great paraded in and proclaimed a new city, a Venice of the North, for the Russian empire. They were there when a hundred thousand serfs died constructing the city out of the rock and woods and marsh. They were there in 1917 when the last Tsar, Nicholas II, was arrested and imprisoned, and a few months later as well when a little man gave a big speech that shook the world. The man, fresh from exile, spoke from a balcony to the crowd below. He proclaimed the freedom of the Russian people and a new dawn for humanity. He was Vladimir Ilyich Lenin, and the city was renamed in his honor.

Adolf Hitler despised Lenin's ideas and despised the city where they were brought to life. Though never publicly announced to the German citizenry, Hitler had decided that Leningrad would not be allowed to surrender. The city's populace was to die along with the doomed city, which would be razed to the ground once it was captured. Random shelling of civilian objectives was authorized, and any inhabitants attempting to flee the city were to be shot.

In early November, 1941, Leningrad was on the edge of catastrophe. Hundreds of people were dying of starvation or starvation-related causes every day, and winter had barely begun. The only scant supplies of food making it into the city were over Lake Ladoga, but the lake was stormy and ice-laden now. Very few boats could make the trip and those that did still had to dodge death from above, for the German fighter planes and dive bombers never ceased in their attacks. When German forces captured the city of Tikhvin, the last remaining supply route was severed and Leningrad teetered even closer to the abyss. The city had enough flour for seven days, cereals for eight, fats for fourteen, sugar for twenty-two. There was no meat.

After the fall of Tikhvin, Hitler spoke of the besieged city at Munich, stating, "No one can free it. No one can break the ring. Leningrad is doomed to die of famine." Indeed, if the city was to avoid a quick descent into oblivion, it would need help. But from where? The battle for Moscow was in full swing as the German's Army Group Centre under Fedor von Bock advanced closer and closer to Russia's capital. South of Leningrad, the great city of Kiev had already surrendered to the German's Army Group South. France had long since fallen, and the Soviet Union's sole ally, Great Britain, was fighting for its life from a relentless Luftwaffe bombing campaign. The United States remained isolationist—unable to keep completely out of the war, but unwilling to explicitly enter it either. Japan, Germany's ally in the Pacific, continued to overtake China and the rest of Asia as the Soviet government kept a wary eye on its far east borders.

So the stars looked curiously on as the Russians and Germans played their deadly game and the people of Leningrad slowly starved. They watched hopes for love and peace recede, taking their place in line behind hopes for food and warmth. The stars wanted to know—as did the rest of the world—what drama would the City of Dramas play out now?

On the eastern horizon, a small sun peeked cautiously over the edge of the earth, and the stars gave way to another new day. Large clouds as white as the freshly fallen snow moved quickly over the still sleepy city. One behind the other, in perfect military order they flew across the sky—over the canals, over the frozen Summer Gardens, over the Winter Palace, and out to sea.

When they were gone, the shelling began. And then the screaming. And the weeping.

Глава Восьмая — Chapter Eight

THE LAKE, THE MOON, AND THE LIES

I live in despair,
  feeding off your fear.
I am the darkness
  that will never disappear.
I am that, which you know not,
  and always will I stay
  in the back of your mind
  til your dying day.
The politics of success,
  breed an emptiness so true.
And the suffering remains
  as the truth escapes you.
In circles goes the mind
  whose eyes cannot see
  that the meaning of life
  is the mystery of me.

Katya awoke to the steady ticking sound playing over the apartment loudspeaker. Rubbing the sleep from her eyes, she was disappointed to recognize where she was. She'd had horrifying dreams of a dark, cryptic figure stalking her, and of her beautiful Leningrad being methodically destroyed by an unseen enemy. She had convinced herself it was just a dream, nothing to be upset about. But now she knew it wasn't a dream. The loudspeaker confirmed it. It plugged into a special outlet in the wall and gave warnings and instructions during air raids. Other times it merely ticked, signifying that the Germans hadn't taken over the city. Yet.

A shell exploded in the distance, as if confirming the ugliness was all too real. Katya got out of bed and crept past the others to get a glass of water. They could only heat one room, so all five of them lived, ate, and slept there together. Katya was the first one up in the morning and was usually out the door while the others were still asleep. Oksana was the next to arise, and lastly Petya. One never knew whether Guzman or Igor would make it out of bed that day.

Katya nourished herself in this short time she had alone. She enjoyed the stillness of mornings: the tender light breaking around the low-lying clouds on the horizon, the softness and clarity of those first few breaths of the new day. If evenings were when the wave of the day finally broke and crashed to shore, then mornings were when that wave was just becoming a wave—tiny, little ripples on a clear, calm lake.

Sitting by the window, she read from a book of poems by Anna Akhmatova for her daily fill of hope and inspiration. The sun was shining through the window, and she slowly turned the ring Felix gave her, watching the sunlight dance off the two small diamonds surrounding the ruby. She missed Felix literally more than words could say. She'd tried writing several poems to express the depth of her yearning to see him again, and none of them were satisfactory. Each night she went to bed, she told herself that the next day would be the one where Felix finally came back. Despite everything, she hadn't lost her faith. She knew they'd be together again.

Her scant breakfast consisted of water and a slice of bread, and she liked to close her eyes and pretend it was summer and she was having a picnic at Tsarkoye Selo. Located in lush countryside just outside the city, Tsarkoye Selo was the summer home of the former Tsars and Tsarinas. Katya had visited there often as a little girl and fondly remembered how the whole area would come alive in June. Lilacs, birch trees, and flowering bushes of every sort would burst forth with blooms, and everywhere one went, a fragrance as sweet as the most expensive perfume would follow.

Hearing Igor stir, she glanced at the bed he shared with Guzman. Neither of them were doing well, but Guzman was definitely the worse of the two. The funny, self-effacing man she knew was long gone, replaced by an incoherent invalid who slept nearly all day and night. He was lying in the same position he was always in—on his back, head turned to the right, arms folded across his chest. Igor used to complain about Guzman's snoring, and so they now slept head to toe next to one another. Though the two of them were over half-a-century apart in age, they both reacted similarly to the lack of food. Neither had been up in the past two days except to go to the toilet. Katya was gradually accepting the fact that Guzman was going to die, but she'd grown far too attached to Igor to let him go so easily. She needed to find a way to get him more food.

"Ahh!"

Katya startled at Igor's bloody scream. He had pushed himself against the wall—as far away from Guzman as possible. "What is it?" she asked. "Did you have a nightmare?"

Igor kept shrieking, holding his hands in front of his mouth.

Petya and Oksana sat up in their beds, though Guzman didn't stir in the least.

"Igor, what's wrong?" Katya asked anxiously as she made her way toward him.

"He's cold," Igor said, looking at Guzman.

"We're all cold, sweetheart," Katya said. "We'll need to get the fire going again."

"No. He asked me to wake him when I got up," said Igor. "So I grabbed his foot and it was cold."

Katya shook Guzman and called his name. When he didn't respond, she knew that he'd died in his sleep.

To her surprise, her first feeling was one of relief. Ever since Guzman had lost his ration card and couldn't get a replacement, Katya had been sharing her meager rations with him. She was only a few days away from using the last of the food her father had stockpiled before he left for Moscow. Then she'd have nothing except whatever her ration card got her.

"It's all right, sweetheart," she assured Igor, holding the frightened boy in her arms. "It's nothing to be afraid of." He buried his face between her neck and shoulder and cried. Kissing him lightly on the temple, she noticed he was hot. "I think you might be running a fever," she said. She retrieved a thermometer, terrified at the thought of him having the flu. In these days, that meant certain death. Not only that, with the cramped quarters and everyone's weakened immune system, it would only be a matter of time until they all got the fatal illness.

With trepidation, she watched the red line in the thermometer rise to 98, then 99, then 100. It didn't stop until it reached 103.

She gave him some aspirin and considered staying home from work, but knew she couldn't.

When Igor saw her repeatedly glance at the clock, he squirmed out of her arms. "I know you need to leave," he said. "You don't have to stay here with me."

"No. You're wrong," she replied, putting her arms around him again. "I do have to stay here with you. That's the only way we're going to make it through this."

She stayed with him for another twenty minutes until he fell asleep, then she finished getting ready herself. Oksana had already left, and Petya was the only one available to look after Igor and take care of Guzman's body. Katya was reluctant to ask Petya for favors. Her relationship with him had changed dramatically after the birthday dinner he'd given her last month. She didn't remember anything from that night, but knew that when she'd woken up she was lying on Petya's bed and her sweater was on the floor. She'd asked Petya what had happened, and he'd replied, "Nothing," but said it with a peculiar grin on his face.

Ever since then, she'd decided to distance herself from him. She'd made a vow to be faithful to Felix and felt ashamed for what she might have done or allowed to happen.

"Petya," she called hesitantly, "would you be willing to take care of Guzman's body today? I need to leave for work."

He didn't answer, but that didn't mean much. He often didn't answer her questions.

"Also," continued Katya, "Igor's running a fever. Could you keep an eye on him? Make sure he drinks water and give him some more aspirin at noon."

Again, Petya didn't answer, but at least he didn't say no.

With a twinge of envy, she hurried out the door for work. She wouldn't mind staying in bed half the day like Petya, but her conscience wouldn't allow it—not while the threat of mass starvation still loomed so large.

She hoped it wouldn't be too windy today. She could handle the crisp temperatures, but the wind always went right through her many layers of clothing and chilled her emaciated body to the core.

"You're late," said Lev as Katya walked into the office.

"Yes, I know. I'm sorry. Igor is running a fever and one of my roommates died during the night."

Lev tilted his head forward and peered over his glasses. "Who was it?"

"Guzman."

He took off his glasses and pinched the bridge of his nose. "Everywhere one goes these days, you see people dying. I had to step over a corpse at the foot of my building's stairwell last night. And I cursed at it—the corpse. Can you believe it? The poor man had died, and I was angry at him for dying where I might trip over his body and hurt myself. Such are the times we live in!"

Katya hung her coat on a hook on the wall and sat down at the table.

"Igor's not doing well?" asked Lev.

"He gets worse every day," she replied. "Just lies in bed all the time or in a chair by the stove. Complains he's always cold, and he chews on those horrid oil cakes. They're so coarse you can't even bite into them. They used to only be fed to cattle."

Lev wandered over to the frosted window and gazed outside.

"He hardly talks anymore. Has no interest in anything," continued Katya. "And he has these deep blue circles under his eyes. It was only two months ago that he was putting on this act trying to impress me—pretending he was older and more mature than he is. But now, he doesn't say anything. He doesn't even throw temper tantrums anymore! It's like he's dead to the world, and I'm at wit's end with him. He's still a kid, with his entire future ahead of him. It's just so unfair."

"And now he has a fever?"

"Yes, and it's quite high."

"I hope it's not the flu."

"It's not," Katya said.

"How do you know?"

"I just know. It isn't the flu. It can't be."

Lev turned to face her. "You're quite fond of him, aren't you?"

She gave a brief nod. Air raid sirens started wailing, but neither she nor Lev had any reaction. They were a daily occurrence. After their standard glance at one another to verify neither wanted to go to the shelter, Katya asked Lev what he thought they should do about the rumors going around the marketplaces.

"You're going to have to be more specific than that," remarked Lev, speaking loudly to be heard over the sirens. "There's more rumors going around than I can count these days."

"The rumors about the sausage being sold at the markets," Katya said, "that it's not entirely from *animal* sources."

Lev grunted. "What do we do about it? Nothing. It's none of our concern. Let the police handle it. Personally, I think there's probably some truth to the rumors. That's what this proud city has been reduced to: cannibalism. You should keep an eye on Igor. I've heard that children are the ones to disappear first."

"Yes, I know."

When Lev lowered his head and began pacing back and forth in front of the window, Katya knew some bad news was forthcoming.

"The director has ordered another ration reduction," he announced with a sigh.

Katya felt a lump settle in her throat. "Oh, no," she said anxiously. "Not again." Every ration reduction meant the deaths of thousands more people. "How much?"

"Workers will be reduced from four hundred grams of bread a day to three hundred. Everyone else will get one hundred fifty grams."

So many people were already dying. Katya shuddered to think of the effect this latest reduction would have. A working adult needed two thousand calories a day, and the current ration of four hundred grams of bread supplied only 25 percent of that—a measly five hundred calories. She didn't even want to think about how many calories three hundred grams would be.

She thought back to the prophecy Igor had told her when he saw all the mushrooms under the tree: 'Many mushrooms—many deaths.' It was clear the prophecy was coming true. The only question was how many deaths. "Must we?" she asked.

Lev held his hand to his ear. "What?"

Katya raised her voice. "I said, must we?"

"We have no choice," said Lev. "Lake Ladoga is beginning to freeze, and we won't be able to count on the supply boats making it across for much longer. And now that Tikhvin has fallen, the supply port won't even have any supplies to deliver soon. We need to tighten our belts to buy some time."

Katya worried about how much further people could tighten their belts. They were already punching new holes in them to keep their trousers up. "What are we going to do once the lake freezes?" she asked. "We don't have enough food in the city to last for more than a week or so."

"Once the lake freezes, we'll be able to drive trucks over the ice. We just need to know when it will be cold enough, when we'll have thick enough ice for the trucks. I don't think I need to tell you we have no margin of error left in calculating the situation. If we can expect the lake to freeze early enough, then we won't have to cut the rations any further."

"You said 'we.' You mean the director wants you and I to figure this out?"

"Yes."

"Why us? How on earth are we to do it?"

"He didn't say."

Katya thought she heard the sound of planes approaching, but she wasn't sure and tried not to let it distract her. "How long do we have?"

"He wants it by six o'clock this evening."

"What? With all their authority and resources, they couldn't find someone more qualified than us? And they expect the answer by tonight?"

"I know. I know," said Lev, shaking his head. "I had the same reaction when he told me, but he was in no mood to hear any argument. The situation is quite desperate. Every hour counts."

Positive she heard planes now, Katya wondered if they bothered Lev like they did her. It was excruciating to know that the enemy could kill you from so far away, without ever seeing your face, without ever knowing that you existed.

Lev was pacing in front of the window once again, leaning slightly forward, hands behind his back. Katya called out his name to ask him a question, but he didn't seem to hear her. "Lev," she called out a little louder, "what if we can't retake Tikhvin?"

He stopped, took a deep breath, and jutted his chin out as he addressed her. "We need to be strong in the face of fear and diligent in the defense of the motherland."

Katya hated that answer. That was what he always said when he didn't want to respond to a question because the answer was too painful. She understood now that if they couldn't retake Tikhvin—and soon—then it was the end. The entire city, all 2.5 million people, would die of mass starvation within a matter of weeks.

One problem at a time, she told herself. *One problem at a time.* "So how do we figure out this data for the lake freezing, Lev? Where do we begin?" She gazed up at the portrait of Lenin as if it could tell her.

Before Lev could answer, a deafening blast exploded outside. It shook the floor and shattered the window into a thousand shards that crisscrossed the office.

Katya instinctively crawled under the table and hugged her knees tight. Then all was muted and hushed. For a minute, Katya had no idea who she was, where she was, or what was happening, but as the dust settled, she started to come to her senses. Through the newly created hole in their wall, she saw that the building across the street was now a pile of rubble.

She heard footsteps running down the hallway, and then the door opening and a voice asking if anyone was there. Katya managed to respond with a weak "yes," and two men stumbled over the toppled chairs and started searching for the voice's owner. Katya recognized them as the Civil Defense Corps workers from next door. With each step, their feet crunched the glass shards scattered over the floor.

Katya was uninjured—fortunate to have been looking away from the window, at the portrait of Lenin. Lev, on the other hand, had been struck by the flying glass and knocked to the floor. Katya feared he was dead. She climbed out from under the table to join the two men kneeling over him. Bright red blood streamed down the side of Lev's face from a dozen or so scratches, but he was still breathing at least.

While one of the men retrieved a stretcher, the other informed Katya that Lev had only superficial wounds and a concussion. He would be all right in a few days. As they loaded him on the stretcher, Katya shook the glass from her hair.

She accompanied Lev and the two men outside, where sunlight bounced off the million fragments of glass in the street and cries for help rose from people trapped in the rubble. As a trio of Civil Defense Corps workers pulled a man out from underneath a big slab of concrete, Katya put her nursing training to work and dressed his wounds. Later on, she'd just finished putting a woman's leg in a splint when her director appeared and pulled her aside. He wasted no time in making it clear that he still wanted the ice data by 6:00 that evening. Katya tried to explain that Lev was incapacitated and that she didn't have the expertise to calculate something like that, but he cut her off. "I have every confidence you'll get the information to me," he said bluntly. "And if not, your commissar and I will have a little chat."

Katya appreciated that he was so open with his threat. At least she didn't have to guess what the consequences of failing to carry out the order would be. She returned to the office, where pink dust covered everything and workers were already cleaning up the glass and preparing to install plywood over the broken windows.

Whatever course of action she decided on, she knew she couldn't stay there. The demand weighing on her was bad enough, but now they were about to block out the sunlight. She needed the sun, earth, and sky more than ever now. She needed to trust that God had not abandoned her and that an answer—if one existed—would be provided. Departing the office, she walked toward the library, hoping to find a chemistry textbook with information on how ice forms. She doubted it would give her the answer, but it seemed like her best, if not only, option.

To clear her mind, she tried to simply breathe the air and notice the sights and sounds around her as she walked. It was easy enough to notice the cold. That was something that never left you. It was only November 12, but it felt like mid-December. Winter had come early.

She'd seen the first snowflakes of the day early that morning. They'd been scattered and casual, drifting through the air aimlessly, but now they were no longer sparse and indifferent. Now, they fell with a purpose. Heavily. Hastily. They accumulated on top of whatever they found: tanks, barricades, trees, steps, bushes. Katya usually loved snowfall. For her, it was like God's love— falling carelessly, compassionately, equally on all. But snow in these times of starvation and struggle meant only one thing. More deaths.

She walked past another newly-constructed street barricade—a barbarous thing made of ferroconcrete and railroad iron. Even the pristine white snow piling atop it couldn't mask its hideousness. Stretching from one sidewalk to the other, it was built to withstand not only tanks, but air bombardment as well. Past it, a sentry at the bridge held up a hand ordering Katya to halt.

"Hi, Nikolai," she said. "How are you doing?"

"Cold," he answered, glancing at her papers as a formality. "You've heard Tikhvin has fallen?"

She nodded.

"We're dead," he said flatly. "We're all going to die here."

"No. Don't say that. We'll get Tikhvin back."

"Before or after we all starve to death?" he asked sarcastically.

"The lake will freeze soon," Katya said, "then we'll be able to evacuate people if the food supply gets any worse." She knew it wasn't feasible to evacuate many people, but she kept that part to herself.

"Yes, that's true," he said thoughtfully. "You've got a point there. When will it freeze?"

"That's what I need to figure out."

"If my grandfather were still alive, he'd know," said Nikolai. "He loved to play hockey, and was the one who decided when the ice was thick enough for us to make our rink. I remember he used to...."

Nikolai's story reminded Katya of Felix telling her about his ice fishing trips with his father. They would drill holes through the ice, then drop their line through and wait for a fish to bite. It sounded rather boring to her, but Felix said he enjoyed it because he got to spend time with his otherwise extremely busy father.

"That's it!" Katya blurted to Nikolai. With a sudden realization, she bade him an abrupt farewell and hopped on a nearby streetcar, heading toward the university.

Felix's father was a brilliant scientist, and one of the few who had refused to be evacuated from the city. She was sure he could help. She just didn't know if he was still alive.

The empty hallways of the university building where Felix's father worked were cold, unlit, and smelled of ammonia and dog feces. Katya could hear the dogs yelping and scratching at the walls of their cages. She was surprised that lab animals still existed. Except for one small pack of stray mutts that she saw or heard in the distance from time to time, it was a rare thing to see cats or dogs in the city anymore. Most of them had already starved to death or been eaten by their owners.

Katya last saw Felix's father three weeks ago at his apartment. She went there once a week to check on him and his wife and help out if she could. Even though he was doing research for the army now, and thus getting the much better military rations, it still wasn't enough. The last time she went, she'd noticed his puffy eyes and sickly, ashen face—the first sign of dystrophy. It broke her heart that not only was there nothing she could do to help, she also didn't have the strength or time to continue making the trip.

With a tepid knock on his office door, she held her breath in the hope he'd answer.

A few seconds later, a faint voice spoke from the other side. "Yes? What is it?"

The man's voice sounded so nasal and strained that Katya couldn't tell if it was Felix's father or not. That he hadn't opened the door didn't surprise her, considering how fearful and paranoid people were these days.

"It's me," she called out, taking a chance that it was him. "Katya."

"Katya?" the man repeated. "Katya who?"

"Katerina Selenaya."

When there was still no response, she added, "Felix's girlfriend."

"Oh, *Katya*," he said, suddenly sounding like the man she knew. He opened the door and held out his arms for a hug. "You'll have to forgive me, my dear. Lately, my brain has been a bit ... umm ... foggy."

His appearance was even worse than the last time she'd seen him. He was almost completely unrecognizable from the man she knew before the blockade started. His whole body was rigid, and his arms and legs shook visibly when he moved. His eyes had sunk so far into his head as to be nearly unseeable.

"Come in," he said. "It's not much warmer in here, but a little at least." His office consisted of a desk crammed into the corner of a small laboratory. In the middle of the room were counters filled with microscopes and beakers and vials. The windows had been broken, and—like Katya's office now—were covered with plywood. Two smoky koptilkas provided the sole lighting for the room.

There was an uncomfortable silence between them that Katya let linger because it was even more uncomfortable to ask the usual questions. She didn't want to look at him and his dimming iron-grey eyes that reminded her too much of his son, and she didn't want to ask how his wife was getting along. But after another long minute, she gave in and did both.

He cleared some papers off a chair and motioned for her to sit. "She passed away last week," he replied.

That was the answer she'd dreaded, but curiously enough she felt indifferent. She had no urge to hug him, take his hand, or even to say she was sorry for his loss. The news was as ordinary as him remarking that he'd bought a frying pan. That she felt so little sympathy disturbed her more than the news itself. "Did she suffer much?"

"Yes. She was in terrible pain."

"Well, it's a good thing it's over then," said Katya, surprised to hear the words coming out of her mouth.

Amidst his uncomprehending stare, she berated herself. Was that the best she could do now? Was that all the compassion she had to offer?

As difficult as that had been, the next question would be even more challenging. Every time they met, they stumbled along in their conversation until one of them got up the courage to inquire about Felix. Conscious of her time constraints, Katya took a shallow breath and broached the subject. "Have you heard anything of Felix?"

He hung his head. "No. Nothing."

"Well, I'm sure he's all right," she said, trying to move on from the subject as quickly as possible. "I think we'll hear something soon. I hear that communication with front-line troops is getting better."

He nodded unconvincingly.

"I don't have much time, so I need to get straight to the point," said Katya. "I'm here because I'm hoping you can help me with some calculations on ice formation."

"I see," he said.

Katya sensed disappointment in his voice, but decided his feelings were less important than the city's survival.

He listened patiently as she explained the situation to him. When she'd finished, he asked, "How much weight would the ice need to hold?"

Lev hadn't specified that to her. "I don't know," she answered. "I guess however much a truck with supplies weighs."

"A truck?" He raised his eyebrows. "You're going to have to wait quite a while before the ice is thick enough to hold a truck. You might better start out with something smaller."

"Like what?"

"You could start out with horses pulling sledges."

"All right," said Katya. "Could you make estimates for both sledges and trucks?"

"Yes, but I'm a bit busy right now. They've got me training dogs to run under tanks."

"Why would they want to do that?"

"They're going to strap explosives around the dogs, then detonate them when they're under the tank."

Katya was aghast. "Oh my God," she exclaimed. She detested the way scientists and the military treated animals, blaming it all on the French philosopher Renee Descartes and his teachings that animals were soulless machines. "So we're forcing animals to fight in our war? What next?"

"We've got to win somehow," he replied matter-of-factly.

His statement sounded so obvious, but Katya couldn't help but think *at what cost? Does being at war mean you can disregard your values and ethics? So long as you win, nothing else matters?*

She opened her mouth to argue with him, but elected against it. "I need to give the information to my director by six o'clock this evening."

He took a pocket watch out and checked the time. "I'll do what I can."

"Please do," Katya implored. "Thousands of people's lives are depending on it."

"I understand."

Not wanting to disturb him while he worked, Katya got up to go. "I'll be back in an hour."

He didn't respond. He was already digging through a thick stack of books piled in the corner.

Startled awake by a pair of hands lifting her legs off the bench she was lying on, Katya cried out, "What are you doing?"

The man immediately put her legs back down. "Oh! Forgive me, comrade," he apologized.

There was another man standing near her head, and he retreated a step as Katya sat up. "We thought you were—" he started to say before pausing.

She saw a cart nearby with three dead bodies stacked on it, then finished his sentence for him. "Dead."

"We're so sorry, comrade," the man who'd grabbed her legs said. He had a gray fur hat pulled down tight over his ears.

Katya figured out that the two men had been gathering corpses from the university grounds when they saw her lying motionless on a hallway bench. "It's all right," she said with a shudder at the cart's bluish corpses. "Just be on your way, please."

"Yes, of course," they said, apologizing once more as they departed down the hallway with their grim cart of death and its squeaky wheels.

Katya checked the time and saw that an hour had passed. She'd meant to do some work while waiting for Felix's father, but instead she'd fallen asleep. It was all her malnutritioned body wanted to do lately. Packing up her notebook, she headed back to the office of Felix's father.

"Just a little longer," he answered in response to her knock. "I'll open the door when I'm done."

She sat in a chair opposite his office and again tried to work, but her thoughts never strayed far from the plight of Igor. She'd made a promise to herself that she'd ensure his survival, but he was inexorably slipping away into the overcrowded arms of the Grim Reaper. If she didn't do something soon, he'd leave her like the others had.

After another hour passed, Katya wondered if Felix's father had forgotten about her. She knocked on his door, and he opened it with a blank expression on his face.

"Is everything all right?" she asked.

"Katya?"

"Yes, it's me," she said, fearing he'd gone blind.

He returned to his cluttered desk and slowly sat down.

"I've been waiting for you to come back. I'm afraid I'll need your help."

She followed him to his desk and peered down at the sheet of paper there. It was covered with his handwriting, but she couldn't make out a single word or number. "How can I help?"

"I've worked out the basic formula," he said, pointing with his pencil at some scribbles on the paper. "Let me show you." Resting the tip of the pencil to the paper, he tried to write, but his hand shook so badly that the result was just more scribbles. "Actually, this is where I need your help. It's difficult for me to write."

Katya took the pencil from his pale hand. "You just tell me what to write."

He coughed feebly, then cleared his throat. "To support a man on a horse," he began, "the ice will need to be four feet thick. And if—"

"Wait," Katya interrupted. "The ice needs to be *four feet* thick to support a man on a horse?"

He squinted at his scribbles on the paper. "No. Sorry. That should be inches. Four *inches*."

Katya felt overcome with dread. Perhaps this had all been in vain. His numbers might be complete nonsense, and if they used them, all the trucks would fall through the ice. "I'm feeling concerned about the accuracy of your calculations," she said gently.

"As well you should be, dear," he replied. "My brain doesn't work as well as it once did. But I can assure you these numbers are correct. I've double checked them, and they agree with my own experience when I used to go ice fishing."

Recognizing she had little choice, Katya asked him to continue.

"At twenty-three degrees above zero, four inches of ice will form in sixty-four hours," he said. "At fourteen above, it will take thirty-four hours to form four inches. At five degrees above, it will take twenty-three hours. Obviously we need more than four inches of ice since we want to haul supplies over the lake. A horse pulling a sledge with a ton of supplies requires seven inches of ice. A truck carrying a ton of freight needs a minimum eight inches of ice. I'm afraid I don't know how much a tank weighs, so I can't calculate that, but I do know that once the lake freezes—I mean *really* freezes—you'll have ice three to five feet thick. Enough to hold nearly anything. If you...."

Katya wrote furiously, afraid of missing some important detail. When he finished, she saw it was already 5:10 p.m. The trip back to her office took her close to her apartment, and she wanted to stop in and check on Igor. If his fever got any worse, she'd go to the hospital later and beg one of the doctors to come see him that night.

Gathering her things, she rushed to the door, nearly forgetting to thank Felix's father. With a cold realization that this was likely the last time she'd ever see him, she puzzled at what to say. Goodbye seemed too shallow, but what more was there to say? It really was goodbye.

After giving him an embrace and a thank you, she recited her current favorite Akhmatova poem. He bowed his head as he listened.

> *Give me bitter years of sickness,*
> *Suffocation, insomnia, fever,*
> *Take my child and my lover,*
> *And my mysterious gift of song—*
> *This I pray at your liturgy*
> *After so many tormented days,*
> *So that the stormcloud over darkened Russia*
> *Might become a cloud of glorious rays.*

Petya awoke from his nightmare with a gasp. His hands gripped the blankets so tightly that his knuckles had turned white, and his whole body was drenched with cold sweat. It was nothing new for him though. It was the same dream, the same image of his parents being shot while he looked on as a four-year-old.

He tried again to recall those two days he'd spent clinging to their side after they'd been killed. What did he do? What did he think? Did he cry? Having never been able to fully remember those two days, he didn't know.

Lying in his bed, staring at the cracks in the ceiling, he wanted to sleep more, but the prospect of returning to that dream kept him awake. It used to be when he was tired and couldn't sleep, he'd toss and turn relentlessly, trying to get comfortable. But he didn't have the energy for that anymore. He didn't even have the energy to get up and load more wood in the stove, even though he was quite cold and knew the fire must be nearly out by now.

He kept a knife under his mattress and deliberated whether to get it out. One of the voices had returned to speak to him and was even more persistent than the last time. "You feel how weak you are? That's because Igor is stealing your strength," it said. "You can't let him do this to you. You can't let him win. Kill him now while you have the chance."

Reaching under the mattress, Petya grasped the cold knife in his hand and decided the voice was right. Oksana and Katya were both at work, and now was the perfect time to kill Igor. All day long the boy had been delirious and talking nonsense from his fever. It would be no surprise if he died. Since Igor was currently sound asleep in Katya's bed, it would be easy to do—probably easier than strangling Oksana's cat.

"Don't use the knife, you fool," the voice hissed. "Suffocate him with a pillow!"

Petya lifted one of his pillows and glanced nervously about the room. Guzman's corpse was still lying in the same position as it had been that morning, and Petya cursed himself for not taking care of it earlier in the day. That's where the voice was coming from, he decided. It was Guzman seeking his revenge.

"What are you waiting for?" the voice demanded. "Kill him now and stop him from stealing your strength!"

"Shut up!" Petya shouted. "Just leave me be!"

Igor opened his eyes and turned his head toward Petya. "What?" he mumbled.

Petya put the pillow down and saw the clock out of the corner of his eye. It was almost six p.m., and Oksana would be home from work soon. "I said, help me get rid of Guzman before Katya and Oksana get home."

Igor groaned and pulled the covers over his head.

"Stop your whining," said Petya. "I can't get him down the stairs alone."

Igor protested again, but eventually got out of bed and helped. Together they dragged Guzman's body down the stairs and outside where the sun had long since set and it was snowing.

While Igor went to get the sled so they pull the corpse to the morgue, Petya leaned against the building and smoked a cigarette. He didn't dare sit down, because it was too much of a struggle to get back up. Just hauling Guzman's body down the stairs felt like running a marathon. Nothing was easy these days. Even getting out of bed was a chore.

Hearing snow being crunched, Petya searched the darkness for who might be approaching. When the sounds stopped and he didn't see anyone, he shrugged it off and focused on his cigarette. He only had a few left, so was trying to enjoy every second of it. He inhaled deeply and examined Guzman's blue legs protruding from the blanket they'd wrapped him in. Petya had already taken Guzman's trousers to wear himself. Petya had lost so much weight that none of his own pants fit him anymore.

"You should have killed Igor when you had the chance," a voice said to Petya.

Kicking Guzman's corpse on the icy sidewalk, Petya said, "Shut up. I'm not falling for any of your tricks. I didn't kill you."

"Whose ration card is that in your pocket?" the voice asked.

"It wouldn't have made a bit of difference if I hadn't taken your ration card," Petya said defensively. "You were going to die anyway, and you know it."

Petya heard the snow crunch again, and then Oksana rounded the corner of the building. She had a smug grin on her face, and Petya wondered how much she'd overheard. With a glance at Guzman's corpse, then at Petya, she entered the building without saying a word.

"She knows! Oksana knows. You've got to get rid of her!" the voice screamed to Petya.

"Damn you," Petya said, kicking Guzman's corpse even harder. "Shut the hell up and leave me alone!"

Someone else approached, calling out Petya's name. He recognized Katya's voice and watched her pretty face emerge from the shadows.

"Who are you talking to?" she asked.

"The Nazis of course," he replied. "Who else would I be talking to?"

Before Katya could say anything more, Igor emerged from the stairwell with the sled. Her eyes opened wide. "What on earth are you doing up?"

"Petya made me help him."

"Petya!" she said with a fierce glare. "He's sick. He needs to be in bed." She took her mittens off and felt Igor's forehead with the back of her hand. "He's burning up," she cried.

After Katya led Igor back upstairs, Petya loaded the body on the sled. Deciding he didn't have the energy to haul it to the morgue, he pulled it instead to the courtyard and buried it under a few inches of snow.

When he made it back to the apartment, his two roommates were conversing around Igor's bed. As Katya put her hat and mittens back on, she gave Petya a look of disgust. "Igor has a fever of one hundred four," she said.

Petya felt a twinge of guilt for forcing the boy out of bed. Had he known Igor's fever was that high, he wouldn't have done it.

"Are you going to the hospital?" Oksana asked Katya.

"No. I need to go to the office," she answered. "I have to deliver some information to my director."

"Whatever it is, it can wait," Oksana said as she put the tea kettle on the stove. "The boy needs to see a doctor. He's been sweating terribly. You see how his sheets are soaked?"

Igor sat up and let loose with a dry, hacking cough.

"You hear that?" asked Oksana.

"I know," Katya said, "but what can I do? My director has threatened to call in my commissar if I don't deliver the information by six p.m. I already took a big risk in coming here. I don't have much time left now." She buttoned her coat up and pulled her scarf tight. "I'll stop by the hospital right after," she said. "It'll only be an extra forty minutes."

Petya sunk into his bed and pulled the covers up to his neck as Katya hurried out the door.

The apartment loudspeaker was broadcasting inspiring words from a poet who was in the infantry: "Comrades, we fight for our freedom! We fight for our honor. We fight on behalf of every man, woman, and child who has been crushed by the fist of tyranny throughout history. Our cause is just. This battle must not be lost...."

When the water boiled, Oksana made two cups of strong-smelling herbal tea. She set a blue cup down—presumably for herself—on the small table where the lamp was and gave the orange cup to Igor. The soldier-poet ended his patriotic exhortation, then an announcer reminded listeners that Stalin would be making an address the next evening at 10:00. One of the numerous marches Shostakovich had written played next, and Oksana hummed along to it.

After a few cautious sips of his tea, Igor gulped down the rest, then curled into the fetal position. He fell asleep a few minutes later.

The voice in Petya's head had started up again, telling him all sorts of things about Oksana. "That hag is planning something for you," it said. "She knows you killed her cat, and now she knows you stole Guzman's ration card. She'll probably tell Katya as soon as she gets the chance."

Petya resolved to act pre-emptively. Before Oksana said anything to Katya, he had to discredit her testimony—make Katya believe the woman had lost her senses and was talking nonsense.

Opening his eyes a crack, he spied Oksana heading to the kitchen. Quietly sneaking out of bed, he poured the tea from Oksana's blue cup into Igor's orange cup, then put the orange cup back in the same place the blue cup had been.

He pretended to be asleep when Oksana came back to the room. Peeking from under his blankets, he saw the puzzled expression on her face as she picked up the orange tea cup and examined it. She then looked at Igor's empty blue cup, shook her head, mumbled a few curse words, then returned to the kitchen.

Petya fell into a dreamless sleep after that and didn't wake up until Katya returned home a couple hours later. The music from the loudspeaker was gone, replaced by the metronome-like ticking that played when no program was being broadcast.

He overheard Katya and Oksana in the midst of a heated conversation near the front door.

"No, but they gave me more aspirin and a can of condensed milk," Katya was explaining. "They said it's probably just a cold and that he'll be all right if he gets some rest."

"You don't get a fever of one hundred four from a cold," Oksana said, obviously struggling to keep her voice down. "He needs to see a doctor."

"Oksana, I tried," Katya said defensively. "All the doctors were busy or resting."

"You should have *insisted*," said Oksana. "You've done enough for them with all your volunteer work that they could certainly do this one favor for you. You let people walk all over you."

"Oksana, you don't understand. They work so hard and get so little time to rest."

"And what about you?"

"Me?"

"Yes, you," Oksana said. "Don't you work hard? Don't you help others all the time? Why is it you don't deserve some help once in a while?"

Petya waited to hear what Katya's answer would be, but there wasn't one, only the never-ending ticking from the loudspeaker.

The wind was ice-cold and whipped over the top of the snow, stinging Felix's cheeks and stabbing into his lungs. He ducked down and tried to settle into his foxhole to better protect himself, but it was useless—as was his being there on the side of the road in the first place.

Olga had ordered him to watch for German activity along the road and then report back at the end of the day. It was a pointless assignment. Felix knew it. Olga knew it. Everyone in camp knew it. There *was* no German activity on the road, and there wasn't going to be. All their tanks, trucks, and cars were frozen solid. When the Germans launched their invasion, they'd expected victory before winter set in. As a result, neither their armies nor their vehicles were prepared for cold weather, especially weather this cold.

Five hours had crawled by and Felix was now almost completely indistinguishable from the snowdrifts around him. Even his recently grown beard was covered white with snow. It was the sixth day in a row that he'd been assigned this absurd order, and in all that time, he hadn't spotted a single thing come down the road, unless you counted squirrels. Perhaps he should start reporting them back to Olga, as Misha had suggested: *Three brown-camouflaged rodents were seen traveling south in loose formation. Appeared nervous and seemed to be searching for something. Unable to ascertain if they were advance scouts, Nazi Sympathizers, or lost troops.*

Lifting his head high, he gazed up the road to the north. The wind had been building a snowdrift there since he left yesterday, and it now stretched completely across the road. It was at least six feet high and twelve feet wide. Felix remembered when he was a kid how excited he would be seeing snowdrifts like that. He and Dima would tunnel into them, make snow forts, and pretend to battle Napoleon's armies. It was always great fun, and they'd stay out there for hours until Dima's mother called them in for hot cocoa.

Far from buoying his mood, the memory actually made him more bitter. He couldn't think about Dima anymore without a pain in his heart. Why was his friend's life cut short, while he, himself, was allowed to live? It didn't make sense to Felix, and he couldn't comprehend how the world could be so capricious and arbitrary.

He fixed his eyes on the giant snow drift once more. The road was completely impassable to anything but a snowplow. He was supposed to stay until sundown—another hour still—but he didn't care. Numb with cold, he'd had enough and began trudging back to camp.

Life as a partisan under Olga's command had become more about fighting boredom than the enemy. They rarely ventured out, and when they did, it was to do what Olga referred to as "intelligence-gathering missions.". Felix mockingly referred to these trips to the neighboring areas as "gossip crusades," and joked that no other military outfit in all of Russia had more rumors in their arsenal than they did. "We've got enough rumors to kill a dozen old widows in one shot," he'd say whenever he wanted to crack Misha up.

The partisans had abruptly fled their former camp a few weeks earlier when Felix had staggered in, breathlessly announcing that two German platoons were approaching. The new camp they'd set up was ten miles farther north. Olga had seized materials from a nearby village and conscripted several farmers to build her a new shelter against the frigid winter temperatures. After installing a hefty stove that provided a great deal of heat, she rarely came outside anymore.

To Felix, it seemed like she just wanted a cozy place to wait out the winter. He hated her cottage and all the comfortableness they'd surrounded themselves with. He despised sitting around the campfire all day long listening to people gossip and chitchat.

Felix, Misha, and Yuri shared a hut together. It was made out of mud, straw, and ice, and a little stove kept it warm. When they'd first lit the stove, Felix had expected the structure to melt and collapse after a few hours, but he came to understand what the Eskimos had known for so long—a little melted snow will freeze again and act as cement between the blocks of ice. The inside of the hut might melt a little, but the frost on the outside would counteract it.

The entrance to the hut was waist-high, and Felix struggled to crawl through it now with his bulky clothing and cold muscles. Misha was perched on his homemade bed smoking a cigarette. "Welcome home, sweetheart," he said, blowing him a mock kiss.

Having long since run out of booze, Misha was, in general, quite miserable. He wasn't so easy going anymore, and his tongue had grown considerably more caustic.

Felix took his coat off, and Yuri helped him hang it by the stove to dry. When Misha offered a puff from his cigarette, Felix accepted. He'd started smoking— for the first time in his life—shortly after Dima died.

The tobacco was harsh, and Felix struggled to keep from coughing. He sat down on his own crude bed, which consisted of several inches of bark and a foot of straw. The bark covered the frozen ground, and the straw served as a mattress. Finding it annoyingly comfortable, Felix considered getting rid of it.

"Misha picked up an extra week of guard duty today," announced Yuri.

"How the hell did you know?" asked Misha. "It just happened an hour ago."

Felix wasn't surprised that Yuri had found out already. "An hour is an eternity around here," he commented. He held out the cigarette for Misha to take back, but Misha waved it away. "What did you do this time?" Felix asked.

"What does it matter?" Misha said crossly. "She just makes shit up if she really wants to get you." He wrapped his arms around his knees and pulled them close to his chest. "I think it's about time someone challenged that bitch's authority."

Yuri arched his bushy eyebrows, then frowned and nodded.

"How about it, Yuri?" Misha said. "You used to be a captain in the army. How about we stage a coup and make you the leader?"

Felix couldn't tell if Misha was serious or just trying to entertain himself.

"It's not that I wouldn't mind," answered Yuri. "I'm tired of sitting around here doing nothing. But leaders can only be leaders if others will follow them. I've been around long enough to know people won't follow me."

"People won't follow you?" Misha said in feigned amazement. "But why? You're such an honest man. And you're certainly no coward. Don't people know that?"

Now Felix knew for sure that Misha was trying to amuse himself. Not a day went by when Yuri didn't mention how honest and brave he was.

"They *should* know that by now," Yuri said, leaning forward and studying the dirt floor.

"Certainly they should," Misha agreed. "Perhaps you should tell them outright so they know for sure. Stop beating around the bush."

"Yes, you may have something there," Yuri said. "Perhaps I've been too subtle." He crossed his massive arms in front of his chest and held his hand to his chin.

The wind picked up outside and blew some snow flurries through the entrance of their hut. Felix adjusted the blanket that served as a door in a vain attempt to keep them out.

"What about you, Felix?" asked Misha.

"What about me?"

"How about you lead our coup."

"Why me?"

"Because you have everyone's respect," Yuri said as he cracked the knuckles of his enormous hands. "Olga has only their fear."

Felix didn't have a chance to reply because Olga's voice shouted his name from outside their hut. "Varilensky! Get out here!"

"What does that witch want now?" grumbled Misha.

"I don't know," Felix said as he put his coat on, "but I'm sick of it." Over the past several weeks, Olga had taken every opportunity to punish Felix for something—usually trivial infractions of rules that she'd made up on the spot. Felix had learned not to argue with her, and simply do whatever ridiculous task it was that she ordered. She had it out for him, he knew, and he didn't want to give her any cause to accuse him of insubordination.

"I heard her complaining earlier that the stew we had for lunch had too much salt," remarked Yuri.

Misha got up and grabbed his coat. "It'll be interesting to see how she blames that one on him since he wasn't even here."

Felix crawled through the small opening of the hut to the sight of Olga awaiting him with pistol drawn. Two partisans who had recently joined flanked her, and they grabbed Felix by the arms.

Olga was grinning. "Why aren't you at your post, comrade?" she asked, her gold tooth gleaming briefly in the pale winter light.

Felix wanted to knock that tooth out of her mouth.

Olga glanced at the faint sun on the horizon. "I gave you direct orders to stand watch on the road a mile west of here until sundown," she continued. "Clearly, you have disobeyed my order."

Yuri and Misha made their way out of the hut, and a few other partisans wandered over to see what was going on.

"That order was bullshit and you know it," Felix said hotly. "Everyone in camp knows it. There hasn't been a single vehicle down that road in a week, and the road is completely impassable now."

Olga raised her voice a notch. "This group will not survive if orders are not carried out as specified," she said. "Infractions must be dealt with swiftly and severely." Olga seemed to say this more for the gathering partisans than for Felix. "This is not your first infraction." Taking out a piece of paper, she began listing every instance, some real, some made up: "You were involved in a fight against your fellow comrades on October 16. You reported six minutes late for guard duty on November 9. You were again late on November 12...."

Felix listened to the charges with ever increasing indignation. When Olga finished, nearly the entire camp had congregated to watch.

"I think everyone will agree that I've been more than patient with you," said Olga. "You've been given numerous opportunities to improve your behavior, but you've chosen every time not to do so. In the best interest of this group and this war, you are to be executed."

"My death will be in the best interest of no one except the enemy," Felix said furiously.

"Enough of your lies and provocations!" shouted Olga. "We're all quite tired of them."

"If I am to be shot, then I'll speak my mind," Felix countered. "All we do is sit around this damn camp while the Germans march on Moscow and starve Leningrad to death. What have we done to fight the enemy lately? We cut one of their telegraph wires. That's it! How are we going to win the war that way?"

"Silence him!" Olga yelled to the partisans holding Felix's arms.

"We don't answer to *her*," Felix proclaimed loudly. "We answer to the Russian people! And right now, I couldn't look a single one of them in the eye and say that I'm doing all I can to defeat the enemy."

"Spare us the lecture!" said Olga. "You're not in charge here. *I* am."

"Leaders need to lead," accused Felix. "And you've done everything but! The only thing you're good at is cursing and making threats. Nobody joined the partisans to escape the war." Felix saw Yuri and others nodding in agreement. "We all know Tikhvin has fallen to the enemy and that the people of Leningrad will perish unless it's retaken. Why aren't we joining the battle there? Why aren't we *fighting*?"

"Take him to the woods!" Olga ordered the two men holding Felix.

"If I die," said Felix, "it'll be at the hands of the enemy, not you!" He kicked his right leg out in front of him, knocking the pistol from Olga's hand. It landed at Natasha's feet, and she picked it up. But when Olga held her hand out for it, Natasha instead stepped back and pointed it at the men holding Felix. "Let him go," she said.

All color drained from Olga's face. After the two men released Felix, Natasha tossed the pistol to him. No one tried to intervene as he aimed it at Olga.

Lifting her chin, she held her arms out wide. "What are you waiting for, kike? Shoot me."

Felix lowered the pistol. "No. I'm not going to shoot you."

"You better," Olga threatened, "because I'm sure as hell going to shoot you as soon as I get the chance."

Felix tucked the pistol inside his coat. "I think it's past time we go our separate ways."

"I'm not going anywhere," she replied.

"But I am. I'm going to join the fight for Tikhvin," Felix said. "I'll leave camp in half an hour."

"Good riddance," sneered Olga. She walked away from the crowd and disappeared into her cottage.

With a sense of sadness, Felix scanned all the expressionless faces staring back at him. He'd been through a lot with them: the incident where Misha helped rescue him and Dima from the Germans, the time he and Dmitry and Natasha rescued the two little girls from the house fire started by Nazi flamethrowers, and, of course, the close call with the landmine with Yuri.

Lifting his head toward the flat winter sky, he spied the setting sun. On the opposite horizon, through the leafless branches of a birch tree, was a full moon.

"Are you really going to Tikhvin?" the voice of a female in the crowd asked.

Felix recognized Natasha's voice. "Yes."

"What difference is one man going to make there?" one of the new partisans asked.

"A hell of a lot more than here," Felix replied.

He didn't want to answer any more useless questions, so he went back to his hut and began packing. He knew what he had to do.

After a few minutes, Yuri came in and started collecting his things as well.

Felix eyed him quizzically. "What are you doing?"

"Going with you, of course."

"You don't have to do that."

"I know," Yuri said. "I want to."

Felix stopped what he was doing. "It's not going to be easy," he warned. "Tikhvin is a long way from here. It'll be cold as hell. And the Nazis will be well dug in."

"Doesn't matter," replied Yuri. "I want to fight. And if you'll lead the way, I'll follow."

Misha came in, saw the two of them packing, then slumped on his bed. A moment later he stood again, blurting, "To the devil with you both!" Then he pulled the blankets off his bed and started folding them. "You think I'm going to stay here by myself? I'd be bored out of my mind. Not that you two are much fun anyway, mind you."

Felix felt pleased he wouldn't be making the journey alone. "With the three of us going, we'll surely tip the balance and send the Nazis running out of Tikhvin," he joked.

Yuri and Misha chuckled.

Felix didn't have much to pack. He had three blankets, two wool undershirts, a sewing kit, a canteen, five packages of canned fish, half a pound of dark chocolate, a loaf of bread, and a razor. He kept his spoon—like all Soviet soldiers did—inside his boot. Stuffing the remaining items in his pack, he was careful not to damage his most important possession: a letter from Katya, given to him the night before he left for the front.

After Felix and Yuri disassembled the stove and packed it away, they were ready to leave. As is the Russian custom before leaving a place, they sat and were quiet for a moment. Then Felix stood and grabbed his pack. "Ready?" he asked.

"Yes," said Yuri, getting down on his hands and knees to make his way out of the hut.

Felix went next, and as soon as he got outside and stood up, Yuri pushed him to the ground and fell on top of him as a gunshot sounded. There was a lot of commotion and shouting, and then four additional loud cracks that echoed through the camp.

It had all happened quickly, and Felix saw none of it. When Yuri rolled off him, Felix began piecing the events together. He saw Olga near the door of her hut sprawled out in the snow, breathing heavily and wheezing with each inhalation. She was still holding a rifle with her right hand. Behind Felix, gathered around the campfire, was a large group of partisans—perhaps the entire camp—and half of them had their weapons pointed in Olga's direction.

Olga must have tried to shoot him, reasoned Felix. She'd missed because Yuri had thrown him to the ground, and then the other partisans had shot Olga before she could take aim again.

Felix was puzzled why so many of his comrades were gathered around the campfire. Then he saw they all had their bags packed, rifles around their shoulders.

Olga was wheezing louder, and everyone was looking to Felix. It took a second for it all to sink in, but he realized he was the new leader of the partisans.

The moon was full. The wind had tapered off. "Let's move out!" called Felix, leading the way.

It was late morning when Petya awoke, and he was surprised to find Katya hadn't left for work yet. He was even more surprised when she moved into the sun's soft light shining through the window and he caught a glimpse of how attractive she still was. Despite her sunken cheeks and ever-expanding forehead, she'd retained that elegant beauty Petya found so irresistible.

He watched her remove a pot of boiling water from the stove and strain it into another pot. When she finished that, she strained it a second time into its final container. Petya counted the containers and saw she'd finished three, but still had five more to go. It was a tedious and arduous process, but one necessary to make the polluted river water drinkable.

All those things one took for granted before the blockade—food, running water, heat, electricity—were gone. Life was very simple now. You had only one goal when you got out of bed in the morning: to get enough to eat to make it to the next day. You didn't have to worry about deciding between tea or coffee, mashed potatoes or fried, or whether to buy chocolates or cake for your friend's birthday. Petya's biggest decision each day was how much of his bread ration to eat for breakfast and how much to save for dinner.

Katya sat on the edge of Igor's bed and took his temperature. Afterward, Igor coughed long and hard, blowing a tremendous amount of phlegm into a handkerchief.

Petya had no sympathy for the boy. Igor got what he deserved. The voice in Petya's head had convinced him that Igor was poisoning him. Petya just couldn't figure out how, since he'd become so careful with his food. Petya kept his bread ration in a special pocket he'd sown on the inside of his shirt, and he ate it only in seclusion.

Katya poured some of the water she'd finished making drinkable into three tea cups. She gave one to Igor, one to Petya, and saved one for herself. Petya peered at the brown water in the cup. It smelled awful—like tea made with acorns and rotten eggs. He pushed the cup away.

"Petya, you need to drink water," Katya said, pushing the cup back toward him. "The doctors say that if you bathe twice a week and drink three glasses of water each day that you can survive for a long time."

"That's how you're being poisoned!" a voice hissed to Petya. "It's the water."

Petya shuddered at the realization. It wasn't Igor that was trying to kill him. It was Katya. She was poisoning both of them. That's why Igor was so sick.

Katya was standing over another pot of water she'd put on the stove, glancing impatiently at the front door every few seconds. Petya considered that he'd vastly underestimated how cunning and devious she was. Could it be she was putting on an elaborate charade? Merely pretending to be kind and considerate all the time? What a clever way that was to hide the fact you were trying to kill somebody.

"I told you she hates you and wants you dead," the voice whispered in Petya's head.

Petya watched Igor to see if he drank his water. He did. The fool.

Then, to his astonishment, Katya drank her water, but Petya surmised she must have only placed the poison in his and Igor's cup.

When Katya went to the kitchen, Petya used the opportunity to pour the water from her cup back into the pot on the stove, and then pour the water from his cup into Katya's. When she returned, he pretended to drink from his empty cup.

"That's better," Katya remarked to him as she took another drink from her cup.

Petya smiled to himself. He'd foiled her little plan. And wouldn't she be surprised when she was the one who got sick instead of him?

After two sharp knocks on the front door, Katya rushed to open it.

"Comrade Doctor," Petya heard her say, "thank you so much for coming. I know you're terribly busy, and I really appreciate you stopping by."

"Yes, well, I don't have much time," a gruff voice answered. "Where's the boy?"

A doctor. That was smart, thought Petya. It was a good way to make Igor's eventual death look like it was from natural causes. And to think, Petya used to believe Katya was such an admirable and innocent soul.

The doctor pulled out an old-fashioned listening tube from his pocket and pressed it to Igor's chest. Then he pressed his fingers into Igor's belly, felt his pulse, inspected his tongue, and concluded authoritatively that the boy had bronchitis. "Make sure he drinks plenty of fluids and gets some rest," he said as he wrapped his scarf around his neck and buttoned up his coat.

Katya thanked him profusely, then got bundled up herself and accompanied him out.

Petya listened to them make their way down the stairs, then he crawled out of bed and went to the mirror to comb his hair. He hardly recognized the stranger staring back at him—the long narrow face, the scruffy neck and cheeks, the clear but hideously pale skin. He hadn't weighed this little—146 pounds—since he was a teenager. He'd unwillingly dropped sixty pounds since the start of the blockade.

His hair was long, greasy, and full of snarls, and he couldn't get the comb through it. It was mid-November, and his last bath had been in September. Abandoning the comb, Petya pulled a hat down tight over his head. Then he put on his boots and two coats and went to get his daily rations.

The first line—to get the allotted bread from his ration card—usually took two hours, but today it took him three. Next, he waited outside in the cold at a different distribution point to get the bread from Guzman's ration card.

As he neared the front of the line, he noticed the normally ill-tempered lady was giving out rations with scarcely a rude word. Petya guessed she probably no longer had the stamina to be explicitly offensive anymore. It was difficult to muster the energy for a lot of things these days. Activities one used to do with ease, without a second thought, were now a tremendous struggle. Lifting one's arm was done only as a last resort. When opening doors, one did so just far enough to squeeze through. Carrying things was out of the question unless it was an absolute necessity. Going up stairs was the most arduous part of one's day and something that had to be undertaken with patience and concentration.

The middle-aged woman two spots ahead of Petya in line was the opposite of those who grew deathly thin. She was puffy. Her arms and legs were like balloons, and her hands were so fat that she had trouble taking hold of her bread ration. If Petya didn't know better, he'd think she was obese. But it was all an illusion. She was as deprived and ill as everyone else.

When Petya got his ration, he stepped away from the others and hid it in a pocket on the inside of his shirt. He wouldn't eat it until he got home and could lock himself in the bathroom. After an apprehensive scan in every direction, he placed Guzman's ration card in the same pocket. He kept his own card in his boot so as to not confuse the two.

To get home, Petya had to walk halfway before he could climb aboard one of the few streetcars still running. The first street he walked down was wide and filled with snow drifts. Petya seemed to be the only one on the street, but he knew better. There were muggers hiding in the alleys, ready to jump you for your ration and ration card. He kept a close eye on each alley, but his attention was mostly on his bread. No matter how coarse and bitter it was, he couldn't wait to get home and take a bite.

He thought back to two months ago when he'd just begun to feel the effects of the blockade. He vividly recalled the first time he went two days without food. The first twenty-four hours had been relatively easy, and he actually felt rather refreshed and energetic at one point. But from twenty-four to thirty-six hours, his legs hurt and he got a terrible headache that wouldn't go away. It burned when he urinated, and his tongue was coated in a thick white film. He had horrendous bad breath, as well as an appalling taste in his mouth.

Once all the discomfort had passed, he'd felt unbearably weak, and if he got up too quickly from lying down, he'd get light headed.

Petya remembered the foods he used to have on a daily basis: buckwheat with butter, borscht, fried eggs. They were ordinary—mundane even—but he recalled them so fondly now that they were elevated to an exalted status, like stuffed sturgeon or Napoleon cake.

Approaching another alley, Petya first glanced suspiciously at the man walking on the other side of the street, then he peeked around the corner of the alley. Seeing nothing except an abandoned, snow-covered car, he started to pass by when a dark figure jumped from behind the car and ran at him. With his disfigured leg, Petya couldn't flee, so he called out to the man on the far side of the street instead.

"Help me!" he cried out as he was tackled to the ground.

His attacker—thin and bony with a black scarf wrapped around his mouth—flashed a knife in front of Petya's face. "Give me your bread and your ration card or I'll kill you," he threatened.

Petya was so frightened he could barely speak. "It's ... in my ... my ...," he stuttered.

The man situated his knee so that it pushed on Petya's stomach. "Give it to me," he growled through the scarf, pressing the long blade to Petya's cheek.

With trembling hands, Petya retrieved Guzman's ration card and handed it over.

"And the bread too!"

"I ... I ... don't have any bread."

The man reached into Petya's pocket and found the bread himself. "You liar," he hissed. "I said I'd kill you."

As the assailant raised his knife over his head, something struck his arm, and the knife went flying into a snowbank.

"Beat it, you coward!" commanded a gruff voice.

Petya's attacker scrambled to his feet amid sharp strikes from a wooden cane. He fled down the alley, then stopped midway and slowed to a walk.

"Are you all right?" the stranger asked as he offered his hand to Petya.

Petya took the man's hand and made his way to his feet. As he eyed the stranger's thick white beard and crooked nose, he exclaimed, "That bastard stole my bread ration."

"That's awful," the man said, shaking his head. "In all my fifty-six years I've never seen such a terrible time as now. People have become complete animals. Hopefully you still have your ration card?"

Petya knew that if he lost that he was as good as dead within a week. Luckily the thief had only gotten Guzman's card, Petya's was still tucked safely inside his boot. "Yes. He didn't get that," Petya replied absently as he brushed snow off himself.

"That's good," the man said. "Give it to me."

The wind was gusting, and Petya wasn't certain he'd heard correctly, but then he looked up and saw a pistol in the man's hand.

"Give me the card now or I'll put a hole in your stomach," the man said menacingly.

Petya could hardly believe it. "Is this a joke?"

"Don't test me," the man snarled. "I've already killed three people. Give me your card and you won't get hurt."

"If I give you my card, I'll die anyway."

"Maybe," the man replied. "But if you don't, you'll die for certain right here and now."

Petya could find no flaws in the man's logic, and he pulled the card out of his boot and gave it to him.

Making Petya lie back on the ground, the man ordered him to count to fifty before standing up. "You get up before that and I'll shoot you."

Petya did as he was told.

"Animals," the man muttered as he walked away. "That's what people have become: animals fighting for their survival."

Petya lay on the cold, hard ground staring up at the gray sky, wondering if God was laughing at him like the kids in the orphanage used to. The wind blew snow off the top of nearby snow drifts and into his face, and he could hear bombs falling in another sector of the city. Their high-pitched whistle was inevitably followed by an earth-shaking boom.

Though he stopped counting at fifty, he didn't stand back up. He wasn't sure he'd get up at all. He was tired of trying. Tired of doing what the voices in his head demanded. His entire life had been nothing but hurt and shame. Feeling his eyes well with tears, he tried to prevent all the pain from rising to the surface. He squeezed his eyes, gritted his teeth, focused on his outrage, but nothing was going to stop it this time. One tear rolled down his cheek, then another, and then the flood gates gave way and the tears flowed like a raging river.

The stove was still warm when Petya arrived home, and he wrapped his hands around it to thaw them out. Igor was in his bed, but he wasn't moving or making any sound and Petya suspected he'd died from the poisoned water Katya gave him. Sneaking close to the boy to see if he was still breathing, Petya caught sight of Igor's chest rising and falling ever so slightly. Deciding he must simply be sleeping deeply, Petya added more wood to the fire and prepared to nap himself.

Noticing Oksana had repositioned her blankets and pillow so her head, instead of her feet, would be near the stove, Petya rearranged her neatly-made bed to the way it used to be. He took special care to ensure there were no wrinkles and that the pillow was only half-tucked under the blankets, like she always did. Then he lay down on his own bed and fell into a deep slumber.

When he awoke forty-five minutes later, it wasn't because of his empty stomach or cold bed. A new voice had introduced itself, and this one claimed to be God. It was a man's voice—deep and full—and it spoke to him calmly, patiently.

Petya thought it would vanish when he woke up, but the voice kept up its continuous stream of mesmerizing monologue. It was particularly convincing, because it was more rational than the other voices. When it explained that it was speaking solely to him and that was why no one else could hear it, that made sense to Petya. When God had spoken to Moses or Joan of Arc, no one else had been able to hear His voice either.

The new voice was vastly different from the others. It even argued with them. When they told Petya he was corrupt and despicable, the voice of God told them they were wrong and assured Petya he was one of His children and therefore worthy and good. And when Petya thought he perceived Guzman speaking to him again, the voice of God convinced him otherwise, telling him it wasn't Guzman, but instead a disciple of the devil and that Petya should never do its bidding.

The voice of God also informed Petya of an important mission he was to undertake. It wouldn't say what the mission was; however, clues would be provided when the time was right.

As sounds came from the hallway, Petya pulled his blankets up tight to his chin. The apartment door opened a few seconds later, and Oksana and Katya came in carrying bundles of wood.

"They delivered a pile of firewood to the courtyard," announced Katya. "Could you help us bring it up before it's all gone?"

It was bad enough Katya was trying to kill him, but for her to then ask for his help was too much. Petya was about to tell her to go to the devil when the voice of God instructed him to help them. He found he couldn't ignore it like he sometimes could with the other voices. The wind was howling outside, and he wanted more than anything to snuggle further into his bed, but instead he got up and joined in the grueling task.

How much firewood one should carry each time was a confounding decision. The more you carried, the fewer trips you had to make. But on the other hand, the heavier the load, the more rapidly you tired. The decision was made for the three of them, because after only a few trips the pile was gone. Everyone living within a block of the delivery had come to take some.

Petya collapsed back into bed, feeling weaker than ever. The voice of God began speaking to him again, telling him it was important to sustain himself physically for his upcoming mission. Petya explained to the voice that he'd lost his ration card, then offered to steal Oksana's.

"No," the voice responded adamantly. "Thou shalt not steal."

"Perhaps you could make me some bread, like that story in the Bible," suggested Petya.

"That would endanger the mission," the voice answered. "If you have no bread, then eat meat instead."

Oksana and Katya were in the kitchen, and Katya called out to him. "Are you talking to us, Petya?"

Petya ignored her and made clear to the voice that he had no meat, nor anything to trade to be able to buy meat at the market. Then, out of the corner of his eye, Petya spied the faint outline of a figure standing in the hallway. Startled, he sat up to get a better look, but it disappeared. He studied the area for a minute, closely inspecting the pair of boots on the dingy floor, the crooked frame of a birch tree forest painting, and an abandoned cobweb near the ceiling. Just when he was about to look away, he discovered the faint bluish outline once again. It was like a hollow person was standing there. There was an edge, but nothing inside.

"But you *do* have access to meat," the voice contended.

"One of you drank it," accused Oksana. "And don't try to deny it!"

Katya rushed in from the kitchen to see what the commotion was about. She'd just been in the room a moment ago and had seen Oksana getting ready for work while both Petya and Igor were still asleep. "What's going on?" she asked.

Petya and Igor were sitting up in their beds, gazing blankly at Oksana. Igor wiped the sleep from his eyes while Petya yawned and stretched his arms.

"I poured myself a cup of water," replied Oksana. "Then I left for a few seconds, and when I came back, it was gone."

"Your cup was gone?" asked Katya.

"No. My cup is still there," she said, pointing at it. "But someone drank the water. And I know it was one of these two scoundrels." She had her hands on her hips and her bottom lip pressed tightly into the top one. Her formerly black hair was now the same dingy shade of white as last week's snow. She'd stopped styling it, and it hung like a wet mop over her head.

Katya inspected Oksana's cup to ensure it was empty. "Igor, did you drink Oksana's water?"

"No," Igor answered. "Why would I drink her water? I have my own." He picked up a chipped white tea cup by his bed and showed that it was indeed half full of water.

"Then *you* must have drunk it," Oksana said, scowling at Petya.

"I was sleeping," Petya said with another yawn. "Besides, why would I drink your water. I could just as easily get my own."

Katya shook her head in pity. She was gradually coming to agree with Petya that Oksana was losing her mind. "Maybe you already drank it and just forgot," she suggested.

"No," Oksana said firmly. "I did not drink it yet. I distinctly remember pouring it, then setting it down, then going to get my coat."

"Just like you 'distinctly' remembered rearranging your bed," Petya said skeptically.

"I *did* rearrange my bed," she cried, then covered her ears and growled. "You're all making me crazy!" Grabbing her coat, she stormed out of the apartment.

Petya tapped the side of his head with his index finger. "You see?" he said to Katya.

She nodded her head, briefly considering asking him and Oksana to move back to their old apartment. They were *both* losing their sanity, and Katya was caught in the middle.

Igor wrapped his arms around his chest and coughed. It was a horrible hacking sound that didn't reflect the fact he was actually getting better. He hadn't had a fever in the past week and was starting to regain some of his energy.

Katya sat down on the edge of his bed and put her arm around him. "The doctor said the cough might take a few weeks to go away," she said. "Just try to bear with it."

When he finished his coughing spell, he blew his nose, then asked unexpectedly, "Is the end of the world coming?"

She again felt sad that Igor had never known their grandmother and her teachings. Katya wished the whole world could have received her teachings. Maybe then this war never would have happened. "I think we're living in very dark times," said Katya. "Times not unlike when Jesus lived. People are scared and clinging tightly to their beliefs, the same as when Jesus walked the earth. The Romans ruled most of the world, including Palestine, and the Jews had become complacent and dogmatic. Jesus shook all that up. He challenged the establishment—not just the Jewish rabbis, but the Romans as well. He taught there was to be no allegiance to any country, ruler, or even rabbi. Instead, one should answer only to God. And—"

"What a pack of lies," Petya called from the other side of the room. "Don't listen to her, Igor. That's not what Christianity teaches at all. It says you get one chance in this world, and that's it. You get it right; you go to heaven. You screw up; you go to hell. It's that simple. To get into heaven, you have to stroke God's ego, sacrifice animals, convert the heathens, and build temples in His honor."

It wasn't easy for Katya to hear Petya's spiteful words on God and religion, and she had to bite her tongue to keep from lashing out. She wanted to practice what she preached, but more than that, she wanted Igor to see firsthand that one didn't have to be afraid of other people's ideas and opinions, that you could hold onto your own principles no matter what everyone else thought.

"I won't let you poison this young boy's mind with that garbage," continued Petya. His eyes were narrow slits beneath his eyebrows. "Religion has been a plague on mankind from the moment someone invented it."

Katya knew the subject of religion triggered something deeply painful in Petya, so she took a deep breath and tried to cultivate gentleness in her words and tone. "I'm curious to hear more about why you think this," she said, turning to face him.

"No other concept has caused more harm and suffering than the idea of an omniscient deity," replied Petya. "Hundreds of millions of people have been slaughtered throughout history—all in the name of Allah, Shiva, Yahweh, Odin, Jupiter...."

Katya did her best to hear past his judgments and find that place in him that was so full of anguish. "You feel outraged when you think of how many innocent people have died in battles, pogroms, and inquisitions because of religion," she guessed. "You value peace and harmony, and feel furious when people resort to violence."

"Yes," he answered quickly. "But it's not only that. Religions tell people what to do, how to think, and what to believe. They're always trying to control you!"

Katya saw Igor taking it all in. "If I hear you right, Petya," she said, "you're full of despair because you value liberty and autonomy. It's important for you to have freedom of thought, freedom of action."

"Of course," exclaimed Petya. "And these damn religions don't give anyone freedom. Instead, they tell you that you should suffer—that you're flawed and evil by nature. They teach you that you're a horrible person *unfit in the eyes of the Lord*. To them, man deserves to suffer, because he has to pay for his sins. And the first sin he commits is to be born!"

"You'd like people to know they're alright just as they are," Katya said. "You're offended when you see someone being told they're inherently flawed and sinful by nature. Is that it?"

For the first time since Petya started talking, Katya saw him pause to take a breath. "I'd like you to know that I do think man is inherently good by nature," she added.

"But that's not what Christianity or Judaism or Islam teach," protested Petya. "They instruct people to judge themselves and judge others. Does that make the world a better place? Does people hating themselves and hating others make the world a better place?"

"No. It definitely doesn't," she said. "I'm certain it was never God's intention to confuse and constrict man with layers of rules and commandments. It was men who did this—fallible humans who sometimes had their own selfish motives. To me, it makes no sense to blame God for the pitfalls of religion or the things that have been done in his name. It's not God's fault."

"And what of heaven and hell?" Petya said, leaning forward. "Don't you think these two silly concepts are just extreme examples of reward and punishment? Do as the authority figure tells you and you go to heaven. Disobey him and you go to hell. Religions are quite adept at control."

Katya was fascinated that through deeply listening to him, she was coming to see how they both wanted the same thing. "You'd like people to be able to make their own decisions without concepts of right and wrong, good and bad."

"Exactly! That's what the world needs. We don't need a new god. We need to get rid of all our existing ones and start recognizing man as holding the key to the future. Humanity is all we need. We don't need Jesus Christ and never have."

Katya felt a shift in the conversation. Petya looked less tense and wasn't in such a rush to speak. "It's important to you for people to have faith in themselves and each other," she said. "You'd like people to believe in themselves, believe in humanity. Right?"

Petya's shoulders slowly inched down from his ears. He nodded his head and leaned back onto his arms, looking poised and at ease.

Katya exhaled and managed a brief smile. "I think the most difficult part of walking the path of spirituality is learning how to sift through all the debris the truth has been buried under," she said. "For example, did you know that for the first two hundred years after Jesus' death, his followers abstained from military service at all costs? They believed in Jesus' teachings that you couldn't destroy evil by destroying your enemies. Jesus taught that only love could overcome hate. It wasn't until the Roman Emperor Constantine co-opted Christianity that all that changed."

Petya shifted his position and sat up straighter. "Has God ever spoken to you?" he asked intently. "What does he sound like? What does he say?"

"I can't say I've ever *literally* heard his voice," replied Katya. "But I suppose if I did, it would be a calm, patient voice that reassured me when things weren't going well, complimented me when no one else would, and told me I was all right just as I am."

Petya—folding his hands and staring at the floor—seemed to contemplate her words as a knock came at the front door.

Answering the door, Katya was taken aback to find a Red Army soldier cradling two heads of cabbage. He was dressed in an officer's uniform with a heavy wool greatcoat, fur collar, and fur hat. "Hello, Katya," he said cordially as he removed his hat.

She recognized him, but wasn't sure from where.

"How is Felix?" he asked cautiously.

Now she knew. He had been Felix's commanding officer when he was doing clerical work for the army.

"I haven't heard from him since he left for the front in early September," she said.

He pursed his lips and was silent.

Katya was amazed at how little he'd changed since she last saw him. Most people you hadn't seen in a few months were barely recognizable. Their skin would be dry, scaly, and tight around the bones. They would speak slowly and easily lose their train of thought. Their gums would be swollen and bleeding, and their teeth in decay. But this man wasn't one of the walking skeletons of the city. He was a military man and an officer, and though he was still probably hungry all the time, he was far from starving.

"Oh, here," he uttered, holding out the two cabbages. "These are for you."

Katya took them and was immediately worried about Petya seeing or overhearing. She didn't want to share them. These life preservers were for her and Igor only.

The man then reached into his pocket and handed her four chocolate bars. "And these too," he said.

Katya was speechless. The gifts were literally gifts of life. "I ... I don't know what to say."

"You don't have to say anything. I only wish I could do more."

She hid the chocolate bars in a pocket and wrapped the cabbages in the blanket hanging around her shoulders. As marvelous as the gifts were, Katya couldn't help but think that they'd only delay the inevitable for Igor. "You know," she said, "there is something else you could do. You could find a position for my cousin, Igor, to increase his rations."

"I'm afraid I can't help you there," he said sheepishly.

Katya hung her head, peering at the big buttons on his coat. "I understand."

He cleared his throat. "I wish I could stay longer but I've got to get to—"

"Wait," she blurted, seizing him by the arm.

He looked slightly alarmed at her hand gripping his sleeve.

"I ... I ... um," she stuttered. "I really need your help." She couldn't believe how difficult that was to say. "I need you to get Igor a position."

"I just told you," he said, "we don't have any open positions." He put his hat back on. "Now if you'll excuse me, I need to—"

"Don't deny me this," Katya persisted, maintaining her hold on his sleeve. "This isn't just a favor. It's a matter of life and death. He's going to die unless he gets more food." She held his gaze with her watery eyes.

He looked away, then said. "I guess I could look around for you. See if anything comes up. What is he doing now?"

"He's not doing anything. He's just a boy."

"A boy? How old?"

"Twelve," Katya said, then quickly added, "but he's very capable."

He hesitated. "I don't think so," he said. "There's not—"

Katya spoke over him. "He can do anything you ask of him. You must have a need for something around there. Every place is understaffed these days."

"Not us." He tried gently pulling his arm from her grasp, but she didn't let go.

"Please," implored Katya. "Surely you can find some small tasks for him to do. I'm begging you."

He scratched behind his ear with his free hand. "I guess it wouldn't hurt us to have a courier to deliver stuff once in a while. Can he walk all right?"

"Oh yes, he can even run." She knew she was stretching the truth with that one, but only because he was still recovering.

"I don't know," he said doubtingly. "Let me get a look at him first."

Katya hurried down her apartment hallway, calling over her shoulder, "I'll be right back. Don't go anywhere."

She first went to the kitchen to stash the chocolate and cabbage. Her hands trembled as she unlocked the heavy padlock that safeguarded her food. With the exception of three sugar cubes and a few potatoes, the inside of the cupboard was bare. The five small potatoes were all that remained from when she traded her fur coat at the market last month.

Igor was the only resident of the apartment whose appearance hadn't changed dramatically. He'd lost weight, but he didn't look like a completely different person like Petya or Oksana. He just looked like a skinny kid.

While Katya combed his ratty hair, she explained the situation to him. "Listen to me, sweetheart. There's a man at the door who could save your life. I'm trying to convince him to give you a job so your rations will be increased. You know how you're always telling me you want to fight the Nazis? Well, this man is in the army, and if you work for him, you'll be helping out with the war effort."

"Really?" said Igor, his eyes widening.

"Yes. He wants to see you, so you need to look as healthy as possible and be very nice to him. Do you understand?"

Igor nodded.

Katya took out a needle from her sewing materials, poked her middle finger, and squeezed a few drops of blood out. Then she rubbed the blood on Igor's cheeks until his pale, sickly skin looked healthily rosy.

"Let's go," she said, nudging him to the front door. "Smile a little and try to look lively."

The officer crossed his arms guardedly as Igor approached.

"Introduce yourself," Katya whispered when they were nearly there.

Igor stood at attention and said, "Comrade Igor reporting for duty, sir!"

The officer smiled and saluted back. "How well do you know the city, young man?"

"Not so well," Igor answered. "I've only been here since August."

"Oh, he's being modest," injected Katya. "He used to go out wandering around the city all the time before they implemented the curfew. I even sent him out on errands myself to buy things for me. He's very reliable."

Igor let loose with another lengthy cough, and Katya nearly panicked at the man's displeased frown. "Don't worry about that, comrade," she said, trying to reassure him. "Igor's just getting over a cold. It sounds much worse than it is."

"I don't know," the officer said. "He doesn't seem—"

"You must take him," pleaded Katya, barely holding back her tears. "He's not going to make it if you don't."

She hated to say that in front of Igor, but it was worth the risk.

The man hesitated yet again, then unexpectedly cleared all expression from his face. "All right, then," he stated. "Maybe next week you could send him over and—"

"How about right now?" urged Katya. She didn't want to leave anything to chance. "He has nothing to do, and there's no time like the present, right?"

"Well ... I guess. Are you ready, son?"

"He just needs to get his coat and boots on," said Katya. She then threw her arms around the man, weeping and thanking him endlessly.

The hard snow crunched loudly under Katya's boots as she walked to work. The temperature had dropped fifteen degrees from the day before, but she was so cold all the time that she barely noticed the difference. The recent unexpected gifts of food and a job for Igor had renewed her spirit and given her hope that things were starting to change for the better. When she got to the office and saw Lev had recovered enough from his injuries to return to his job, she was convinced things were indeed improving.

"Good morning, Lev," she said. "How are you feeling?" Besides some scratches on his face, he actually looked healthier than before.

He looked up from the table where he was seated. "Ah Katya, good morning. Nice to see your friendly face again. I'm feeling much better, thank you. They feed you quite well in the hospital, and I needed the rest even more than I knew. As soon as this ringing stops in my ears, I'll be as good as new."

She sat down next to him and cleared some space on the cluttered table.

"Congratulations on getting the ice formation data to the director that day," Lev said. "It couldn't have been easy."

"It wasn't," she said. "I made it back to the office ten minutes after six and our kind, sweet director still called in my commissar to tell her of my 'failure to perform to the best of my abilities.'"

"And?"

Katya understood he was asking if she'd received any punishment. "That's it," she replied. She'd been let off with a strict warning: do exactly as you're told from now on or you'll be relieved of duty. The significance of the threat was not lost on her as losing a job meant you also lost its commensurate ration.

"He's not an easy man to work for," commented Lev. "Short on appreciation; long on criticism. And he expects you to carry out every order unquestioningly." He emphasized the last word, then got up and started pacing in front of the plywood where the window once was.

The pacing meant more bad news, Katya knew, and she wondered what it could be this time. When it came to the food supply or the war, there was never any *good* news. Military victories were as rare as a full stomach. Had the Germans broken through the lines somewhere again? Had another warehouse been hit by a bomb?

"All right, Lev," she said after watching him pace for a few minutes. "Out with it."

"What?"

"The bad news."

"How did you know?"

"We've been working together a while now and there's been enough bad news that I know when it's coming," she replied. "So what is it?"

"You're not going to like it," he said, staring at the floor. "The director has ordered a fifth ration reduction."

Katya covered her mouth with her hand and felt her breath go out of her. "For the troops?" she asked cautiously.

"No," he said glumly. "It's for the civilian population."

Placing her hands over her ears, she shook her head in disbelief. "No! He can't cut rations *again*," she cried. "People are already dying by the thousands. He might as well just hand out death certificates."

Lev sat down across from her and arranged random stacks of paper.

"He has to cut the troops' rations instead," she insisted. "Those on the front-line already get *twice* as much bread as we do. Plus, they get meat!"

"I don't like it either," Lev said with a sigh. "But those are our orders and we need to get started, because there's a lot to do. He wants it implemented on the twentieth. That only gives us the rest of today and tomorrow to get ready."

"Is he in?" asked Katya.

"Why?"

Katya knew he wouldn't have asked why if their director wasn't in, so she rushed out of the room toward his office.

"Katya, don't be a fool," Lev called after her.

On her way down the hall, she folded her hands in prayer and saw her grandmother in her mind's eye. The elderly matron was sitting in her favorite rocking chair, knitting and telling Katya about Jesus' Sermon on the Mount. Of the eight Beatitudes, Katya had always felt an affinity for the last one: "Blessed are they who are persecuted for the sake of righteousness, for theirs is the kingdom of heaven." It had given her great comfort when she was a child to know that no matter what happened to her dissident grandmother here in the Soviet Union, she was assured of a place in heaven in the hereafter. As Katya silently recited Jesus' eighth declaration now, she realized it was the first time she was doing it not for her grandmother, but for herself.

After a hasty knock on the director's door, she entered without waiting for him to answer. The diminutive director was sitting in a chair with a homely, barrel-chested officer standing next to him. With the aid of two kerosene lamps, they were leaning over a table looking at a large map of Leningrad and the surrounding areas. Soviet positions were marked in red, German positions in black. Katya didn't know how he'd managed the lamps since the rest of the city had long since run out of kerosene.

"Comrade Selenaya, what is it? Can't you see I'm busy?" her director said irritably.

"Sorry for the intrusion," she replied, regretting her words as soon as they came out of her mouth. She wasn't sorry in the least. "I'd like to speak with you about your orders for the latest ration reduction."

Her director had a long, thin nose, and by the way his nostrils flared, she knew he was greatly annoyed. "There's nothing to discuss," he said curtly. "Continue with the preparations."

Despite her trepidation and shakiness, Katya stepped closer to the two men. "I'd like you to reconsider the order," she said, "because I cannot carry it out in good conscience. You've ordered the deaths of tens of thousands of people."

The officer—bald headed and bespectacled—arched his eyebrows and folded his arms in front of his chest.

"It's a temporary reduction," Katya's director responded. "As soon as the situation improves, civilian rations will be returned to their current levels."

"But you can't make the civilian population shoulder the entire burden of the cut," she argued. "You've got to cut the troops' levels."

"Cut our troops' rations?" he said with a glance at the officer. "You should be ashamed of yourself, Comrade Selenaya. They're putting their lives on the line every day for you, and this is how you want to repay them?"

"I know the situation," Katya said confidently. "They can absorb a cut. Leningraders can't."

"We have a job to do," he replied, raising his voice and motioning to the officer next to him. "And that is to see to it that we win this war."

"I thought your job was to see to it that Leningrad didn't starve to death," Katya said as calmly as she could.

He leapt from his chair, nearly knocking over one of the lanterns. "Leave this office now and carry out the order you've been given," he snarled.

"No."

The officer grunted, dropping his arms to his sides. With a hostile stare, Katya's director announced, "Then you can consider yourself relieved of duty. I won't have anyone on my staff who disobeys direct orders."

"When orders are unjust, we have a moral obligation to disobey them," she retorted.

"Get out of this office now!" he shouted in response.

Katya reluctantly turned toward the door, but then stopped and asked over her shoulder. "So that's it? The decision to cut rations has already been made?"

Her director paused, just slightly, before saying yes, and this gave Katya the information she was hoping for. His hesitation meant that he hadn't yet presented his recommendation to Comrade Zhdanov and the Leningrad Defense Council. No decision concerning Leningrad was ever final until they said so.

If the cut was to take place in two days, then the Defense Council would have to formally approve the decision that very night to allow one day to issue and implement the order. Having delivered last-minute documents from time to time at their previous meetings, Katya knew where and when they met. She also knew that her director's recommendations were usually approved as a mere formality.

She had to ensure that didn't happen this time.

Clouds had moved in and blotted out the moon and stars by the time Katya arrived at the bunker. The guards at the entrance shined a light in her face, asking why she was there. Trying her best to come across as cordial and at ease, she told them that she needed to deliver some last-minute documents again. They remembered her, and after checking her papers and searching for weapons, they let her pass to the inside.

The bunker was buried deep in the ground and fortified with thick layers of concrete. She opened the heavy door and strode purposefully down the narrow corridor. There were still more guards to come, and she had no idea how she was going to get past them and into the meeting. When she'd delivered documents previously, she'd had to hand them over to a guard to take in. Hardly anyone was ever allowed into the all-important gatherings where the fate of Leningrad was decided.

Four unsmiling guards eyed her every step as she approached the entrance to the meeting room. Katya took a deep breath, picked the one who looked the least unfriendly, and explained that she once again had important documents her director needed right away.

"Give them to me," the man responded and held out his hand. "I'll take them to him."

"No. I can't this time," Katya said. "I have specific instructions to deliver them myself."

The man eyed her skeptically, then disappeared into the room and came back out a minute later. "He said he's not expecting any documents."

"Well, he must have forgotten," insisted Katya. "Why would I come all the way here if he didn't need them?"

"I suggest you leave now," the guard said coolly. "This is a secure area. Unauthorized personnel are not allowed to be here."

"He's going to be very angry when he realizes he needed these documents," said Katya.

"You may leave the documents if you wish, but you need to go or else I'll be forced to put you under arrest."

"Very well," she replied. "Will you give me a moment to retie my scarf? It's terribly cold out there tonight." Before he could respond, she unwrapped her long scarf from her head and neck. She didn't really need to retie it, but the task would buy her a minute to think of another way into the meeting.

The guard tapped his foot impatiently as she slowly wound the scarf around herself. When more than a minute had gone by, he lost his patience and ordered one of the other guards to escort her out. Before the guard could reach her, the door to the meeting room burst open and a pasty-faced, middle-aged man smoking a cigarette emerged. He looked worn down, but was by no means like one of the walking corpses Katya saw so frequently these days. He still had plenty of meat on his bones.

The guards quickly came to attention, and Katya knew it was he—Zhdanov—the boss of Leningrad. "Is there any paper in the toilets?" he asked hoarsely.

One of the guards had been reading Leningradskaya Pravda, and he handed the newspaper to Zhdanov.

Katya called to him before he got very far. "Forgive me, comrade. I know your time is precious, but this is very important. I'm wondering if you're completely aware of the all the implications of the latest ration reduction."

He seemed taken aback by the question. Plucking the cigarette from his mouth, he answered, "I'm quite familiar with the facts. We don't want to cut rations again, but we have little choice."

In fear of being thrown out before she could argue her point, Katya spoke rapidly. "To cut civilian rations to the levels proposed is murder," she said boldly. "I beg of you to revise it and have the troops shoulder some of the burden."

"We already reduced the troops' rations a week and half ago," Zhdanov said. "I don't remember the exact amount, but their levels need to be maintained—"

"Yes. I know they were cut," Katya injected. "But they're currently receiving six hundred grams of bread plus one hundred twenty-five grams of meat. Rear-unit troops are getting four hundred grams of bread and fifty grams of meat. It's not much, I agree, but it's no comparison to civilians. Right now factory workers only get three hundred grams of bread, and everyone else gets a miserable one hundred fifty grams. No civilians get any meat."

He arched his thick eyebrows. "How do you know this information?"

Just then Katya's director emerged from the meeting room and gaped at her. "What are you doing here?" he asked, moving between her and Zhdanov. "Guards, remove her immediately."

They grabbed her by the arms and started taking her to the exit.

"My apologies, comrade," Katya heard her director say. "I was unaware—"

"Does she work for you?" interrupted Zhdanov.

"She used to," he replied. "She was let go this morning for insubordination."

"She looks familiar," Zhdanov said. "I swear I've seen her before."

"She's Grigori Selenii's daughter."

"Katya?"

"Yes, that's her name."

"Oh my, she's all grown up. I remember when she was just a little girl. Comrade Selenaya," he called out. "Come back here."

The guards let go of her arms and she briskly returned.

"You probably don't even remember me," said Zhdanov. "I used to bounce you on my knee when you were just a girl. My goodness how you've grown."

Katya didn't remember him, but believed his story. Her father knew many people and was constantly inviting them over to their apartment.

"I'm sorry about your father," Zhdanov said sincerely. "He was a good man."

Katya gasped. "He's dead?"

Zhdanov nodded. "Forgive me. I assumed you knew. He suffered a heart attack in Moscow."

Katya wasn't completely surprised by the news, but it still shook her. She thought of Igor and how he was her only living relative left now. Though she wanted to cry, she held it back.

Zhdanov turned to Katya's director. "She was just telling me that front-line troops are still getting six hundred grams of bread and one hundred twenty-five grams of meat. Is this true?"

"Yes, comrade, that's correct."

"For some reason, I was under the impression they were getting much less than that," Zhdanov said, scratching his chin. "Your proposal to cut civilians' rations by so much without cutting the troops' by a single gram makes little sense to me."

"You've said before, comrade, that our number one priority in food distribution was to sustain the troops protecting the city."

"What point is there in protecting a city if all its people are dead?" asked Zhdanov sharply.

Katya's director opened his mouth to speak, but then seemed to think better of it.

"I think we need to reconsider this latest reduction," continued Zhdanov. "Don't you agree?"

"Yes, comrade," he said meekly.

Zhdanov took another drag from his cigarette then dropped it to the ground and snuffed it out with his boot. "If you can't make recommendations that are in the best interest of Leningrad, then perhaps I should get someone else." He glanced at Katya. "Like Comrade Selenaya here."

"That won't be necessary," Katya's director said. He cast a malevolent glare in her direction. "I'll be more careful with my recommendations."

Felix cursed under his breath at whichever partisan behind him had allowed himself to be spotted. It had complicated things, but he couldn't expend energy on worrying about it. He needed to get his rifle into position before the light of the moon returned. He spread out more in the thick snow so his arms were better supported, then took aim at the machine-gun nest ninety feet away. The moon crept over the edge of the monstrous black cloud and Felix found his target—a dim figure with binoculars looking out from behind the sandbags.

Felix had figured out that many German positions along the Tikhvin front were vulnerable to attacks at night, especially when the wind howled or the snow fell so heavily one could barely see. The Germans didn't seem to expect an attack at three in the morning in the biting cold. Apparently it wasn't part of their rules of engagement. In fact, Felix found that the more uncommon his tactics, the more successful their attack.

He clenched his jaw over his loose tooth in order to feel his own sour blood in his mouth. Whenever he tasted blood, he thought of Dima—impassioned, starry-eyed Dima who'd wanted to change the world and himself for the better. But the Nazis hadn't given him that chance, and now Felix was going to see to it that *they* got no more chances. He dedicated every fiber of his being to eliminating the Nazi infestation of his homeland. The Germans were no longer fellow humans, but vermin that needed to be exterminated, just like the cockroaches that had invaded Katya's apartment last summer.

With a gentle, practiced squeeze of the trigger, a bullet from Felix's rifle penetrated the man's hand and then cheek. First the binoculars, and then the man fell from sight.

One less cockroach.

The other German soldier quickly engaged the machine gun and bullets flew frantically in every direction. They struck all around Felix, but he remained still. Even when one of the bullets burned a hole straight through his left arm, he did not move.

As the tat-tat-tat of the machine gun wound down and more German soldiers arrived, Felix closed his eyes and thought of Katya. Was she still alive? Or had the lack of food or a German bomb taken her to the next world? Felix wanted nothing more than to marry her and live a peaceful life. He wanted to make passionate love to her in the evening and wake each morning to see her lying next to him. He wanted to have children—a little boy who looked like him, and a little girl who looked like her. He wanted to take trips to the countryside to pick mushrooms and teach his son how to swim in the river. He wanted a normal, uneventful life with friends, family, pets, and poetry.

Feeling his face flush and a warmth rushing through his freezing body, he opened his eyes and saw the snow by his arm turning red. With the bitter realization that the damned cockroaches wouldn't let him have that life, he set his sights on the machine-gun nest again. Through his scope he spotted two more of the accursed insects yelling and gesticulating to one another. After taking aim at the vile head of the first one, Felix adjusted downward for its throat instead. If he hit it just right, the bullet would go straight through and strike the other one standing next to it. He took in a breath and let it out slowly as he squeezed the trigger once more.

His shot hit the mark perfectly and two more cockroaches fell from sight.

The moon disappeared, and additional German troops fired a flare into the sky before ducking into the machine-gun nest. Felix searched for more targets, but they were all hidden.

One thing he knew for sure is that more cockroaches would be coming. Where you saw one, there were at least ten more you couldn't see.

Pushing on his sore tooth, he pictured Dima in his mind, from the shy smile of his boyhood to the bloody, broken body he helped carry last month. Then Felix jumped to his feet and charged at the machine-gun nest with a savage, vengeful scream. Bullets whizzed by him—one grazing his cheek below his right eye—but death was the only thing that was going to stop him now.

He gripped a grenade in his right hand, and when he was close enough, threw it through one of the narrow openings in the nest. It exploded with a muffled thud, and then the gunfire stopped and all was eerily quiet.

Peeking his head around the sandbags of the entrance, Felix spied six lifeless cockroaches in a pile. As he stepped inside to collect their guns and grenades, an officer in a Death's Head helmet unexpectedly stirred and spoke.

Felix didn't like seeing its face, didn't like the fact it had two eyes, two ears, a nose, and a mouth, like him. And he especially hated hearing its grotesque language.

With a newly acquired Nazi pistol, Felix fired two shots into the creature's exoskeleton. "Back to the devil," he muttered to it, then resumed gathering weapons.

Outside, a dozen and a half German troops hastily advanced on the newly formed breach in their lines. Felix took up a position behind some of the sandbags and started shooting. A few more cockroaches went down, but he couldn't tell if he'd hit them or if they'd dove for cover.

A fearsome roar of shrieks, howls, and shouts built behind him, and when Felix turned, he saw his comrades rising up from the snow like a hungry pack of wolves. The partisans charged forward, their battle cry rising like a wave. And for a change, it wasn't the Russians who were in panic and falling back in disarray.

Still savoring the thick, salty taste of blood in his mouth, Felix took aim and shot two cockroaches in the back as they retreated. He wanted to take out more, but there weren't any in his line of fire. Sprinting from the machine-gun nest to a better spot, bullets whizzed by his head. He'd lost all fear of combat. The only thing that mattered to him anymore was killing as many cockroaches as possible.

It had been a tremendous struggle for Petya to sever the arm at the elbow, and he was now thoroughly exhausted. He rested as the fire in the stove gradually came back to life. When the coals were bright orange, he roasted the meat until it was black and charred.

Opening the window, he scooped up some freshly fallen snow into a large pot and set it on the stove. When the snow had melted, he poured the water into a tea cup, then sat down on his bed to eat. The meat was tough and hard to chew, but tasted good nonetheless.

The voice of God in Petya's head had assured him it was not a sin to eat the flesh of another. The only thing that mattered to the voice was that Petya maintain his strength for his upcoming mission. When Petya questioned the voice about the mission, it answered only that it would be revealed in such a way that Petya alone could figure it out.

The lock on the front door clacked as someone opened it from the outside. A few seconds later, Katya entered the dimly lit apartment. Before she even took her coat off, she sniffed loudly and asked Petya where he got the meat.

"From the market," he lied as he ate the last bite.

Katya scanned the room frantically. "Where's Igor?"

Petya shrugged. He was reluctant to say too much, because he knew the trees were eavesdropping.

"You don't know where he is?" asked Katya.

Petya shook his head.

"Have you seen him today?"

He nodded.

"Why can't you speak?"

Deciding she needed to know about the trees recording every word, Petya went up close to her. Motioning to the leafless trees that stood like petrified demons outside their window, he whispered, "They're listening."

Katya glanced out the window. "Who's listening?"

"*They*," he whispered intently, pointing his finger directly at the nearest tree.

Katya took a step away from him.

"Don't be afraid," he reassured her. "They can't hurt us as long as we have this." Petya showed her the shield he'd made with a tin can and piece of string. "I haven't determined how to stop them from eavesdropping," he said, "but they definitely can't hurt us."

"She doesn't believe you," a voice hissed in his head. "You're an imbecile! A ridiculous, disfigured fool! That contraption you made is ludicrous. It doesn't do anything."

"Silence!" the voice of God thundered in response. "Pay no attention to him," it advised Petya. "He is an apostle of the devil, and that is why he says these shameful things. Listen only to me. I am the only one who cares for you, the only one who loves you. You have scared Katya and endangered the mission by telling her about the trees. Apologize."

"Katya, I'm sorry," he said, moving closer to her again. "I shouldn't have told you that. Just forget what I said. All right?"

She nodded. For every step he took toward her, she took an equal step away. "Sure, Petya. I'll just forget it," she said unconvincingly.

"You are such an idiot," a voice accused Petya. "She thinks you've gone completely mad."

"I'm not crazy," asserted Petya. "I know this looks strange, and you don't understand it, but I can explain."

Katya had now backed up to the wall and could go no further.

"You remember we talked about religion and God a while back?"

She stared at him speechlessly.

"I asked you if God ever spoke to you directly."

"Yes, I remember," she said, clenching her hands tightly below her chin.

"Well, I hear him," Petya said excitedly. "He speaks to me."

She dropped her jaw and hesitated. "What?" she finally said. "*Who* speaks to you?"

"God," answered Petya. "God speaks to me. He told me no one else can hear Him. Only me."

"You ... hear ... God," she repeated slowly.

"Yes. And He's coming back."

"Who's coming back? Jesus?"

"Look," he said eagerly as he pulled out the piece of paper he'd found in his old apartment's mailbox.

Katya read the crude handwriting aloud: "Only God can save Leningrad. Pray to Heaven. The Time of the Apocalypse has come. Christ is now in the peaks of the Caucasus."

"You see?" Petya said. "I'm not crazy."

"This is from the Old Believers and Molokans that were pushed into the city by the war," explained Katya. "Everyone has been getting these notes. It's not just you. I got one myself."

Petya sighed in relief that he wasn't the only one God was communicating with. "You got one too? Let me see."

"I can't. I already used it to light a fire."

He recognized she was lying, but couldn't fathom why. She was a good Christian, and he'd expected her to be enthusiastic and support him.

"Well, regardless," said Petya, "I realize now I've been living a life of sin, and it's important we repent before it's too late." He wanted to tell her about his dishonesty, about his stealing the package meant for her and Guzman, but it was more difficult than he thought. The words didn't want to come out. Admitting his deception meant admitting he was a fraud and a pariah to society. "Katya, I ...um ... I," he began.

"Shut up, you fool!" a voice hissed in his ear. "You don't have to tell her a damn thing. She can't prove anything!"

Footsteps echoed from the outside hallway, then the door unlocked and Oksana came in. Katya rushed to her side. "Hi, Oksana. How are you doing? How was work today? Here, let me help you with that bag."

With a look of bewilderment, Oksana held fast to her bag.

"Would you like me to make you some of that herbal tea?" Katya inquired. "It was terribly cold out today, wasn't it? Did it affect your arthritis?"

Petya retreated to the window to study the trees again. He felt relieved that his confession had been postponed.

"The cold was indeed awful today," said Oksana, unbuttoning her coat. "I can barely move my hip. It feels like it's frozen."

Katya helped her take off her coat. "Oh, I can just imagine. It must be absolute torture for you to go up and down those stairs. Have you seen Igor today?"

"To be honest," Oksana said, "I don't know how much longer I can do it. I'm not a schoolgirl anymore. I've asked to be evacuated, but I don't think those bastards give a damn about an old woman like me."

Katya hung Oksana's coat on a hook, then said, "I'm sure everyone's doing their best. Have you seen Igor lately?"

Oksana sniffed at the air. "What's that smell? Is that meat?"

"Yes. Petya had some."

"Where the hell did he get it? He has no money."

"That you know of," Petya said from the other side of the room.

Katya put her face directly in front of Oksana's, exclaiming, "I asked if you've seen Igor."

"I saw him this morning," she finally answered, "before I left for work. Why?"

Katya approached Petya, demanding anew to know where Igor was.

"How should I know?" he replied.

"Damn you!" she screamed in response. "What have you done with him?"

"He's probably just working late," Petya offered meekly.

Snatching her hat and coat, Katya fled the apartment.

"Where are you going?" Oksana called after her.

"To look for Igor!"

Petya sat on the edge of his bed and began putting his boots on.

Oksana eyed him curiously. "You're leaving too? Where are you going?"

"To help her look," he replied flatly.

The room kept shrinking—getting smaller and smaller as the weather outside got colder and colder. Every day, beds would be moved another centimeter closer to the small stove in the middle of the room. It was so crowded now that two people could only get by one another if one of them sat down.

The stove—with its flue stretching to the edge of the room and out the window—was called a burzhuika and nearly every apartment in Leningrad had one. When Katya awoke, she stretched her hand hopefully toward the stove to see if it was still warm. No matter how many layers of clothes or blankets she had on, she was always cold of late. Resting her hand on the stove's side, she was disappointed to feel it wasn't even lukewarm.

She'd awakened from a magnificent dream: she and Felix were in the Kazansky Cathedral getting married. With all their friends and family clustered round, Felix had just lifted her white veil and kissed her.

In vain, she attempted to return to the dream and once more feel his lips on hers, his warm breath on her cheek, and the palpable scent of his skin. Folding her hands in prayer, she asked God to ensure Felix's safe return. Then she got out of bed, pulling one of the blankets with her and wrapping it tightly around her shoulders.

They had a small pile of kindling in the hallway that she could use to start a fire, but she could find neither paper nor matches. Careful not to wake her sleeping roommates, she went to Guzman's apartment where she'd seen some matches a while back.

She found them right where she'd last seen them, on top of the now legless piano. She also spied a wadded-up piece of paper and brought it along with the matches.

Petya snored loudly as she stuffed the paper in the stove and stacked a few twigs on top of it. It had been a fitful night of rest and she was glad it was over with. Still half-asleep, she lit the paper and watched it burn as if in a trance. One of the paper's edges turned bright orange, then quickly faded to black and disintegrated. There was handwriting on the paper and Katya saw Shostakovich's name scrawled on the bottom. She felt disappointed that

Dmitry had written Guzman and not her. Then the paper shifted and uncrumpled and she was able to read a few fragments of the letter:

> ... *items are meant for you and Guzman equally* ...
> ... *the vodka or cigarettes, for* ...

She tried to get the letter out of the fire, but it was too late. The whole thing was engulfed in flames.

Staring blankly into the fire, she thought back to the birthday dinner Petya had surprised her with a few weeks ago. He had mysteriously acquired caviar and vodka, but wouldn't tell her where or how he'd got them. And of course he had suddenly started smoking cigarettes after complaining for a month that he didn't have any and couldn't afford any. Items like cigarettes that temporarily numbed the pain of the constant cold and hunger were in high demand. They were the second most sought after good at the markets, right behind the most coveted item: vodka.

She felt certain the items had been meant for her and Guzman—not Petya and Guzman—but had no proof. She didn't want to believe Petya capable of stealing something so precious, something that could determine whether one lived or died. If he'd done that, she didn't know if she could forgive him. Intense indignation coursed through her veins just thinking about the possibility.

From under the covers of his bed, Igor tossed and turned and let out a muffled moan. Katya glanced his way, then at the empty bed where Guzman used to sleep. A neighbor had found the poor painter's mutilated body buried under a thin layer of snow in the courtyard. Katya hated to suspect Petya of being the one who'd hacked off the arms and legs, but where else could he have gotten the meat he'd been eating lately? She turned her head uneasily to the other side of the room where Petya slept. He had at least six blankets wrapped around him, and only the bridge of his nose and his thick black eyebrows were visible. It seemed like he was always in bed, as if he thought he could hibernate his way through the blockade.

She was afraid of him. With each pound that dropped from his now gangly frame, so too did an ounce of his sanity. If these were normal times, he'd be in a mental institution. But these were anything but normal times. Millions of people the world over were trying to kill one another. Scientists and engineers worked day and night to devise more efficient ways of eradicating people en masse. Men operated mechanized killing machines that prowled the ground, the sky, even the sea. And those who were the best at it—who killed the most people—were given medals and honors.

In truth, Katya decided, the whole world had lost its sanity, and Petya fit right in. *She* was the one who was a lunatic. Her, and her cockamamie notions of peace and understanding, were the misfits.

As she started bundling herself up to go outside, she deliberated how to prove Petya had stolen a package meant for her and Shostakovich's friend. Had Guzman received more food, the amiable painter might still be around telling his wry jokes and meandering stories.

She was heading to the hospital to get her old nurse position back. If she was going to survive the winter, she had to get the worker level of rations. The non-worker level she was on now—a measly two slices of bread a day—wasn't enough to sustain her.

It could be worse, though. If her former director had gotten his way and not cut any of the troops' levels, she and every other non-working adult, child, and elderly Leningrader might be dead already. The two slices of bread kept her alive at least.

The editorial in the newspaper announcing the recent reduction—the fifth—stated in stark language its necessity:

> *It is not possible to expect any improvement in the food situation. We must reduce the norms of rations in order to hold out as long as the enemy is not pushed back, as long as the circle of blockade is not broken. Difficult? Yes, difficult. But there is no choice....*

Lake Ladoga had finally frozen and the Road of Life, as it was now called, was teeming with drivers hauling food and ammunition into the city. Tikhvin was still in German hands though. Unless the Red Army could retake that city and its all-important railroad junction, there would soon be no more supplies to deliver.

While Katya trudged to the hospital, she dreamt about food. It had become her favorite pastime. She liked to imagine eating all those ordinary foods she used to take for granted. Like raw carrots. Pretending to hold one in her hand, she marveled at its vibrant shade of orange. And how sweet it tasted! In her mind's eye, she took bites in unusual ways: from the sides, from the opposite end. What a miraculous vegetable! It was like tasting the whole universe: the rain that watered it, the sun that shone on it, the ground that nourished it. That it grew in the earth and you could just pluck it out and eat it was a wonder of the imagination.

She envisioned radishes, tomatoes, fried onions. And mashed potatoes! She'd give a year of her life for some thick, creamy potatoes with milk, butter, and garlic right now.

Katya had come to realize how little she'd truly appreciated food in her life. It had always been available. Even in times of short supply, she'd never gone hungry for days on end. Full of regret for having ever taken food for granted, she vowed to never again eat it carelessly or thanklessly. She would no longer nibble another morsel while working or thinking of something else. She'd appreciate every nourishing bite and concentrate solely on the food's taste, texture, and smell.

Around the corner of the next block, the somber, hulking hospital came into view. Rumbling up the street toward it was one of the never-ending stream of camouflaged trucks that dumped the wounded off. As it came to a stop near the front door, Katya approached and waited for the driver to emerge. She hoped for the off chance it was delivering supplies, and not more wounded. But when she heard the familiar, dreadful moans emanating from the back, she knew what its cargo was. The driver hopped out, announcing he had six wounded soldiers. When he opened the door to enter the hospital, Katya saw the beds crammed together in the hallway were all full. That meant there was no room for these injured men and they'd have to remain in the truck—possibly all day—until the nurses could free some beds.

As she made her way to the hospital administrator's office, she saw several patients making candles. When she inquired, they explained to her that the hospital had run out last week. One of the wounded men had suggested that those recovering would be grateful for something to do, so why not let them make candles? The idea had worked brilliantly so far.

The hospital administrator was also the lead doctor, and Katya had to wait for him to finish an operation before speaking with him. When he finally came out of surgery, he took off his blood-covered apron, threw it in a hamper, then invited Katya into his office.

On top of his well-organized desk were two orderly stacks of papers, an electric lamp which he obviously hadn't been able to use in quite some time since there was no electricity, and a black bowl with a lid. He motioned for Katya to sit, then sat down himself, asking, "How are you getting along, my dear?"

"I'm alive," she replied. "Which is more than a lot of people can say."

"True. True," he said, running his fingers along his grey mustache. "I wish I could convince some of my patients of that wisdom. I just had to amputate a leg. I was hoping I could save it, but the gangrene was too bad." He took the lid off the black bowl, and the room filled with a delicious aroma. He poured some of the soup into a tea cup and handed it to Katya. "Here," he said, "have some of this. There's even some meat in there."

Instinctually, Katya opened her mouth to protest. She was going to say she couldn't accept such a generous offer, that his job was so important, and that he needed it more than she. But before any words came out, she put the cup to her lips and drank.

He took a large spoon out of a desk drawer and began to eat. "So what is it you want to talk to me about?" he asked in between noisy slurps.

"I'd like my old position back," she said.

"You want to be a nurse again? I thought you had an administrative position overseeing the food supply."

She took another sip of the soup, trying to determine the meat they'd used. She guessed it was probably horse. "I don't have that position anymore."

"What happened?"

"I'd rather not talk about it."

He wiped broth from his mustache, insisting, "I'd really like to know."

She sighed wearily. "I was let go because I had a disagreement with the director."

"It must have been one hell of a *disagreement* for him to let you go."

Noticing a little piece of carrot in her soup, Katya smiled. "He's the type of person who demands people carry out his orders unquestioningly," she said dully. The soup tasted heavenly, and she was looking forward to eating food of this quality every day.

"I see," he commented, running his fingers thoughtfully along his mustache once more.

Katya drank the last of her soup. "But that's all over. I'm actually excited to be a full-time nurse again. I've missed it."

"I'm not sure how to tell you this," he said hesitantly, "but we don't have any room for you."

Katya couldn't hide her shock. She'd expected her request to be a mere formality, that he would welcome her back with open arms. "You're *always* understaffed," she pointed out. "I know that. You know that. That's why I come and volunteer in the evenings."

"There's no question we could use more help," he said, peering at his desk, "but we're constrained as to the number of personnel we can take on."

Katya found it peculiar he wouldn't look her in the face. "When I left, you told me you were very sorry I was leaving and that I was the best nurse here. And now you won't take me back? Were those words just lies?"

He shook his head. "It was the truth. I'd love to take you back, but I can't." Wiping dust off the corner of his desk, he repeated, "I just can't."

Though her eyes were filling with water, she wouldn't allow herself to cry. "I overheard two nurses earlier saying they were going to Tikhvin next week to serve on the front there. You're definitely going to need help then."

He held his hands out for her tea cup, and she passed it to him. "Katya," he said sadly, finally looking at her. "I think you should try other places, perhaps a different hospital. We're not going to be able to take you on here."

"Why?" she exclaimed. "I don't understand. Is there something you're not telling me?"

He rose from his seat and closed the door to his office. "Listen, Katya," he said in a low voice, "you've made some powerful enemies with whatever you did. I've been warned not to take you back. I'm sorry. I wish there was something I could do."

Feeling suddenly dizzy, Katya hastened out of his office to get some fresh air. She made her way quickly down the hallway toward the exit, but felt lightheaded and short of breath and had to stop. With no place to sit, she leaned against the wall, hoping the sickly feeling would pass.

In a makeshift bed near her, a wounded man began to whimper. Within a minute, it developed into an outright scream, and Katya held her hands over her ears to block it out. When that didn't work and no nurses responded, Katya approached and asked what was bothering him.

"My leg," he hollered, thrashing his head from side to side. "My left leg is killing me!"

"Where does it hurt?" asked Katya as she lifted the blanket to get a look.

"Where I was shot," he said. "Just below the knee."

She hurriedly pulled the blanket back down. The man had no knee. He had no left leg at all. It had been amputated, and they must not have told him yet.

Morphine was in short supply, but Katya found some and gave him a small dose anyway. She couldn't bear his screaming.

He calmed almost immediately, and she watched the tension melt from his face. "You're an angel," he said with a slight smile. He had sparkling blue eyes and light blonde hair that hung down to his eyebrows. "The pain was awful. It was like it was on fire, like someone was pouring boiling water on it."

Katya had heard about this type of thing before—ghost pains, they called it—but this was her first experience with it. "And the pain it gone now?"

He nodded.

While she debated whether or not to tell him he had no left leg anymore, a high-pitched whistle screeched through the sky outside. A second later, an explosion shook the ground and a thin mist of dust fell from the ceiling.

"I felt safer at the front," the man said. "At least you could duck in your foxhole. Here, there's nowhere to hide."

"I guess I've gotten used to it," said Katya. "The Germans rarely let up. They're either firing on us with their artillery or setting the city on fire with those awful incendiary bombs."

She turned to go, but he grabbed her by the arm. "What does my leg look like?" he asked. "It's not too bad is it? I used to teach dance—the foxtrot, waltz—at the university before the war."

Katya thought briefly of Felix and how he'd taught her the waltz. She couldn't bear to answer the wounded man's question. She didn't have the strength right now.

Fortunately, he changed the subject. Taking her hand, he said, "It's been a long time since I've seen a beautiful woman. It feels good."

She tried to force a smile, but couldn't.

"Do you know about the other guys from my unit?" he asked. "We were sent to Tikhvin. Talk about a slaughterhouse...."

"I don't know," she answered as she arranged the blanket so it covered him better in the drafty hallway. "You'll have to ask one of the other nurses." The air smelled of body odor and chemicals, and she couldn't take much more. She had to get away.

"Could you check for me? I'm in the Volunteers. First Division."

A flush of adrenaline flooded her body. "You're in the Volunteers?"

"Yeah, what's left of us anyway."

"What regiment?"

"The Second."

The room wanted to spin, and Katya had difficulty stopping it. "You wouldn't happen to know a Felix Varilensky, would you?"

He gazed pensively at the wall, then shook his head. "No. Don't believe I knew anyone by that name. What platoon was he in?"

Katya shrugged. "I know he joined in early September, if that helps any."

"Hmm," he said. "There were only three platoons then, and I knew everyone from the First and Third Platoons. He must have been in the Second. Poor guy."

Katya felt queasy at his words. "What do you mean?"

"Last time I saw them was when we moved up together during the failed offensive on the ninth of September."

"The ninth of September," Katya repeated. "That was the day he went to the front."

"The Second Platoon was the one that didn't fall back," he continued.

She pulled her hand out of his and blurted, "I don't understand."

"We got orders to fall back to our previous lines, because we were overextended and the Germans were counterattacking," he explained. "But the Second Platoon didn't fall back. They stayed where they were."

"And then what?"

"Then the Nazis reclaimed the territory," he said matter-of-factly.

The room spun, and Katya had to hold onto the bed to keep from falling

"I'm sorry," he added. "They fought heroically that day. They'd captured more territory than anybody."

"What are you saying?" she cried. "You don't know that they're dead! They could have escaped, or the Germans could have taken them prisoner—"

"There was nowhere to escape *to*," he declared. "And the Nazis had stopped taking prisoners on that front long before that."

She swallowed hard to keep down the rising nausea in her throat.

With a wince, the man complained that his leg was starting to ache once more, but Katya had already turned and was marching down the hall toward the exit.

"Wait!" he shouted. "Can't you check my leg for me? It's hurting again."

Katya glanced over her shoulder and caught sight of him trying to sit up, but she kept walking. Before reaching the door, she heard a grisly shriek. It echoed down the hallway and penetrated her like the bitter winter wind. "My God! My leg! It's gone! They cut off my damn leg!"

She flung open the door and dashed outside where the cold air hit her like a gale force wind. Reeling backward, she grasped for something to hold onto. Her hands found a cold, uneven wall that stopped her from falling. Leaning against it, she tried to catch her breath, then discovered what the wall was made of: corpses. Dozens of them were stacked like firewood, one atop the other.

She backed away, gaping at the frozen blue bodies, then fell to her hands and knees and vomited on the snow.

When Katya arrived home, she collapsed onto her bed without taking her coat or boots off. It was a little past noon, and she could hear Petya in the kitchen talking to somebody. When he came into the room a minute later, she realized he was alone and had been talking to the voices in his head again.

"Do you have any of that vodka left?" she asked.

He shook his head.

"Any cigarettes?"

"No. They're all gone too."

"Maybe you can tell me where you got them, so I can go buy some," she said.

He came closer and sat down across from her. She wondered what lie he'd come up with this time.

"Katya, I have committed a grave sin." He said the words slowly, as though unfamiliar with them. "Shostakovich sent a package to you and Guzman, and I stole it. The vodka, cigarettes, and caviar were all meant for the two of you." He took a deep breath. "I'm very sorry for what I've done. I know it was wrong, and I'm asking for your forgiveness."

She perceived a puncturing sensation inside her chest, as though something had pierced her heart. But she was indifferent to it. Making no reply, she instead stared numbly at the ceiling.

"Katya? Did you hear me?"

Rather than being full of anger and indignation like she expected, she felt hardly anything.

"If you need time to think about this, I understand," added Petya. "I know the news must be quite jarring for you."

She observed her breath as it flowed up her nose, down her throat, and into her lungs. Besides being cold, the air was dark and heavy. "No. I don't need any more time," she said distantly.

Petya audibly exhaled. "Thank you so much," he said. "You don't know how hard that was for me to say. Bless you for having the heart to find forgiveness. If anyone's going to heaven for sure, it's you, Katya."

She turned her head toward him. "I don't forgive you."

His mouth fell open and all color drained from his face. "What?" he asked dumbly.

"I said I don't forgive you. I can't. You've written my tombstone."

"No, I haven't," he protested. "You're going to make it through this. God told me to make it up to you, and I will."

"And how will you do that?"

"I don't know," he answered. "But *I will* do it. I'll make it up to you. Say you'll forgive me."

"I can't," she said, rising from her bed.

As she left the apartment, he called after her, "I never expected this from you!"

Hanging her head, she whispered to herself, "Neither did I."

She wandered aimlessly through the devastated city. Nothing had any color. Everything was only a lighter or darker shade of grey. The sun—sinister and spiteful—glared off the snow and stabbed her in the eyes.

Passing by a cemetery, she saw a heap of cadavers piled up outside its front gate. There were no coffins, just thin, pitiful bodies wrapped in rags. The dead were amassing faster than they could be buried.

With a bitter taste in her mouth, she contemplated how much longer it would be before she joined them. She was freezing, starving, and trapped in a city on the brink of unmitigated disaster. In a single day, she'd been denied her old job and its life-saving ration card, Petya had betrayed her in the worst way imaginable, and she'd been told that the love of her life, Felix, was in all likelihood dead.

She found herself in a park that her parents used to bring her to as a child in the summer to feed the ducks. She recalled how cute the ducklings were as they waddled out of the Neva River and took the bread from her tiny, outstretched hand. Out of the corner of her eye, she glimpsed the bench where her parents used to wait for her. Seated on the bench now was a corpse covered in snow. It was frozen in place, looking out at the river, whose water did not flow.

The Neva River was silent and still. It too was a prisoner of Leningrad.

Глава Девятая — Chapter Nine

THE COLDEST WINTER

My love is like a shadow
      forever following you.
There, behind you
      around you,
I always surround you.
Look for me when winter dances with your heart,
      And steals your warmth
      Because it's what you most need
      To visit that place where the ice stops you.
Do not fear the fall.
You'll find me there, but do not call
      My name
Is written everywhere.
I'm always there,
      a baby's breath away,
      the sun of May…
There, behind you.

The myriad charred remains of destroyed German equipment were like roadkill littering the ditch of a busy highway. Felix and the partisans walked from one piece to the next, searching for anything they might be able to salvage before they headed back behind enemy lines. It was unclear whether the vehicles and equipment had been destroyed by the Germans retreating from Tikhvin, or by the rapidly advancing Soviet forces.

It was December 12, and it had been an eventful month thus far. With fresh troops from the far east, the Red Army had mounted a successful counter-offensive on the Moscow front. Around the same time, the troops on the Leningrad front managed to retake Tikhvin and were hurriedly putting the Leningrad supply route back together.

Felix lit a cigarette and leaned against one of the burned-out vehicles. It was a dreary winter day, and the sun hadn't been able to completely melt the thick fog from earlier that morning. The fog had painted all the trees and bushes an immaculate white, and if it wasn't the middle of a savage war, it would be beautiful.

Leaning his head back, Felix exhaled smoke into the frigid air. As he put the cigarette back to his lips, he heard that haunting intonation from the forest again. He tensed his shoulders, straining to block it out as a tiny shiver spiraled up his spine. It had been happening more and more of late. He would hear something that no one else seemed to, and it sounded distinctly like someone—or something—calling his name. It was just as unsettling to him as looking into another person's eyes and knowing they're going to die soon. Whatever it was, Felix didn't want to hear its plea, because he knew somehow that if he did, he would have to answer it.

Misha wandered up the road, coming to a rest on top of the jutting front wheel of the vehicle Felix leaned against.

Felix scanned the forest once more for a clue as to the strange sound. Finding nothing, he turned to Misha. "What time is it?"

Misha retrieved a German pocket watch from inside his coat. "It's almost noon."

In mid-December, the sun set before four o'clock in the afternoon. Felix calculated how much more ground they could cover in the few remaining hours of daylight.

Lighting a cigarette, Misha asked, "Did you hear about the Americans?"

"What about them?"

"The Japanese bombed one of their ports in the Pacific, sunk just about their entire fleet."

Felix took a long drag on his cigarette. "Good," he said. "Now we shouldn't have to worry so much about our eastern border. The Japs will be busy fending off the Americans."

Misha nodded and blew smoke out his nose. "I guess they're our allies now, the Americans. Think they'll help us march on Berlin?"

Felix quoted a famous line from Tolstoy's *War and Peace*, but substituted America for Austria. "Oh, don't speak to me of America. Russia alone must save Europe."

Misha grunted. "That's what I think too. But there's all sorts of talk about them sending us troops and supplies."

"I'll believe that when I see it," said Felix.

"You don't think they'll help us?"

Felix flicked the butt of his cigarette into a snow drift. "We've been fighting a couple million Nazi troops for half a year now, and they haven't lifted a finger to support us. Seems to me they're content to sit over there in their protected kingdom and watch. You know how they love to be entertained."

A Soviet infantry patrol with dogs marched single-file down the road in front of them. The men were dressed in white camouflage, and even the dogs had swatches of dirty white sheets wrapped around them.

"Find anything?" one of the men called out to Felix and Misha as he passed by.

Misha shook his head. "Nothing."

The dogs were exceedingly thin and had strange devices strapped to them. Felix guessed they must be the 'suicide dogs' he'd heard so much about—the ones who were trained to run under German tanks, detonating the explosives on their backs.

Felix loved dogs, and only a few weeks ago would've been outraged to see them being used in such a way. Now he looked at them with a practiced dullness, deciding that ethics and morality were luxuries one couldn't afford in times of war.

The unmistakable buzzing of a plane filled the sky, then the plane dropped below the clouds and approached. It was a rare sight these days as most German planes had been grounded because of the bitter cold. Men started to scatter—taking shelter behind the destroyed vehicles or lying flat on the snow-covered ground. Felix was the only one who didn't make any attempt to hide. He stayed where he was at, lighting another cigarette and watching the plane draw near. It was a small fighter plane, and it opened up with its machine guns when it was within range. The bullets struck all around Felix, but he didn't flinch. Instead, he leaned back and blew smoke in the sky as the plane flew overhead.

The pilot didn't circle back for another strafing run, and everyone came out of their hiding places. Natasha was the first to come up to Felix. "Why do you do that?" she asked crossly.

He shrugged. How could she possibly understand?

"Don't you care if you live or die?"

Felix gazed at her pretty face, admiring her emerald green eyes. He knew she was fond of him, not because he noticed it himself, but because Misha kept telling him so.

"No. It's not that," he said flatly. "If I was meant to die today, then I'll die. No use fighting against it."

With a mischievous smile, she scrunched up her nose and said with a wink, "Maybe you just need a good reason to live."

Despite her layers of drab clothing, Felix could tell she had a great body. He fixed his eyes on her thin, seductive neck, but then pushed his desire out of mind. Anything that didn't have to do with defeating the Germans was irrelevant to him.

Walking to the middle of the road, he gave the signal to move out. He wanted to cover another four miles of the road before they called it a day.

The partisans gathered round and tramped forward, forming an oblong circle with Felix leading the way. If it weren't for the rifles, one wouldn't be able to tell them apart from the countless masses of fleeing refugees. Both groups moved across the wintry wasteland with a distinct weariness, an aloof indifference to the death and devastation surrounding them. Stepping around bomb craters and frozen corpses in the road was not only an everyday occurrence, it was mundane.

Felix's partisans had earned a name for themselves in the battle to retake Tikhvin. They had performed exceptionally well under his leadership, providing crucial victories against the Germans' left flank and suffering a mere two casualties for their efforts. They had performed so well, in fact, that they weren't broken up as Felix expected they'd be. The lightning fast victories the Germans had compiled in the early months of the war had thrown the organization of the Red Army into chaos, and it was often the case that Soviet field commanders siphoned off members of partisan units who weren't officially on the books.

It was no secret that the Soviet leadership wanted to strengthen the partisan movement in order to wreak havoc behind German lines. As part of this initiative, Felix was made a lieutenant and his partisans were fully recognized. In addition, they were assigned a political commissar whose job was to provide "guidance" and "motivation." Their commissar, Comrade Volkhov, was a short man with a red, patchy beard. He wore wire-rimmed glasses and was disarmingly sincere considering the work he did. His surname, Volkhov, meant wolf and didn't fit him at all.

When the partisans came to a German cemetery next to the road, they stopped to look at the rows and rows of wooden crosses marking the graves.

"It's nice to see the fruits of our efforts," remarked Volkhov dryly.

Felix didn't share his zeal. He'd heard about the mass graves they were digging in Leningrad. They dumped bodies—one to two thousand per day—in them as a matter of routine. Yet these revolting cockroaches each got their own individual grave. Felix wanted to dig them all up. They didn't deserve to be buried in sacred Russian soil.

Approaching from the opposite direction were three soldiers on skis pulling a machine gun on a sled. Trailing them was a group of German prisoners—eighteen wretched men with their hands tied and heads hung low. Six rifle-bearing Soviet soldiers marched behind them.

In the second to last row, one of the prisoners was having trouble walking. His face, chubby and childlike, was covered with purple bruises and dried blood, and he had no gloves or coat. Holding his arms tightly around himself with his hands tucked under his armpits, he shivered uncontrollably.

Watching him stumble once again, Felix realized why he was having so much trouble. He had no boots. His feet were wrapped with pieces of cloth, and not only did they offer no traction, but there were so many layers that they provided no flat surface on the bottom.

A few steps past Felix, the young man fell to the ground and one of the guards rushed to his side. Felix assumed he was going to pull him back to his feet, but instead he kicked the prisoner in the ribs.

"Get back in line, you son-of-a-bitch!" shouted the guard.

Every time the prisoner tried to get back to his feet, the guard would either kick him or strike him with the butt of his rifle so that he fell back down.

The scene transpired only a few yards from Felix, but he saw it as if from a great distance. Something in his belly felt sharp and prickly, and though he was disturbed by what was happening, he did not intervene. Instead, he convinced himself that the German got what he deserved. The man had come to Russia of his own accord to kill and destroy, and now he was reaping the seeds of hatred he'd helped cultivate.

After a few minutes of attempting to get back to his feet and being beaten back down, the German gave up and curled into the fetal position on the hard snow of the road.

"You won't get back in line, huh?" the guard said sarcastically as he pointed his rifle.

Felix turned away, peering at the grove of birch trees across the road. He heard the forest again—that mysterious sound like someone calling his name. Then he heard two shots echo through the dismal winter sky.

He felt an itch above his stomach, like a rash or a hive, except it was on the inside. At first, he used his tremendous powers of concentration to try to ignore it. When that didn't work, he removed one of his mittens and reached his hand inside his clothes. But no matter how long and hard he scratched, it didn't seem to make a difference. The itch wouldn't go away.

And the forest wouldn't shut up.

Petya had already wrapped his scarf tightly around his face, leaving only a thin gap for him to see through, and yet it still did nothing against the air that was so cold it hurt to breathe. He walked carefully so as not to slip and did his best not to think about the winter weather that was the fiercest he'd ever known.

There weren't many people on the streets this early in the morning, but he knew there would be a long line at the bakery. People began arriving there well before it opened.

As Petya passed a red trolley frozen in place in the middle of the street, he thought back to when the trolleys were still running and how much he'd taken them for granted. He'd always been miserable riding them—complaining fervently about how crowded they were. But after having to walk everywhere for so long, he vowed to never gripe about them again, if only they'd get them running once more.

With his disfigured leg and pronounced limp, Petya had to be especially cautious on the treacherous streets. With no manpower to spare, every alley and avenue was covered with three to four feet of compacted ice and snow. If the city survived until spring, there was going to be a monumental mess to clean up.

Upon reaching the still-unopened bakery, Petya counted twenty-three people in line. Of those, nineteen were women and four were old men. He took his place at the end, arriving a few seconds before a sickly boy who looked to be about ten-years-old.

When Petya made it up to the counter an hour later, he presented his two ration cards: his own and Katya's. The somber woman inspected the slips of paper, then handed them back along with two hunks of bread. Stepping off to the side with the intention of placing each ration and card in a different pocket, he became confused and forgot what he was going to do. This all-too-frequent occurrence unnerved him, but he'd learned that if he didn't fret about it and just waited, that it would come back to him eventually.

He overheard the boy behind him who was now at the counter. "It *is not* expired," the boy exclaimed. "Give me my bread!"

"I can't," the woman said tiredly. "That card is no good anymore. Tell your mother she needs to get a new one."

"Give me my bread!" the boy screamed, starting to cry.

Finally recalling what he had intended to do, Petya put the bread and ration cards in separate pockets, then walked away, pretending he hadn't heard any of the boy's conversation. He didn't get far before that confounded voice in his head told him to stop. There was a right and there was a wrong, and it was Petya's duty as one of God's disciples to set things right. Not that he wanted to; the voice told him he *had* to.

The boy was kicking the front of the counter, refusing to move away. Although there were a dozen people in line behind him, none of them said a word nor attempted to intervene. Petya called to the woman, "Let me see the card." She gave it to him, and he saw that it was indeed expired. All cards had to be renewed from time to time in an attempt to stop people from using stolen or forged cards, or cards that belonged to the dead. When Petya had his ration card stolen, he'd had to wait until the next renewal to get another one. Going without a ration card for eleven days had been beyond difficult. It had very nearly killed him.

"There's a renewal tomorrow," said Petya. "Can't you give him some for now and he'll get it renewed tomorrow?"

Her gaunt face, framed by a fur hat and dark scarf, stared vacantly in response. Just when Petya didn't think she was going to answer, she replied in a weary, well-rehearsed voice, "Comrade, I am accountable for every slice of bread. If I give any to people without the proper authorization, then I could face the firing squad."

Petya knew it was useless to argue with her, not only because what she said was true, but because she couldn't very well bend the rules with so many people watching.

Taking out his own bread ration, he broke off a quarter of it and handed it to the boy. Then he led him off to the side and announced to the rest of the people in line, "If anyone else would like to help by giving him a piece of your ration, we'll be waiting here."

After ten people had gone to the counter, three of them stopped by afterward and donated a portion of their ration to the boy. Then Petya took him by the hand to escort him home.

"It's dangerous for a young child to be walking around alone," said Petya, wondering where the boy's mother was and why she'd let the card expire.

After a few minutes, they came to an intersection thick with snowdrifts and the boy led them down the street to the right. The block seemed to be deserted, with hardly any footprints in the snow.

"I'm Petya. What's your name?"

"Kolya."

Petya noticed the boy—like many Leningraders—had swollen and bleeding gums. "How is your mother doing, Kolya?"

"She's tired," he answered after a few seconds. "She's sleeping right now."

Their conversation, with long pauses and few words, was typical for the times. It simply took too much energy to speak.

Petya squinted against the bright sun glaring off the ice and snow. At the next intersection, the boy pulled his hand away. "Our building is down there," he said, pointing to the next block. "Thanks for the bread."

Once he crossed the intersection, the boy glanced suspiciously over his shoulder at Petya from time to time. Petya pretended to be walking in a different direction, and when the boy stopped spying on him, he changed course and followed after him. The boy turned into an alley, disappearing from Petya's sight. At the alley's opening, Petya saw three abandoned cars piled high with snow. Taking out the long kitchen knife he now carried at all times, Petya followed the boy's tracks around the first car and then in between the second and third. The footprints led to a partly demolished building and a small hole in the wreckage.

Petya was quite sure now that his previous hunch was correct. The boy was an orphan living on his own. His mother had probably died of hunger or else in one of the bombings, and his father was likely at the front. There were orphanages all over the city to care for the multitudes like him, but many children wouldn't go there voluntarily because they were afraid they'd never see their parents again if they did.

He made his way through the rubble, down a set of snow-covered stairs, and to a warped red door that couldn't be closed completely. Petya pushed the door, but it only opened ten inches before it got stuck on something. Putting the knife in his coat pocket, he pushed harder until it opened enough for him to squeeze through.

"Kolya?" he called out in the darkness. "It's me, Petya."

No answer.

"Kolya, I know you're here. Come out."

"What do you want?" asked the boy.

"I want you to come over to me so we can talk," answered Petya. He didn't understand how the boy could possibly live in this dark and cold place. A snowdrift half-a-foot high angled in from the door.

"About what?"

Petya searched the darkness for where the boy might be hiding. "About something of considerable significance to you."

"Huh?"

Petya rephrased it. "About something important."

When he still didn't hear the boy coming, he added, "If you come out, I'll give you a piece of candy." He didn't really have any, but hoped the trick would work.

A few seconds later, the boy appeared in front of him. "Where's the candy?" he asked before coming any nearer.

"It's here in my coat." Petya stuck his hand inside his pocket and pretended to struggle to get something out. When the boy moved closer, Petya lunged at him, catching him by the arm. The boy cried out and struggled to get away, but Petya was too big for him. He dragged the boy, kicking and screaming, from the basement to the outside.

"What do you want?" yelled the boy. "Where are you taking me?"

Petya kept a tight grip on the boy's arm as he led him toward the nearest orphanage. But when he approached the dismal brick building, bitter memories of his own time there came back to him. He decided he couldn't subject Kolya to the same taunting and ridicule he'd underwent. But neither did Petya know what else to do.

Back in the apartment, Petya found Katya in her usual spot—sitting in her chair facing the front door. She rarely moved from there, no matter what convincing argument Petya or Oksana came up with. She was pensively tapping a pencil to a page, which meant she was writing poetry.

After nudging the boy forward, Petya introduced him. "Katya, I'd like you to meet Kolya."

She peered up from the journal in her lap and said a confused hello.

"Hi," Kolya replied shyly without lifting his eyes from his boots.

"I found him living by himself in the basement of a destroyed building," Petya explained as he led him past her down the hallway. "He's going to stay with us now."

Kolya came to a stop next to the coffee table and briefly gazed about the room.

"Don't worry," Petya said as he patted him on the head. "I'll take care of you. You'll like it here."

Kolya shrugged and sat down on one of the beds.

The apartment had more light than it should have, and Petya saw that his barricade over the window had been tampered with. The blanket had been pulled to the side and sunlight was streaming in. He'd erected the contraption last night in an attempt to keep the trees from spying on him.

"Did you do this?" he called to Katya.

"No," she said, without looking back at him.

Petya's thinking started to get jumbled again, and he took some long, slow breaths to sort out the onslaught of thoughts. Once he regained his focus, he asked her who did it.

"You know who," she replied.

Petya did indeed know. *The trees!* "Did you see them?"

She shook her head.

"Did you hear anything?"

Again, she shook her head.

Petya was both amazed and frustrated. "This is inconceivable! How do they do it?" he muttered under his breath. He'd spent two hours constructing the barricade, even adding a series of tin cans on a string that would alert someone to any attempted tampering. How could the trees have done it and Katya not heard anything?

As he started repairing the damage, a familiar voice resounded in his head. "This is not necessary," it said. "*I* will protect you. The only defense you need against these demons is faith in me."

Petya knew there was no point in arguing with the voice of God. It always won. It had drowned out all the other voices, and Petya felt powerless to challenge its decisions.

Obeying its command, he dismantled the barricade, and the sun's hazy light filled the apartment once more. The walls, black and dingy from the smoke of the stove and lantern, had been stripped clean of their wallpaper. It had been made known that the glue holding wallpaper up was partially edible, and Petya, Oksana, and Katya had torn down all the wallpaper in the apartment and made glue soup.

Petya poured himself a cup of water that emptied their last container. He still had difficulty accepting that the water wasn't poisoned, but the voice of God assured him it was safe to drink. It assured him of many things: that Katya was not, and never had been, trying to kill him, that the war with the Germans was a pivotal part of the Apocalypse, and that Petya was a good person—a sinner, no doubt—but still a good person at heart.

Holding his breath so he wouldn't smell it, Petya took a sip of the brown water. It tasted awful, but getting enough fluids was an absolute necessity in these times. He took another drink, then divided the rest into two cups, taking one to Kolya and the other to Katya. As usual, Katya ignored him, so he set the cup down on the floor next to her chair. "You need to drink more," he urged. "You're the one who was always telling *me* that."

Her skin, once so smooth and alluring to Petya, was now dry, scaly, and stretched tight over her face. Her eyes, once so spellbinding, were now impossibly large and unnatural. Her whole body was wasting away. In any other time, one would guess she had some debilitating disease. But her only sickness was hunger and its devastating consequence: malnutrition.

Two weeks ago, Petya had caught a glimpse of her as she gave herself a sponge-bath. He remembered how her ribs stuck out and her breasts were shrunken to the point of non-existence. He'd experienced no lust whatsoever in watching her. But then he hadn't felt any sexual desire at all in several months. That too was a consequence of starvation.

Retrieving Katya's bread ration for the day, Petya held it out to her. She set her pencil down, took the bread, and began scraping crumbs off its edges. Then she picked up a small saucer from the floor, wiped the crumbs on it, and set it back down next to a small hole in the wall. A scrawny mouse lived inside the hole. Katya had nicknamed it Prince Myshkin. It would come out in the late afternoon to eat the crumbs, and Katya would talk to it. With Igor no longer around, it seemed to have become her closest friend and confidant.

Ever since Katya had tripped over a corpse in the stairwell and sprained her ankle badly enough that she couldn't walk, Petya had been getting her rations for her. It had been over a week, and even though she rarely acknowledged his efforts, he wasn't resentful. He felt tremendous pity for her. Her prospects for getting a job and regaining her health didn't look good. He knew she'd checked every hospital in the city and that none of them would take her, no matter how understaffed they were.

Petya believed some people deserved what they got—himself, for instance. He was a horrible person. Selfish. A liar, and harsh judge of others. And he was paying for it now. But Katya? She was a good person and didn't deserve this.

"Are you sure you don't want to lie down for a while?" Petya suggested to her. "It's best if you keep your ankle elevated. Sitting in this chair all day long isn't helping."

She didn't respond right away, but Petya had learned to wait. Reaction times weren't what they used to be.

He knew why she was always waiting there, staring at the door. She expected Felix to walk through any minute, as though he'd just stepped out to go get a newspaper.

"Katya, he's not coming back," Petya said piteously. "There's no point in waiting here."

"You're wrong," she answered. "I've been calling him."

Petya had no idea what she was talking about, and suspected she didn't either. Her mental acuity had been in steady decline. "Don't you remember? The soldier at the hospital told you. The Germans killed everyone in his platoon."

"He *is* coming back, and we'll be together again," she insisted. "I know it."

Petya sighed dejectedly. It was no use arguing with her.

The room felt colder than usual, so he went to the stove to check the fire. Just as he feared, the fire was nearly out. He wanted to chastise Katya for it, but knew that wouldn't be right. Kindness was not just a nice thing to do, the voice of God had told him it was a prerequisite for getting into heaven.

He trudged over to his old apartment and grabbed another stack of his writing. Then he went next door and gathered the last few pieces of wood from Guzman's piano. The firewood deliveries had ceased in early December, and they'd soon have to start chopping up their chairs and coffee table.

After wadding up a page of his writing, Petya placed it in the stove and arranged the wood over top. He always took a fiendish pleasure in watching his poems, prose, letters, and essays catch fire. It was like subtracting parts of himself from this grievous world.

Noticing Kolya hadn't drank his water yet, Petya gently urged him. "Drink that."

The boy did as he was told. Then came a strange knock at the door. Strange, because it sounded like someone was kicking the bottom of the door with their boots. Katya dropped her pencil and paper and stood up. "Yes?" she called out.

"Open the door," a voice responded. "It's me."

Katya limped to the door and unlocked it, then Petya watched a ghost walk into the apartment.

"What are you doing here?" asked Katya, obviously displeased.

"I thought you could use some firewood," replied Igor.

Petya stared in disbelief. He was sure he'd killed Igor two weeks ago.

"I told you to stay away," Katya said. She glanced over her shoulder uneasily at Petya. "It's not safe here."

"I was worried about you," protested Igor as he set the firewood down. "Wanted to make sure you were all right."

Katya held out her arms and the two of them embraced.

Petya thought Igor looked quite healthy for a ghost, certainly better than when he'd last seen him. His cheeks had some color, and his lips weren't quite so thin anymore. What Petya couldn't figure out was why—not to mention, how—a wraith had been carrying a load of firewood.

"Well, since you're here," said Katya, "come in and tell me how things are going."

She pulled the hat from his head, and his ears jutted out, just the way Petya remembered the boy from their first meeting back in August. It was gradually sinking in for Petya that he must have dreamed he killed Igor. The boy in front of him was no apparition.

"How's your courier job going?" Katya asked as she led him into the apartment toward the stove. "Do you like living there?"

Igor began telling her how it was hard to sleep at night because all the men snored so loudly, but then he saw Kolya. "Who's that?" he asked.

"That's Kolya," Katya answered. "Kolya, this is Igor."

Kolya lifted his head and said a meek hello.

"What's he doing here?" asked Igor.

"Petya is going to take care of him," she said. "But we'll talk about that later."

Igor reached into his coat and pulled out a can of condensed milk, a small piece of chocolate, and some loose tea. "I brought some food," he said. "I thought we might celebrate."

Petya's eyes grew wide at the sight of the tea.

"Celebrate what?" asked Katya. "Is the war over?"

Igor frowned. "No," he said. "It's New Year's Eve."

Katya arched her eyebrows in disbelief, then gazed questioningly at Petya.

Petya nodded his confirmation that Igor was correct. Petya had already told her that morning that it was New Year's Eve, but her short-term memory seemed to be failing her lately.

"Oh," she said hesitantly. "Then, of course, we'll celebrate—that we're still one step ahead of death."

Igor smiled. "Do you have any food for our celebration?"

Like most Leningraders, Petya, Katya, and Oksana had stopped sharing their food with one another a long time ago, but New Year's Eve was an exception.

"We have a plethora of provisions," Petya said half-jokingly as he rummaged through his coat pockets. "We have bread, and also *fish*," he exclaimed holding up a small tin of sardines.

"Wow," said Igor. "How did you get that?"

"And I have two potatoes I've been saving," added Katya.

Petya thought she'd lost her senses again, but then she went to the kitchen and proved him wrong—returning with two fist-sized white potatoes.

While Igor arranged all the food on the coffee table, Petya rehearsed all the things he had to do in order for them to have tea. They were out of water, and since he'd already collected all the snow from the roof and windowsills, he'd have to go to the river.

"Where are you going?" Igor asked as Petya buttoned up his coat.

"We need water," he replied. "Keep an eye on Kolya for me."

Igor dropped his jaw and gawked. Petya didn't blame him. Petya had never helped out with getting water when Igor was still living with them. But things were different now.

As soon as Petya closed the apartment door behind himself, Katya asked Igor to get her thermometer. Then she approached Kolya and commanded him to stick his tongue out. She'd already seen his swollen, bleeding gums, and puffy eyes which usually meant dystrophy.

"How long have you been living on your own, Kolya?" she asked as she inspected his small pink tongue that was covered with brown dots and a white film.

"My mom never came home from work last week," he answered.

"Your father's at the front?"

He nodded. His lips were so narrow and white that it didn't appear as though he even had any. "He hasn't been back to visit in three months."

Katya let out a small whimpering sound like a hungry puppy. She'd seen so much of this, but her heart still ached each time. She took his temperature, and breathed a sigh of relief when it indicated he didn't have a fever. Giving him a kiss on the forehead, she pulled him close and hugged him. "You're going to be all right, Kolya," she said. He wrapped his small arms around her neck and buried his face in her shoulder.

The boy's face and dark, curly hair were similar to Felix's, and Katya guessed that Felix had probably looked a lot like this little boy at one time. "Go sit next to the stove to warm up," she whispered in Kolya's ear.

He kept his arms wrapped tightly around her neck, refusing to let go. Katya imagined for a moment that he was her son, and Felix the father. Then she burst into tears.

"What's wrong?" Igor asked anxiously.

"What is *not* wrong?" she whispered in response. As the last tear slipped down Katya's gaunt cheek, Kolya released his hold and went to the stove.

After regaining her composure, Katya called Igor into the kitchen to speak to him in private. Her ankle hurt and she felt weak both physically and emotionally, but she knew what had to be done.

Summoning what little strength she had left, she instructed Igor to take the boy to the orphanage a few blocks away. "Kolya is sick," she said in a low voice. "They'll be able to look after him."

Igor wrinkled his pug nose. "I thought you said Petya was going to take care of him."

"Petya means well," she said, "but he can't take care of him. He's sick himself."

Igor nodded slowly. "I understand."

Katya ran her fingers through his hair. "I see they've given you a bath."

"I didn't want to," he whined, "but they made me. All soldiers have to take baths at least once a month."

"So you're a soldier now?"

He stuck his chest out and stood up tall. "Yes. And if I keep doing such a good job, my commander said I could be promoted to sergeant before the war is over."

Katya smiled. "Just don't forget you're going to college one day."

"I won't," he said. "That's the only way you can become an engineer."

"You're going to be an engineer? I thought you'd decided on being a pilot?"

"No. Pilots can't put the city back together," he explained. "I'm going to be an engineer so I can help rebuild the bridges and buildings the Germans destroyed."

Katya reflected again on how Igor was her only living relative left. Her own aspirations of happiness may well rest on his shoulders if she didn't survive this winter. She believed each person carried not only the fears and failures of their ancestors, but also their strengths, hopes, and dreams. Every night, she prayed for Igor's safety, wellbeing, and success in life.

Wrapping her arms around him affectionately, she held him tight. "I love you," she whispered, "no matter what you become."

"I love you too," he said.

Before leaving the kitchen, she cautioned him not to tell Kolya where he was being taken. "In fact," she said, "hold his hand so he can't run away when you get close. He probably won't want to go, but it's the best place for him."

To relieve her throbbing ankle, Katya hobbled over to Kolya and sat down beside him. "I want you to go with Igor," she instructed the boy. "You're sick, and he's going to take you to a place where they can help you."

"I ain't going to no hospital," said Kolya.

"Don't worry," she said, looking him in the eyes. "He's not taking you to a hospital."

Igor—a head taller and ten pounds heavier—led Kolya by the hand toward the door. "It'll be all right," Igor said reassuringly.

Katya smiled to herself at Igor's tenderness and confidence. He'd changed so much since he first came to live with her.

"See you soon," Igor called to her as they left.

Katya locked the door behind them. She still didn't like Igor going about the city on his own, but felt comforted by how well he knew the streets, and also that he was young and could run. She doubted there were any muggers or cannibals in the city who were willing to expend energy on running after someone.

Exhausted, she sank down on her bed, propping her leg up on a pillow. She felt haggard and cold, but not hungry. Her appetite had vanished a week ago—a bad sign, she knew. Her body was failing, and there wasn't much that could be done about it. She had trouble remembering and thinking clearly. Her muscles didn't always do what they were asked, and when she looked in the mirror, she saw a frightening, skeleton-like stranger staring back.

After losing her job last month, she'd spent a week checking every hospital in the city. None of them would take her, forcing her to look for work elsewhere. Another two weeks went by before she finally managed to convince a sewing shop to take her on. There, she'd spent all day in a large unheated room that caused her face and legs to go numb with cold. But it gave her the ration level she needed to survive, and that was all that mattered to her.

Her supervisor, Katya came to find out, was a former classmate of Oksana's and she kept Katya on even after Katya sprained her ankle and could no longer make it into work. Then, last week, she'd stopped by Katya's apartment unexpectedly, announcing the bad news that they were being audited by the food czar and could no longer keep her on the payroll. That meant Katya would be reduced once more to the non-worker ration level.

It was getting harder and harder to find the energy to keep fighting. After she grudgingly accepted she might not live to see the spring, her view of the world began to shift. She wrote letters to every person—whether alive or dead—who she felt resentment toward. She asked for forgiveness, and also told them she forgave them any of their misdeeds. Her grandmother's words from long ago were her guiding light: "If you forgive others the wrongs they have done to you, God will also forgive you."

And though it was an arduous, painful process, she'd even managed to forgive Petya.

Pulling the covers over herself, she didn't want to ever get out of bed again. She closed her eyes, picturing Felix doing those endless push-ups on their picnic the day before the war started. She felt the hot sun, smelled the scent of freshly-cut hay on the breeze, and saw Felix's athletic V-shaped back, his muscular arms, and the tiny beads of sweat around the short hairs on the back of his neck. He'd been so strong, so sure of himself, so confident the world was perfect just as it was.

She wondered if he still felt that way.

Raising her arm to her face, she gently brushed her cheek, imagining it was Felix's hand. "Where are you, my love?" she said aloud. "I need you."

A trip to the river for water was never an easy, short, nor particularly safe journey. The most difficult and most dangerous part was descending to the river. The great granite stairs leading to the river were covered with thick ice. Several times Petya had seen women slip and fall. Some of them never got back up.

Pulling his sled along the wide, empty street, he'd occasionally see another person doing the same. Their sled would either be loaded like Petya's with clanking pots and pans, or with one of the ubiquitous blue corpses that seemed to outnumber the living these days.

At the riverbank, Petya saw the stairs were icier than ever and contemplated riding the sled down the bank. The slope was quite steep and there was no way to stop. You could end up drowning in one of the bomb craters in the ice. Or you might die a slower death if you fell off the sled and hurt yourself. You certainly couldn't count on any of the hospitals to help. They were already packed to capacity, and the doctors rarely performed operations on Leningraders because they were so undernourished that their blood wouldn't clot.

After debating the pros and cons of each method of descending to the river, Petya decided sledding down wasn't much riskier than the icy stairs. He went to the least steep section of the riverbank, slid the pots and pans down on their own, then sat on the sled and aimed for a pair of snow-covered corpses lying next to one of the holes in the ice. He gave himself a little push, and the sled took off quickly. In a matter of seconds, he collided with the dead bodies and was thrown off the sled. Fortunately, he wasn't hurt, and he made his way to his feet and gathered the pots and pans.

In the distance, he could see one of the Navy's battleships. Every ship in the Northern fleet—what remained of it anyway—was stuck in the ice, completely immobile. They were still manned, though only partially, and their big guns pounded at the enemy lines from time to time. German planes had tried repeatedly to sink the ships.

Petya wound his way around the numerous corpses until he found a hole in the ice that wasn't frozen over. Dipping his can into the hole, he waited to hear a splash. Then, once the rope got sufficiently heavy, he pulled the can up and dumped the brown water into one of the pots. He'd have to repeat the tedious procedure many times in order to fill all the pots and pans.

The second most arduous part of his journey was yet to come. Once the pots and pans were full, he had to take them one by one up the icy steps, then situate them on the sled so that a little bump wouldn't overturn them and make the entire trip for naught.

When Petya returned to the apartment two hours later, Igor helped him bring the pots and pans of water up the stairs. Then Katya helped him boil and strain enough for their evening's festivities. Oksana arrived home as they were finishing and surprised them all with a bottle of Georgian wine. "They gave it out at work," she announced. "We were hoping for food, but it's better than nothing."

There was a lump of blankets on Igor's bed, and Petya had assumed that Kolya was buried under them sleeping. It wasn't until he went to check on the boy that he realized he wasn't there.

"Where's Kolya?" he asked everyone.

"Who?" replied Oksana.

Petya took a deep breath to try to calm the fear inside. Had he imagined the whole thing? Did the boy not really exist? He grabbed Igor by the arm. "Where's Kolya?" he demanded, his eyes frantic.

"I don't know," cried Igor as he struggled to free himself of Petya's grasp.

"Where is he?" Petya shouted, clutching Igor's arm even tighter.

"Kolya ran away," Katya called from the other side of the room.

"Why didn't you stop him?"

"We tried," she answered, "but he got away."

Petya was overcome with sadness and grief. He'd made up his mind to take care of the boy, and now, through his negligence, Kolya was gone. He put his ragged brown coat on to venture outside once again. "I'm going to find him. I think I know where he ran to."

"No. Don't," urged Katya, wringing her hands.

"I have to," he said as he walked out the door. "He's just a boy. He won't survive on his own."

Petya trekked all the way back to the abandoned building, but was unable to find Kolya. After searching other nearby buildings as well, he returned home heartbroken. Katya endeavored to console him, saying Kolya was likely picked up by a policeman or a Civil Defense Corps worker.

"He'll be fine," she insisted. "He's probably already celebrating New Year's."

Petya didn't believe her, and it wasn't until the voice of God said he'd watch over the boy that Petya felt better.

Their New Year's festivities got underway shortly after 8:30 p.m. Their feast—that was anything but—consisted of Petya's tin of sardines, several dense hunks of bread, a can of condensed milk, a piece of chocolate, two potatoes, a bottle of wine, and some loose-leaf tea. Though there had been rumors that extra rations of canned meat or fish, butter, sugar, chocolate, or maybe even vodka would be given out in celebration of New Year's, none of it transpired.

Petya ripped four pages from a dictionary and passed them out to serve as plates. They'd stopped using real plates a long time ago, because water was much too valuable to be expended on washing dishes. When Katya rose from her chair and went to the stove, she gazed about the room with a confused expression. Petya had noticed this quirk becoming more pronounced the last few weeks. She'd started to tote pencil and paper everywhere so she could write things down to remind herself of what she was going to do or say.

"What is it?" Igor asked her.

Katya took her paper out, but Petya could see there was nothing written on it.

"I forgot what I was going to do," she replied.

"Perhaps get the potatoes," suggested Petya.

"Oh yes," she exclaimed. "That's it. Thank you." She pulled the blackened, cracked potatoes from the coals and set them on the coffee table with the rest of their food.

For a short time, the four of them forgot their grievances against one another and enjoyed food, drink, and conversation. It took only a few sips of wine to feel drunk and warm. Igor came up with the idea to put the condensed milk on top of the stove and add the chocolate to it. Once the chocolate melted, they added water and stirred it all together to make some weak hot chocolate.

Halfway through their meal, the building shook from nearby explosions. The Germans were shelling the city again.

"Can't they leave us alone for *one* minute?" grumbled Oksana. She had her head wrapped in a white kerchief, and in the dim light of the candles she resembled a mummy.

When the shelling ended, the metronome-like ticking from the radio suddenly stopped, and everyone quit talking. One by one, their heads turned to the faded black paper cone of the speaker. Nothing replaced the ticking. Was it the end? Had the Germans finally broken through? Would the street warfare begin now? Or would they wake in the morning and find the Germans in control? Petya felt simultaneously horrified and relieved at the prospect. Then a voice came over the speaker, stating: "Moscow speaking." The sound of the Kremlin chimes played after that, and a few seconds later, the national anthem.

As the music played, Oksana raised her glass in a toast. Her arms were as thin as the branches they put on the fire, and her hand trembled so badly it threatened to spill wine over the edges. "God willing," she said, lifting her hand another inch higher, "we will prevail."

They all touched their glasses one to the other and drank.

"We will indubitably prevail in the end," Petya said as he set his glass back down on the coffee table. "God is on our side."

"If that's so," Igor snapped, "then why doesn't He snap His fingers and send all the Nazis to hell?"

"He doesn't work that way," Petya replied stoically.

"Why not?" asked Igor as he peered at Katya.

"I don't think we should be asking if God is on *our* side," Katya said. "We should be asking if *we* are on God's side."

The building shook again amidst a loud salvo of artillery fire. The shells weren't incoming this time, though. The ships frozen in the Neva River were firing, letting the enemy know that the upcoming year was going to be just as miserable for them—hopefully more so.

By eleven o'clock, everyone but Petya was in bed asleep. It was the shortest New Year's celebration he'd had since he was four years old, and he felt cheated. He stayed up and gathered the used tea leaves from everyone's cup, spooning them into a small tin can. Then he added water and set it on the stove to boil. He hoped that if he boiled the tiny black leaves long enough he'd be able to have one more cup of tea.

While he waited for the water to boil, he listened to the radio. Someone was giving a patriotic speech about never giving up, about fighting the enemy with your last breath. Petya heard the words, but felt no inspiration. He expended all of his energy just making it from day to day. There wasn't much left for emotions.

When his cup of water still hadn't boiled after fifteen minutes, Petya threw in some of the precious firewood Igor had brought. In these frigid days and nights, it seemed like you could add all the wood in the world to that stove and it still wouldn't put out enough heat.

Misha had somehow managed to get enough liquor for the partisans to throw a New Year's Eve party. The alcohol was another homemade concoction nearly twice as strong as vodka. Though it looked like cognac, it tasted terrible, and if you drank it straight, your throat would burn then feel raw. But nobody cared about that. Their festivity was about the here and now. They celebrated because they were alive. No one took that for granted anymore.

The partisans had honed their ingenuity and resourcefulness in outwitting hunger, the elements, and the Germans, and a group of them were now using that inventiveness to decorate a small evergreen in honor of the New Year. They adorned the tree with whatever they could make or find: miniature snowmen carved out of ice, painted pine cones on strings, shiny stars cut from tin cans, captured German medals pinned directly to the branches. At the top of the tree, they placed a miniature version of the red flag of the Soviet Union.

It was close to midnight and the moon gleamed in the sky like one of the shiny ornaments on their tree. Felix—cigarette tucked neatly between the middle two fingers of his right hand—relaxed against the wall of snow and ice behind him. Gazing at the moon, he casually blew three perfectly formed smoke rings into the crisp air. "I agree," he remarked to Volkhov. "It's rather hopeless at this point."

They were talking about the fierce battle to retake Mga. Having already lost Tikhvin to the Red Army, the Germans seemed especially determined not to be defeated there. If they lost Mga, their stranglehold over Leningrad would come to an end.

"I think we've lost momentum," added Felix. "I don't see the lines around Leningrad changing until spring brings warmer weather."

Felix's partisans were not engaged in the battle for Mga. They were still near Tikhvin, awaiting orders of where specifically they were to go behind enemy lines.

Most of partisans were gathered around the campfire drinking. It was a cloudless, windless evening, and Misha was the life of the party. Having covered a pocket comb with cigarette paper, he held it to his mouth and played the national anthem. After that, he led everyone in singing a round of "Dark Night," an appropriately melancholy song for the times:

> ... ♫ *You are waiting for me, standing by the crib,*
> *and wiping away the tears so no one sees.*
> *I am not afraid of death. I met him a few times in battle.*
> *And even now he is circling around me ♪* ...

The next song they sang was the ever popular "Katyusha," about the Soviet Union's top secret mobile multiple rocket launcher that was much feared by the Germans:

> ... ♫ *Fly toward the clear sun*
> *And to the warrior on a far away border*
> *Bring Katyusha's greeting ♪* ...

Near the end of the song, Misha crouched to the ground then leapt in the air, then bent low again and alternately kicked each leg as high as he could—performing the traditional Ukrainian Gopak dance clumsily, but with enthusiasm. By the time he finished, there wasn't a single person who wasn't howling with laughter.

When the stroke of midnight came, the night sky erupted with hoots, howls, and gunfire. Misha wobbled over to Felix and Volkhov and held out a bottle of booze.

"Happy New Year," exclaimed Misha, slapping Felix on the back.

Volkhov—the only sober one of the bunch—crossed his arms. "This is ridiculous," he said crossly. "What's there to celebrate? You think 1942 will be any better? It'll probably be just as miserable—maybe even more so—than '41."

"We're not celebrating," Misha said in mock seriousness. "We're commemorating socialism's impending triumph over fascism."

"You're drunk," replied Volkhov.

"Thank you," Misha said, slurring his words. "I've been trying very hard tonight to reach that supreme state of bliss."

Felix took a drink from the bottle and nearly gagged. The other bottles he'd drank from had either been diluted or mixed with something. Misha's wasn't.

Misha leaned back until he nearly fell over. "Look at that," he said, a sense of awe in his voice.

"At what?" asked Volkhov.

Misha pointed up at the sky. "The stars, man! You can't look at the stars when you're dead. Don't you get it?"

"No," Volkhov said, "and you don't either. We're fighting a war."

Natasha emerged from nearby shadows and stood in front of Felix. She had a red nose, glossy eyes, and a seductive smile on her lips. "How about a New Year's kiss?"

Felix had drunk his fair share that night, and without much thought he put his arms around her waist and leaned forward to give her a short kiss.

"You certainly can't kiss women when you're dead either," Misha commented dryly to Volkhov.

After a second or two of kissing, Felix pulled away. But Natasha didn't. She squeezed her arms around him and pressed her lips back to his. Felix resisted at first, but then gave in, and they kissed long and hard. The softness of her lips and the feel of her tongue on his filled him with desire.

"What are you trying to do?" he asked with a grin when she finally let up.

"Give you something to live for," she said teasingly as she pressed her lips back to his.

He hadn't thought of intimacy in such a long time, and this animal instinct, this primordial appetite of his body, washed over him now like a tidal wave. Even through her many layers of clothing, he could feel her breasts pressing against him. His breath became short, and he could suddenly think of nothing other than sex.

"How about we go to my hut?" offered Natasha. "We can be alone there."

Unable to find his voice, Felix nodded. He couldn't remember why he'd paid so little attention to her obvious interest in him. He envisioned how amazing it was going to be to touch her naked body and hold her tight to him.

Inside her hut, they resumed kissing. Felix worked his hands through layer after layer of clothing, until he came to her soft, enticing skin. She shuddered as he ran his fingertips up the side of her waist.

They were there embracing and caressing for many minutes when someone from outside the hut shouted, "Felix! Are you in there?"

Felix recognized Yuri's voice, but decided not to answer. Both he and Natasha were nude from the waist up, and Felix was blind with desire.

"Are you sure he's in there?" Yuri asked somebody.

"Yes. I saw him go in there," answered Volkhov.

"Felix! We have a New Year's present for you," Yuri hollered.

"Give it to me later," Felix called as he pulled Natasha's supple body close to his.

"No," replied Yuri. "This one can't wait."

Felix reluctantly pulled away from Natasha. "Wait here," he whispered. "I'll be right back."

Natasha kept her arms around his neck. "Don't go."

"I'll be quick," he said, giving her another kiss. "I know Yuri, and he's not going to leave me alone until I do this." He dressed quickly and went outside.

Yuri—big grin on his lips—was waiting with his rifle pointed at a young German soldier. "Here's your present," he announced.

Felix sighed disappointedly. He'd hoped to just grab some sort of gift of food or tobacco and then return to Natasha.

Yuri was wearing his white camouflage and a dark fur hat with an inch of snow piled atop it. Volkhov stood to the left, and their commissar looked like a dwarf next to the massive Siberian.

"Where did you get him?" asked Felix.

The German soldier's eyes darted from speaker to speaker.

"On the road just south of us. There were two of them. I think they were lost."

"Where's the second one?"

"He was a little *stubborn*," said Yuri. "Didn't want to cooperate."

Felix understood that meant Yuri had shot the man. "All right. Let's see if this one can tell us something interesting. Take him to our hut. Comrade Volkhov, could you summon Sergei?" Sergei was the newly joined partisan who spoke German.

"I already did. He's waiting in our hut," Volkhov answered as he did an abrupt turn and led the way. He took long strides for his size, and his boots made small, precise indentations in the snow.

The hut Felix shared with Yuri, Misha, and Volkhov was the largest of them all. In addition to being the place where they slept, it also served as a meeting and gathering place. When Felix crawled inside now, he found it full of drunk and boisterous partisans eating chocolate and exchanging black humor jokes. He was about to kick them out, but then changed his mind. There was no other hut big enough to accommodate them, and the wind outside had started gusting ferociously. Besides, they deserved to enjoy themselves after all the bloodshed and misery they'd endured the past few months.

After clearing people out of a corner of the hut, Felix instructed Yuri to put the prisoner there. The German sat on the ground with the tense Siberian towering over him.

"Relax," Felix advised Yuri, though he knew it wouldn't do any good.

Yuri kept his tight, unflinching grip on his rifle and continued to point it at the German while Volkhov took his place next to Felix. Their translator, Sergei, sat between them and the German prisoner.

Felix motioned to a candle near them. "Put that one out," he said to Sergei.

"But why, comrade?" asked Volkhov. "It's not very light in here as it is."

Felix hated being in such close proximity to cockroaches, and the light made it worse. "Do it," he commanded irritably.

After Sergei blew out the candle, Felix asked him, "Have you been a part of many interrogations?"

"A few," their translator answered.

Volkhov had a pencil and thin notebook in his lap. "I haven't done any," he disclosed. "I'll defer to you for now."

Sergei asked the German a question, got a response, then addressed Felix and Volkhov. "His name is Friedrich von Manstein."

"Damn you," Felix cussed. "I didn't ask for his name."

"Sorry, comrade," apologized Sergei. "I just assumed—"

Felix didn't like to be reminded that the cockroaches had names. "Ask him where he was going tonight," he said gruffly.

Sergei conversed back and forth with the German for a minute until Felix asked impatiently, "Well?"

"He won't say," said Sergei, raising his voice to be heard over the din in the hut.

With Volkhov's eyes on him, Felix muttered under his breath. He didn't want to be doing this right now. "Tell him we'll kill him if he doesn't answer us."

Sergei spoke with the man, then reported back. "He says we're going to kill him even if he does answer."

Natasha entered the hut and asked Felix how much longer the interrogation would take. He could smell she'd put on perfume, and his sexual desire roared back to life.

"As long as it needs to take," Volkhov said to her as he wiped his glasses on his shirt.

Felix arched his eyebrows and gave Volkhov a testy, sidelong glance.

"My apologies, Comrade Lieutenant," Volkhov added hastily. "She was obviously talking to you." He put his glasses back on and looked away.

"Tell him we'll give him a drink of alcohol and a cigarette if he tells us how many men they have defending the big hills south of here," Felix said to Sergei.

Sergei translated, then reported back, "He says to give him the booze and cigarette first. Then he'll tell you."

Felix hollered for the men playing cards in the opposite corner to pass him their bottle. Then he gave it to the German and motioned for him to drink.

The youthful prisoner was dressed poorly for the cold weather. Instead of a winter coat, he wore an autumn jacket with a rain coat over top. His gloves were thin, and his thick, full beard was more likely out of necessity than anything else. There was a fresh scar on his left temple that looked like a bullet had recently grazed him. Felix reveled in the thought it might be from the rifle of one of his partisans. They'd been harassing the Nazis for the past several weeks.

Upon taking a gulp from the bottle, the German's face turned red and he fell into a coughing fit. Everyone in the hut laughed.

"That's Siberian tea!" someone shouted. "Keeps you warm at night!"

"He probably thought it was beer!" said another.

Once everyone had stopped laughing, Felix addressed Sergei. "Tell him he'll get the cigarette after he answers us."

The German spoke at length, and Sergei translated. "He says there's ten men—"

"What?" interrupted Volkhov, holding his hand to his ear.

"Quiet down!" Felix ordered everyone.

Sergei started again. "He says there's ten men there: two groups of three near the road, and a group of four on the right flank. He claims the left flank is currently undefended."

"He's lying," Volkhov said to Felix. "We know for a fact they have at least fifteen men defending those hills. We've spotted that many. Who knows how many more we haven't seen?"

Felix knew that. It was why he'd started with that question—to see if the man was going to tell the truth.

"Tell him he's lying and we know it," said Felix.

The noise level had ratcheted up again, and Sergei spoke loudly over it, "Tell him *what*?"

"Felix," Natasha said, tugging on his sleeve, "come on. You should do this tomorrow."

Felix smelled Natasha's perfume again and felt his patience dwindle even further. He closed his eyes briefly and imagined taking her numerous layers of clothing off one by one.

"I think he'll be more willing to tell the truth after a night without food or heat," he said to Volkhov. Then he stood and shook his head at how loud and chaotic it was in the hut.

Yuri furrowed his bushy eyebrows at Felix. "Are we giving up? Is he not cooperating? You want me to shoot him?"

Natasha wrapped her arm around Felix's. "You're finished?" she asked with a smile. "You're going to do it tomorrow?"

Felix glimpsed her cute face and saw how pleased she was. "Yes, might as well," he answered, putting his mittens on. "We're not getting anywhere."

The crack of a gun suddenly rang out, and everyone ceased talking and turned toward Yuri. The prisoner slumped sideways to the ground, a pool of blood forming around him.

"What the hell!" yelled Felix, glaring at Yuri.

"I asked if you wanted me to shoot him," Yuri said defensively. "And you said, 'Yes, might as well. We're not getting anywhere.'"

"I wasn't talking to *you*!" said Felix as he knelt by the man to check the pulse in his neck.

With Volkhov's help, Felix rolled the wounded man onto his back. It didn't take him long to find the small hole with bright red blood gushing out. There was nothing to be done. The German would be dead in a matter of minutes.

The edge of something white on the inside of the man's jacket caught Felix's attention, and he pulled out a faded photograph.

In disbelief, he stared at it with his mouth agape. It was a picture of a young woman with a long graceful neck, sad brown eyes, and angelic dark hair that naturally framed her face. Felix was convinced at first it was Katya, and only after gaping at the photograph in depth was he able to find the subtle differences informing him the woman was German. Still, he couldn't pull himself away from it.

When Volkhov came and took the photograph from Felix's hand to inspect it, Felix fled from the hut. Overcome with emotion, he had to get away from everyone and everything.

He tramped deep into the woods where he could be alone with the evergreens and falling snow. Chastising himself for ignoring the forest's persistent call to his heart, he opened himself now to what it had to say.

Contrary to what he thought he'd hear, both the message and messenger were comforting. It was the same feeling he got when he was a kid lost on the playground and heard his mother's buoyant voice calling him to her outstretched arms.

He listened for an hour, contemplating what was said about the universe, his life, and his current tribulations. In the end, he could see plainly that he had a choice to make: either succumb to bitterness and contempt, or face the darkness he feared.

Leaning his head back so that the snow fell onto his face, he closed his eyes and saw both Katya and the German woman in the photograph peering down at him—waiting, it seemed, for him to emerge from a thick, black cocoon that he was just now beginning to see surrounded him.

After tossing and turning all night, Felix was glad when morning finally came. He lit a candle and placed it at the foot of his bed, then tried to pack his things quietly so as not to wake Yuri, Misha, and Volkhov. When he came to Katya's letter, he held it to his nose and inhaled. Though she'd placed a lilac flower in it, he could no longer smell its fragrance. Unfolding the letter carefully, he admired her elegant, flowing handwriting. In the top corner, she'd drawn a picture of a unicorn flying toward a crescent moon.

When Yuri began to stir, Felix quickly folded the letter, tucked it in his pocket, and finished packing. Before he could leave, Yuri turned his big head toward him and asked, "Where are we going now?"

Felix had planned on slipping out unnoticed and just leaving a note behind, but now he decided to tell. "I'm going to Leningrad."

Misha yawned, then commented, "Very funny. Seriously, where are you going?" He sat up in bed, then groaned and held his head in his hands. "Everyone's probably a bit hung over. Can't we stay put at least one more day?"

Volkhov, now also awake, said, "I don't recall us discussing any plans for moving out today. Did we finally get our orders?"

"No. Not yet," replied Felix. "You might as well stay put until they come though."

"Son-of-a-bitch," Misha muttered. "You're serious, aren't you? You're leaving."

"Comrade, what is this about?" asked Volkhov.

Misha chugged water from his canteen, then asked, "How the hell do you think you're going to get to Leningrad?"

"Over the Ice Road," Felix answered.

"Over Lake Ladoga? That's crazy," said Yuri.

Volkhov sat up and put his glasses on. "You might make it to the lake, but you won't get across it. If the Germans don't stop you, then your own comrades in the Red Army will."

"He's right," agreed Misha. "They're not going to let you cross the lake, and they're sure as hell not going to let you in the city. I'm speaking from experience here. I was nearly sent to the firing squad when I entered the city without permission back in August."

Felix pulled his pack on over his shoulders. "I know this is difficult to understand, but it's something I have to do."

"What on earth is this about?" Volkhov asked again.

Misha fixed his eyes on Felix. "This isn't about that girl you left behind, is it?" Felix nodded.

"Sorry to be blunt," said Misha, "but she's probably dead."

"You don't know that," replied Felix. "I have to go there."

"Your country needs you here," declared Volkhov, emphasizing the last word.

"*We* need you here," Yuri chimed in.

"This has nothing to do with any of *you*," said Felix adamantly.

Volkhov pointed to the ground. "The fight is in this location, comrade. It's not in Leningrad."

"Yes. Listen to him," added Yuri. "He's right."

"You don't understand!" Felix shouted.

"That's true," said Volkhov. "So help us understand."

When Felix didn't elaborate, Volkhov continued, "Comrade, you believe in equality? In justice? Freedom? Because that's what this war is about. We're not engaged in a battle just to chase the Nazis off our land. We're fighting on behalf of the entire world against evil. You're not going to turn your back on that, are you?"

Felix slumped his shoulders forward. Volkhov had hit on his weakness.

"You've been blinded by your personal desires, by your infatuation with this girl," said Volkhov. "The goal is to lift man up to fulfill his potential. Love has no role to play. Devotion, romance, compassion—they're all dead. They're tired clichés, useless concepts, that have no value anymore. You're stuck in that, in those fairy tales from the past, and you've got to pull yourself out of it. The only sentiment that's helpful these days is hate. Hate is fuel. It keeps you alive. If we don't out-hate our enemies, then we won't win this war."

Felix's current internal struggle was as violent as any physical battle he'd been in. He swung one way and then the next, until Katya's voice resounded in his head with the last lines of the poem she'd read to him on that warm summer day last June: *Love is the beginning, and Love is the end, and here in the middle is where we must mend.*

He had to go to her, and he had to go now. He'd never been so sure of anything in his life.

"I'm going," Felix said with finality as he grabbed his rifle. "I hope none of you try to stop me." He was referring specifically to Volkhov and looked at him now.

Volkhov got up from his straw bed and frowned. "In the short time I've known you," he said, "you've earned my respect. I won't try to stop you, but know, too, that I can't defend your decision if you're caught."

"I understand," Felix said. He handed Volkhov an envelope addressed to Katya. "Could you send this out in the next batch for me?"

Volkhov took it and nodded.

Felix had written several letters to Katya, though he had his doubts as to whether any of them made it to her. He began tightening his coat and boots, getting ready for the arctic weather outside. Volkhov went to the other end of the hut with the letter, and Yuri began rummaging through his belongings looking for something.

After tying his scarf snug around his neck, Felix took a deep breath and said to his three comrades, "I hope we'll meet again one day after this madness is over. We'll drink a bottle or two and tell some jokes." As he headed toward the door, Yuri grabbed him by the arm.

"You'll need this," said Yuri, sticking something in Felix's hand.

Seeing the rubles, Felix felt grateful. He had no money himself, and it was hard to come by these days. "Thank you, my friend," he said.

"It's nothing," responded Yuri with a wave of his arm.

Felix knew better. He stepped forward and embraced the big Siberian, whispering, "Take care of yourself."

"Wait," called Misha. "Let me go with you."

"No," answered Felix. "They need you here."

As he pulled the blanket hanging at the doorway aside, a gust of wind blew snow and frigid air into the hut, and extinguished the candle at the foot of Felix's bed.

Misha set out twenty minutes after Felix left, following his tracks in the snow until they ended at the scattered tents of an infirmary erected on a frozen meadow. The dismal field hospital didn't have much to offer in the way of care. The first tent Misha entered—cold and with a sickening smell—was full of sallow, expressionless soldiers with chest wounds. After a hasty retreat, Misha checked the next tent and found Felix sitting next to a stove warming his hands on a cup of tea.

Misha sat casually next to him, then leaned over and exclaimed, "Wow. Fancy meeting you here."

Felix glanced up from his tea, but if he was surprised, he didn't show it. "Why are you here?"

"I was thinking what a long journey it would be, and how you'd surely get bored," replied Misha. "You're not exactly a barrel of laughs on your own, you know."

Felix motioned with his head to the other side of the tent. "There's some cups over there," he said in a detached tone.

After getting a cup and filling it from the large, homemade samovar, Misha returned and asked, "What do you think? Are you impressed I found you?" It had been two hours since Felix had departed the partisans' camp.

"No," answered Felix. "I know you're quite capable. If you set your mind to do something, you'll do it."

Misha squirmed uncomfortably. He'd been raised on criticism and felt awkward with praise or anything even approaching it. Unable to look Felix in the eyes, Misha instead focused on the pink scar on Felix's cheek where a bullet had grazed him in one of their many battles to retake Tikhvin.

Though he tried not to show it, Misha was intensely jealous of him. Felix had a way of being in the world that Misha didn't. Felix was authentic and sincere at all times, as if he had nothing to hide. And despite them doing mostly the same exact activities as one another, Felix undertook them with a sense of purpose. Try as he might, Misha could find no purpose in his own life.

After gulping down the hot tea like it was a shot a vodka, Misha gave a satisfied sigh and said, "What are we waiting for? Let's get going. Leningrad, here we come!"

The besieged city of Leningrad was two hundred miles east of Tikhvin. Felix and Misha's first goal was to reach the town of Kabona on the edge of Lake Ladoga. Next, they'd need to gain access to the frozen lake, hitch a ride across it, then onto the road to Leningrad, and, lastly, make their way into the city itself.

It took them seven days to get to Kabona: one to get arrested on the way there, two for Misha to cajole and bribe the guards into letting them go, and four for the actual trip.

Formerly, Kabona had been an unmemorable, sleepy village near Lake Ladoga, but was now rapidly being transformed into a bustling port. Before the war, Misha had driven through there when it was still a typical Russian village, with a few hundred inhabitants working as fishermen in the summer and lumberjacks in the winter. Today, everywhere Misha turned his head, he saw newly built warehouses and barracks, myriad tents housing the road maintenance crews, drivers, and anti-aircraft garrisons. In between all the soldiers and civilians walking to and fro were hundreds of trucks, ambulances, and staff cars heading for the lake.

Once past the village huts and their barking dogs, Misha and Felix beheld the frozen expanse of Lake Ladoga—the largest lake in Europe at 125 miles long and nearly 80 miles across.

Although there were several roads leading to the lake, they were all being funneled into one central gateway where Red Army soldiers halted every vehicle and inspected the papers of each occupant. Misha and Felix tried to hitch rides with trucks beforehand, but none of the drivers would take them through a checkpoint. The best they ever offered was: "Maybe on the other side...."

After having no success at three of the four checkpoints, Misha and Felix approached the last one warily. At the previous three, the soldiers wouldn't even talk to them upon learning they didn't have the proper authorization to travel across the lake.

The traffic had thinned considerably, and the two soldiers Misha and Felix headed toward had no trucks waiting in their line.

"Let me do most of the talking," Misha advised Felix as they approached. He studied the faces of the soldiers, hoping for something different than the fatigued, indifferent expressions they'd seen thus far.

"Papers," the shorter soldier demanded, holding out his hand.

Misha had tried to forge an official order, but it hadn't fooled any of the others. Nevertheless, he took it out and handed it over.

After glancing at it for only a few seconds, the man gave it back. "That's not getting you onto the lake," he said.

"What do you mean?" Misha asked with feigned surprise. "Those are official orders from our commanding officer, Major Lestov."

"That may be," the man replied. "But they're not getting you past this checkpoint."

"Comrades, this is a critical mission," said Misha gravely. "Could you tell us what exactly you need to allow us past?" He hoped for an opening to negotiation or else some information on what they might do next.

The soldier pulled his rifle from his right shoulder and put it on his left. "Get a valid pass," he said dryly.

"And how do we go about that?"

The man shrugged. "That's your problem."

"Please! This is very important," exclaimed Felix. "I need to get to Leningrad as soon as possible. What's it to you if you let us pass?"

Misha cringed at Felix's heartfelt but tactless plea.

"We're under strict orders from our commanding officer," the soldier replied. "Personally, I don't give a rat's ass if you want to kill yourself trying to cross the lake."

"Don't give me that!" Felix said hotly. "*You* are the one standing here who won't let us pass. No one else."

Felix's words had the opposite of their intended effect, as Misha knew they would. The men hardened their position and threatened Misha and Felix with arrest.

For all Felix's leadership skills and bravery, he was clueless when it came to contentious situations like this that required finesse, charm, and guile. But

Misha was all too happy to help—pleased he was better than him at one thing at least. He convinced Felix to step back about fifteen yards while he had a few words with the two men.

"You'll have to excuse the Lieutenant," Misha explained. "His girl is in Leningrad, and we all know the situation there."

Both men nodded their heads gloomily and seemed to soften a little.

"They say three to four thousand die every single day," Misha continued, "so you can see why he's eager to get there."

"We sympathize, but without the appropriate orders you aren't getting past this point," the taller one said. "I suggest you turn back around and—"

"Whoa, let's slow down here," interrupted Misha, pulling out a pack of cigarettes. "There's no reason why we can't discuss this a little and make sure we understand one another, right?"

The two men eyed Misha's pack of cigarettes like it was a can of caviar. Having already made sure the pack contained only five cigarettes, he took one for himself, then offered one to each of them. With a quick glimpse in every direction, they accepted the offer.

Misha lit his cigarette as the two men hid theirs in their pockets. "So what's the ration situation like around here?" he asked.

The taller one slowly shook his head as the shorter one responded. "It's getting a little better."

"They give you plenty of bread?"

"Yes. Just hardly anything to go with it."

"That's not right," commented Misha, offering them a puff of his cigarette. "They probably save the good stuff for themselves."

The taller one nodded. "I saw the Major eating salted pork yesterday," he said to his partner. Taking turns hiding behind one another, they each took a drag on Misha's cigarette.

"You guys have a harder job than just about anybody," declared Misha, gazing about the barren, windswept area. "If anyone deserves better rations, it's you guys. They should try your job for a week—standing on your feet all day long in this freezing cold day in and out." Misha pulled out his flask, turned away, and held it behind his back. "Go ahead," he said over his shoulder. "I'll keep a look out."

They each took a sip and coughed afterward. "It's good stuff, huh?" Misha said with a grin. "That'll warm you up in no time." He set his pack on the ice, searched through it, then withdrew a small parcel wrapped in paper. "Perhaps the two of you might also enjoy this," he said. He unwrapped it and allowed them a peek at the cream-colored lump about the size of a tin of sardines. "It'll make that bread taste ten times better."

"Is that butter?" asked the taller one.

"Not *just* butter," Misha said. "It's sweet cream butter. The best you've ever tasted."

The shorter one reached for it. "Let me taste it."

Misha pulled it away. "Absolutely not. I don't work that way." He wrapped it back in the paper. "You can have the whole thing if you let me and the Lieutenant pass."

When neither man responded, and instead looked to the other for the answer, Misha knew he had them. "Comrades," he said, "what's there to think about?"

Finally, the shorter one said sheepishly, "Throw in a pack of cigarettes, and we'll look the other way for a minute."

"I would, except I'm down to my last pack," said Misha, retrieving it from his pocket and showing them its contents.

Pushing up his bottom lip, the man said shrewdly, "Too bad for you. Give it to us or no deal."

Misha sighed. "You drive a hard bargain," he grumbled, handing it over. He actually had several more packs of cigarettes hidden in his pack.

The man smirked, revealing two missing upper teeth.

Misha then gave them the parcel along with some advice. "I suggest you keep that well-hidden. I'm sure you know the penalty for bribery." He imitated the sound of a gunshot.

"Just get going," the soldier said gruffly as he hid the parcel in his pocket. "Before we change our minds."

Misha motioned for Felix to hasten, and when he arrived the two soldiers pretended to be busy inspecting something near their checkpoint.

"Quickly," Misha urged Felix.

"How did you get them to let us pass?" Felix asked incredulously.

"I bribed them with some butter," he replied, quickening his pace.

"Butter? I didn't know you had any."

"I didn't," Misha said. "It's just soap. That's why we need to hurry."

Felix laughed, and the two of them jogged toward the line of vehicles that had passed checkpoints and were about to head across the lake.

When they were far enough away from the checkpoint, they slowed to a walk, and Felix asked, "Why did you really decide to join me on this journey?"

"I already told you," said Misha. "Figured you could probably use some company and a little help every now and then. You'd still be under arrest if it weren't for me, and you certainly never would have gotten past that checkpoint by yourself."

Felix nodded. "True. It took a little while—maybe because you were always drunk when I first met you—but I've learned I can count on you. You always come through. I want you to know that I regard you as more than just a fellow soldier. I consider you a friend."

Misha felt a little choked up. Felix's remarks were a perfect example of why Misha had decided to join him, despite the obvious risks. "And I guess it's nice that I don't have to pretend when I'm around you," he said thoughtfully.

They walked in silence for a few seconds, then Felix said, "I'm glad you're here."

Again, Misha felt overcome with emotion. Nobody had ever said that to him before—amazing what a few kind words could do.

"We'll get to Leningrad," Misha said unequivocally. "One way or another, we're gonna get there."

Cramped tightly one next to the other in the cab of the truck, Felix struggled to get his arm out from behind Misha's to get a drink of water from his canteen. He had no idea how Misha had managed to convince the truck driver to take them over Lake Ladoga, but he'd discovered Misha was proficient at that sort of thing. If a situation came up that involved bartering or bribery, Felix knew to let Misha handle it.

They were in the ninth of a twelve-truck convoy, and their convoy was but one among a never-ending stream of convoys going to and from Leningrad. Twenty-four hours a day, seven days a week, the trucks rolled on.

The jittery driver wasn't talkative and kept his left hand on the door as if he might jump out at any second and let the truck go on without him. Using his teeth, he pulled the mitten off his right hand and retrieved a cigarette from his coat pocket.

Noticing his last two fingers had been severed below the knuckle, Felix asked, "What happened?"

"The first truck I drove didn't have any heat," he said matter-of-factly.

Felix didn't understand at first, but then figured it out. Frostbite. After sitting motionless in an unheated truck for hours on end with nighttime temperatures dipping to forty-five degrees below zero, the man had to have two of his fingers amputated.

"Lucky they gave you this truck," Misha commented. "It's got a good heater. What did they do with your old truck?"

The driver pointed below them.

"What do you mean?" asked Misha. "It's in the lake?"

"A few weeks after I started, there was a thaw," he said. "I jumped out just in time."

Now Felix understood why the man kept his left hand on the door at all times.

"I take it you didn't fall in the water," said Misha.

The driver shook his head. "You fall in the water, you're dead in less than ten minutes."

They came upon a hand-painted sign that spelled "Road of Life." Next to the sign was a snow-covered car sticking halfway out of a bomb crater in the ice. Every hundred feet along the road there was a small, colorful flag sticking out of the snow. The driver said they were markers to help them follow the road. If you saw a red flag, that was a warning to take a detour around a thin spot in the ice. In addition to the flags, there were traffic controllers every few hundred yards directing the convoys. The men wore white camouflage robes that stretched all the way to the snow, covering their dark boots. They had snub-nosed guns slung around their necks and wore extra cartridge belts slung across their chest in a X formation.

Spying a board on the ice with a little flag fluttering in the wind above it, Felix asked, "What's that?"

"Means there's open water there—a bomb crater," the driver answered. "It'll be frozen over again in a day or two, then they'll remove the board."

The driver hit the brakes suddenly to avoid slamming into the truck in front of him. There wasn't much space between the trucks in the convoy, and neither were they allowed much, the driver explained.

"What are you hauling?" asked Misha.

"Food," said the driver.

"Well, that's what they need, I've heard," Misha remarked. "How are things going in Leningrad?"

The driver motioned with his head toward a caravan of cars and trucks heading the opposite direction. "Right there's your answer," he said glumly.

The vehicles were all stopped, because the truck at the front of the line was apparently experiencing some mechanical difficulties. While one man leaned over top of the engine, another was lying on the snow underneath. Felix and Misha craned their necks to get a better look. Just like the trucks in their convoy, all the vehicles in the caravan had been painted white for camouflage. The large army truck at the front was crammed to capacity with thickly bundled civilians fleeing the city. They peered back at Felix and Misha with ungodly big eyes and thin faces. Seeing the red and white frost marks on their cheeks, Felix knew they were already half-dead. He shuddered to think that the whole city might be like that—full of emaciated skeletons on the verge of death.

Behind the truck was a bus that had been outfitted with heat. Puffs of smoke came out of a tin chimney in its roof. After the bus was a carload of people. Though the car could comfortably fit seven, Felix counted eleven people packed into it. "What's that big tank on the laps of the people in the backseat?" he asked.

"Probably gasoline," said the driver.

Felix could hardly imagine how miserable they must be: packed in so tight that they couldn't move, gasoline fumes filling the air, stuck in an unmoving vehicle on a road of ice where the outside temperature was well below zero. On top of all that, the Germans might attack with their long-range artillery or planes at any moment. He was beginning to understand what the driver meant when he'd said, "Right there's your answer." No one would submit themselves to the harsh conditions the people in this caravan were experiencing unless what they were leaving behind was even worse.

In a second truck behind the car, four men were dragging a body out and toward a round crater filled with blue water. The men had to stop and rest every few yards as they lugged the corpse over the ice. Felix could hardly comprehend it. He alone could pick up that thin corpse, toss it over his shoulder, and carry it to the crater in a matter of seconds. What had happened to these people? Were these just the extremely ill who were being evacuated? Felix could not—would not—believe that the whole city was filled with feeble invalids like this.

"I've heard dystrophy is rampant in the city," Felix said to the driver. "Are all the people in these vehicles sick with it?"

"Some, I imagine," he replied with a shrug.

"Where are they going?" inquired Misha.

"To their graves, most likely," the driver answered. "Most of them are too far gone to be saved."

"But I heard they increased the rations," Misha remarked.

"Too little, too late," said the driver.

Felix had to close his eyes. He couldn't take it all in. What if Katya was already dead? She was thin to begin with. She had no fat reserves to call upon.

After another twenty minutes, the traffic slowed to a crawl. Abandoned cars and trucks lined the road—victims of either the cold weather, the perilous road, or the German Luftwaffe. As their convoy came to a complete stop, Felix and Misha got out to stretch their legs and smoke a cigarette.

Scrutinizing the truck's camouflage, Felix was impressed at first with how well it blended into the endless white around them. But then he noticed the shadow. It was a cloudless day, and sun never got very high this time of year. There was no way German planes could miss the hundred-foot long shadows the trucks made.

A pair of nurses with sheepskin coats were skiing near them. They had red crosses on their left arms, submachine guns around their shoulders, and pulled small sleds packed with medical supplies.

Misha nudged Felix with his arm. "Girls," he uttered lustfully.

The nurses heard and stopped when they reached him. "That's *Lieutenant*," the second one said, "and you'll salute before addressing me."

Misha came to attention and promptly saluted. "My apologies, Comrade Lieutenant."

"Do you know what the holdup is, Comrade Lieutenant?" asked Felix.

"There's only one lane open ahead," she said. "There's a bomb crater in the road that hasn't frozen over yet."

"Those certainly look warm," Misha said, referring to their sheepskin coats.

"They are," the first one responded, "but they don't smell so good."

Felix eyed the long procession of peasant sledges approaching. Tired horses with bony ribs and hoar-frost encrusted fur pulled each straw-filled sledge.

Suddenly, the driver of their truck jumped out of the cab with his automatic submachine gun. "Down!" he yelled, running away from the truck.

Felix was confused. Surely the sledges weren't a part of some German trap.

The nurses skied away as the peasants halted their sledges and threw dirty white sheets over the horses. Two people emerged from the straw in the back of each sledge and dashed away.

Then Felix heard it. Planes.

He and Misha sprinted away, then dove to the ground as bombs whistled through the air. They exploded on the ice and sent geysers of water streaming into the sky.

An anti-aircraft battery Felix hadn't noticed before began pounding at the planes. The big guns were hidden behind walls of ice blocks and a heavy snow-laden net that sunk low over the top. Everything was camouflaged in white. Even the guns had been painted white.

The low-flying planes with black crosses on their wings roared over Felix and Misha before beginning a giant loop for another pass. While they did that, a second wave of planes dropped their bombs on the columns of trucks and sledges. Felix watched as one of the sledges, horse and all, suffered a direct hit and disappeared into the lake. As the deafening sounds of explosions and rushing water filled the air, Felix rolled onto his back and fired frenetically at the planes.

When the third wave came, Felix could see out of the corner of his eye that several trucks were damaged and on fire. Squealing bombs fell through the sky and shook the ice when they struck.

Having completed their loop, the first wave of planes now began strafing the convoys with their machine guns. The bullets hissed as they hit the ice. One of the horses neighed wildly, and Felix watched as its rear legs slumped to the ice. The sledge's driver rose to his feet, shaking his fist at the German planes and cursing them at the top of his voice. A second later, bullets cut him down and a pool of blood formed around his lifeless body.

It wasn't until the third wave of planes came around for their strafing run that the anti-aircraft guns finally hit one. The plane's left wing was split in two, causing the plane to spin out of control. It hit the frozen lake with a tremendous thud that made lightening-like cracks in the ice.

"Yeah! Take that you bastards!" Felix heard someone shout.

Once the anti-aircraft guns stopped firing, Felix heard plenty more shouting, but they weren't shouts of victory or vengeance, but of agony. Numerous people had been wounded in the attack.

Half of the dozen trucks in their convoy were on fire. The ice was dotted with craters where the dark blue water of the lake stood in stark contrast to the whiteness all around. The truck Felix and Misha had been riding in wasn't on fire, but it had been struck repeatedly by the planes' machine guns. Felix doubted it would be going anywhere for a while, if at all.

"Looks like you're going to have to dig into your bag of tricks and get us another ride," Felix said to Misha.

When he didn't hear Misha's usual quick-witted response, he turned and saw Misha was still lying in the thick snow. "Misha," he hollered. "It's over. They're gone. You can get up now."

Still no response.

Felix swallowed uneasily. "Misha!" he called out even louder as he walked toward him.

As he got nearer, he saw the awful red snow under Misha's head. Kneeling next to him, Felix gently rolled his unresponsive friend over. Misha's right eye was drenched with blood. One of the nurses skied over and joined Felix. She worked without her mittens, placing her fingers in her mouth from time-to-time to keep them warm.

"He's still alive," she explained, "but he needs to see a doctor. We have to get him to a medical station right away."

"We passed one not too long ago," said Felix.

"Yes, that's the closest one," she confirmed. "It's about a mile and a half from here."

Felix wavered, gazing to the other side of the lake where Leningrad was. If he went back with Misha, he'd be delayed for several hours, perhaps even a day. But his indecision lasted only a few seconds. He knew what he had to do.

All the trucks were either out of commission or stuck in line, so that left the sledges as the only means of transportation to the medical station. Circling carefully around the wide cracks in the ice that led to bomb craters, Felix made his way toward the sledge drivers. Four of them were gathered near the horse that had been wounded. They'd already put it out of its misery, cut its belly open, and pulled out its internal organs. While two men dumped the inedible parts down one of the bomb craters, the other two tied the horse's carcass to one of the sledges. Its meat would not be wasted.

When Felix arrived, one of the sledge drivers was finishing shoveling fresh snow over the blood stains the horse had left on the ice. "Help me bury those two men," the man said to Felix, nodding toward two bodies a short distance away.

Together they dragged the two bloody corpses to the nearest crater and dropped them in.

"Did you know them?" asked Felix.

"I was transporting them in my sledge."

"So you have some free space now?" Felix asked hopefully. "Can you take me and my comrade who's been wounded to the nearest medical station?"

The man shook his head. "My orders are to return immediately once I've finished. There's others waiting."

Felix tried to think of what Misha would do or say to coax the man into saying yes. "We have some cigarettes we could give you."

"I don't smoke," he said indifferently and began to walk away.

"Wait," Felix said, taking him by the arm. "My friend is badly injured. He needs to get to a medical station right away."

The man peered warily at Felix's grasp on his sleeve, declaring, "There'll be a sledge along shortly to pick up the wounded."

"No. He can't wait."

"He'll have to," the man said, trying to free his arm. "I'm not going that direction."

Felix refused to let go. "I'll make you a deal," he said.

"What kind of deal?"

"You agree to take us to the medical station," he said and paused.

"And?"

"And," Felix continued, "I promise I won't shoot you."

The stoic man raised an eyebrow. "Where's your friend?"

Felix led the way to Misha, and together they loaded him into the back of the sledge. After Felix hopped in and covered Misha and himself with straw for warmth, the driver cracked his whip, and the horse started forward.

It was an agonizingly slow trip. The horse moved just slightly faster than Felix could have walked. When they finally arrived at the medical station, it was dark, and Misha was still unconscious. A pair of stout nurses came out of an ice hut and helped roll Misha onto a stretcher and get him inside. A young female doctor inspected his eye and proclaimed they needed to operate. They took Misha behind some curtains, then told Felix to go to the hut next door and check if they had room for him to sleep there that night.

Felix lay awake most of the night thinking either about Katya or Misha. When he got up and left the hut, the sun was just beginning to rise, which meant it was about ten in the morning.

Seeing one of the nurses walking from one ice hut to another, he called to her inquiring about Misha.

"He just woke up," she answered. "The doctor is with him now, but you can go see him in probably fifteen minutes if you like."

Relieved at the news, Felix lit a cigarette and relaxed. When he was nearly finished, a truck with a humongous black pot in the back pulled up. After honking the horn a few times, an elderly woman driver climbed out. Felix smelled something delicious—perhaps stew—and realized this truck was the field kitchen.

"Good morning, young man," the woman said. "Are you hungry?"

"Always," replied Felix. He never got to eat three meals a day anymore. He ate when he could and if he could. It was usually the case that he got one meal a day, then snacked on some bread before going to sleep.

The woman looked him up and down. "I can tell you're not from Leningrad."

"No, but that's where I'm going," said Felix.

"Well then you better get your fill now. Ain't no food in the city." She retrieved a large ladle from the cab, then hoisted herself up to the back of the truck. When she opened the lid on the pot, a cloud of steam rose up. "You got a bowl?" she asked as she stirred.

"No."

"I've got one you can use, but you have to give it back to me before I leave." She scooped a large helping of stew into a tin bowl and handed it to Felix. "There's some bread in there," she said, pointing to a bin next to the little fire under the pot. "Just pull that door up."

Felix opened it and saw a hundred thick slices of black bread. He could tell right away that it was good quality. After taking one and settling onto a snowdrift, he pulled his spoon out of his boot and started to eat.

The nurses, three in all, came out of the first hut, and half a dozen soldiers out of the second and third huts. They all had bowls in hand.

When everyone had been served, the woman began packing things up to go to her next stop. Before she left, Felix approached and gave her the bowl back. She did a quick scan, then slipped Felix a few extra pieces of bread. "You'll need this if you're going to Leningrad. Be safe."

Felix thanked her, then she got into the truck and pulled away with a roar of the engine and a cloud of exhaust. No sooner had the truck left than another one took its place. The driver hollered to Felix to help carry a wounded man inside, and after Felix had done so, he went to check on Misha. He found his friend in a corner on a straw bed. A pretty, young nurse with blonde hair was feeding him stew one spoonful at a time.

"I can do that," Felix said to her, holding out his hand for the bowl. "I'm sure you have plenty of other things you need to do."

"Thank you, comrade," she said, giving him the bowl.

Misha frowned. "What are you doing?" he asked after the nurse was out of hearing range. "She completely adored me."

Felix chuckled. He was glad Misha seemed to be himself already. There was a patch covering the eye that had been wounded, but other than that, he looked fine. "How are you feeling?"

"I've got one hell of a headache," answered Misha, "but the doctor tells me I'm lucky to be alive. She pulled one piece of shrapnel out. She thinks there might be another one, too, but said she couldn't find it."

"Is your eye going to be all right?"

Misha shook his head. "What eye? She took it out."

"I'm sorry," Felix said sincerely.

"Don't worry about it. This could be a good look for me," joked Misha. "Women love war heroes. And plus I've always wanted to be a pirate." He laughed at his joke then sat up in bed. A second later he got a glazed look on his face, and his head wobbled from side to side.

A nurse rushed to his side and laid him back down. "Comrade, I told you not to try to get up. You've had a concussion."

"Looks like I won't be going anywhere for a while," Misha said to Felix.

"How long will it take?" Felix asked the nurse.

"A few days minimum," she answered. "Possibly a week."

The driver Felix had helped a few minutes ago stood near the doorway buttoning his coat and pulling on his mittens.

"Off so soon?" called the nurse next to Felix.

"Yes," the driver answered. "Leningrad needs me."

"You're heading to Leningrad?" asked Felix eagerly.

The driver nodded. "You want a ride?"

Felix hesitated, glancing at Misha.

"I know what you're thinking," Misha said. "You don't have to wait for me. I'll be all right."

"You sure?"

"Of course."

"Yes. I'll go with you," Felix said to the driver.

"I'm leaving in five minutes," the driver replied and left the hut.

Felix turned back to Misha, enfolding his hands around the fingers of Misha's left hand. "Listen," he said earnestly, "you've done a lot for me, and I want to thank you for—"

"No. Stop," injected Misha. "It was nothing."

"You don't even know what I was going to say."

"Let's just say 'til next time' and shake hands."

Felix reflected for a few seconds. "No. I'm not going to do that. We might not ever see one another again, and I don't want to regret anything."

"Don't make me cry, you son-of-a-bitch," said Misha half-jokingly.

Felix grinned. "Misha, you've helped me and supported me every step of the way, and I wouldn't have made it this far without you. You've been a good friend, and—"

"Oh, come on," Misha interrupted. "I'm just a drunk, a fool."

"No," Felix said adamantly. "You're not."

Misha was quiet, then slowly turned his head and said, "Thank you."

Felix gave Misha's hand one last squeeze and got up to leave. "I won't forget you."

Misha wiped a tear from his eye. "Damn you. You did it anyway."

"Goodbye, my friend," Felix said with a smile. "Take care of yourself."

"You too," replied Misha. "Hey, do me a favor on your way out. Ask that nurse if she'll finish feeding me."

Felix laughed. "All right. I will."

It was morning, and Petya was on his hands and knees on the sidewalk in front of their building. He was looking for clues in the ice underneath the snow. It was a tedious process—scraping away inch after inch of compacted snow until the ice underneath could be seen—but he was convinced that was where God had left him instructions as to his mysterious *mission*.

After Katya casually mentioned to him a few weeks ago that God's message is everywhere, Petya had been using a magnifying glass to study the ice formations in the frost on their apartment windows. Unfortunately, he hadn't been able to find a single letter or number there. When he'd asked Katya what words *she* saw, she'd replied that God didn't communicate in Russian.

Having already found several Russian letters in the ice on the sidewalk, Petya now knew she was lying. As he carefully scraped away another patch of snow, he recognized the Russian letter "К". Of course the crack in the ice could've been a random squiggle that by chance looked like a "К," but that's exactly what God would want the average person to think. His message was meant only for Petya, and Petya knew that squiggle that looked like a "К" was no mere coincidence.

It was a cloudless, windless day, and though the morning sun was shining brightly, it was still bitterly cold outside. Each time Petya exhaled, his breath obscured his vision.

After the "К," he found a "Д," and was especially pleased to have found two letters in one day. He'd add them to the ones he'd found on previous days: "А," "З," "Ц," "Х," and "Я." That afternoon, he'd see if he could arrange the letters into a word.

As he got up from the sidewalk, his left suspender came unhooked from his pants. He'd lost 83 pounds since the start of the blockade, and suspenders were the only way he could keep any of his pants up. His weight—finally stable at 123—was undeniably better than most. Many a man in the city considered himself fortunate if he weighed over 100.

After refastening the suspender, he went to check the large bulletin board in the middle of their block. There were a number of pieces of paper on it, most of which Petya had already seen:

Missing: Five-year-old girl with black hair and brown eyes. Was last seen walking from here toward Nevsky Prospekt...

For Sale: Phonograph and records, man's leather boots and fur coat, baby crib...

Will remove corpses for food...

The last one was his. He'd put them up all over the city. It was the only way he was making it through the blockade. All the able-bodied men were at the front, and most Leningraders—whether man or woman—simply didn't have the strength to take dead bodies down stairs and then pull them on sleds to the morgues or cemeteries.

Petya scanned the notices until he found a new one. On January 8— today—the Young Communists were having a winter coat and clothing collection for war orphans and soldiers at the front. As soon as Petya figured out what the notice was about, he stopped reading and attempted to move on to another one. But it was too late. That confounding voice in his head informed him he had to help. It was useless trying to fight it. If God told him to do something, he had no choice but to obey. Although he already had a lot to do that day, he resigned himself to the fact that he now had even more to do.

When he arrived back at the apartment, Katya was in her usual place seated in a chair facing the front door. Petya squeezed by her, looking over her shoulder as he did so. She was drawing another one of her endless sketches of Jesus. That was all she seemed to do lately.

Each picture she drew was the same in one astonishing way: Jesus would be smiling or laughing. Having only ever seen paintings of Jesus in agony—with a crown of thorns on his head, being crucified, or both—Petya didn't know what to think, and the voice of God in his head was strangely silent on the subject. When Petya had asked her once to explain her drawings to him, she'd responded simply, "Jesus was the epitome of peace and joy, and that's what he tried to teach others."

After retrieving his journal, Petya sat down across from Oksana, who was lying in bed moaning softly. She'd taken a turn for the worse in the past week and hadn't been able to make it to work. She complained incessantly that her stomach hurt, saying she surely had an ulcer and was going to die. Petya hoped she was right. After all, half the food you ate these days was inedible, and ulcers were indeed fatal.

He wrote the letters "К" and "Д" in his journal, then retrieved a large brown bag for the coats and clothing he hoped his neighbors would donate. He started at the first apartment on the fourth floor, but hesitated before knocking. The woman that lived there didn't like Petya and didn't try to hide it.

After explaining why he was there, she opened her door an inch, but kept the chain locked. "You?" she said suspiciously. "I don't believe it. What are you up to?"

"I just told you," Petya said wearily. "They're having a coat and clothing drive for war orphans and soldiers at the front. There's a notice on the bulletin board. The Young Communists are sponsoring it."

"I still don't believe you," the woman said. "You probably just want to sell whatever I give you on the market. Now go away." She slammed the door shut.

Petya trudged down the stairs and back to the bulletin board, took the notice down, then returned to the woman's apartment and knocked on her door again. She wouldn't open it to him, so he slid the notice under her door.

A minute later, she opened the door, keeping the chain locked, and squeezed a coat out the three-inch crack between the door and the doorframe. "Even if you are lying," she said, "ain't nobody gonna pay you a kopeck on the market for this old coat anyway."

"Thank you. You are a most kind and munificent woman," Petya said sarcastically and moved on.

At the next apartment, a man whose name Petya had forgotten opened the door and leaned against the frame as Petya told him about the coat drive. The man was covered with boils—another of the many results of malnutrition. Petya noticed he even had boils on his fingers, several of them lanced and unhealed.

The man invited Petya in, then disappeared into a bedroom. Though it was dark inside the apartment because the windows were covered with plywood, Petya could make out two women packing things into suitcases. Without his asking, they disclosed that they were being evacuated tomorrow. They were supposed to have left two days ago, but apparently the car that was to have taken them had broken down.

The man donated a generous amount of children's coats and clothes, and Petya learned why: both daughters had died the week before.

On the next floor, an apartment door opened as Petya was approaching. The Lusinkii's lived there, and Petya saw their eldest son—an officer in the navy—emerge. He looked comparatively healthy, as did most of his family. They certainly weren't flourishing, but neither had they lost anyone to starvation or disease. Petya didn't know how they did it, but they were not alone. Death was busy knocking on nearly every door in Leningrad, but by no means all.

Petya asked if they wanted to donate any clothing or coats, but they said no and promptly closed the door.

No one responded to Petya's knock at the door across the hall, so he moved on to the next one where the Karpovskii's lived. The man's wife answered, listened to Petya's request, then invited him in and led him down a short hallway. Beyond another door that opened into the kitchen, she lit a candle so they could see. The candle's light glittered off the frost-covered walls, and she pointed to the floor by a boarded-up window. A corpse lay there.

"You can have his coat," she said. "He doesn't need it anymore."

Petya didn't have to ask who it was. He knew it was Mr. Karpovsii. "When did he die?"

"Day before yesterday."

Dead bodies, even in apartments, did not stink or decompose because of the bitter cold.

"I can take care of the body for you, if you like," said Petya.

"How much?" asked the woman.

"A day's bread ration."

The woman gazed thoughtfully at her husband's body, then said, "No. I can't do it."

"You're just going to leave him here then?"

"Yes. I can't give up an entire day's ration."

As she spoke, Petya observed how badly decayed her teeth were. It was the same all over the city. There wasn't a single body part that didn't suffer from the effects of starvation.

"You're a neighbor," Petya said. "I'll do it for half the ration. How about that?"

She nodded, went into another room, then returned a minute later with the bread. It looked like considerably less than half, but Petya wasn't going to argue with her.

Pulling the coat off the cadaver, he handed it to the woman. "Put that outside your door for me. I'll come get it later." Then Petya grabbed the corpse's frozen legs, pulling the body out of the apartment to the hallway. There, he let it lie while he went to retrieve a sled and give Katya half of the bread he'd just received.

He was surprised when he didn't find Katya sitting in her chair in front of the door. Instead, she was in her bedroom dragging herself from one side to the other. Her ankle had healed some, but she still walked with almost as big a limp as Petya did. She seemed to be gathering things into a bag, and though he was curious, he didn't bother asking her why. He knew she wouldn't answer him. She took the bread he offered her, then closed the door on him.

Petya worried that no matter how much food she received now that it wouldn't help. There were tens of thousands of people like her—firmly in death's grasp, their bodies too depleted of nutrients to ever regain their health.

Once Petya dragged the body of Mr. Karpovskii down the stairs to the outside, he loaded it on the sled. But instead of taking it to the morgue or the cemetery, he made for a small shed in the deserted courtyard across the street. All the apartment buildings there had been destroyed by German bombing campaigns, and the shed was the only structure still standing. Petya unlocked the padlock he'd put on the door, then dragged the body inside.

Clearing away disembodied, sticklike arms and legs, he lifted the corpse onto a workbench, then closed the door behind him.

This was his butcher shop—complete with a variety of knives and a small ceramic stove. Without this place, Petya figured he would have starved to death weeks ago. In addition to consuming the meat, he'd also begun selling it at the Haymarket, labeling it "Horse Sausage."

The Haymarket, made famous by Dostoevsky's novel, *Crime and Punishment*, was the biggest marketplace in the city. Everything and anything was sold there: boots, coats, clothes, sleds, bread, and, of course, "meat." Most everyone knew what the meat was really made of, but chose to pretend it was actually whatever the seller said it was: horse, dog, cat....

As heads were the body parts most likely to speak to him, Petya covered Mr. Karpovskii's face with a rag. Then he left the shed, making sure the padlock was secured, and returned to his apartment building.

Stuffing all the coats and clothing into his brown bag, he tied it to the sled and started for the collection center. The Germans had started shelling with their long-range artillery again, so Petya listened to the explosions and high-pitched whistling of the shells for a while to see where they were coming from. The

Germans were systematic in their bombing, and you could tell what area of the city they were targeting and whether your trip would be safe.

All along his journey, Petya saw the old-timers—thin and seemingly on the verge of death—at their posts waiting for an air raid alarm. There hadn't been any bombing runs by German planes since mid-December. The rumors were that it was so cold the fuel in the planes had frozen. But that didn't mean the old guards didn't still have to sit in the freezing cold, at their posts by gates, doorways, in halls, or stairwells.

The Germans stopped their shelling when Petya was about halfway to the collection center, and all was ghastly quiet. He hated the silence. It wasn't only that that was when the voices usually spoke to him, but it also just wasn't right that such a large city could *be* that quiet.

Just as Petya feared, a voice began speaking to him. It was the voice of God, and it was telling Petya how pleased He was that so many of His children were being returned to Him in heaven as a result of the war.

"But there is one who has not come home yet," the voice said. "One that I miss deeply."

Petya knew who the voice was referring to. It wasn't the first time God had expressed his longing to be reunited with Katya.

"I am tired of waiting," the voice lamented. "I want her returned to me. Today."

Petya wanted to argue. He wanted to fight, or at least plead, instead of just giving in. But what did it matter what he wanted? In the end, the voice would win. It always did.

The warmth inside the truck's cab, along with the methodical rocking and steady hum of the engine had lulled Felix to sleep. He had a strange dream of being entombed in a coffin so big that he could stand up and walk around. When he awoke, it left him feeling discombobulated, and he fretted about not making it into the city yesterday, instead of today, January 8. The trip across the lake to Leningrad had been slow going from the start. The traffic was heavy, and they'd spent a great deal of time not moving at all.

Felix watched as five huge snowplows approached from the opposite direction, creating another road.

"Good," said the driver in his thick Georgian accent. "We need another road. The Nazis have pretty much ruined this one."

"They certainly seem determined to put an end to this supply route into the city," remarked Felix.

"Yes, but we're more determined to keep it open," the driver said. "They can keep on destroying our roads, we'll just keep building more. They'll never win."

"How are you so confident?"

"Because we'll never give up," the driver said matter-of-factly. "The Nazis aren't going to win unless they kill every last one of us." He cranked the big steering wheel to the left to avoid a piece of wreckage sticking out from the side of the road. "This is our home. It's where we're meant to be."

His comments didn't surprise Felix. He'd noticed a slow but steady shift in people's attitudes since those first few months of the invasion. You rarely met anyone these days who was ambivalent about the war. People had bonded together in a common cause: the defeat of the Nazis by any means. It was no longer a conflict of opposing ideologies. It had become a patriotic war.

For Felix to be seated in a warm place with nothing to do was a rare thing, and he drifted off to sleep once again. When he next awoke, he saw trees outside his window. "We're off the lake?"

The driver nodded. "We finished with that a while ago."

"How much farther?"

"Not much," the driver replied, pointing ahead of them.

Leaning forward and peering through the windshield, Felix was astonished to see Leningrad's skyline coming into view. He must have been sleeping longer than he'd thought, because once you crossed the lake, it was still a long distance before you reached the city.

He pulled out his pack of cigarettes, but then remembered he only had three left and decided to save them. In lieu of money—of which Felix had none left—the driver had accepted Felix's last full pack of cigarettes as payment for the ride.

As they approached a small collection of ice huts, Felix glimpsed two nurses with the customary red crosses on their arms carrying a wounded man into one of the huts. The closer they got to the city, the more Felix could see how viciously its once beautiful skyline had been ravaged by the German planes and long-range artillery. He tried to prepare himself mentally for the devastation that had been inflicted on his beloved Leningrad.

Shortly after veering around a snow-covered truck tipped over on its side, they passed by two figures trudging away from the city, heading in the direction of the lake. One of them was wearing a man's fur coat that was much too big for him, and Felix wondered if the man had lost that much weight or if maybe the coat didn't belong to him. He was pulling a small brown sled with some bundles strapped to it. The fur wasn't as dark as most similar coats, and it also had an interesting pattern of stripes. It looked vaguely familiar to Felix, and he thought for a second he might know the man, but he couldn't see his face because it was wrapped in a dark scarf.

The other person appeared to be an old woman. She was stooped, wore a wool shawl, and had rags wrapped around her boots. Felix had seen the rags, or pieces of carpet, wrapped around feet before. It was an attempt to prevent frostbite.

"Where are they going?" asked Felix.

"To the lake," the driver replied. "I see them all the time. They're evacuating on their own. They try to hitch a ride with us when we're headed back across."

"Do you pick them up?"

"Sure, if they can give me something—some cigarettes or bread, you know."

"And those who don't have anything to give?"

"Aw, come on. Everyone's got a least a little something. If they don't want to give us anything, then they can walk."

"Walk where? All the way across the lake?"

"That's their problem. We're not even supposed to pick them up in the first place."

Felix watched the two fade into the distance. It would be dark soon, and he wondered where they'd sleep that night. He wondered too at the wretchedness of their lives in the city to risk such a trek, for it was a journey where the odds of dying were probably far greater than the odds of living. He'd seen the lifeless bodies alongside the road proliferate the closer they got to Leningrad. He'd assumed they were victims of bombings or shellings, but now he knew the truth.

When the outskirts of Leningrad spread out before them, the driver stopped the truck. "This is where you get off," he said. "They don't let us carry passengers into the city."

Felix buttoned up his coat, thanked the driver, and hopped out of the cab.

"A word of advice," the driver said before Felix shut the door. "Keep your wits about you if anyone approaches. Especially stay away from the river."

"What do you mean?" asked Felix. "I already told you I don't have any money."

"It's not your money these people are after." The driver bared his teeth and pretended to bite his own arm.

Felix closed the truck door, unsure what exactly the driver's gesture meant.

With a glance at the faint sun low on the horizon, Felix calculated it was about three p.m., meaning he had one hour of daylight left. The walk to Katya's neighborhood would take several hours, so he got out a piece of bread and ate it slowly as he hiked.

The section of the city he started out in wasn't familiar to him. Piles of rubble lay in the street, and for some reason he kept smelling turpentine.

Blackened, burnt buildings and dead trees jutted from the ground, looking as though they'd tumble over after the next big gust of wind. Snowdrifts reached to the second-floor windows of some buildings. A multitude of streetcars and automobiles were frozen in place and partially—or in some cases, completely—covered over with snow. It was so quiet that Felix imagined his footsteps, crunching the hard snow beneath him, might be heard a mile away.

Not encountering a single person for the first forty minutes, he felt like he was traversing the ruins of an ancient abandoned city. After witnessing block after lifeless block, he began to wonder who could possibly survive here.

Then he saw them—dark figures lumbering down alleys and around snow drifts. Three of them surprised him as he rounded the next corner. They wore black masks over their faces, with peepholes cut out for their eyes. Felix instinctively reached for his gun, but realized they weren't out to rob him. They wore the masks to protect themselves against the mind-numbing cold.

When an artillery shell exploded nearby, Felix dove to the ground. He noticed none of the others did though. They just kept on walking as if nothing had happened. Not long after that, he came across three soldiers on pass from the front to visit their families. He asked them for directions, departing hastily when he spied two women in militia uniforms approaching.

"Your papers, please," Felix heard one of the women ask the three soldiers. Then she called to him, "Comrade, where are you bound?"

Felix quickened his pace. He had no pass, no orders to be in the city, and if he was caught, he could be sent to the firing squad for desertion.

She called to him again, a little louder, but Felix pretended not to hear. He ducked into the next alley, and when safely out of sight sprinted away. Emerging from the other side, he forced himself to resume a meager walking pace. It was apparent to him that no city dwellers were capable of running—or even walking briskly—and he didn't want to draw undue attention to himself.

A five-ton truck rumbled down the street and slowed as it approached a corpse. Stopping a few yards past it, two men got out and pulled the tarp from the back, revealing a chaotic pile of dozens of cadavers. They picked up the corpse and threw it on top of the others, then poured something where the body had been lying. A second later, Felix smelled turpentine and realized they were using it as a disinfectant. That was why the whole city reeked of it.

An hour after the sun had set, Felix expected the city to become busier. Five p.m. was when all the workers would head home for the day, but there were no masses of people walking the sidewalks. There were no streetlights, no trolleys, no cars. Above him, the moon shined its pale light on the plump, gray anti-aircraft balloons hovering at varying altitudes. He still struggled to pinpoint where exactly he was in the city. Not only were familiar buildings no longer there, but there were no street signs or block numbers. They'd all been painted over.

Nearly everywhere he looked in this part of the city, he saw corpses: on the sidewalks, streets, in the doorways of buildings, even sitting up on curbs, frozen in place. He counted them for a while, but stopped after reaching fifty.

The chilling thought that Katya may have suffered the same fate stopped him in his tracks. Perhaps she had already starved or froze to death. Or been a victim of the relentless German bombing. The more he contemplated it, the more foolish he felt for thinking otherwise. He hadn't received any letters from her. He hadn't—in fact—heard anything from anyone suggesting she was still alive. The logical conclusion was that she was dead. But his heart told him otherwise. Somehow it knew she was still alive.

Hearing a familiar squeaking sound that he discerned as coming from the runners of a sled, Felix recalled fondly how he used to go sledding as a child. But the sled's owner coming toward him now was not a young boy, but a thin, elderly man. And on top of his sled was a small blue body. Though wrapped in a blanket, the girl's long brown hair had spilled out and trailed behind in the snow.

The man dropped the sled's rope next to a park bench and stood motionless as Felix passed. Half a minute later a militiaman emerged from an alley in front of Felix and shouted, "Halt!"

Felix—heart pounding—froze in place. There was nowhere to go.

The militiaman took his rifle from his shoulder, then marched right past Felix toward the man with the sled.

"Halt!" the militiaman said again. "You are destroying government property."

Felix turned and saw the gaunt man had torn a plank from the bench, presumably for firewood.

With a sigh of relief, Felix resumed walking. He noticed that all the apartment buildings he passed—even the ones still intact—looked deserted. Not a light. Not a sound. Where were all the two and a half million inhabitants of this city?

Coming upon a tremendous fire that lit the surrounding area as if it was still daytime, Felix considered whether to stop and help those gathered put it out. But he saw that the chain of people were not trying to douse the flames. They were retrieving possessions from the building: a samovar, a kerosene stove, blankets....

He'd heard about the scourge of fires that afflicted Leningrad. It wasn't just the Germans and their incendiary bombs; hardly any of the makeshift stoves people used were installed properly. Every month these stoves started hundreds of fires, which resulted in hundreds of buildings burning to the ground. There was no water to put the fires out.

Felix asked one of the men at the fire the way to Kazansky Cathedral. It was only upon hearing the directions that Felix determined the person was female, not male. He couldn't tell by sight alone whether these walking skeletons with their skin stretched tight over their face were man or woman.

Before departing, he noticed a group of people with buckets coming toward the fire. He assumed they were bringing water from somewhere to extinguish the flames, but it was the opposite. The fire was melting snow and ice, and the people were going to collect the precious liquid into their pails to take home.

In a few more blocks, Felix started to recognize his surroundings—partly because some of the wrecked buildings had been covered over with plywood and painted to look as though they were still intact.

Three hours after beginning his trek from the outskirts of the city, he finally reached the Kazansky Cathedral. It gave him some comfort to find it undamaged. The cathedral's two giant wings remained resting on the ground, and Felix thought that if it hadn't flown away yet, it never would.

The moon was still shining, and he expected to see its light glimmering off Kazansky's shiny cupola, but the top of the cathedral had been painted a dark color as camouflage. Everything in the city looked strange to him, as though he was an unwitting character in a science fiction story. Places that were once familiar were now mysterious and foreboding. It was both the city he knew so well, and a sinister place full of ruins, corpses, and ghoul-like people.

As he approached Katya's block, he was relieved to see her building was still intact. It hadn't caught fire or been bombed. There were dark streaks down the side of the building, but they weren't from smoke, Felix knew. People didn't have the energy to take their bedpans and garbage out. Instead, they threw it out the window into the street.

Felix felt his way up the stairs in the pitch-black stairwell. The building, like the entire city, was absurdly quiet, and the only sound he heard was his own footsteps. With a queasy stomach, he reached the third floor and carefully inched down the hallway. He felt intensely anxious about seeing how thin and sickly Katya must have become, but his biggest fear was not seeing her there at all.

Taking a deep breath, he prepared to knock at Katya's apartment, but noticed the door hadn't been closed all the way. It was open a crack, and he could hear an unfamiliar man's voice inside.

"None of this is personal," the man said. "I don't even want to be doing this, but it's necessary for me to be able to continue."

Opening the door noiselessly, Felix snuck into the apartment. Although it seemed like the man was having a conversation with someone, Felix never heard anyone answer.

"There is one thing I want to apologize to you about," said the man. "I'm not quite sure how to say it though."

From the apartment's dark hallway, Felix spied candlelight from somewhere up ahead. Moving silently and slowly, he crept along the wall until he could see around the corner.

The room Felix used to know so well was barely recognizable to him now. There was a stove in the middle and three beds crammed in tight around it. The walls—stripped of wallpaper—were stained black, and a stovepipe snaked through the room to one of the windows.

The man had his back to Felix and was leaning over someone lying flat. The person on the bed wasn't moving, and the bed was covered with blood.

Felix stepped into the room. "Who are you?" he demanded. "What are you doing?"

The man—wrapped in layers of blankets from head to toe—stopped what he was doing.

The light from the candle flickered, and Felix repeated his questions.

"It's all right, Felix," the man answered as he turned around. "It's God's will, all part of the mission."

That the man knew Felix's name alarmed him, because he had no idea who he was talking to. As he moved closer to get a better view of the stranger's face, the man lunged at him with a bloody knife. Felix caught his arm and easily flung him down onto one of the beds. Then he grabbed the knife out of the man's hand and threw it across the room.

The stranger made no effort to get back up, instead staying where he was and declaring, "She waited for you."

Felix glanced at the emaciated, bloody corpse on the bed with the blanket covering its face. Everything began to swirl. "*Who* waited for me?" he asked. "What are you talking about?"

"She never gave up on you," the man continued. "Even after they told her you were dead, she sat in that chair staring at the door every day—just waiting for you to walk through."

Felix staggered toward the dead body. Nothing made sense to him. Who was this man speaking to him? Who was the corpse with the long hair? Tearing the blanket away, he stared in disbelief at the familiar face.

Then he went to the man, grabbed hold of the blankets wrapped around him, and lifted him in the air. "Why did you kill her?"

"I didn't kill anyone," the man replied. "Oksana was already dead when I got back."

Felix examined the man's face closely, noting a little black mole on his cheek. "Petya?" he asked skeptically.

The man nodded. "Yes. It is I."

"Where is Katya?" Felix asked in a quivering voice.

When Petya didn't answer, Felix lifted him even higher. "Where is she?"

"Hopefully in a place far better."

"Damn it, Petya! I'm not going to ask again. I'll throw you across the room if you don't tell me. Now where is she?"

"Gone."

"Where?"

"To find you."

Felix let go of his blankets, and Petya fell back onto the bed. "She went to find *me*?" he asked incredulously.

Petya held up a piece of paper. "When I got back an hour ago, I found this."

"Give it to me," Felix said, snatching it from his hand.

Petya,
By the time you read this, I'll be gone. I've decided to go across the lake to find Felix. I know he's out there somewhere and that we'll be together again. I took the brown sled. Please say goodbye to Igor for me and give him the letter I wrote him.
– Katya

No sooner had Felix finished reading the letter than he realized why that fur coat he'd seen earlier had seemed so familiar to him. It was Katya's father's old coat—the one he'd bought from the fur trader outside Archangel, the one he used to wear before he'd gotten a new one last year. Because it was a man's fur coat, Felix had assumed the person heading toward the lake was a man, but now he was sure it was Katya. He'd just missed her!

He fled from the apartment, stumbled down the stairs, and crashed into the door to the outside. Barely able to breathe, he ran into the night, grasping his chest, struggling to get enough air into his lungs so his heart wouldn't burst.

He raced back the same way he'd just come—running and running until his legs were exhausted.

Dark, heavy clouds converged on the city. The streets were empty.

The sun had just set, and Katya watched as her companion fell to the snow-covered road for the second time in less than ten minutes. Coming to a halt next to her, Katya hoped the woman would be able to get back up again. Katya did not have the strength to assist her in any way. It was all she could do to put one foot in front of the other and not fall down herself.

After much effort, the woman made it back to her feet. "I'm so damn cold," she muttered.

Katya didn't know the woman. They both happened to be heading to the lake and had decided to accompany one another. "Why don't we trade coats?" suggested Katya. "I'm warm enough for now, and we can switch back once we reach a shelter and you're able to warm up."

"Are you sure?"

Katya took off her fur coat and handed it to the woman. It made her feel good that despite her wretched condition, she could still help someone. Compassion was about the only thing she hadn't run out of.

"My goodness," the woman said as she wrapped herself in the fur. "It's so big."

"It was my father's," explained Katya as she pulled on the woman's ragged old coat.

Once they'd finished exchanging coats, they recommenced their sluggish pace along the road. The trucks coming at them from the lake arrived in a steady stream, though trucks going the same direction they were heading were few and far between. Katya didn't bother waving at them to stop anymore. She'd learned that she didn't possess anything they wanted, and none of them would give her a ride for free.

It wasn't even another five minutes before Katya's companion fell again—this time into the thick snow on the side of the road. Katya pulled her sled up close and sat on a snowdrift next to her.

"I can't make it any further," announced the woman dully.

On the side of the road, the snow was particularly deep. "I can't help you up," said Katya.

"I know, dear," replied the woman. "I don't expect you to. This is where I'm going to die."

Katya didn't argue with her. She'd considered collapsing onto the soft snow and doing the same thing herself a few times already.

"Those truck drivers should have given us a ride," the woman said bitterly. "I worked as a schoolteacher for twenty-seven years, and not once did I ever ask for a pack of cigarettes or a loaf of bread to teach a child."

Katya stayed by her side for a long time, until the woman told her in a whisper, "You may as well get going, my dear. You've got a long journey ahead of you."

Katya agreed. There was nothing she could do.

"Will you bless me before you go?" asked the woman.

As the wind picked up and it started to snow, Katya made the sign of the cross and whispered a short prayer. Then the woman closed her eyes, and her breathing became shallow. Having witnessed a number of deaths when she was a nurse at the hospital, Katya could tell death was imminent. She wanted to get her fur coat back, but realized it was too late. The woman couldn't take it off, and Katya was much too weak to get it off of her. It was only with great effort that Katya had even been able to stand up again.

Grabbing the rope of her sled, she began walking once more. She had no idea how much further it was to the lake, but hoped she was at least past the halfway point.

The only way she'd made it this far was by focusing solely on the next segment of her journey. She thought only of reaching the next goal—something within sight, like an intersection, a building, or a tree. To contemplate her final destination was too daunting.

She passed by corpse after corpse, but they had no effect on her. She never imagined she could be so indifferent to death, but after seeing it day in and out for so long, she'd lost all fear of it. Being constantly hungry, tired, and cold, death seemed more like a welcome slumber than a frightful annihilation.

Before even leaving the apartment, Katya understood how much risk this trip would entail. It was a one-way journey, but one worth the gamble. It was ironic to her that the final push she needed to undertake it was an even greater fear of staying. She knew if she didn't leave that she'd die in that apartment. Either Petya would take that final plunge into insanity and murder her, or she would simply succumb one night to the cold and the hunger.

Catching herself reaching for her last edible item—lipstick—she said silently, "Wait until you reach the lake. Then we'll have a bite and a nice rest." Though she'd started using the term "we" to refer to herself, she had no idea why.

When the sled's rope fell from her hand for the fourth time, she knew she needed to come up with another method. It wasn't only that she had so little strength, it seemed the commands from her brain were either being ignored by the intended muscles or else getting lost along the way. In addition, her joints ached even more than usual and she found herself stumbling over her own feet and forgetting where she was and why she was out here.

The difficulty with thinking was nothing new. For the last month or so, she found her concentration lasted no more than a few seconds. It was similar to being really drunk: one would decide to do something and get ready to do it, then forget what it was.

The best solution, she decided, was to tie the rope around her forearm. As she was preparing to do it, she saw a truck barreling down the road in her direction. The road was narrow here, so she moved to the side as far as she could and pulled her sled off the road. But as she did so, she lost her hold on the rope, and the sled drifted away and down a ditch.

Sitting down on a snowbank, she stared at the sled. It was only thirty feet away, but it may as well have been thirty miles. Off the road, the snow was exceedingly deep, and though its top was hard, she knew it wouldn't support her weight and that she'd sink down to her waist. She had no energy to get upset about losing her documents and clothing that were on the sled. The tragic event was merely something that had happened, and that was it.

Willing herself up to her feet, she started walking again, vowing not to stop until she reached either the lake or a shelter.

Dark clouds moved in, blotting out the moon and stars, and the wind gusted with sand-like snowflakes. As the trucks thinned out, then stopped altogether, she was sure another blizzard was coming.

After a half-hour of plodding forward, her legs gradually came to a halt. She hadn't told them to. They just stopped, then suddenly gave out from under her. She fell to the side, landing in the thick, fluffy snow alongside the road. It was so very comfortable, and she had no desire to get back up.

Her grandmother's presence felt particularly close, and Katya noticed that her breathing was no longer automatic. If she didn't consciously tell her body to take a breath, it wouldn't. Removing a mitten, she stuck her right hand inside her coat. When her fingers got to be too thin to hold the ring Felix had given her, she'd put it on a string and wore it around her neck. She held fast to the ring now, recalling the dance where she realized for the first time she was in love with him.

No words had been spoken. No heartfelt letters had passed between them. It had happened innocently, spontaneously. When the band began playing a waltz, Felix left his group of friends behind and purposely strode across the room directly to her. He bowed, just slightly, and held out his hand in a regal manner. Accepting his invitation, she put her hand in his and they walked to the middle of the dance floor. With confidence and charm, he placed one hand on her hip and held her right hand in his at shoulder height, then smiled and looked her in the eyes, as if to say, "Ready?"

Her heart said yes, but her legs felt like rubber. He moved his left leg forward, but she didn't move backwards, and he crushed her toes with his shoe. The pain was sharp, but she found herself laughing in spite of it. Felix apologized profusely as she confessed that she didn't know how to waltz. "Close your eyes," he'd told her. "I'm going to lead, and you only have to follow. Relax, and don't try to guess what you need to do. Just react. When you feel me moving toward you, step back with your right leg. Keep your arms firm. Don't let my chest come any nearer to yours than it is now."

And then they began, ever so slowly to waltz. One-two-three. One-two-three. Katya kept her eyes closed the whole time, letting herself be carried away by the music and Felix's firm grasp. They glided across the floor— spinning, swaying, Felix counting softly in her ear, "One-two-three. One-two-three."

There was only that moment. Nothing else existed. Just her and Felix and the music moving as one. At that moment she knew beyond words that she was madly in love with this man and that her life would never be the same.

Although her right hand was now starting to get numb from the cold, she refused to let go of the ring. Placing her left hand over her right, she closed her eyes even tighter, trying to return to that night when her heart was as big as the dance hall. Tears of sorrow welled in her eyes, and the icy wind froze them to her eyelashes.

Felix had no idea how long it had taken him to make it back to the place where he thought he'd seen Katya with the sled. He only knew that it had been snowing for the last hour and was incredibly cold. The wind stung his face and caused his cheeks and eyebrows to go numb, and the ice-cold hairs on the inside of his nose felt like needles poking him on each inhalation.

There had been a long line of trucks coming from the lake, and their headlights had provided him with a nearly constant source of light. Since the trucks had thinned out, he'd had to rely on his flashlight more often as he checked the bodies lying along the side of the road. There was one at least one every hundred feet or so.

Only a short distance past where he thought he'd seen Katya, Felix spotted the fur coat with the familiar pattern of stripes. It was half buried under the sand-like snow, on a body that did not move.

"Katya!" he yelled as he rushed forward. Urgently brushing some of the snow off, he called her name repeatedly and shook her by the arm. But there was no response from the rigid, lifeless body. When he pulled away the scarf covering her face, he saw—to his horror and relief—that it wasn't Katya. It was an old woman.

A flood of emotions threatened to overwhelm him. Fear: if someone else had Katya's coat, did that mean Katya was dead? Regret: why couldn't he have stood firm and made her leave on that train back in August? Guilt: why had he taken so long to come back for her? Hopelessness: if she wasn't wearing that unique fur coat, how could he possibly find her?

He sat back on the snow, unsure what to do next. He could head back toward Leningrad to find some place to sleep for the night, or continue on in the hope that Katya might still be out there. This woman didn't have a sled after all, and he distinctly remembered seeing the person with the fur coat pulling a sled with some bundles strapped to it. His gut told him to keep going, to continue on toward Lake Ladoga, but the rational part of his brain argued it was pointless.

A truck stopped nearby, and the driver hopped out to urinate. Felix asked him if he'd seen any people walking toward the lake.

"Sure, I see 'em all the time," he answered. "Poor souls. Hardly any of 'em ever make it."

"Tonight though," Felix said. "Did you see any tonight?"

"Tonight ... hmm," he replied. "Not sure. The days all kind of blend together."

Felix groaned disappointedly, then noticed how thirsty, hungry, and tired he was.

"You need a ride into the city?" the driver asked as he climbed back into the cab.

The wind was blowing harder, the snow falling heavier, and Felix opened his mouth to say yes. But before the word came out, his gut instinct overruled him, stating in no uncertain terms: *Don't give up. Not now. Not ever.*

Waving the driver off, Felix marched on, checking every body he saw. He worried Katya could have collapsed and that he might pass her by, so he was careful not to skip any of the dark lumps lining the road. He'd stop, brush off the snow, then shine his flashlight on the face. Although he could easily tell the old from the young, he had to study the face intently to discern any more than that. They all looked remarkably similar.

After he'd walked about two miles from the spot where he'd thought he'd seen Katya, exhaustion—both physical and mental—took its toll on him. The wind was gusting and blowing snow horizontally, pelting him in the face and making it difficult to see. He'd checked dozens of bodies, and they were all dead and frozen.

When he came to another corpse on the side of the road, he didn't want to stop and check it. There was no sled nearby, and he was tired of disturbing the dead. They deserved to rest in peace.

He dropped onto the snowbank a few yards past the body and retrieved the flask Misha had given him. As usual, the liquor burned his throat, but his numb-with-cold body welcomed the warming sensation. His stomach growled, but there was nothing to be done about that. He'd eaten the last of his food several hours ago.

With a bleary sigh, he rose to check the body, hoping it might have some bread or food they'd failed to eat before dying. There was a time when taking things from the dead would have been reprehensible to him, but he'd seen so much death that he had little reaction to it anymore. Corpses were as ubiquitous as flies in the summer, and the dead had no need of things like food.

The body had only an inch of snow over top of it, so Felix guessed they hadn't died too long ago. As he brushed the snow off, he saw the person had both of their hands tucked inside their coat, just below their chin. The left hand covered the right, as if they were holding something precious. Felix pulled each arm out so he could see what it was they were holding. He was amazed at how easily the arms moved. The person couldn't have been dead long at all. Rigor mortis hadn't even set in.

Using his flashlight, he saw the person was holding a ring hanging from a necklace. The ring had a small ruby in the middle and a petite diamond on each side. Felix recognized it, of course. It was the ring he'd given Katya on that day long ago before he'd left for the front.

Unable to take in the significance of it all, he stared at the ring with his mouth agape. Then he placed his hand on the scarf covering the person's face and braced himself. He removed it slowly, studying the face inch by inch. It took several seconds after he'd pulled the scarf away for him to be sure. She was thin and pale and had those awful red and purple marks that indicated frost bite, but despite her taut skin and humongous eyes, Felix recognized her.

"Oh, Katya," he bawled. "My precious!" He laid his head on her chest and held her. He was too late. She was gone.

He pressed his lips to her cheek. "My love," he cried softly, barely able to get the words out. Her skin was cold, but he'd expected it to be colder. He removed a mitten and stuck his frozen fingers in his mouth to unthaw them. Then he held his breath and cautiously felt for a pulse in her throat. And there it was—the faintest pulse he'd ever felt. She was alive!

With quivering hands, he took out his flask and poured a little liquor in her mouth. Then he got out both blankets from his pack and wrapped them tight around her. He desperately hoped to see a truck and get a ride, because it was critical that she warm up. But the trucks, already few and far between, had stopped completely.

Felix remembered from his ride into the city that there was a collection of ice huts a mile or two away. He'd seen two nurses pulling a wounded soldier into one of the them, so it might have been a medical station. He picked up Katya—horrified at how light she was—and began the trek.

The road was slippery because the falling snow didn't pack, and underneath it was patches of ice. Additionally, Felix's legs were weak and worn out. It was all he could do to keep from stumbling.

He carried her in front of him with both arms, trying to keep her face close to his. After half a mile, he stopped and poured some more alcohol down her throat. She responded by coughing, and it was the most wonderful sound he'd ever heard.

"Katya," he called over the roaring wind.

She moaned and moved her head feebly.

"Katya, open your eyes."

Her eyelids remained closed, but she mumbled something.

Felix moved his face even closer to hers. "What?" he asked, pulling her scarf down away from her mouth. "I couldn't hear you."

"You're a wonderful dancer," she said weakly.

Felix still wasn't sure he'd heard her correctly. A *dancer*?

"Katya, it's me. Felix."

"I know," she said, opening her eyes a crack. "Who else would it be?"

Felix wasn't sure she saw anything. Her eyes appeared unfocused and seemed to be looking past him.

"Where did you learn to waltz like that?" she whispered.

Felix didn't understand and thought she was delusional.

She squinted her eyes at him, then commented, "You have a white beard."

He was sure she'd lost her senses, but then realized that his beard probably *was* colored white from the snow.

"You look like Father Frost," she said.

A joke. *She told a joke*! Felix laughed. It was the funniest, most wonderful wisecrack he'd ever heard her say. She was going to be all right. He just knew it. "Yes, that's right," he said with a chuckle. "I'm Father Frost. Ho-ho-ho. And I brought a present for you, little girl."

She somehow managed a slight, short-lived smile. "Oh Felix, I knew I'd find you," she said. "I just knew it."

The wind blew snow as fine as table salt directly into Felix's face, and he bent his head forward as he carried her. "Yes, you found me. Everything's going to be fine. We're together again."

"I'm really tired," she said. "I'm going to sleep a little."

"No," Felix said emphatically. He knew what falling asleep meant for someone in her condition. It wasn't slumber she'd be surrendering to, it was death. "You need to stay awake, Katya. All right?"

She didn't answer and had already closed her eyes.

"Katya," he shouted, "promise me you won't fall asleep."

He leaned his right ear as close as he could to her mouth and heard a barely audible mumble: "Aaa promiss."

"Good. You don't have to speak," he told her. "Just listen to me. Stay awake and listen to me."

Knowing he had to talk about something that would keep her attention if he was to have any hope of keeping her awake, he searched his mind for memorable moments they'd shared together.

"Remember that day we skipped school and went to the museums?" he hollered over the wind. "We'd arrived at school at the same time, and it was the first nice day of spring. Neither of us wanted to go to class, and right before we walked into the classroom, you said, 'Let's get out of here.' I thought you were joking, but you were serious, so I asked, 'Where?' And you said, 'Anywhere. Anywhere, but here.' So we did it. We had such an incredible day. I still remember eating chocolate ice cream in the park, and that one painting we saw that we both loved. It was...."

Felix tried to cover every detail of the story, both to keep it interesting and to stretch it out as long as possible. As soon as he finished telling it, he started on another story.

The wind no longer gusted. Now, it blew hard nonstop, and hard, little snowflakes found their way past Felix's scarf and down his back. The storm had become a full-fledged blizzard.

The physical toll of the trip on Felix continued to mount. It had been seven hours since he'd been sitting comfortably in the warm cab of the truck on his way into the city. Since then, he'd been walking, running, trudging through deep snow, stepping carefully on slippery surfaces, and carrying his beloved in his arms against a ferocious headwind. The blinding snow and lack of light made it nearly impossible to see, and if it weren't for the large snowbanks on either side of the road, he would've easily lost his way. He stumbled more than a few times, and wanted badly to rest for a few minutes, but wouldn't allow it. There wasn't a minute to spare in getting Katya medical attention.

After telling several stories, he struggled to come up with new ones. Neither his body nor his brain was functioning particularly well.

"Oh, I know," he said after a brief pause. "How could I forget this? Remember that time you stole your father's bottle of brandy, and Dima picked the lock on the door to the roof of his apartment building? The three of us sat up there all night long talking and staring at the stars. We ended up falling asleep on the roof, and you had an exam the next morning. You ran into class twenty minutes late, you told me later, and somehow still got an A on the test. Do you remember that, Katya?"

Miniature icicles hung from where his breath warmed his scarf. He put his ear close to her mouth again and thought he heard something like a "yes" or a small laugh, so he continued on.

An hour later—just as Felix's endurance was breaking down and he'd run out of stories—he saw the snow-covered truck tipped on its side that signaled the ice huts were only ten to fifteen minutes further.

"We're almost there, my love," he assured her. "Just a few more minutes, then everything will be all right." He didn't hear a response from her.

When the ice huts at last came into view, he caught sight of someone exiting one. "Is there a medical station here?" he yelled to them. "A doctor? Or nurse?"

"Yes," replied the man. "In that next hut. Follow me."

The man led Felix to the medical station and helped him pull Katya through the waist-high entrance. Then they laid Katya down on one of the crude, wooden beds as two nurses arrived to tend to her.

Felix collapsed in sheer exhaustion onto the floor of the hut. He sat against the wall and watched one of the nurses put a blanket over Katya while the other checked her pulse and listened to her chest with a stethoscope.

"Should I go get the doctor?" asked the first nurse.

"No," answered her colleague as she folded her stethoscope and stuck it in her pocket.

Felix made it back to his feet as the nurse pulled the blanket up over Katya's face. "What are you doing?" he demanded.

"I'm sorry, comrade," the nurse said sympathetically.

"What do you mean, *you're sorry*? I brought her here so you could help her. Give her a transfusion or something!"

"Comrade, she's deceased. There's nothing we can do."

"No!" shouted Felix. "She can't be dead!" He pulled the blanket from Katya's face and felt her throat for a pulse. When he couldn't find one, he put his ear next to her nose to listen for her breathing. Nothing.

"Comrade, it's no use," the nurse said, trying to pull him away by the arm.

Felix shook off her grasp. "There has to be *something* we can do!"

"There's nothing," the nurse said resolutely. "She's in God's hands now."

The finality of the words stopped him. *In God's hands now.* A tear slid down the side of his nose and caught in his beard. Wiping his watering eyes with the back of his hands, he bent toward Katya's pale face. He pressed his lips to hers, and for the first time ever, there was no response. Her lips were thin and cold, and he knew then that it was over. She was gone.

He slid her mittens off, wrapped his hands around hers, and rested his head on her heart. In between his sobbing, he sang that silly nursery rhyme she was so fond of:

♫ *Silly as a duck, what dumb luck, we're meant to be together, meant to be to-ge-ther* ♪ ....

Then he felt crazed and mad with hate. He went outside to scream. But at who? At what?

He yearned to *do* something, to let it out. He wanted to throw back at life all the ugliness that had poisoned him deep within. He opened his mouth wide to cry, or roar, or curse, but no sound came. There was nothing he could do or say that was going to change anything. There was only that infuriating recognition that he was trapped. There was no escape from this pain. No escape from death. No escape from sorrow.

He spread his arms wide and fell straight back into the thick snow. Everything he held dear in his life had been taken from him: his hopes and dreams for the future; his beloved city; his best friend, Dima; and now the love of his life, Katya.

It was as if the universe—knowing he wouldn't take that pilgrimage willingly—had shrewdly pushed him from behind into the abyss. He was in freefall on that most frightening of human journeys: the Descent.

The snow continued to fall, slowly knitting a blanket of white over him. Felix felt the earth trying to reclaim him in some way, and he didn't resist. He welcomed it.

Глава Десятая — Chapter Ten

THOSE WHO WOULD NOT BE DEFEATED

A Blue Jay chirps outside my window
as I contemplate why the door to my room
is always open.
I'm expecting no one.
I didn't even expect the Blue Jay.
I think I should shut the door.
No sense in leaving it open.
And then I hear it…
Laughter.
It bounces off the walls,
up the stairs,
and into my uncomprehending ears.
I ask it what it's doing here.
But laughter only laughs. It doesn't understand.
"Don't leave me," I say.
And it doesn't.
And we sit together for a while,
remembering those endless summer nights,
those endless summer dreams,
with our youth, and our convictions,
that our endless lives would always be just that.
I look away—only for a moment—
and laughter slips away.
I am bitter,
but leave the door open anyway.

The middle-aged dentist, sighing in exasperation, set his flashlight and tool down. "You're going to have to hold still for me to be able to do this," he griped in his heavy Lithuanian accent.

Felix had developed an acute toothache that morning that blurred part of his vision. He was on leave from the front specifically to have this Leningrad dentist examine it. Taking a deep breath, Felix relaxed his jaw and facial muscles.

"That's better," said the dentist.

It was the same tooth that had been knocked loose so long ago when he'd tried to stop the fight between Dima and Yuri. It had never really healed. Nor had Felix wanted it to. He was grateful for the constant source of pain, because it served as a distraction to the cruelty and confusion that defined the times he lived in. It also blocked other pain—whether physical, mental, or emotional—from his mind.

The dentist poked at his teeth and gums with a sharp metal object, commenting, "Ah yes, I see the problem."

For weeks on end, Felix had lived with that painful tooth as he wandered aimlessly in the depths of sorrow. He was hesitant, even now, to get rid of the tooth. It was like a childhood friend who'd shared in the defining moments of Felix's life. But these days their relationship offered little more than familiarity, and Felix knew it was time to move on. He was ready. Ready to feel again.

The dentist set one tool down and picked up another that resembled a pair of pliers. "Are you sure you don't want a little alcohol to numb the pain? This is going to hurt."

Besides some strong alcohol you could swish in your mouth and then swallow, the dentist had no anesthesia. Felix wouldn't have accepted it, even if he did. It was important to him to feel every ounce of the pain when this tooth was removed.

The dentist stuck the plier-like tool in Felix's mouth and clamped down. "Ready?"

Felix heard the dentist, but didn't reply because he was already far away, busy creating a different world in his mind. A world in which there was no hate, shame, or depravity. A world where poetry and legends were more important than money and philosophy.

After the dentist yanked the tooth from his jaw, Felix thought he'd die from the excruciating pain.

The dentist put a small piece of cloth in Felix's mouth when he was done. "Bite down on that," he said, "but not too hard. It'll help stop the bleeding."

Though glad it was over with, Felix also felt a great sadness. It was like saying goodbye to a way of life he'd grown accustomed to.

"Well, my son, you're just about all grown up now," proclaimed the dentist with a chuckle. "A 'mature adult' as they say."

Felix struggled to speak while still biting down on the cloth. "What do you mean?"

Washing his hands over a bucket of water, the dentist answered, "Your wisdom teeth are coming in."

It was March and the great cleanup of the city had begun. Felix passed by thousands of Leningraders laboriously clearing away snow, slop, and corpses from the thawing streets. The workers were weak, thin, and nearly all women. They used crowbars and hammers to chop the ice, snow, and debris from the sidewalks, then carried it on flat sheets of plywood to the Neva River. When the icy river finally thawed, its water would be toxic, but that was a problem for another day.

The ration situation had finally stabilized. Bread was plentiful. One could even get sugar, butter, and meat. The devastating months of January and February were behind them now, and Leningraders were daring to hope again. They hoped they'd already endured the worst and that the blockade would be broken soon.

Felix passed by a bulletin board where a woman was putting up the latest issue of the Leningradskaya Pravda newspaper. In his former existence, he would've stopped and read every article. But he was no longer interested in their sensationalist stories. Concerned that they distorted his view of the world, he'd gone a week without reading any newspapers. He'd liked it so much that he'd stopped listening to the news on the radio too. He found his whole demeanor changed. He felt lighter and had more clarity on what he was supposed to be doing with his life. He spent his time now in conversation with the trees and animals and snowflakes. He didn't always understand what they were saying, but it was immensely gratifying trying to figure it out.

He passed by a long line of people waiting to get inoculations at a school building. With spring fast approaching, it was feared that epidemics would break out and kill the remaining Leningraders who had miraculously made it through the winter. Vaccines for typhus, cholera, plague, smallpox, and others were flown in from Moscow. Every hospital and school served as an inoculation station. Those too weak to make it there would get their shots at their home by visiting nurses.

A breeze picked up and it started to snow—big, wet, milky-white snowflakes filling the sky. As one passed by his ear, he heard a whisper. He didn't bother glancing around him. He knew who it was.

Wherever he set his eyes now, he saw Katya. She was in the monuments, bridges, canals, and the Neva River. Her voice floated on the wind. Her eyes looked back at him from everyone he met. She was everywhere—inseparable from the city and people she loved. Everything she believed in was still here, and Felix awoke each morning knowing she was in his heart, her spirit guiding him with every step he took.

Approaching the Kazansky Cathedral, Felix observed a small group of people gathered out front. A beautiful, haunting piece of symphonic music was coming from the outside loudspeakers, and he stopped to listen. He was enchanted by the unfettered confidence of the piece. It was clear the composer had mastered his craft, and also that he'd been deeply inspired when he wrote it. New ideas crashed through the music like giant waves, the tone changing seamlessly from vibrant to fearsome to dread and back again. The brass and percussion thundered in, then faded away, only to return in a more dire form later on.

Felix didn't try to find any meaning or symbolism in the music. He was weary of ideology, theory, and contemplation, of always wanting to know what something meant. He'd had dozens of epiphanies over the years, and had been convinced each time it was the one that would irrevocably change his life. But none of them ever did, and he'd learned to take everything with a grain of salt now.

The music moved him to reflect on the proud and courageous people of Leningrad, how they'd refused to give up. He recalled the time at the end of January when the power stations had run out of fuel, halting the city's last remaining water-pumping station. Without water, the bread bakeries couldn't operate. A call went out for help, and two thousand Young Communists answered it. They formed a chain, passing buckets of water from the river to the nearest bakery. They kept up the strenuous work in the biting cold for hours on end, saving thousands of lives.

Then Felix recollected the truck drivers who'd tirelessly transported food into the city—risking their lives every minute they were on the ice, driving until fingers and toes had to be amputated. He thought of the starving workers who'd continued to produce shells and bullets in the frigid factories, of the soldiers on the front lines who'd fought day after day against the Nazis, the cold, and their own hunger. All in order to save Leningrad. There were so many who had sacrificed everything, including their lives, for the sake of their country. Felix was overcome with appreciation and awe at their bravery and selflessness.

Bits and pieces of the music sounded familiar to Felix, and he asked a fellow soldier standing near him what it was. "Shostakovich's Seventh Symphony," the man replied. "It's being performed in Moscow."

It was then that Felix knew Russia and the rest of the Soviet Union would ultimately prevail over the Germans. Shostakovich had composed that symphony while living in Leningrad under siege, and now it was being performed for the whole world to hear. It was a testament to the fact that they'd absorbed the deadliest blow any army had ever inflicted on another, and they were still standing.

When the symphony ended, Felix walked on. The pain from his tooth was fading, gradually being replaced by a squeamish sensation in his stomach. He'd felt it for most of his life, but always thought it signified a weakness. The night Katya died, he'd learned otherwise. Her death had triggered something in him. A part of him he hadn't even known existed came to life. It was a fierceness, centered in his belly, that gave him profound strength to keep his heart open to the world no matter the circumstances. He could openly speak of his grief and sorrow, and he could listen to others express theirs. It was all part of a greater conversation to him, one he had daily with things both living and non-living.

As he'd lay there on the earth that night, being covered over with falling snow, he'd had the terrifying realization that the life he was living was not really his. It did not belong to him, but to something larger, something he had yet to fully comprehend. He'd struggled to find the words, ultimately settling on Divine Mother Nature. It was She who had brought him into the world, and the price of that precious birth was steep: it was that everything and everyone he held dear belonged to Her, and She would reclaim them all, sometimes one by one, sometimes a thousand at a time.

He understood after that night that he was always meant to be in complete servitude to Her. He'd known that as a small child, but had somehow forgot as he grew older. It took him nearly fifteen years to come full circle, to regain that knowledge of who he was and was always meant to be. That one night of unbearable angst and sorrow had accomplished what would have otherwise taken him decades to perceive. Because of that great and awful secret that had been whispered to him when he reached the bottom of the pit of despair, he could no longer look at anyone the same as before, for nothing was ever what it appeared to be.

It was going to take a lifetime of vigilance for it to sink into his being completely. All Felix knew right now was that he accepted the world exactly as it was, and it gave him a sense of peace that he'd never known before.

Peace so great, it burned through the darkness around him.

Epilogue

It was the first sunny, pleasant day in May, and the five university students sat restlessly at a table next to an open window. Greenfinches rejoiced from the treetops, and pigeons strutted along the sidewalk looking for crumbs. Kyra, one of the students, had a big bag of puffed corn and threw a handful of it out the window for the pigeons.

"So everyone knows their role for the presentation, right?" asked Igor.

The others nodded.

"Then we're done," exclaimed Kyra. "Now let's get out of here!"

Papers were hurriedly shoved in bags, books were shut with loud snaps, and the doors to the outside were flung open with abandon. Kyra was the first one out, skipping and raising her arms toward the bright blue sky. "Oh, how I love spring!" she sang. Dropping her books and bag to the ground, she lay down and sprawled on the grass, while the others shared cigarettes and told jokes around a bench under a big tree.

Igor joined Kyra on the grass, pensively watching the passing cars and trolleys on the street. Kyra squeezed his ankle to get his attention. "Kiss me," she said.

With a grin, Igor leaned over and touched his lips to hers. She wrapped her arms around his neck and pulled him down so that he fell on top of her, and they both laughed for a long time.

"Are you going with us for the picnic?" asked Kyra. "We're celebrating Sasha's eighteenth birthday. We'll go right after the parade."

"No. I can't," Igor answered. "I've got other plans today."

Kyra pretended to pout. "You're no fun," she said teasingly.

Igor felt hot in the sun and rolled his sleeves up beyond his elbows. He had hard, muscular forearms, and Kyra ran her fingers along them.

"You're at least coming to the party tonight, aren't you?" she asked.

Igor made his way to his feet. "Yes. I'll be there."

"You better be," she warned playfully as Igor departed.

On his way past the others gathered around the bench, Igor plucked a half-finished cigarette from his best friend's lips, then smoked it himself as he continued on.

"I'll get you for that," his friend jested. "Just when you least suspect it too."

"Eight o'clock sharp!" Kyra called to Igor. "You better not be late."

A tiny wisp of a cloud floated through the sky, and Igor shielded his eyes from the sun to peer at it. Today was a special day: May 9, Victory Day. The whole country took this specific day off every year to celebrate their victory over the Nazis in WWII. The ninth of May meant even more than that to Igor though. It was the day he chose to give thanks to a person who had changed his life.

As he passed under branches filled with blooming white flowers, he recalled a story Katya had told him about an oak tree, and how it was never really born and thus never died. The tree was a culmination of things that had come together in unison: an acorn, fertile soil, water, and sunlight. If any one of them was missing, an oak tree would not form. But nature's sole goal was to generate the conditions for life, and a mature oak tree created the seeds for its own continuation.

The sentiment comforted him, not only because it implied that Katya had not ceased to exist simply because her heart had stopped beating, but also because it meant nothing existed of its own accord. The survival of everyone depended upon the existence and support of everything and everyone else.

Igor cherished this idea of interconnectedness—that he himself was one of the conditions responsible for bringing new things into being. This was the most important lesson Katya had helped him learn, and—like her—he strove every day to bring forth beautiful things that would hopefully bloom into joy, love, and laughter.

After passing through the ten-foot-tall iron gates of the cemetery, Igor turned to the right toward the familiar bush with the bright pink flowers. He put his nose close and inhaled their fragrance, then snapped off a small branch of flowers.

As he walked alongside the graves and tombstones, he thought back to that horrible time when nearly half of the city's population perished due to starvation, cold, or the enemy's bombs. The number still staggered him: over one million people dead in such a short amount of time.

The Great Patriotic War, as it was now called, had been a war like no other. Unprecedented in its savagery, and so too, in its bravery. Igor pulled out the medal he'd been given as a survivor of the blockade. Every Leningrader who had made it through that hell had been given one. He held it tight in his hand and was reminded of how many times the Red Army had tried to break the blockade. He recollected the Ice Road and how there were as many as sixty routes over it at one time. They'd even built an entire railroad over the frozen Lake Ladoga one winter. For nine hundred days they'd endured the siege, until the tide finally shifted irrevocably and the Soviet Army burst forth and didn't stop until it reached Berlin.

Up ahead at his intended destination, Igor spied a lone figure kneeling on the ground. He knew who it was. Igor saw him there at the tomb on this day every year. It was Felix Varilensky. Everyone knew him—the decorated war hero wounded on nine separate occasions. Old ladies kissed him on the cheek. Children sang nursery rhymes about him. A poster of him receiving the Order of Lenin medal adorned the interior of every Post Office building in the city.

All to Felix's embarrassment, Igor knew. They talked once or twice a year, and one thing Igor was always amazed at was Felix's humbleness. He didn't like all the praise and attention, and didn't think he deserved it. He wasn't proud of what he'd done in the war, but neither did he regret it. It was something that had happened, and it was over. "Why can't we just leave it at that?" Igor had heard him say more than once.

Not wanting to intrude, Igor stopped and leaned against a tree to wait. Felix was on his knees, in between two graves, speaking in a soft voice and rubbing his eyes with the backs of his hands. He made the sign of the cross, then folded his hands together in front of him and stayed that way for a long time.

An attractive young woman with brown, shoulder-length hair, a light-blue dress, and a yellow sun hat approached in the distance. She held the hands of two small children, one boy and one girl, and was walking slowly so they could keep up. Each child held a dandelion with their free hand. When the woman neared Felix, the children let go of her hand and started running. "Daddy! Daddy!" they shouted.

Felix caught them in his arms, then picked them up and spun around in circles while they laughed and squealed. The woman came up and kissed Felix on the lips, then the four of them started for the cemetery's exit.

Catching sight of Igor, Felix waved and called to him to stop by for dinner sometime next week.

Igor waved back as he made his way to the grave. It was covered with fresh-cut flowers: red roses, purple lilacs, white daffodils, and two yellow dandelions. Igor added to the mix the pink flowers he'd picked, then sat down and pulled a small brown book from his bag.

He thought back once more to those days that changed his life. The misery, the despair, the destruction. And yet through it all, he remembered mostly just the kindness of one person.

"You see," he said aloud, holding up the book in front of him. "I told you last year I'd get your poems published. It's been receiving acclaim since it came out last month. Anna Akhmatova herself even wrote a glowing review of it."

He opened the book and began reading from the first poem. He read for an hour and a half, not stopping until he reached the last part of the last poem, his favorite:

I follow the path and come across a great lake of joy,
and see it's fed by this abundant river of sorrow.
This maddening dichotomy has evaded me for so long:
One cannot exist without the other.

Upon leaving the cemetery, Igor strolled leisurely along the Neva River. Everywhere one looked now there was new life: birds singing as they flew from tree to tree, green buds sprouting from the dark soil, trees and bushes overflowing with colorful flowers. The air was filled with the scent of linden trees just coming into bloom, and a pigeon on the sidewalk in front of Igor hooted softly before flying away.

People were lined up along the bridges and riverbanks to watch the ice from Lake Ladoga pass through. It was an annual event that every Leningrader looked forward to watching. Igor found an empty spot along the railing and stopped for a minute. The gray water was full of ice floes of various sizes that shifted and squeezed and forced their way downriver.

A group of small children, no more than four years old, passed by Igor. They each held part of a rope being pulled by a gray-haired, thick-waisted woman. Ducks were gathered nearby, and a little girl with brown eyes and brown hair let go of the rope and ran after them.

"Katya!" the woman at the front of the rope scolded her. "Come back here!"

The little girl stopped, looked back, and frowned. Then the frown turned into a mischievous grin, and she turned and raced for the ducks as fast as her tiny legs could carry her.

Igor smiled at the little girl running and giggling and the old woman chasing after her. He was underneath a large oak tree, its brown leaves still clinging to the branches, just as they had all winter long. A breeze picked up, and one of the leaves finally let go. It sailed slowly toward the earth, gracefully coming to rest on a large ice floe making its way out to sea.

A second gust shook free an acorn stuck in the branches, and it bounced off Igor's head and landed at his feet.

RESOURCES

The following excellent books have been referenced in the writing of this novel:

Erickson, John & Ljubica, *The Eastern Front*, Carlton Books Limited, 2001.

Salisbury, Harrison E., *The 900 Days: The Siege of Leningrad*, Da Capo Press, 1985.

Shostakovich, Dmitry, *Testimony: The Memoirs of Dmitry Shostakovich*, Harper & Row, 1979.

Skrjabina, Elena, *Siege and Survival: The Odyssey of a Leningrader*, Southern Illinois University Press, 1971.

Wayne, Kyra Petrovskaya, *Shurik: A Story of the Siege of Leningrad*, Lyons & Burford, 1970.

ALSO BY JV LOVE

There Ariseth Light in the Darkness: A Novel of First Century Galilee

Three wandering souls. One miraculous teacher. A story of love and forgiveness...

In ancient Palestine, three survivors struggle to find solace in a world of injustice and repression. Azara is studious, headstrong, and committed to her ideals. Jonah is pure and virtuous, but his heart has been darkened by the evils of man. And Vitus is a Roman soldier battling for order and progress when he is unexpectedly confronted with a different kind of war...

Separated by miles of dangerous lands, and decades of turbulent history, these three wandering souls set off on a journey beyond their imagination. Their travels will test their faith and culminate in an encounter with a mysterious rabbi from Galilee—a teacher who upends their lives with his revolutionary message of love and compassion...

A man called Jesus of Nazareth.

Author JV Love blends meticulous research with an absorbing, heartfelt story. There Ariseth Light in the Darkness is an epic biblical adventure that sweeps readers into the lives of its unforgettable protagonists.

"This dazzling story transformed my understanding of that time and place, of what happened there, how it happened, and what it means for the personal and global challenges we face today." — Susan Johnson Hadler, author of *The Beauty of What Remains*

Excerpts from reviews on Amazon
"The book was exceedingly fresh, surprisingly full of action, and a loaded story that led to legitimate self-reflection." – Tod M.

"The teachings of Jesus never really resonated with me before reading this book. Having the context of real life at that time has shifted my whole perspective. On top of this, I loved the characters, and their stories. Well written, entertaining, and informative. This is a great book!" – NR

"Very inspirational. I loved this book." – Anonymous

The Sea Is Not Black: A short story set in post-Soviet Ukraine

This short story noir showcases author JV Love's first noteworthy fictional narrative. A dark, moralistic tale set in mid-1990's Ukraine, it gives an account of a tormented "New Russian" named Anatoly. It is only a few years after the collapse of the Soviet Union, and Anatoly finds himself haunted—both literally and figuratively—by his past. As he strives to maintain his fragile grip on reality, he is driven to revisit the place where his fateful decision took place.

Available on Amazon.

Made in the USA
Monee, IL
22 September 2021